D0371889

VERY MERRY MYSTERIES

A Mystery Guild
Lost Classics
Omnibus

VERY MERRY MYSTERIES:

REST YOU MERRY
by Charlotte MacLeod

CORPUS CHRISTMAS
by Margaret Maron

A HIGHLAND CHRISTMAS
by M. C. Beaton

Mystery Guild
Garden City, New York

REST YOU MERRY
Copyright © 1978 by Charlotte MacLeod

CORPUS CHRISTMAS
Copyright © 1989 by Margaret Maron

A HIGHLAND CHRISTMAS
Copyright © 1999 by M. C. Beaton

All rights reserved.

ISBN 0-7394-2970-1

The characters and events in this book are fictitious.
Any similarity to real persons,
living or dead, is coincidental.

Manufactured in the United States of America.

CONTENTS

REST YOU MERRY

INTRODUCTION

by Joan Hess

I FIRST MET Charlotte MacLeod in the Fayetteville (Arkansas) public library in the early 1980s. She was not pouring tea for patrons, or even stamping due dates in dog-eared books, but instead was shelved in a most genteel fashion. I was on my weekly prowl for mystery novels, and was intrigued enough by the title *Rest You Merry* to pull out the book and read the first few pages. Half an hour later, I was sitting on the floor, giggling madly at the eccentric characters and improbable (but not incredible) situations. After having been glared at by more decorous patrons, I forced myself to stop reading long enough to check out the book and drive home, where I could curl up on the sofa and laugh out loud.

There were more encounters with Charlotte at the library, and when I'd read and reread all her books, I chanced upon Alisa Craig. My whoops of delight nearly caused my expulsion from the hushed environs of my favorite local hangout. And then, at a mystery convention, I found myself being introduced to a gracious lady with bright eyes, pink cheeks, a mischievous smile, and a very proper hat with a discreet feather. We became friends, and later, close friends. She became a mentor, freely offering me advice and criticism (of the kindly sort). Occasionally, she scolded me, but never without cause. Her public demeanor never wavered, but as you will discover as you read this and other Peter Shandy novels, as well as the Sarah Kelling series and those written as Alisa Craig, Charlotte does have a bawdy streak.

Rest You Merry is the first of the series and introduces us to Peter Shandy, a mild, somewhat shy professor at Balaclava Agricultural College, where he is renowned for his hybrid rutabaga. He leads a quiet bachelor's existence in a cul-de-sac with other faculty members, and would like nothing more than to be left alone. Alas, in the first paragraph, he is confronted by the perpetually pushy Jemima Ames, who insists for the seventy-third time in eighteen years (as Peter tells us) that he decorate his home with Christmas lights for the annual campus Illumination. Peter cooperates in a hilariously subversive way, and manages to set off mayhem and madness on the heretofore serene campus.

Rereading *Rest You Merry* in preparation for writing this note, I was once again amused and bemused by Charlotte's Dickensian way with names. The president of Balaclava College is the gruff, ill-tempered Thorkjeld Svenson, who rules with a heavy thumb and roars with frustration at his hapless victims. The oafish Chief of Police is aptly named Ottermole. Campus security is headed by a dubious fellow named Grimble. There are many more, but I will leave you to find them yourself and giggle, snicker.

Don't allow yourself to think that Charlotte's novels are nothing more than comedies. They are, at some level, drawing-room comedies from the late nineteenth and early twentieth centuries, but they are much more, sharp satires written with such depth and clarity that I, as a writer, find myself overwhelmed by her mastery. The characters, as oddball as some of them may be, remind me of people I've encountered, for better or worse. A tad exaggerated, perhaps, but intensely real. Thorkjeld may intimidate faculty, staff, and students, but he is, in his own way, rather adorable. Peter never underestimates Thorkjeld's perspicacity, nor do we. I can understand Peter's mild attempts at what he presumes are pranks, as well as Jemima's admirable but nevertheless annoying attempts to fill the college's coffers to provide funds for scholarships. Good intentions in Charlotte's novels often lead to bodies scattered hither and yon, with violence tactfully left offstage. Romantic entanglements take place behind closed doors. But as I said, Charlotte does have a bawdy streak. You're on your own.

Another thing that struck me as I reread *Rest You Merry* was Charlotte's boggling erudition in matters of research. When Peter muses about possible sources of toxins, he runs through a variety of possibilities before he reaches a conclusion. As readers, we are not bored with his meandering thoughts, nor treated to dissertations about the various levels of toxicity of common plants—but it might behoove us all to think twice before Charlotte offers any of us a cup of tea. She would have no problems burning down a building or cataloguing a library collection of obscure poets. I was stunned, and personally shamed, by her range of knowledge. Later, I learned she could not only quote the famous and the infamous, but also could warble the most risqué pub songs.

So here is Charlotte MacLeod, a woman in a demure felt hat who can reduce us to hysterical laughter and amaze us with her wit. Sensible, silly, sharp, gentle, nipping here and there, but never with malice aforethought (okay, maybe as an afterthought).

Now, enjoy!

—Joan Hess
July 2001

ONE

"PETER SHANDY, YOU'RE impossible," sputtered his best friend's wife. "How do you expect me to run the Illumination if everyone doesn't cooperate?"

"I'm sure you'll do a masterful job as always, Jemima. Isn't that Hannah Cadwall across the way ringing your doorbell?"

With a finesse born of much practice, Professor Shandy backed Mrs. Ames off his front step and shut the door. This was the seventy-third time in eighteen years she'd nagged him about decorating his house. He'd kept count. Shandy had a passion for counting. He would have counted the spots on an attacking leopard, and he was beginning to think a leopard might be a welcome change.

Every yuletide season since he'd come to teach at Balaclava Agricultural College, he'd been besieged by Jemima and her cohorts. Their plaint was ever the same:

"We have a tradition to maintain."

The tradition dated back, as Professor Shandy had taken the trouble to find out, no farther than 1931, when the wife of the then president had found a box of Japanese lanterns left over from some alumni ball of more prosperous days. Combining artistic yearnings with Yankee thrift, she decided to stage a Grand Illumination of the Balaclava Crescent on Christmas Eve. The professor had come to feel a deep sense of personal injury because it hadn't rained that night.

The Grand Illumination, blotting out for one night the drabness of the Great Depression, had been such a smashing success that the college had repeated the event every year since, with accumulating embellishments. Now during the entire holiday season the Crescent became a welter of twinkling lights, red sleighs, and students in quaint costume chanting totally superfluous injunctions to Deck the Halls. Those faculty members whose houses faced the Crescent threw themselves into the jollification. No energy shortage dimmed the multicolored blaze because the college generated its own power from methane gas.

From near and far came tourists to bask in the spectacle and be milked by the lads and lasses of Balaclava. Students sold doughnuts and mulled cider from whimsical plywood gingerbread houses, hawked song sheets, ran parking lots, or put on the guise of Santa's elves and hauled people around on old-fashioned sleds at a dollar a haul. Pictures appeared in national magazines.

However, the photographers always had to shoot around one dark spot on the gala scene. This was the home of Peter Shandy. He alone, like a balding King Canute, stood steadfast against the tide.

In the daytime his stubborn refusal to assist at the Annual Fleecing didn't matter so much. The small house of rosy old brick, framed by snow-covered evergreens, looked Christmasy just as it was. Still, it was this very picturesqueness that galled the committee most.

"You could do so much *with* it," they moaned.

One after another, they showered on him wreaths made of gilded pine cones, of stapled computer cards, of stuffed patchwork, of plastic fruit, of lollipops wired to bent coat hangers with little scissors attached so he could snip off goodies as desired. He always thanked the donors with what courtesy he could manage, and passed on their offerings to his cleaning woman. By now, Mrs. Lomax had the most bedizened place in town, but the small brick house on the Crescent remained stubbornly unadorned.

Left to himself, Peter Shandy would willingly have made some concession to the event: a balsam wreath or a spray of holly on the front door, and a fat white candle guttering in the parlor window after dark. He rather liked Christmas. Every year, he sent off a few decently restrained cards to old friends, attended those neighborhood parties he couldn't in decency avoid, and went off to visit relatives.

Cousin Henry and his wife, Elizabeth, were quiet people, older than Peter, who lived a three hours' journey by Greyhound from Balaclava Junction. They would thank him for the box of cigars and the basket of assorted jellies, then sit him down to an early dinner of roast beef and Yorkshire pudding. Afterward, over brandy and the Christmas cigars, Henry would show his stamp collection. The professor had little interest in stamps as such, but found them pleasant enough things to count. Late in the afternoon, Elizabeth would serve tea and her special lemon cheese tarts and remark that Peter had a long ride ahead of him.

Agreeably stuffed and warm with familial attachment, the professor would slip back into the brick house somewhere around nine o'clock in the evening and settle down with a glass of good sherry and *Bracebridge Hall*. At bedtime he would step out the back door for a last whiff of fresh air. If it was a fine night, he might feel the urge to stay outside and count stars for a while, but for the past couple of years the Illumination Committee had scheduled fireworks, which wrought havoc with his tallies.

Altogether, too many of Shandy's Christmases had been blighted by the overwhelming holiday spirit around the Crescent. On this morning of December 21, as he stood automatically counting the petals on the bunch of giant poinsettias snipped out of plastic detergent jugs which Jemima had just forced upon him, something snapped. He thrust the loathsome artifact at Mrs. Lomax, grabbed his coat, and caught the bus for Boston.

On the morning of December 22 two men drove up to the brick house in a large truck. The professor met them at the door.

"Did you bring everything, gentlemen?"

"The whole works. Boy, you folks up here sure take Christmas to heart!"

"We have a tradition to maintain," said Shandy. "You may as well start on the spruce trees."

All morning the workmen toiled. Expressions of amazed delight appeared on the faces of neighbors and students. As the day wore on and the men kept at it, the amazement remained but the delight faded.

It was dark before the men got through. Peter Shandy walked them out to the truck. He was wearing his overcoat, hat, and galoshes, and carrying a valise.

"Everything in good order, gentlemen? Lights timed to flash on and off at six-second intervals? Amplifiers turned up to full volume? Steel-cased switch boxes provided with sturdy locks? Very well, then, let's flip on the power and be off. I'm going to impose on you for a lift to Boston, if I may. I have an urgent appointment there."

"Sure, glad to have you," they chorused, feeling the agreeable crinkle of crisp bills in their hands. From a technical point of view, it had been an interesting day.

Precisely forty-eight hours later, on Christmas Eve, Professor Shandy stepped outside for a breath of air. Around him rolled the vast Atlantic. Above shone only the freighter's riding lights and a skyful of stars. The captain's dinner had been most enjoyable. Presently he would go below for a chat with the chief engineer, a knowledgeable man who could tell to the last pulse how many revolutions per minute his engines made at any given speed.

Back on Balaclava Crescent, floodlights would be illuminating the eight life-size reindeer mounted on the roof of the brick house. In its windows, sixteen Santa Claus faces would be leering above sixteen sets of artificial candles, each containing three red and two purple bulbs, each window outlined by a border of thirty-six more bulbs alternating in green, orange, and blue.

He glanced at his watch and did rapid calculations in his head. At that precise point, the 742 outsize red bulbs on the spruce trees would have flashed on for the 28,800th time—a total of 21,369,600 flashes. The amplifiers must by now have blared out 2,536 renditions each of "I'm Dreaming of a White Christmas," "I Saw Mommy Kissing Santa Claus," and "All I Want for Christmas Is My Two Front Teeth." They must be just now on the seventeenth bar of the 2,537th playing of "I Don't Care Who You Are, Fatty, Get Those Reindeer off My Roof."

Professor Shandy smiled into the darkness. "Bah, humbug," he murmured, and began to count the stars.

TWO

THE ENORMITY OF what he had done did not hit Peter Shandy until he was halfway through breakfast on Christmas morning. Then his right hand froze in the very act of conveying a forkful of excellent pork sausage to his expectant mouth.

"What's wrong, Mr. Shandy?" asked the sympathetic purser. "Not getting seasick on us, are you?"

"It's the engines. They've stopped."

Though this was not the real cause of Shandy's perturbation, it happened to be true. For no apparent reason, the ship's great pulse had suddenly ceased to beat. The engineer threw down his napkin, made a blasphemous utterance, and leaped for the companionway. The captain rushed to the bridge, followed in order of rank by his first, second, and third mates. The steward cleared his throat deferentially.

"Well, Purser, it looks as if you and Mr. Shandy will have to finish the sausages."

"Please present my share to the ship's cat with the compliments of the season," replied the professor, "I believe I'll go try on my life jacket."

He was not particularly alarmed. Compared to what might be in store for him back at Balaclava Junction, the prospect of sudden death by drowning was not without some attraction. Also, there seemed no immediate danger, especially since they had been traveling southward along the coast. A sea anchor was thrown out to keep them riding comfortably until seagoing tugs could arrive to tow them to port. A helicopter flew overhead taking pictures for television. Shandy stayed out of camera range and meditated on his infamy.

An honorable man withal, he could see only one course of action, and he took it. When they put in at Newport News to dry-dock, he repacked his bag, bade farewell to his new-found comrades, and caught the next Greyhound to Balaclava Junction.

It was, as the bus driver remarked at rather too frequent intervals, one hell of a way to spend Christmas. Eating a greasy cheeseburger at a rest stop, Shandy thought of Elizabeth's roast beef and Yorkshire pudding. Jolting along slick roads in freezing sleet, he brooded on her lemon cheese tarts. Dozing fitfully, stiff and chilled, he would wake to regret those sausages he had donated to the ship's cat, and drop off again to dream there was somebody waiting back in the brick house on the Crescent to cook him a hot supper.

There wouldn't be, of course. Mrs. Lomax was away visiting her married daughter over the holidays and she wouldn't have worked today in any case. As he alighted in the chill dawn of December 26, not a leftover reveler, not even the tar-and-feathering committee he half expected, was to be seen. The professor turned his coat collar as high as it would go and began the precipitous climb to the Crescent, wondering at what point he would be confronted with the blinking and bellowing evidence of his ill-judged prank.

He wasn't. The brick house stood dark and silent. He might have known the doughty men of Balaclava would cope with trivia like locked doors and break-proof power boxes. Some student in the Engineering School doing a minor in felonious entry must have thrown the switches.

Relieved, yet nettled at finding his aesthetic bombshell so competently defused, Shandy jabbed his key into the lock, swung open the front door which his accomplices had wrapped like a giant Christmas present with a tumorous growth of pixie mushrooms in the middle, and stumped inside.

He took off his coat, hat, and muffler and hung them in the hall closet. He took off his galoshes and also his shoes, for his feet had swelled from cold and too long sitting. He wiggled his toes. In spite of everything, it was good to be home.

Now for some food. In sock feet, the professor padded down the narrow hallway. The faculty dining room wouldn't be open for hours yet. In any event, he had no wish to venture out from sanctuary so hardly attained. There must be something edible in the kitchen. Hot soup would be just the ticket. Shandy was quite good at opening tins.

Intent on sustenance, he failed to watch where he was going. A sharp pain pierced the sole of his right foot, the floor moved, and he landed flat on his back.

Peter Shandy was not hurt, for the floor runner was thick, but he was extremely put out. Remembering what the engineer had said on finding the engines had stopped, he addressed the same remark to the men from

Boston, and turned on the overhead light to hunt for whatever they had so carelessly dropped where he would be sure to step on it.

He borrowed another expletive. The cause of his downfall was a marble, one of his own, that had been given him long ago by a niece of Elizabeth's. This elfin sprite, Alice by name, had loved to visit at the brick house. Alice was married now and living far away, sending him snapshots of her babies instead of the paste-and-crayon creations over which she had so lovingly labored in years gone by.

Most of Alice's gifts had disintegrated, but Peter Shandy still kept her thirty-eight fried marbles in the little glass bowl they had come in. He counted them over sometimes, remembering a little girl's breathless account of how the fascinating inner crackling was achieved.

It was a blue marble he had stepped on. There were seven blue marbles, four light and three dark. This was a dark one, hard to see against the figured runner. That explained his downfall, but not why the marble was on the floor instead of the parlor whatnot.

Temporarily diverted from his quest for soup, Shandy stepped into the living room. More marbles rolled under his unprotected feet. All thirty-eight must have been spilled, but how? The Boston workmen had been deft and efficient. Furthermore, they'd had no occasion to go near the whatnot, which stood well away from any door or window, in the same corner where he'd found it when he first took over the house from a departing professor eighteen years before.

He recalled having made a final tour of the rooms just before he'd left, to make sure all parts of his plan were duly consummated. He couldn't remember noticing the marbles on the whatnot, but he'd surely have felt them underfoot. Could some tiny animal, a mouse or squirrel, have pushed them off the shelf? It would have to be a muscular rodent. Anyway, he'd better pick them up before he took another toss.

The bowl lay on the carpet, luckily unbroken. Shandy went crawling around the floor, counting aloud as he dropped the errant spheres into their receptacle.

"Thirty-four, thirty-five, thirty-six, and the one I stepped on in the hall. Must be another somewhere. Yellow with brown streaks."

But where? The rooms were small and uncluttered. Even crouching down and squinting along the pile, Shandy could detect no crackly gleam. He searched the hallway, moved chairs, at last thought to look behind the sofa. He didn't find his marble. He found Jemima Ames.

The assistant librarian was dead, no question about that. She was lying on her back, looking up at him with the same cold, fishy stare he'd seen when she handed him the bouquet cut from detergent bottles. Her mouth was slightly open, as though she might be about to deliver one last exhortation about the duty of a Crescent resident, but she never would. There was a settled look about the body, as though it had been there for some while.

The manner of her death seemed plain enough. A small stepladder brought from the kitchen lay beside her, her head propped against the edge of its flat metal top. As to why she'd climbed the stool, a plastic Santa Claus face lying across her chest gave silent answer. Feeling like a murderer, Shandy padded over to the telephone and rang campus security.

"Grimble, you'd better get over here. This is Peter Shandy."

"Yeah? Where you been?"

"I was—er—called out of town unexpectedly."

"Didn't happen to take Miz Ames with you, by any chance?" Grimble evidently thought he was being funny.

"No, but I—er—have her with me now. That's why I'm calling."

"Hang on. I'll be right over."

Shandy put down the receiver. Grimble had been on the lookout for Jemima, therefore she must have been reported missing on Christmas Day, or even the day before. That could mean she'd been lying here almost the whole time he'd been gone. It would take her husband at least twenty-four hours to realize Jemima wasn't where she ought to be.

In the midst of his perturbation, the professor was ashamed to realize he was less upset over having inadvertently killed his best friend's wife than he was over not having got to heat his soup. Blaming himself for his lack of proper feeling, he nevertheless made a tentative move toward the kitchen. Then he stopped.

He might be in an even worse spot than he thought he was. Had Jemima still been alive when he skipped out of town and took ship for foreign parts without telling anybody he was going? His opinion of the assistant librarian, her ridiculous title, and her eternal badgering were well known. Everybody else thought she was a pest, too, but nobody else had gone to such lengths to spite her, and nobody else had her corpse behind his sofa.

He had little time to brood. The security chief was already hunting among the mushrooms for his knocker.

"Come in, Grimble. Come in. Good of you to get here so quickly."

"Sure, Professor, any time. Where is she, and what's she been up to?"

"Well—er—I think the circumstances speak for themselves."

"Why can't Mrs. Ames speak for herself? She generally does." The security chief wouldn't have dared say such a thing if he hadn't been seriously annoyed. "Where is she?" he repeated.

"In here. Behind the sofa. I didn't move anything."

"You mean you—oh, my God!"

Grimble stood goggling down at the corpse for at least a minute. Then he shoved his cap forward and scratched hard at the base of his skull.

"What do you know about that? Looks as if she butted in once too often."

"Yes." Professor Shandy found that his lips were so dry he had trouble articulating. "Apparently she took exception to my—er—decorations."

"Well, now, I don't want to hurt your feelings, Professor, but some of the folks around here do think you've kind of overdone it. They think you're trying to outshine 'em, see?"

That was the one possible interpretation of his outrage that Shandy would never have thought possible.

"Of course," Grimble went on kindly, "most of us figure you're just making up for all the times you wouldn't be bothered. I think it's kind of cheerful myself, with the music and all. Even Professor Ames noticed that part. First time I ever seen him take any interest in the Illumination. Too damn bad he couldn't take a little more interest in his wife."

"How long has she been missing?" asked the professor with his heart in his mouth.

"Best I've been able to find out is that she went to a party at the Dysarts' last Thursday night. You know that big wingding they always throw at Christmastime."

"Yes. Come to think of it, I was intending to go myself. I quite forgot to let them know I wouldn't be there. I shall have to make my apologies."

Realizing he had an iron-clad alibi, Shandy became voluble. The invitation had been for eight o'clock, and at that hour he was in Boston, picking up his ticket to board the *Singapore Susie*.

Grimble wasn't interested. "Well, anyway," he cut in, "she stayed at the party till half past nine."

"Was her husband with her?"

"Hell, he don't remember where he was. Home with his nose in a book, or up at the soil lab making mudpies, most likely."

"I expect so," Shandy agreed.

Timothy Ames never left his study if he could help it, except to teach a class or immure himself in his soil-testing laboratory. He was deaf as a haddock and hopeless at small talk, so there was nothing unusual in Jemima's attending a social event without her spouse.

"Where did she go when she left the party?"

"Looks to me as if she come straight here. She was wearin' that purple cloak thing she's got on now, they said. Professor Dysart says he helped her on with it an' saw her out the door. Prob'ly tripped on the end of it an' that's how she upset the ladder. She was all steamed up about these decorations of yours, they said. Must o' got a few drinks under her belt an' decided to come an' take 'em down. See, she's got one o' them Santa Claus faces on top of her. It's the sort o' thing she'd do."

"Yes," said the professor sadly, "it is. I ought to have known better. I feel personally responsible for this terrible—"

He intended to add "accident," but the word wouldn't come out. Professor Shandy was a truthful man, and there was that missing marble still to be accounted for. Should he explain that odd circumstance to Grimble, or should he not?

On the whole, he thought not. The college security force was trained to cope primarily with unauthorized prowlers and overexuberance within the student body. Chief Grimble was a man of good heart but limited intelligence. The police would have to be called in anyway, so he might as well tell his story where it would do some good. The sooner the better. He was feeling more exhausted every second. But Grimble was making no move.

"Would you like to use my phone?" he prodded.

"Don't you think we ought to go over and tell Professor Ames ourselves?" said the security chief. "He'd never hear the telephone in a million years."

"Yes, but aren't we supposed to notify the police first? We do have an unexplained death on our hands."

"What's so unexplained? She fell an' bashed in her skull."

"Still, don't you have to observe certain—er—formalities?"

"Search me. All I know is that the president's goin' to raise holy hell if this gets into the newspapers."

Grimble wasn't so stupid, after all. The Grand Illumination was slated to last through New Year's. At least half the student body had given up the chance of spending Christmas with their families in order to run the parking lots, the sleigh rides, the refreshment stands; to sculpt the giant snowmen, sing the carols, build the bonfires, sweep the skating ponds, or put on costumes and stand around in picturesque attitudes for the benefit of those golden calves, the tourists.

Proceeds were handled on a fifty-fifty basis: half to the student, half to the college. Many of these young people depended on Illumination earnings to help pay their tuition. The college used its half for scholarships and loans. It was excellent business both ways and the president would have good reason to be upset if unfavorable publicity kept visitors away. A braver man than Grimble, or than almost anybody, might well think twice, and perhaps a few more times to be on the safe side, before inviting the wrath of Thorkjeld Svenson.

Nevertheless, Shandy replied, "Then we'd better let him know at once."

"He's off skiing, thank God," said Grimble. "I guess I better get hold of Fred Ottermole down at the police station. He's not a bad egg."

"Yes, do that. Er—while we're waiting for him, why don't I make us a cup of coffee?"

"Great idea. Three sugars in mine, if you can spare it."

The security chief stuck a thick finger in the telephone dial, and Professor Shandy at last managed to reach his kitchen.

THREE

WITH A HOT drink and a couple of stale doughnuts under his belt, Shandy felt queasier but less defeated. He managed to greet Chief Ottermole with a decent mixture of distress and dignity.

"This how you found her?"

Ottermole was a large, youngish man wearing a sheepskin-collared leather jacket over his uniform. He refused to take it off, perhaps because he realized the added bulk enhanced his already impressive appearance. He had his gun, his flashlight, and his notebook at the ready, but his ballpoint pen wouldn't write. Professor Shandy lent him a pencil and answered his question.

"Yes. I haven't touched her. She was obviously beyond help."

"How did she get here?"

"I wish I knew. I've been away since Thursday evening myself. I hadn't been in the house more than a few minutes before I called Grimble."

"How come him instead of me?"

"We always call security when anything goes wrong. It's just habit."

"Um. Where were you?"

Shandy drew a long breath and chose his words carefully. "As you can see, I'm a middle-aged man of quiet habits. Living here on the Crescent, I get the—er—full impact of the Grand Illumination. I expect you don't have to be told what that entails."

"I sure don't," said the policeman gloomily. "Okay, so you cleared out."

"Exactly. I—er—had contributed my share of the decorating—"

"Oh, boy, you can say that again! How the hell did a guy like you even get those eight reindeer up on your roof?"

"Actually, I didn't. Being without experience in such matters, I simply hired some decorators and told them to—er—decorate."

"Oh yeah. People have been kind of wondering how come you picked out all those funny colors. S'posed to be artistic or something, huh?"

"Er—they seemed to know what they were doing. It took a great deal longer than I'd thought it would. I had made arrangements to go off on a short cruise over the holidays, and was supposed to be in Boston by seven o'clock in the evening. Since I couldn't very well go off and leave the workmen unattended, I had to stay in the house till they'd finished. By that time I'd missed the six o'clock bus, so I asked them to give me a ride, which they were quite willing to do. What with one thing and another, it got to be a scramble and I forgot to tell anybody I was leaving. That didn't seem to matter much, because the men assured me the mechanisms were perfectly safe and I knew the neighbors would keep an eye on the place. They always do."

"So you figure this woman came in to check things out? What would she be doing up on a ladder?"

"Presumably she was altering the decorations in some way. Mrs. Ames was chairman of the Grand Illumination Committee, and she took her responsibilities with great seriousness. I suppose that Santa Claus object she seems to have taken down was—er—bothering her."

"How could she get in? Don't tell me you went away and left your door unlocked, with tourists milling around here thick as flies on dog-do in August."

"Oh no, I'm always careful about locking up. I don't know how she got in, unless Grimble opened the door for her."

"I never," said the security chief. "What the hell, Professor, you people are always leaving keys around at each other's houses and forgetting to take 'em back. She prob'ly had one herself."

He and Ottermole exchanged grins over Shandy's head. The security chief shrugged.

"Doesn't look as if there's any mystery about what happened here. Everybody in town knew Mrs. Ames. She wouldn't let a little thing like breaking and entering stop her if she thought there was something that needed to be fixed. Only thing surprises me is that she bashed her own head in, when there were so many people around who'd have been glad to do it for her."

Ottermole grinned again. "If you repeat that, I'll shove you in the clink. Well, I guess we might as well get the wagon up here."

"The sooner the better," said Grimble nervously. "I just hope to Christ we can get her out of the Crescent without anybody spotting us.

Boy, Professor, I'm sure glad you got home when you did. Say, how come you're here at all? That must have been some short cruise."

"It was shorter than we expected," the professor explained. "The ship developed engine trouble and had to put in at Newport News. You may have seen the—er—thrilling rescue on television. Since there was no telling how long she'd be disabled, I decided I might as well give up the idea and come back. She's the *Singapore Susie*, if you care to make sure I was actually aboard. I can write down the names of the captain and officers for you. I'm afraid I never did learn who the men were with whom I rode to Boston. However, I do have the firm's invoice in my desk, and could easily find out."

"That's okay, Professor. I guess we can take your word for it. Mind if I use your phone?"

"Not at all."

Ottermole went into the study and dialed. "Hello, Doctor. Sorry to get you up, but we've got a little problem up here at Professor Shandy's house on the Crescent. No, he's okay, but he just came home from being shipwrecked and found Mrs. Ames dead on his parlor floor. Yeah, some days you just can't win. Looks to me as if she fell off a stool and cracked her skull. She was in here fixing the Christmas decorations. Okay, I'll tell him you said so. Look, do you think you could get over here right away? Eddie Grimble's having a bird. He wants to take her out before the gawkers start coming. President Svenson wouldn't like the publicity, he says. Good. See you."

He hung up. "Relax, Eddie. Dr. Melchett's on his way. Soon as he gives us the go-ahead, I'll have Charlie Forster bring that old pickup of his around."

Ottermole went back to the telephone and chatted with one of his cohorts until the doctor arrived. Melchett's examination took about thirty seconds.

"She died instantly of skull fracture at least three days ago. The wound in the cranium is consistent with the shape of the object she fell on. Anything else you need to know?"

"Nope. That wraps it up. Thanks, Doctor."

"I'll drop off a certificate at the station on my way to the hospital."

Melchett left, and within a few minutes, a plain blue pickup truck arrived. Two men wearing noncommittal nylon jackets carried out a large brown paper parcel. The townsfolk, too, were sensitive to the good will of Thorkjeld Svenson.

Peter Shandy attended the swathing of Mrs. Ames with anxious care. He was still fretting about that marble. He had thought it must be under the body, but it wasn't. At last he had to tell Chief Ottermole what he was looking for.

"That was how I happened to find her, you see. I stepped on one of the spilled marbles and took a rather painful toss in the hallway. Then I thought I'd better pick them all up before I fell again. But after a thorough search, I've found only thirty-seven out of the thirty-eight."

"Wait a second. Are you saying you know for a positive fact how many marbles were in that dish?"

"Of course," said Professor Shandy, astonished to be asked such a question. "The missing marble is yellow with brown streaks. I wish you'd have the undertaker look for it among her—er—personal effects."

"Sure. I'll tell Harry you haven't got all your marbles."

Shandy refused to be baited. "Thank you. They were given me by a little girl of whom I'm very fond. I shouldn't wish to hurt her feelings by appearing to be careless of her gift."

The child in question was now twenty-six years old, but he hoped such an explanation might persuade Ottermole that he was less cracked than his marbles. Apparently, it did.

"Oh, I get it," said the chief. "Well, I guess we'd better put this show on the road. Say, you know Professor Ames a lot better than I do."

"Yes, Tim and I are old friends. I'll tell him, if you want."

"Thanks a lot. That's one job I'll gladly pass up any day. See you later, Ed. So long, Professor. Don't find any more bodies."

"I earnestly hope never to find another. But you will tell them about that marble, won't you? I know it sounds trivial at a time like this, but if the child should come and find one gone—"

"Look, I know all about it. I've got kids of my own."

The policeman climbed into the back of the truck. Ed Grimble stayed where he was, looking at Professor Shandy and scratching the back of his head.

"Say, Professor, I don't suppose it's any of my business, but that story of yours about the marbles, I don't get it. You used to have that little girl of your cousin's here sometimes, but, hell, that was a long time ago. She must have kids of her own by now."

"Three," said Shandy. "You're quite right. I expect Alice has forgotten all about her fried marbles. I was only—er—trying to add verisimilitude to an otherwise implausible request. Do you ever have hunches, Grimble?"

"Once in a while. Like I had a hunch right now you were givin' Fred Ottermole the business."

"It's important that he hunt for that missing marble. If it turns up in

Mrs. Ames's clothing, we can safely assume she knocked over the dish herself. If it doesn't, we'll have to re-examine our data."

"What are you driving at, Professor?"

"Grimble, I do not understand how those marbles got spilled. I was the last one out of here Thursday afternoon, and I'll swear they were on that whatnot over in the corner then, not because I noticed them particularly, but because I didn't. Small round objects on the floor have a way of making their presence felt." He rubbed his left buttock thoughtfully.

The security guard shook his head. "I don't see what you're so fired up about. Mrs. Ames was a big woman, and she had that damn fool cape flappin' around her like a washing in a windstorm. She must o' been hell on bric-a-brac."

"I grant you that, but why should she have gone anywhere near the whatnot? As you see, it's out of the path from the door to the window, and she knew her way around this house well enough."

The Restaurant Management students ran a superb catering service and Shandy was never stingy about doing his fair share of entertaining. Jemima had always come with Tim to his parties, and dropped in altogether too often between times to bullyrag him about one thing or another.

"You see." He pointed to the ostensible cause of her death. "She even knew where to find that step stool, which belongs in the kitchen, though she could perfectly well have stood on a chair."

"Cripes, I don't know, Professor. Maybe fumbling around in the dark—"

"But it would not have been dark. With all those candles and whatnots in the windows, the place must have been lit up like—er—a Christmas tree. That is, assuming the lights were on. I gather somebody has been manipulating my switches."

"Well, what happened was, everybody started getting on my neck about the music. It was drowning out the carolers and the bell ringers and driving the neighbors nuts, if you'll pardon me for saying so. We tried to get hold of you to tone things down a little, but you were nowhere to be found, so I told Jamie Froude from maintenance to jimmy open that switch box your guys had attached to the side of the house here, next to the light meter. That way, we managed to turn off the music. Some people wanted us to douse the lights, too, but the little kids were getting such a kick out of the blinking Santa Clauses and all that I said to Jamie, 'What the hell, they came to see lights, didn't they?' So all we did was adjust the timers so the damn things wouldn't blink so fast, and gave the night watchman instructions to shut 'em off when he made his one o'clock rounds. Since then, we've been turning everything but the sound on manually every afternoon at dusk and having the watchman throw the switch after everybody leaves. Your place is the hit of the show."

"My God," murmured the professor. "So the long and the short of it is, if Jemima came any time before one o'clock in the morning, the lights would be on, and if she came afterward the place would be in darkness."

"That's right. Now that you mention it, I shouldn't think a woman would want to go prowling around somebody else's house in the middle of the night by herself."

"Neither should I, in this instance. Mrs. Ames was more a charger than a sneaker. I daresay she'd intended to tackle me at the Dysarts', and when she found I wasn't at the party, she came straight here. We'll have to make inquiries."

"You can if you want to," said the security chief. "I'm not sticking my neck out for no yellow marble."

Professor Shandy sighed heavily. "I suppose I can't blame you. No doubt it's all a mare's nest. I've been traveling all night and perhaps I'm not thinking straight. You might as well go along about your business. I'm going to fix myself a bite of breakfast, then go over and try to make poor Tim Ames understand what's happened."

FOUR

THERE WERE A couple of eggs in the fridge. Shandy fried them and made himself another cup of instant coffee. Then he took a hot bath and a shave. After that, he felt a trifle less like the way Jemima Ames had looked. He put on a light gray shirt, a dark gray suit, and a reticent tie, not because they were appropriate for the errand he had to perform but because he owned no other sort of clothing, aside from the corduroys and flannel shirts he kept for field work.

Standing in front of the mirror, he brushed his graying hair. He wore it trimmed rather short, making no effort to cover his bald spot. Peter Shandy liked to be neat and he wore garments of excellent quality which lasted for years and saved fuss in the long run, but nobody could have called him a vain man.

He'd never felt that he had anything to be vain about. He was neither short nor tall, neither fat nor lean. His face was not regular enough to be handsome or ugly enough to be interesting. He thought of it mainly as a place to park his glasses. He put them on, went downstairs for his gray felt hat and gray tweed ulster, and set out to find Timothy Ames.

How was old Tim going to take the news? It was foolish to speculate, since Shandy would find out soon enough, but natural to be concerned. Ames was his oldest and closest friend at Balaclava. The soil specialist had been the first to understand and sympathize with Shandy's ideas for developing improved strains of plants. Over the years, his help had been invaluable. Together, the pair of them had worked, studied, rejoiced, grieved, and fought quietly but tenaciously for research grants, for added laboratory space, for better equipment, for all the perquisites true scholars need but grandstanders are apt to get.

They had won more often than not because Thorkjeld Svenson was no fool and because they got results. Shandy, Ames, and the college had all made a killing on the Balaclava Buster, a giant rutabaga so prolific and so nutritious as cow feed that it alone generated most of the manure to produce the methane that ran the college power plant, not to mention a stream of royalties from seed companies far and wide.

The Buster was their greatest but far from their only triumph, and in all the eighteen years of collaboration, their relationship had been marred by only one minor rift. This concerned an extra-fast-sprouting viola which Shandy had wanted to call Agile Alice, while Ames held out for Jumping Jemima. Dr. Svenson had finally appointed himself arbiter and they settled perforce on Sprightly Sieglinde, in honor of Mrs. Svenson.

Shandy wished now that he hadn't been so pigheaded. Jumping Jemima was by far the best name of the three. Except that it was too apt. He thought of that dented-in skull and wished he hadn't eaten those eggs.

The moment of truth was at hand. He went up to the Ameses' front door and began his accustomed fusillade. No ordinary knocking could attract Tim's attention.

Today, however, Professor Ames must have been on the *qui vive*. Shandy had been hammering a mere three minutes or thereabout when his old comrade appeared.

"Pete! Glad to see you."

This was no idle platitude. Ames was grinning like a jack-o'-lantern, slapping him on the back, and going into a fit of chortling that threatened to land the man writhing on the door mat. Shandy got them both inside fast and shut the door. A public display of mirth was hardly the thing in a fresh-made widower. It was after seven o'clock by this time. At least one neighbor must be up and watching from a window. Seldom did any event around the Crescent go unobserved or unremarked, even in Illumination time. That was what made it so hard to believe that not one of them knew Jemima had been inside the brick house for three days.

Reminded of his painful errand, Shandy tried to speak. Tim was in no mood for doleful news.

"That," he gasped, "was the funniest—God, Pete, I've prayed for twenty-seven years that somebody would have guts enough—" he found an unused chuckle or two, got them out of his system, and wiped his eyes. "How in hell did you ever have the nerve?"

"I don't know," Shandy replied in perfect honesty. "I just did."

"You're a great man, Pete. Care for a drink?"

"Bit early, isn't it?"

Professor Ames considered the question. "Maybe you're right. How about coffee, then? I don't think I've had breakfast yet. Come to think of it, I'm not sure I ate any supper. Want some eggs or something?"

"No, I've just finished. I'll cook for you, though."

Shandy was no brilliant performer in the kitchen, but he was less incompetent than his friend, as the state of the never very neat room testified.

"Been keeping bachelor quarters," Ames explained as he pottered about, searching in vain for a clean frying pan. "Jemima's off somewhere. This time of year she's generally some damn place or other, but lately she hasn't even come home to sleep, far as I can tell. I asked Grimble if he'd seen her around and he got all excited. Asked me when she was here last. How the hell am I supposed to know?"

"When did you first miss her?"

"Yesterday afternoon at exactly three o'clock. I remember that because Jemmy phoned from California to wish us Merry Christmas. That reminded me we hadn't done anything about Christmas dinner and the presents were still sitting on the table. We hadn't intended to make any big thing of the holiday with both the kids gone and her so wrapped up in that goddamned Illumination, but I did think she might stick her nose in long enough to open her packages. I wish to Christ she'd turn up. We're out of everything. Now I can't find any coffee."

"Look, Tim, why don't you come over to my place?" said his friend in desperation. "I've got coffee. We can—er—talk about Jemima there."

He involuntarily turned his head away as he finished the sentence, so that Ames had no chance to lip-read more than the invitation, which he seemed ready enough to accept. He put on a threadbare tweed jacket which was the only outer garment he ever wore, winter or summer, and shambled alongside Shandy, across the Crescent.

Regrettably, the sight of those eight plastic reindeer set him laughing again. Shandy could only hope that whoever was watching would decide after the news of Mrs. Ames's death got around that her husband had been hysterical with grief.

After the gloom and clutter of Tim's place, the brick house seemed a cheerful haven in spite of the brown paper parcel that had so recently been taken out of it. Professor Shandy had never thought a great deal about his home before. He'd liked the previous tenant's old-fashioned furnishings well enough and made few changes, except to weed out the clutter and bring in some of his own, mostly books and potted plants he got to do research on and kept around for company. There was also a handsome water-color portrait of the Balaclava Buster, the work of a lady botany professor who had hoped to reach her colleague's heart through his rutabaga. Cross-pollination had not been successful. The lady married somebody else and Shandy continued his comfortable bachelor's life with

Mrs. Lomax keeping him tidy and the faculty dining room keeping him fed.

Insofar as he thought of the future at all, he'd pictured himself going on more or less as he'd been doing. Now for the first time he wondered whether that would be possible.

He had always managed not to get personally involved in any of the blood feuds that had raged around the Crescent during his occupation, but he knew only too well how high passions could run over acts far less outrageous than the one he had committed. He had not meant to kill Jemima, of course, but he had deliberately and with malice aforethought made savage mockery of the Crescent's most cherished tradition and the college's chief extracurricular money-maker. If Tim had the wit to see his act for exactly what it was, so would the rest of the faculty and so, even more to his peril, would those Stymphalian birds, the faculty spouses. And it was inconceivable that President Svenson would mistake his motive.

Shandy wasn't worried about losing his job per se. He had tenure, to begin with, and it would take something like an act of Congress to remove him. Moreover, President Svenson would not hasten to kill, so to speak, the gander who laid the golden eggs. There was always the chance Shandy might hatch another Balaclava Buster.

In any event, his own share of royalties from that and other successful experiments, coupled with his salary as a full professor and his relatively modest life style, had made Peter Shandy a rather wealthy man. He could retire tomorrow, if it came to that.

But he didn't want it to come to that. Fifty-six was ridiculously young to step down. He would miss his work, his colleagues, his students. He would miss the sociabilities of campus life, tiresome as he sometimes found them, and he would miss his house.

Yet he knew perfectly well that if the full force of his peers' disapproval was turned on him, it would be impossible to stay here. His life would be made miserable in countless little ways. His lawn would die, his spruces get budworm, his power would fail and his pipes would freeze and nobody would know why. Secretaries would forget to notify him of faculty meetings, hostesses would absent-mindedly leave him off their guest lists, his students would transfer. At the faculty dining room his food would be served cold and late and no colleague would dare to share his table. By the end of the next semester, he would either have quit of his own accord or turned into a curmudgeonly recluse. And he'd have nobody to blame but himself.

Well, at least he'd given old Tim a good laugh. How much was his friend going to enjoy the joke, when he learned it had cost him a wife?

Shandy fussed around his own immaculate kitchen, heating water and laying out what he could find in the way of eatables. Then he motioned Ames into what Mrs. Lomax insisted on calling the breakfast nook.

"Sit down, Tim, sit down. I'll get the marmalade. Oh, and what about some fruitcake? Elizabeth always sends me a fruitcake."

"I know Elizabeth always sends you a fruitcake. What the hell's wrong with you, Pete? You're flopping around like a hen with its head cut off."

Shandy sat down opposite him and propped both elbows on the table for support.

"The fact is, Tim, I have some bad news for you."

His guest set down the mug he'd got halfway to his lips.

"Pete, it's not—not the Portulaca Purple Passion? Oh, my God, don't tell me those seedlings have damped off?"

"Oh no! It's—" Shandy started to say, "It's not that bad," but caught himself in time. "It's Jemima, Tim. I found her."

For a long time, Ames showed no reaction. Shandy began to wonder if he'd heard. Then he said, "You mean she's dead, don't you?"

Shandy nodded. His friend bent his head and sat staring down into his coffee mug. At last he picked it up, drank off the cooling liquid, and wiped his mouth with a fairly steady hand.

"How did it happen?"

"I don't know."

Now that the barrier was broken, Shandy found it easy enough to keep going. "I came home this morning—I'd been gone since Thursday evening—and found her stretched out behind the sofa with her skull fractured. Dr. Melchett said she'd died instantly, if it's any comfort to you. She'd been there pretty much the whole time I was gone. She had on that long purple cape and an evening skirt. It looked as though she must have come in to take down those cursed decorations, and had a fall. She'd apparently brought in a little stepladder from the kitchen here—"

"What for?"

"To stand on, they assumed."

"Who assumed?"

"Grimble and the police chief, a chap named Ottermole. Know him?"

"Snotty young bastard about four sizes too big for his britches? I damn well ought to."

Ames breathed fire through his luxuriantly haired nostrils for a while, and Shandy recalled that it was Ottermole who had taken away Tim's driving license.

"Look here, Pete, I wish to hell you'd quit pussyfooting. All that 'apparently' and 'they assumed' . . . why don't you just say the sons of bitches misread the evidence, which is exactly what I'd expect a pair of nincompoops to do. Show me where you found her."

"Finish your breakfast first."

The widower shoved a whole slab of fruitcake into his mouth, and got up from the table. Chewing hard, he followed Shandy into the living room.

"The sofa wasn't pulled out as it is now," Shandy explained. "We had to move it to get at the—at Jemima."

"Show me."

Shandy pushed the heavy piece of furniture back into its usual place, parallel with the window, a few feet out from the wall.

"And the stool was how?"

"Like this." He laid the small ladder back where he'd found it. "And Jemima was lying on her back with her head resting against the top edge, and this Santa Claus thing on top of her. Shall I demonstrate?"

"Yes."

Shandy joggled himself into position as best he could.

"Is that how she was lying," Tim asked, "in a straight line with the stool?"

"Just about. She wouldn't have been able to fit any other way. There's only about three feet of width back here."

"Mh. How did you happen to find her?"

"Now, that's something that puzzles me, Tim. I stepped on a marble."

Shandy went over to the whatnot and picked up the little dish Alice had given him so many years before. "I don't know whether you've ever noticed these, but Elizabeth's niece gave them to me a long time ago. You remember she used to visit me sometimes?"

"Of course I remember. Nice little kid. Damn sight better behaved than my own."

"Er—at any rate, I've always kept this bowl of marbles here on the whatnot. There were thirty-eight."

Ames nodded perfunctorily. He took it for granted Shandy would know.

"When I got home this morning, the marbles were scattered over the living room floor and out into the hall. I might not have noticed, since I was cold and hungry and in a state of—er—general perturbation, but one of them tripped me up. So I went hunting for the rest. At first I didn't think to look behind the sofa because it seemed impossible any could have got there. The base is solid right down to the floor, as you can see, and besides, the floor slants a bit in the opposite direction. It's an old house, you know. But I knew I was one short and I'd looked everywhere else, so—"

"Did you find the marble?"

"No. I've asked them to search her clothing. It might be in her pocket or somewhere. But, drat it, Tim, I don't see how she could have spilled those marbles. There was no need for her to go anywhere near the whatnot."

"What gets me is that step stool," said Ames. "What the hell would she bother to drag that in here for? These ceilings aren't very high, and Jemima was a big woman. She could have reached that mask easily enough from the floor. You try it. You're taller than I am."

"And she was at least a couple of inches taller than I."

Shandy went to another window and reached up. He had no difficulty in touching the plastic ornament.

"There, see," said the husband. "Anyway, it wouldn't have been like Jemima to bother about that stool. Damned awkward place to put it, for one thing. She'd have been more apt to shove the sofa over against the window and jump up on that, if she needed to, which she didn't. Jemima spent half her life leaping around on the furniture. That was why I wanted to call that viola the Jumping Jemima. Remember the one we had the fight about that time? I was trying to get back at her about some damn thing or other, I forget what. Water over the dam now. Well, that's one less thing on my conscience, thanks to your pigheadedness."

"Thanks to me, she's dead," said Shandy bitterly. "If I hadn't lost my temper with her and pulled this damn fool stunt, she wouldn't have come here in the first place."

"You sure she came by herself, Pete?"

The two old friends looked into each other's eyes. Shandy shook his head slowly.

"The only thing I'm sure of is that I found her dead in my house. Melchett says—"

"That horse's ass would say whatever he thought Dr. Svenson wanted to hear. You know that."

"Yes, I know. And Grimble says she probably came straight here from the Dysarts' party, about half past nine on the evening of the twenty-second." Shandy's lips twisted. "At least that gives me an alibi. I was running away to sea by then."

He gave Ames a brief rundown of his short-lived adventure aboard the *Singapore Susie*. His friend nodded.

"Stroke of luck for you, Pete. At least you're in the clear. Leaves me in the soup, of course."

"You?" Shandy stared at him in astonishment. "Tim, if you were going to murder your wife, you'd have done it a long time ago."

"That's opinion, not evidence."

Nevertheless, Professor Ames's grin returned for an instant. "She was an awfully exasperating woman to be married to, Pete. She was the world's rottenest housekeeper, she minded everybody's business but her own, and she never once shut her mouth that I can remember. Nevertheless, being her husband had its good points. For one thing, it stopped me from thinking of my deafness as an affliction."

He emitted an odd little wheeze that would under other circumstances have become a chuckle. "It's good to have one friend I can say rotten things to without feeling like a skunk."

"That's not so rotten," Shandy replied. "Hell, Tim, you do have to live with your deafness. Living with anybody but Jemima, you'd have felt constantly frustrated at the thought that you might be missing something by not hearing what she said. With a less assertive woman, your conscience would have driven you to make social efforts that are hard for you to handle. As it was, you could do as you pleased and still have somebody to send out your shirts. I'm putting it badly but you know what I mean. I suspect there are a few people around here who might have envied your situation."

"I know damn well there are. I may be deaf, but I'm not dumb. Don't suppose one of 'em killed her out of spite?"

"That's a supposition I shouldn't care to make without something to back it up," said Shandy. "Er—are you quite sure somebody did in fact kill her?"

"Christ, Pete, you've been sure of that fact yourself, from the moment you found her, and don't try to tell me you haven't. I can read you like a book. What was your first impression?"

"That somebody had been clever," Shandy admitted. "Smart-aleck clever. The spilled marbles were a piece of utterly tasteless embroidery. I suppose they were supposed to create the impression that she'd been blundering around in the dark, possibly because she'd had one too many at the Dysarts'. Jemima did like a drink, you know."

"I ought to. I've been accused often enough of driving her to it. But she never got drunk, Pete, not that way. Her face would get red and she'd start telling somebody off or hurling the furniture around. That's why I'm so sure this scene was staged. She wasn't clumsy, she was belligerent. She'd have been much more apt to just reach up and rip those lights down regardless of any damage to the woodwork, or else to stomp all over your upholstery in her muddy boots. Where do you keep that stool, anyway?"

"In the back hall closet. Once in a while, when Mrs. Lomax feels especially put-upon, she gets it out and starts performing some herculean feat that involves a great deal of grunting and groaning and climbing up and down and sloshing soapsuds around. Except for those few times, I don't believe it gets used very much. I'd wondered about that myself. It did seem out of character."

"Damn right it does. More of your tasteless embroidery. I agree with you, Pete. We're dealing with somebody who's clever but not very intelligent, which in my opinion includes just about everybody on the goddamn faculty. What do you think, Pete? You know 'em better than I do."

"That's open to challenge. I socialize more than you, because I'd be a lonely man if I didn't, but I'm not on particularly intimate terms with any but the Enderbles. Why do you think it has to be a faculty person?"

"Well, hell, Pete, it has to be somebody who knew Jemima well enough to want to kill her."

"Yes, but was she killed as herself, so to speak, or for some reason—er—exclusive of personality factors?"

"How should I know? All right, I'll grant you she didn't make the usual distinctions between town and gown when it came to butting in and making a nuisance of herself, but I'm going on the evidence. We have to assume, at least in my opinion, that she was murdered by somebody who knew how steamed up she was over this joke of yours, who knew how to get into your house, and who knew where you keep your step stool."

"I'll grant that. And also by somebody who knew I'd gone away. Since I left in a hurry without even notifying Grimble, that does seem to narrow the field."

"To some extent, at any rate. I think we can take it as given that every single resident of the Crescent was peeking around the curtains by the time you climbed into that truck. I know I was."

Despite his preoccupation with the hypothesis of his wife's murder, Ames chortled again. "Damn, that was the most amusing afternoon I've spent since President Svenson lost his footing while he was showing the Secretary of Agriculture how we make methane gas. It was an awful disappointment when I saw you were carrying a suitcase. I'd hoped we could get together during the evening and enjoy the reactions."

"I wish we had!" cried Shandy. "Tim, I can't tell you how sick I am about this ghastly business."

"Hell, Pete, you don't have to. I expect I'll feel pretty rotten myself, once I get used to the idea that she's really gone. After all, damn it, Jemima was my wife. I didn't like her very much, but I sort of loved her, in a way. Personal feelings aside, I think what we ought to bear in mind is that if you hadn't provided a convenient parking place for her body, another would have been found."

"Then you think the murder was premeditated."

"It must have been. Look at this room. Do you honestly believe anybody could have brought Jemima in here alive, bumped her off with the blinds up and all those lights in the windows and God knows how many people milling around outside, gone through that folderol with the step stool, thrown marbles all over the floor, and got away without one person's looking in and noticing what he was up to? In the first place, Jemima wouldn't have been all that easy to kill, unless you made damn good and sure to sneak up on her and land one clean blow that did the job. And it had to be done in the right spot, with the right kind of weapon. Even that jackass Melchett would have noticed any real discrepancy between the shape of the wound and the shape of the stool, wouldn't he?"

"Yes, and so should I, and there wasn't. The only alternative suggestion is that there actually was a quarrel and somebody shoved her from in front, so that she fell and struck some hard object similar to the stool."

"Who, for instance? Name me one person in Balaclava Junction, except for President Svenson and that behemoth he's married to, whom Jemima couldn't have licked with one hand tied behind her back. Anybody who tried to knock her down would have to be mopped up with a blotter."

"Er—in any event, the incident would have caused a stir, since it must almost inevitably have taken place in front of witnesses. I see your point. The tidiness of the room and the—er—staging of the scene indicate that Jemima may have been killed elsewhere and brought here sometime after the lights were turned out."

"Can you think of any other logical explanation?"

"I can't think at all any more." Shandy slumped down on the sofa and buried his face in his hands. "Dear God, I'm tired."

"Sure you are, Pete."

Ames whacked his friend on the shoulder. "Why don't you take a nap? I've got to call the kids, then I suppose I'd better get downtown and find out what they've done with her. I'll get back to you later."

"Thank you, Tim. I'll be here."

Shandy let his old friend out, locked the door, and went upstairs to his bedroom. He ought to call the Dysarts. He ought to go with Tim. He ought to have his head examined for ever having started this terrible chain of events. What he did was to fall asleep.

FIVE

PROFESSOR SHANDY SLEPT a good deal longer than he'd meant to. By the time he woke, stiff and chilly, the early dusk was already gathering. So, evidently, was the crowd. He could hear a babble of voices down in the Crescent, and a preliminary ripple of bongs from the chapel carillon. As he lay collecting his wits and easing his cramped muscles, the bedroom was suddenly bathed in multicolored light and those accursed Santa Claus faces began flashing on and off. Grimble must have thrown the switch. Cursing, he sat up and reached for his shoes.

His intention was to take down those hideous masks and jump on them, but as he reached for the first one to hand, a shrill young voice from below piped, "Aw, mister!" He settled for drawing the blind, realized the cloth would be apt to catch fire from being pressed against the hot bulbs, and had to put it up again. From his folly, there was no escape.

At least he could flee temporarily to the faculty dining room. Both he and Tim would feel better with a hot meal under their belts. He'd go round up his old friend.

It was curious, now he thought of it, that the police had not fetched the husband over here this morning, instead of trundling Jemima's body straight downtown without even letting Tim know where it was. True, he mustn't have had to look far. Balaclava Junction had only one undertaker, who belonged to the same lodge as Grimble and Ottermole and would surely get the business. Still, they might have asked Professor Ames's consent before turning his wife over to Harry the Ghoul. The fact was, people did not take Tim seriously as a human being.

Shandy could understand why easily enough. Ames was not totally deaf. He did own a hearing aid, but peculiar bone formations in his ears sometimes caused the device to act as a built-in scrambler. One never knew whether he was hearing the right words, the wrong words, or a jumble of unrelated sounds. He could lip-read very well, but was so near-sighted that he had to get close to the speaker, and so shy that he didn't always care to do that.

Perhaps as a result of his affliction, Ames concentrated so fiercely on his own subject that he was usually oblivious to everything else, thus a natural butt for all the absent-minded professor jokes. Even his appearance was almost risible: diminutive, gnarled, bald on top and hairy everywhere else.

Jemima, probably not on purpose but out of her own need to be important, had fostered the myth of her husband's general uselessness outside his particular field. His children liked him well enough as a sort of family pet but never seemed to accord him the respect due a father. Yet Professor Ames was an exceedingly bright, capable, and above all logical man. Whoever had done this dreadful thing to Jemima didn't know that.

Shandy couldn't honestly see that this narrowed the list of suspects much. Not many people did know, aside from himself and President Svenson and perhaps a few of the more observant students. It was always hard to tell what students took in and what they didn't.

This was no time for such musings. Shandy put on his good gray overcoat and good felt hat and added a dark red cashmere muffler Alice had sent him, for there was a chill in the air that penetrated the walls of the brick house, probably because he'd set back the thermostat earlier and forgotten to turn it up again.

He remedied his omission before starting out. Tim might want to come back and sit awhile, and it would be good to have the place comfortable for him. It was too bad they'd have to put up with that lurid glare, but he realized at this stage that his only hope of averting general obloquy was to brazen it out and pretend he thought his decorations handsome. Instead of being obliged to declare open warfare, his neighbors could work off their resentment by despising his rotten taste behind his back.

That meant he would have no defense next year, assuming he managed to stay, against whichever Illumination stalwart caught up Jemima's fallen torch and offered to decorate his house for him. It was, he supposed, only a fair price to pay. Perhaps the *Singapore Susie* would be repaired by then, or he could fly out and spend the holidays with Alice, as she'd been begging him to do ever since she got married. Maybe Henry and Elizabeth would enjoy an expense-paid trip as a Christmas present, instead of the accustomed cigars and jellies.

He doubted it. They were a pair of contented old fogies, such as he himself had so short a time ago looked forward to becoming. Sighing, Professor Shandy opened his front door and eased himself out into the maelstrom of merriment.

"Watch it, Professor!"

He leaped just in time. One of the sleds, carrying a gaggle of shrieking tourists and propelled by a blond Amazon in a bulky red sweater, no pants to speak of, and heavy rib-knit green tights, hurtled down the sidewalk.

The sled pullers knew perfectly well they were supposed to keep the sleds off the walkways and never let go of the towropes, but the rule was constantly being violated, especially by those of the girls who were pretty enough to think they could get away with anything. Professor Shandy was by no means indifferent to feminine pulchritude, but beefy blondes left him as cold as he would have thought those minuscule pants left them. He would have a word with that young woman if he could ever get her to stand still long enough and if he managed to find out who she was. They all looked much alike in those ridiculous costumes, which were meant to represent Santa's elves. He wouldn't even have known this one was female if she'd been obeying another of the rules and wearing the knitted face helmet that was supposed to go with the costume.

Muttering, he elbowed his way through the strollers and gapers, and managed to reach Ames's house more or less unscathed. Before he'd even started knocking, Tim opened the door.

"Hi, Pete. I thought you'd be over. Been watching out the window."

"Good thing you were. I'd never have been able to make myself heard above this God-awful racket. It gets worse every year."

"You contributed your share. God, that was funny."

Ames made the statement automatically, showing no inclination to throw another laughing fit. Shandy could understand why.

"How did you make out with Ottermole?"

"All right, I guess. He asked me a lot of damn fool questions about when did I see her last and so forth. Seemed to think I was mentally defective because I couldn't tell him. But, damn it, that was the way Jemima operated. She'd breeze in and change her clothes or grab a basketful of junk for one of the booths, go charging out again, and stay till the last gun was fired and the smoke cleared away. We've had separate rooms since the kids moved out, so how the hell would I know whether or not she came in to sleep? Asked me if the bed was made, for God's sake. Nobody's made a bed in this house for thirty-seven years. Well, maybe that's a slight exaggeration. I guess she used to change the sheets now and then, but you can bet your sweet Alice it wasn't while the Illumination was going on. You want a drink?"

"I daresay I could use one. I was going to suggest that we go over to the dining room."

Ames snorted. "You sound like Jemima. 'If you want any dinner, you'd better go up to the college. I have more important things to do than stand around a kitchen.' Of course she'd spend all day baking those damn fool coconut cowpats for the cookie sale. I never knew why it was she could handle everybody's job but her own. Now, where the hell did she put the whiskey?"

He maundered off, searching for a bottle that would likely as not be empty if he ever found it. Shandy didn't offer to help. He only hoped Tim would tire of hunting soon and they could get out of here. The dismal confusion of the Ames house had always depressed him, but it seemed even deadlier now without Jemima's boisterous presence actual or impending.

Could he possibly be missing the woman? He supposed it was possible. Tim had said, "I didn't like her, but I sort of loved her, in a way." That was more or less how he himself had felt about her; not love, certainly, nor friendship, but the grudging fondness one had for one's tiresome but well-intentioned relatives.

For a wonder, Tim managed to locate not only the whiskey but a couple of clean tumblers. Shandy pretended he was glad to get the drink, because old Tim was so pleased with himself for succeeding at this essay in housewifery. How in God's name was he ever going to manage here alone?

"Have you called the children?" he asked.

"Called the Oceanographic Institute to see if there was any way I could get hold of Roy. They say he's still at sea, headed for Ross Bay. They're going to send a wireless to the ship. Best they can do right now. Later they'll try to set up some kind of radio relay so I can talk to him at the base."

"That's good. What about Jemmy?"

"She doesn't think the doctor will let her come. Baby's due in a few days. Jemima was going to fly out. Had her ticket all bought. All Jemmy could say was, 'Now Mummy can't be with me.' I didn't think she'd take it so hard. Suppose it is sort of a jolt, way the hell and gone the other side of the country with none of her own folks around her."

"Why don't you go on Jemima's ticket?"

"Huh? Me? What the hell could I do?"

"You could be with her."

"For what that's worth."

"It might be worth more than you think, Tim. Why don't you call her back and suggest it?"

"I wouldn't even know what to say."

"Say you'll go as soon as the funeral's over, if she wants you to."

"What if she doesn't?"

"Then you stay here."

"You make it sound easy."

"Why shouldn't it be? She's your own daughter, isn't she?"

"Oh yes, no doubt about that." A smile flickered across the gnomish face. "Jemima had her faults, but that wasn't one of them. All right, Pete, if you say so."

"Want any help getting the number?"

"No, I can manage."

Ames set down his tumbler and went to wherever the phone might be lurking. Shandy stayed where he was. He didn't want to hear the hurt in his old friend's voice if Jemmy turned her father down.

Apparently she didn't. Ames came back looking sheepish but happy.

"She's tickled pink. Told me when the plane leaves and says I damn well better be on it because Dave's taking time off from work to pick me up. Laying down the law just like her mother."

"I'm glad, Tim," said Shandy with all sincerity. "It will be a great thing for both of you. I can keep an eye on the house while you're away."

"Hell, she's got that fixed, too. Some old-maid aunt of Dave's was there, bringing over her plants. She just got fired from her job or some damn thing and was leaving town anyway, so Jemmy had the bright idea of sending her here to housekeep for me."

"Why not? You probably won't have her underfoot for long. There's nothing to keep a woman in Balaclava Junction unless she decides to marry you or take over Jemima's job on the Buggins Collection."

That last was a particularly nasty thing to say and Shandy was at once sorry he'd said it, but Tim well knew what a sore point the Buggins Collection had always been with him.

Back in the 1920s, some distant connection of the founder took exception to the fact that Balaclava Buggins had preferred his first name to his last. In order that the family name might be preserved in college, he bequeathed his personal library to the institution with the proviso that it be housed as a separate unit and known as the Buggins Collection.

As he left only a small sum to maintain the collection, and as the books had nothing to do with agriculture, they were dumped into a room at the back of the library building and locked up until such time as somebody got around to straightening them out.

The college grew. The librarian got busier. The Buggins Collection got dustier. Once in a while, somebody would unlock the door, sneeze a few times, shake his head, and lock it again. The books couldn't be circulated, or even consulted, because they had not been catalogued. Nobody cared because nobody wanted to read them anyway, until Peter Shandy joined the faculty.

Professor Shandy had a pleasant, old-gentlemanly taste for verse as distinct from poetry. He had grown up on Macaulay, Joel Barlow, and John G. Saxe. He could never read "Jim Bludsoe of the Prairie Belle" without choking up on those immortal lines, "I'll hold her nozzle agin the bank/Till the last galoot's ashore." He could recite "The Dinkey Bird goes singing/In the amfalula tree," although he had not done so since Alice grew up.

He thought of the treasures in rhyme that must be lurking among those cobwebbed piles, and wished to Christ somebody would get busy and straighten them out. He would gladly have taken on the job himself in his spare time, but Porble the librarian never let anybody have the key to the Buggins Room because the books couldn't be circulated since they hadn't been catalogued and it was against library rules for nonstaff people to go in there and mess around.

So Shandy, once tenure had made him bold, started chanting at faculty meetings, "We ought to do something about the Buggins Collection." First it was a joke, then a bore. Nothing happened until he did what he should have done in the first place and voiced his concern to Mrs. Svenson at a cocktail party. Jemima Ames, who had a knack for popping up in the wrong place at the worst time, overheard and at once volunteered herself as assistant librarian for the Buggins Collection.

Sieglinde Svenson knew Mrs. Ames as a tireless worker in college causes. She spoke to Thorkjeld. President Svenson knew there was money in the Buggins fund that couldn't be touched for any more useful purpose. He did not know Mrs. Ames's total inability to stick to anything she was really supposed to do, so he hired her.

At the time of her demise, Jemima had held the appointment for almost a year. She had requisitioned card files and made great play with Library of Congress lists. She had spent much time and energy promoting a contest to design a special bookplate for the Buggins Collection which nobody bothered to do because there were no prizes and which would in any case have been redundant as the late Mr. Buggins had already put in his own bookplates. She had flaunted her title and talked of the great work to be accomplished, but not one book had got dusted, much less shelved.

If Shandy had in fact been the one to slaughter Tim's wife, it would have been the Buggins Collection that drove him to it. Since nobody else gave two hoots about the old books, however, some other frustration must have triggered the deed.

But how could he know frustration was the motive? Jemima had been putting people's backs up for years, and nobody had murdered her before.

"More whiskey, Pete?"

"Er—no, thanks." He set down the glass he'd emptied without realizing it. "I think we ought to get along to the dining room, or they'll have nothing left but turkey hash. To tell you the truth, I've been wondering why anybody wanted to kill Jemima. I mean, wanted to so badly that he or she actually did it. Oh, damn, you know what I'm trying to say."

"I know, Pete. She could be the most exasperating woman on earth, but she wasn't basically ill-natured. I've been wondering about that myself."

"Did you tell Ottermole we'd decided it was murder rather than accident?"

"No, I thought I hadn't better. He thinks I'm about one step ahead of the funny farm anyway, and I figured he wouldn't listen to me. He's convinced he did a brilliant piece of detecting."

"I expect he wants to think so, anyway. The townees don't want to run afoul of Svenson any more than we do. Did you manage to find the marble?"

"No sign of it. I made Harry the Ghoul search her clothes while I stood there and watched. That was another thing that made Ottermole sure I was rounding the bend."

"I'm sorry."

"What for? Damn it, I'm sorry, too, but not about what that jackass thinks of me. Come on, Pete, we might as well tie on the feed bag."

SIX

THEY PICKED THEIR way among the cider-swiggers and gingerbread-nibblers, the sliders and the strollers, up the slippery, trodden Crescent toward the college. Shandy marveled that so many humans were willing to drive long distances over secondary and often tertiary roads for the privilege of being fleeced by Balaclava's car-park bandits and joggled by fellow gapers as they milled around ankle-deep in slush. To his horror, he could see that Shandy's Folly was indeed the hit of the show.

"Boy, whoever lives in that place believes in giving us our money's worth," he heard one tourist exclaim. "I'd hate to have their light bill."

The professor winced. He hadn't thought of that. Power from the Cookie Works, as it was irreverently called, was not precisely cheap. No wonder Svenson encouraged the Illumination in all its excesses. The college must do a tidy business in electrical fees on top of everything else. Shandy observed as much to his companion.

Tim didn't hear. He was rambling on about his own problems, mouthing words without realizing no sound was coming out. This often happened. Shandy nudged him in the ribs.

"Speak up, Tim."

"Eh? Oh, I was just sounding off about Harry the Ghoul." Undertaker Goulson was well liked in town, but the nickname was irresistible. "He was pestering me about what I wanted Jemima laid out in. Showed me a bunch of fancy dresses with no backs to 'em. Most indecent things I ever saw. Told him I wouldn't stand for anything so disgusting, and so I won't. Pete, I can't handle this thing. I wish to God Jemmy could have come."

He kicked at frozen slush and took another tack. "I don't know if it's occurred to you, Pete, but we're going to be about as popular around here as a couple of skunks at a lawn party. All the people who couldn't stand Jemima when she was alive are going to feel guilty and blame us for her getting killed. You'd better come to California with me."

"No, I'll stand the gaff. You had nothing to do with it."

"I let her lie there for three days. They'll call me a callous brute. Suppose I was."

"No, you weren't," said his friend loyally, even though he knew the neighbors must be saying that and a great deal more. Confirmation appeared in the shape of Jemima's staunch ally, Hannah Cadwall, bearing down on them with blood in her eye. Knowing his only defense was in attack, Shandy beat her to the draw.

"Hannah, we came out looking for you."

His outright lie stopped her in her tracks. Shandy pressed his advantage.

"Tim was just saying we need a woman's help in this terrible time. I expect you've heard about our—er—tragedy?"

Mrs. Cadwall nodded, not quite sure how to reply. Professor Ames nodded, too, and had presence of mind enough to leave the talking to Shandy.

"Perhaps you wouldn't mind walking along with us to the dining room. I'm trying to get him to eat something," Shandy added in a conspiratorial murmur.

"Why, of course. Anything I can do—such a dreadful—still can't believe she's—" Mrs. Cadwall's earnest incoherencies were a welcome switch from the reproaches she no doubt had ready framed. She did show a distressing tendency to lead the shattered widower by the arm, but that would have to be borne. If he could get her to see Ames as victim instead of villain and himself as a well-intentioned blunderer, public opinion might still be swayed in their favor, because Hannah was a talker and so was her husband. Shandy eased the tremolo stop out another notch.

"Unfortunately, he won't be able to have either of the children with him. Roy's at the South Pole and Jemmy's about due to have her baby, as you doubtless know. She's so dreadfully cut up about her mother that Tim's promised to go out there right after the funeral. Rather heartbreaking, don't you think?"

Mrs. Cadwall obliged with a sniffle. "Poor soul, whatever will become of him? Jemima was so—so—"

"Indeed she was. It's a sad loss for us all. I'll confess to you, Hannah, as an old friend, that I'm having strong guilt feelings about this awful thing. After that—er—little talking-to you two gave me, I—er—tried to make amends, as you must have realized. You can't say I didn't try."

"No, you certainly tried," Mrs. Cadwall had to concede.

"Chief Ottermole feels that Jemima must have been in the process of—er—modifying my efforts when she slipped and fell. I'll never forgive myself." That last bit, at any rate, was not humbug.

"Now, Peter, there's no sense in your brooding over what can't be helped. In a way, I suppose it's as much my fault as yours. I nagged at you enough about decorating. Next year, I'd be glad to—"

"It's right this minute we need you most, Hannah. Do you think you might possibly be willing, as Jemima's—er—closest friend and confidante, to do her a last favor?"

"Oh yes, anything!"

"Tim was just saying—Tim," he bawled into the widower's ear, "why don't we ask Hannah about the dress?"

Ames, who had been lip-reading as best he could, picked up his cue.

"Goulson wants to know what to lay her out in. Tried to talk me into some piece of nonsense he's got down there. Didn't look like her style. Can't you pick out something of hers that she liked, that she'd feel comfortable in?"

The last words came out jumbled, probably because his teeth were slipping. Hannah took it for emotion and was won.

"Leave it to me, Tim. I'll straighten out Harry the Ghoul. Shall I order the flowers, too? The florist's his brother-in-law and they'll skin you alive between them if you don't put your foot down."

"Hannah, you're a good friend. You go ahead and do it the way you think Jemima would have wanted, and send the bills to me."

Mrs. Cadwall blew her nose. "Peter," she choked, "see that he eats a good dinner."

There was a fair amount of shoulder-patting and hand-squeezing before Mrs. Cadwall sped off on her errand of light. This took place directly in front of the dining hall and was witnessed by a satisfying number of faculty members. Ames almost queered the performance by remarking, "God, Pete, you played her like a violin," but fortunately he forgot to turn up the volume. Shandy got him inside fast and asked the waitress in properly subdued tones for a table in a quiet corner.

They got through the meal rather quickly. The student waitress was brisk and efficient. Those fellow diners who came over to offer condolences didn't linger at the table. It was never easy to make small talk with Professor Ames, and the subject was not a pleasant one.

"The funeral?" Tim answered the question for the sixth time. "It's tomorrow morning at ten o'clock in the college chapel. Don't want to drag it out and put a damper on the Illumination. Jemima wouldn't have liked that."

He sighed and picked up his dessert fork. The inquirer took the hint and left.

Tim was looking awfully tired, Shandy thought. This must be a terrible strain on the deaf man, so used to living in his own silent world. Probably the best thing would be to get him straight home. For Shandy himself there could be no rest. Among other things, he must call on the Dysarts, not only because he owed them an apology but because he wanted to know more about Jemima's last actions of record.

He signed the check, left a lavish tip feeling that he'd better get as many people as possible on his side, and shepherded his old friend back down the hill. Neither of them said much until they were inside the house that its late mistress had bedecked so exuberantly without and allowed to remain such a dismal mess within.

"Do you mind staying here alone, Tim?"

"Why the hell should I? Anyway, I expect Hannah will be along pretty soon to get that dress. I forgot to give her my key."

"Speaking of keys, I've been wondering whether you or Jemima had a key to my house."

"Damned if I know." Ames glanced around the cluttered room helplessly. "If we did, it's buried somewhere. It wasn't on her, anyway. She wasn't even carrying a key to this house. She knew I'd be here."

"Then I wonder how she got in. She or whoever took her. I could find no sign of forced entry."

"Maybe they picked the lock."

"They're supposed to be the nonpickable kind. You have to use a key both coming and going. Tim, that's another mistake! I had to use my own key to get in. If there was no key on her, how in hell did the doors get locked? I think we'll have to go back and try to pound some sense into Ottermole's head."

"Can't be done; Pete, believe me. He'll claim the door was unlocked and you didn't notice or the key was there and you hid it or some damn bunch of horsefeathers. He doesn't want a murder during the Grand Illumination and he's not going to have one and that's that. Oh, Christ, Pete, I can't handle this."

"All right, Tim. You concentrate on getting through the funeral and out to be with Jemmy. I won't do anything you don't want me to."

"At this stage, I don't know what I want except a few hours' sleep. I'm not going to ask you to sit on this. You're a scholar. If one of your plants died, you'd think it was part of your job to find out why. If somebody gets killed in your house, the same principle has to apply, I suppose. You know I've always worked with you as best I could, and I'm not backing off now, especially when it's my own wife that's dead. I'm just asking how much you think you're going to accomplish by raising a ruckus when you're already in the doghouse for trying to sabotage the Illumination. You know damn well that's what you had in mind and so does everybody else around here who isn't an utter jackass, regardless of your fancy footwork back there with Hannah Cadwall. Aren't they going to think this is just another scheme to stir up trouble because your first one laid an egg?"

Shandy hunched his shoulders. "You've never given me bad advice yet, Tim. I'll wait until I have something more tangible to show. Er—you're not by any chance planning on cremation, are you?"

"No, we have a family plot up near Groton. I'm having her buried there as soon as the ground can be dug. In the meantime, they'll keep her in some damnable cold storage vault they've got somewhere. So we can get at the body without having to order an exhumation for the next couple of months, I daresay. That what you had in mind?"

"Er—yes. Though the cause of death seemed obvious enough. Tim, I can't leave this awful business lying on my doorstep. Surely it won't hurt to keep nosing around in a quiet way?"

"It might hurt a great deal, if the wrong person got wind of what you're up to. You know yourself that students in Poultry Management are always squeamish about killing their first chicken, but after that they take it in stride."

"For a man who doesn't talk much, you have quite a gift for words, old friend. I'll try not to wind up in the soup." Shandy rewrapped his muffler. "Florence Nightingale is about to ring your doorbell. I'll leave you to her."

"Thanks, pal. Care to walk me down to the funeral? I'm supposed to get there early so people can cry over me."

"I'll pick you up at a quarter past nine."

Shandy opened the door for Hannah Cadwall, pressed her hand and was rewarded with a watery smile, and went out to breast the tide of jollity once more. He had no scruples about leaving his friend with Hannah, as Tim could always turn off his hearing aid.

That remark of Tim's about chickens was uncomfortably perspicacious. He hadn't thought of the possibility for himself. There seemed to be a great many things he hadn't thought of. At least he ought to be safe enough making his apologies to the Dysarts.

"Watch it, Professor!"

There was that accursed girl again, trundling some squealing wretch over the iced-in ruts on her confounded sled.

"Watch it yourself, young woman," he snapped. "You're supposed to keep those sleds out of the walkways."

She sped past before he got the words out, with a provocative waggle of her backside. Some other bogus elf, anonymous in a knitted mask, yelled from one of the gingerbread houses, "Don't be a party-pooper, Professor. How about a hot cider to melt that cold, cold heart?"

"I've just finished dinner, thank you," he replied with what fragment of dignity was left to him. "However, I'll take a packet of those—er—coconut cowpats."

The Dysarts went in rather heavily for whimsy.

"You'll never regret it," the student assured him, accepting a five-dollar bill and returning a shockingly small amount of change.

"I regret it already," the professor replied, gazing in dismay at the pittance in his glove. "In any event, I don't intend to eat them myself so the worst will be spared to me. Er—speaking of survival, can you tell me the name of that—er—blond bombshell who keeps trying to run me down with her sled? I've been wondering if she does it out of personal animosity or near-sightedness."

The elf stared through its yarn-fringed eyeholes. "You mean you don't know Heidi Hayhoe?"

"Obviously not. Is there any reason why I should?"

While the elf was still groping for words, its stand was suddenly inundated by a horde eager to exchange cold cash for hot cider. Shandy grabbed his bag of cowpats and fought his way loose.

The Dysarts lived in the last and largest house on the Crescent. Actually, it faced Shropshire Avenue, the road that meandered down from behind the college to cross Balaclava Junction's Main Street. However, the Crescent counted the handsome fieldstone and clapboard residence as its own because it did the neighborhood credit. So, most people felt, did the Dysarts.

They were the only faculty couple who did mad, sophisticated things like hopping down to New Orleans for the Mardi Gras or over to Milwaukee for the Oktoberfest. They were the only people in town who owned a Porsche and among the few who knew how to pronounce it. They also owned a beat-up old Volkswagen.

Nobody needed two cars in a village where everything was within walking distance, but that was part of the Dysart mystique. Adele made a point of driving the VW to the supermarket about once a month. The elderly vehicle was apt as not to break down in the parking lot and give her an opportunity to demonstrate that she was just a harried housewife like the rest of them. Adele was the one with the money.

She also had a great many teeth. Professor Shandy was always aware of Adele Dysart's teeth, but never more so than now, as he handed over his sack of bucolic ribaldry and stammered out his apologies for having cut their Christmas party without notice.

"I was—er—called out of town unexpectedly."

"So we heard, only that wasn't the way we heard it. Hiya, Pete."

Bob Dysart surged forward. Bob always surged. He reminded Shandy of the *Singapore Susie*, now that the professor was in a position to make the comparison.

"Have a drink and tell us all about it."

"There's—er—not a great deal to tell. Thanks, I will. A small scotch and water, if you don't mind. About half of what you'd consider a reasonable allowance for an elderly lady in poor health."

Bob dispensed liquor as he did everything else, in a big way. Shandy did not wish to complete his roster of social gaffes by having to battle his way back up the Crescent half sloshed. He picked his way among the Dysarts' assortment of furniture, avoided the camel bench and the chair made entirely of buffalo horns, and settled on a wicker throne with a back like a peacock's tail. The seat wasn't too bad, and he wouldn't have to look at what was behind him.

"How's that?"

His host thrust a tumbler with a large orange D on it into his hand. Shandy tasted the mixture with apprehension and decided to let the ice melt a little.

"Fine, Bob. I suppose you've heard the—er—terrible news?"

"We've heard Jemima Ames fell and cracked her nut, if that's what you mean." Bob made a thing of calling a spade by a more vulgar name. "As to whether it's terrible, I haven't made up my mind."

"Pay no attention to him, Peter," said Adele. "He's in one of his Oscar Wilde moods. I think it's perfectly awful myself. Poor Jemima was such a vibrant personality."

"That depends on how you define vibrant," her husband quibbled. "Constantly in motion and not getting anywhere but making a lot of noise about it, like a tuning fork? If that's what you mean, I agree absolutely."

"That's not bad, sweetie. Perhaps you'd better go write it down. Bring me a bourbon on your way back."

"You've already had a bourbon."

"I've had two, but who's counting? Tell me, Peter, was she all bloodied up and horrible?"

"No, nothing like that. Just—er—lying there."

"Oh."

Adele struggled not to look disappointed. "Hannah told me she tripped on a ladder or something while she was trying to take down those fantastic Santa Clauses of yours. She said she was going to, you know."

"Did she? No, I didn't know."

"You would have, you bad kid, if you hadn't skipped out on my lovely party. Who's the woman?"

"What woman?"

"The one you went to spend Christmas with. Why else would you walk out on me?"

Shandy felt himself gripped by another of those hellish impulses.

"Er—her name is Susie. In strictest confidence, of course."

"I won't breathe a word," said Adele with an earnestness that fooled nobody. "What's she like?"

"Well—er—she's very fond of the water. You say Jemima was trying to take down my Santa Clauses? I think they're rather colorful myself."

"They're that, and then some," roared Bob. "Come on, Pete, you can't kid us. Everybody knows what you were up to."

"That's distressing. I'd hoped I might be able to—er—persuade you otherwise."

"Forget it, pal. Feeling was running pretty high at the party. No higher than the guests, I have to admit."

"You know what happens when Bob makes the punch," said Adele. "I'm not sure whether it was the cherry brandy or the tequila this time."

"Too bad I missed it," said Shandy, unable to repress a shudder. "Then Jemima was a trifle above herself, so to speak?"

"No worse than anyone else," Adele started to say, but her husband cut in.

"No use trying to paint the lily, Dell, or whatever it is you do to the damn things. Pete would know, I expect. Jemima was drunk as a skunk, to coin a simile. Don't you remember how we all stood at the window watching her weave herself down the path with that purple cape flapping out behind her? Christ, we laughed ourselves sick."

"Well, don't do it again," said his wife. "Peter, you wouldn't believe the mess I had to cope with next morning. Next time you drop one of your time bombs into the punch bowl, sweetiekins, you clean the bathrooms."

"Isn't she cute, Pete? How's your drink? Ready for the dividend?"

"No, thanks. I'm still working on the—er—principal. I wonder if you have any idea who let her in?"

"Who can remember?" Adele replied. "Either Bob or myself, I suppose, or else she just barged in without ringing the bell. She'd do that."

"I meant into my house," Shandy explained. "She couldn't have barged in there because I'd locked up carefully before I left."

Dysart shrugged. "She must have found a key somewhere. I know Adele and I are always leaving them with the neighbors when we go away and so does everybody else. You probably gave her one yourself at one time or another."

"I'm quite sure I didn't. Jemima wasn't particularly reliable. Anyway, Mrs. Lomax generally takes care of the place while I'm gone."

"She didn't this time."

"No, but—"

"Damn it, Pete, there's no use making a mystery over a little thing like this. You've passed one out to somebody or other so long ago you've forgotten about it, that's all. What about the Feldsters? They're the most logical, being your next-door neighbors."

Shandy didn't think so. Mirelle Feldster had been trying for fifteen years to take poor, lonely Peter Shandy under her motherly wing. He couldn't believe he'd ever have been fool enough to give her a key to his house and not get it back. Still, there was always the possibility she'd managed to get hold of one somehow.

"Were they at the party?"

"Sure. Everybody was but you and the Cadwalls, naturally. I'll bet a nickel it was either Mirelle or Jim who gave Jemima the key. You can imagine how they're feeling about this cute trick of yours, with eight plastic reindeer leering straight into their bedroom window. Must be putting old Jim right off his stroke."

"If you ask me, he quit stroking a long time ago," Adele put in, but Shandy paid no attention.

"But you don't actually remember anyone's mentioning a key?"

"Hell, I don't remember anything at all with any great degree of clarity from about half past eight on," said Dysart.

"I'll drink to that," said his wife.

"That and whatever else comes handy. You were feeling no pain yourself, tootsie."

Shandy was not about to let them get sidetracked. "But you do recall Jemima's leaving, Bob? Who let her out?"

"You mean held the door and waved 'by-'by? I didn't. I believe I went upstairs with her to get her blanket and war bonnet mainly because I had to go to the bathroom and the one downstairs was in use. I presume she got down on her own while I was making my tinkle."

"And I know I didn't," said Adele. "Contrary to what my loving husband is trying to make you believe, I was cold sober. I wouldn't dare be anything else in front of that crowd. I couldn't go to the door with Jemima because I had something in the oven. She'd come to me a few minutes before and said she must be going and I said she couldn't go yet because she hadn't had any of my squid puffs."

"Your what?"

"Squid puffs. It's a Greek recipe. They have to be timed to the minute. I rushed out to put a batch under the broiler and the next thing I knew, Bob was yowling, 'Hey, everybody, get a load of the mountain going to Mohammed.' So I glanced out the window and there was Jemima lumbering down the path to the short cut. I must say I was a bit miffed, when I'd gone to that much bother especially for her."

"Do you happen to remember the exact time?"

"Yes, I do, because I was timing the puffs. I had to take them out at precisely nine twenty-nine. Funny how things like that stick in your mind."

"That's right," said Bob. "The carillon started ringing while we were still gathered around the window, laughing our fool heads off. God, that was funny!"

"Don't kid yourself, darling," cooed his wife. "The others just went along with your lousy joke because you were buying the booze, which needless to say you weren't. I hope you don't honestly believe you're fooling anybody about who pays the bills around here."

The conversation had worked around to where the Dysarts' badinage usually did wind up sooner or later. Shandy set down his still nearly full tumbler and got up.

"I'm afraid I'll have to be going. I promised Tim I'd make some phone calls for him. The funeral is tomorrow morning, you know, at ten o'clock in the chapel. You'll come, I hope?"

"So soon?" shrilled Adele. "I haven't done a thing about flowers. God, I wonder if Harry the Ghoul is answering his business phone? Maybe he can wake up the florist or something. It would have to be a Sunday! Why didn't you let me know earlier?"

"Cool it, Dell," said her husband. "They'll be around. Those guys would never miss out on a chance to make a buck. You can count on us, Pete. Adele's got a new black mink coat Santa Claus brought her, and she's itching to show it off. Think you can find the door?"

"I expect likely. Thanks for the drink."

"Thanks for the cowpats. See you tomorrow."

SEVEN

SHANDY WALKED THOUGHTFULLY down the path to the short cut. This was the way Jemima had come. It would be. Jemima was a great taker of short cuts. He tried to picture her in front of him as Dysart had described her, a great mass of purple wool weaving and flapping.

It wouldn't work. The path was neatly shoveled since Adele was a great one for getting male students to do odd jobs around the place, although she had to be circumspect in her requests because Mrs. Svenson set a high standard in student-faculty relationships. Still, the shoveler hadn't exerted himself to dig any wider than he had to. There simply was not room for a big woman to weave and flap without toppling into the piled-up snow at either side, and Shandy could find no spot where the smooth bank was disturbed.

She couldn't have been so far gone as Bob made out. That didn't mean anything in particular. It was typical of the assistant professor in electrical engineering to make believe his parties always turned into orgies. In fact, they tended to be rather circumspect affairs, all things considered, including Mrs. Svenson's principles and the president's temper.

At any rate, Jemima had indeed left the Dysarts' under her own power just before half past nine with the avowed intention of vandalizing Shandy's house. He ought to have asked whether anybody else left with her, but thought that was unlikely. Grimble would have mentioned the fact, and Bob wouldn't have missed a chance to drag a second reveler into his story.

Besides, if the killer was also a guest at the party, he or she must surely have had sense enough to hang back long enough to allay any possible suspicion. Jemima would need a fair amount of time to unlock the door and make her way through the different rooms, and it wouldn't take more than three minutes or so to get over to the brick house after her, using the crowd for cover. One would only have to say, "I came to help," wait till her back was turned and strike her down, then set the stage and go away. Somebody primed on tequila and cherry brandy might easily think it a clever touch to spill the marbles but forget to leave the telltale key with the corpse.

Still, he couldn't figure out how anybody could have got away with juggling that outsize body around his living room with the blinds up and tourists glued to the windowpanes, or why anybody would want to try. It would be so much easier to kill her right here in the shrubbery.

His path led straight into an enormous hedge between the Dysarts' and the house that actually was first on the Crescent. Old Dr. Enderble never liked to cut down the bushes because many birds and little animals nested and fed in what had, over many years, become a dense tangle. Once in a while, Mrs. Enderble sneaked out with her sewing scissors in her apron pocket and snipped off a few really bothersome twigs. When the Dysarts bought the adjoining property a few years ago, Bob had made savage attacks on the overgrown shrubs, heedless of his neighbors' protests. Then he found out the Enderbles were adored by everybody in town and decided he'd only been pruning out dead wood to encourage new growth. Sure enough, he had. One would have no trouble hiding a corpse in that copse, Shandy thought, and was immediately appalled at himself for the frivolity.

Perhaps it wouldn't have been all that easy, not if you didn't want the body found right away. Quite a few of the guests at the party must have used this short cut both coming and going. So, most likely, had some of the visitors and even perhaps one or two of those obnoxious sled-pulling elves, although they were enjoined to keep off private grounds. It was never completely dark, even in here, with the white snow reflecting hundreds and hundreds of multicolored lights all around the Crescent. In any event, John Enderble couldn't have helped spotting that garish purple cloak when he came out at dawn to check his bird feeders.

Furthermore, how could a plausible accident be staged out here? There was no large boulder or stump or fence post along the path on which she might seem to have struck her head in falling. She couldn't be dragged into the bushes without leaving a trail and giving the show away.

Shandy still couldn't tell whether somebody had slain Jemima on impulse and then arranged the cover-up, but he was more and more inclined to think the crime had been planned in advance. But why kill Jemima Ames? True, everybody in Balaclava Junction except perhaps Mary Enderble must have entertained the notion at one time or other, but would it actually be possible to stay furious with the woman long enough to do her in? Her methods could drive anybody to exasperation, but her motives were always benevolent enough. Even the Illumination was a worthy cause, as the professor had to keep reminding himself. The agony would be over soon, but the money it earned would continue doing good work for months to come.

Now, there was an angle to consider. Had Jemima found out that somebody was helping himself to more than a fair share of the Illumination funds? The setup was supposed to be reasonably foolproof, but with so many people involved in such a freewheeling operation, there had to be loopholes. Ben Cadwall would know, being the comptroller. So would Hannah Cadwall, no doubt, and Hannah was Jemima's bosom buddy. Could one of them have spotted a fiddle and not told the other?

That might depend on who was doing the fiddling. If it should happen to be the comptroller's wife, friendship wouldn't keep Jemima from ripping her to shreds as a matter of principle. It was Jemima, as everybody but Tim himself knew, who'd ratted to Ottermole that her husband's failing eyesight made him incompetent to drive any longer, regardless of the fact that the car was one of Ames's few pleasures outside his work. If she'd do that to Tim, she'd do anything to anybody.

It would be interesting to know where Hannah Cadwall was at half past nine on the night of December 22. Bob had said she and Ben weren't at the party, and Shandy wouldn't have expected them to be. The comptroller did not approve of the way Professor Dysart flung his wife's money around.

Of course the Dysarts' personal finances were none of the comptroller's business. A great many of the things Ben poked his nose into were none of his business, but that fact never stopped him from wanting to know, nor from preaching from whatever text he considered relevant to the circumstance. People listened to Cadwall because he was in a position that made him dangerous to ignore, but his holier-than-anybody manner had not endeared him to his neighbors and colleagues.

Was it in fact possible to be as righteous as Ben Cadwall acted? If he was, could any woman endure that much respectability without at last feeling something snap? Shandy wasn't prepared to believe that Hannah had embarked on a life of crime just to spite her husband, but he wondered if she mightn't be building up a private nest egg as a step toward striking out on her own.

As to killing Jemima, Hannah would certainly have had the best chance. It wasn't possible that Jemima Ames hadn't sounded off to her best friend, as she had to the Dysarts' guests, about going over and ripping down Shandy's decorations. They might even have planned to do it together, Mrs. Cadwall being appointed to get hold of a key while Mrs. Ames put in her appearance at the Dysarts'.

It would be quite within Cadwall's character to own a personal set of keys to all the houses on the Crescent. Although these were owned by the people who lived in them, the land they sat on belonged to the college and they couldn't be resold except to other faculty or staff. That, and the fact that they all got their power from the college plant, was sufficient reason for the Svensonian fiat that each householder must leave a door key with the security office. It would be no problem for Grimble to make duplicates, and he'd do it if Cadwall asked him to. Grimble would not disoblige the man who signed his pay checks.

Grimble was, in fact, altogether too co-operative for Shandy's taste. He was pretty sure the key that let Jemima in must have come from the security chief, either directly or indirectly. The only alternative was Mrs. Lomax, and she was not only pea-green incorruptible but out of town. Besides, she'd talk. The professor had a hunch that Grimble, if suitably compensated, would not.

It wasn't fair to make such a judgment, however, without checking out the office first and finding out whether it was possible simply to steal a key. There were a lot of things that had to be found out. He'd start tomorrow. Right now, he was feeling too abominably tired. Was it that lethal drink of Dysart's, or the fact that he was fifty-six years old?

Why did he have to keep brooding on his age all of a sudden? He and Jemima were born in the same year. Jemmy had organized a joint birthday party for him and her mother while she was still living at home. He'd been pleased at being included, even though he had to wear a paper crown and blow out a lot of candles that kept relighting themselves. Jemmy had a regrettable taste for practical jokes. That baby of hers would probably be born wearing a false nose and celluloid buck teeth. Shandy was glad Tim would be with her when it happened. The poor old coot needed a laugh to cheer him up.

Getting Tim to the airport, that was another chore for his list. Either of the Dysarts would no doubt be glad to take Ames in the Porsche, but they both drove like maniacs and smoked like fiends. Tim would be a wheezing hulk by the time they arrived. He was in no great shape now. Shandy would rent a car from the garage downtown and make the trip as comfortable as possible for his old friend. It was the least he could do, after what he'd done.

But what the flaming perdition had he, in fact, done? That was the crux and quite likely the nexus of the entire situation. Did his misbegotten whimsy precipitate this outrage, or only provide a handy cover for something that was going to happen anyway?

Shandy got little time to ponder. He was barely inside the brick house, contemplating a spot of badly needed relaxation with Robert W. Service when the front door buckled slightly. Only one person could knock like that. Now he knew how Rome felt when the Visigoths arrived.

"Come in, President," he said.

The invitation was superfluous. President Svenson was already in, filling the tiny hall from side to side and from floor to ceiling. If the hall had been large, the effect would have been the same. No space ever seemed big enough to contain Thorkjeld Svenson. Wearing a sweater and cap of untreated gray sheep's wool knitted for him by his wife, Sieglinde, probably with an assist from the Norns, he looked like a mountain gone astray from its bedrock.

"Shandy, what are you up to?"

"I've been wondering that myself." There was no use trying to beat around the bush with Svenson. "Sit down, won't you?"

"No. Grimble tells me you've killed Mrs. Ames."

"Does he, now? I wonder why."

"Because he's a jackass, I suppose," the president replied thoughtfully. "What happened?"

"She's presumed to have broken in here to remove my—er—decorations on the way home from the Dysarts' Christmas party, and had a fatal fall."

"Why presumed?"

"I think somebody murdered her."

"Why?"

"If you mean why was she killed, I don't know. If you mean why do I think so, I have sound reason."

Shandy told of the spilled marbles, the superfluous ladder, and the key that should have been with her body but was not. Svenson ruminated awhile.

"Police didn't notice?"

"They didn't want to notice. Grimble and Ottermole are both scared to death of offending you."

"Damn well better be. You told Ames?"

"Yes. He agrees with me, particularly about that step stool. He says his wife would have stood on the sofa."

"Urgh."

The president pondered some more.

"My wife would never stand on a sofa," he pronounced finally.

Shandy wondered what sofa could hold her, but thought it wiser not to ask. "Mrs. Svenson is a lady of great dignity," he said.

"Yes, and she's going to bean me with a skillet if I'm not back in time for supper. Mrs. Svenson is not going to like this, Shandy. I don't like it either."

His voice rose to a full gale. "Damn you, Shandy, you've already tried to sabotage the Grand Illumination. If you involve the college in a public scandal over Jemima Ames, I'll personally shove a Balaclava Buster straight down your throat and out your other end."

Professor Shandy had to stand on tiptoe and lean over backward to look his superior square in the eyes, but he managed.

"As far as I'm concerned," he roared back, "you can take the Balaclava Buster and squat on it till you both rot. There's been murder done in my house and I'm not going to stand for it. If you didn't carry your brains in your backside, you'd realize you can't afford to either. Didn't your grandmother ever tell you about the rotten apple in the barrel? Don't you know the meaning of the expression 'moral decay'? You let one member of your faculty get away with a thing like this, and you know what's going to happen to the whole college?"

Svenson's jaw dropped. "How do you know it's a member of the faculty?"

"I don't. It could be a student or someone from Buildings and Grounds or your own secretary, but I don't think so. It has to be somebody who knows the Crescent and the people well enough to have heard Jemima planning to enter my house. I assume it's somebody who could find a way to steal a key from Grimble, unless he's in on the deal, too, which wouldn't surprise me because I think he's a sneak and a liar as well as a jackass, as you so rightly pointed out."

"Urgh. I'll have to think this over. And you can damn well watch your step. All right, Shandy, since you started this mess, you can just go ahead and clean it up. You get it done fast, with no embarrassment to the college, or you'll wish to God you'd never come back. I may carry my brains in my backside, but I also pack one hell of a clout in my fist. Happy New Year."

The president went away. After a while, the walls stopped reverberating. Shandy fixed himself a nightcap and sat down with Robert W. Service, but "The Shooting of Dan McGrew" was pallid stuff compared to what he'd been through this day. To cap it off, he had defied Thorkjeld Svenson and was still alive.

For how long? That aspersion on the president's intellect was not only uncouth and unworthy a man of letters, but also damnably ill judged. The insult had been adroitly turned against himself. Svenson knew perfectly well that the team of Ames and Shandy could never misread the available evidence so egregiously as to think Jemima had been murdered if she hadn't, and that it would be morally indefensible as well as administratively irresponsible to let such a crime go unpunished. But Svenson would have handled the dirty work himself if Shandy hadn't given him a glorious excuse to dump the responsibility.

Sitting here hoping Mrs. Svenson had in fact crowned her husband with a griddle would avail nothing. Shandy put down his book and tried to organize his thoughts. His brain had turned to mush. He went to bed.

EIGHT

JEMIMA AMES'S FUNERAL made a gloomy anticlimax to a festive weekend. People were huffed at the short notice. They acted flustered and hustled and impatient to get on with their planned activities. Since they couldn't very well take out their resentment on the corpse, they pinned it to Peter Shandy. Only the fact that Tim stuck to him like a leech averted a mass cold-shouldering. The widower was fully aware of what was happening and displayed a Machiavellian streak in getting around it.

"Don't know how I'd have managed without old Pete here," he was telling Sieglinde Svenson. "Rotten thing for him, coming home and finding her like that."

"It is a terrible loss for us all." The president's wife knew better than to commit herself. "Your wife was a truly dedicated woman."

She did not try to expand on what Jemima was dedicated to, but gave the widower a sad, ineffable smile, barely touched Shandy's hand with two fingers of her woolly gray glove, and sailed on like a majestic ship of the line. She was wearing a plain blue tweed coat, a blue Angora beret, and enormous black leather boots. Glittering armor would not have been appropriate to the occasion, though it was generally supposed she had a suit at home.

Hannah Cadwall, as mistress of ceremonies, had prepared a collation to which a chosen group were invited directly after the obsequies. Shandy went perforce, hoping for a drinkable cup of coffee to take away the chill that had gripped him ever since he happened to catch the president's eye.

To his surprise, he found not only coffee but a pitcher of bloody marys and a cold buffet that stopped not far short of being lavish. Ben Cadwall was dispensing refreshment with an unwontedly free hand, in the happy knowledge that Timothy Ames would have to foot the bill. Bob and Adele Dysart were munching and sipping along with the rest.

That they'd accepted an invitation was not remarkable. The Dysarts would say yes to anything that in any way resembled a social event. What was astonishing was that Ben had let Hannah invite them. Shandy thought it over and came to the conclusion that the Cadwalls must feel some sense of obligation for all those invitations they'd declined. This was a way to pay back the Dysarts at no cost to themselves.

Unfortunately, the idea struck him as funny. Shandy made the appalling blunder of laughing aloud, then had to pretend he was choking on a crumb. There seemed a general decision to let him choke, but Mirelle Feldster's motherly impulses got the better of her.

"Here, Peter, drink this. We don't want any more accidents around here."

The professor couldn't think of anything to say to that, so he drank the coffee she'd brought without speaking. Mirelle was not one to tolerate a silence for long.

"I must say, Peter, I'm surprised you popped into the house long enough to find poor Jemima, you're such a gadabout lately. I'm also just a bit puzzled as to why you haven't thought fit to tell your old friends about getting engaged to that woman in Baltimore."

Shandy set down his cup. "You haven't heard who she is, by any chance?"

"I'm waiting for you to tell me."

"They say the—er—husband is always the last to know. Would you mind passing on any further information that comes your way?"

"Are you trying to tell me it isn't true?"

"Mirelle, I cannot imagine how that yarn got started," said Shandy with a glance at Adele Dysart, who was carefully avoiding his eyes, "but I assure you that I am not going to marry any lady from Baltimore."

"Maybe it isn't Baltimore," said Mrs. Feldster archly.

"And maybe she ain't no lady," yelled Bob Dysart, who could generally be counted on to make an awkward situation worse. "Eh, Pete, you old rip?"

"Tim," said Shandy, "don't you think it's time we got started? You mustn't miss that plane."

That set off a chorus of "Who's going to drive him to the airport?"

"I am," said Shandy.

"But you don't have a car," Adele Dysart protested.

"I'm renting one from Charlie Ross. It's all arranged."

"I didn't even know you could drive. I'm beginning to think there's quite a lot I don't know about you."

"Aren't we all?" murmured Mirelle Feldster. "Tim, who's going to look after your house while you're gone? I'd be glad to run over once or twice a day."

"No need," said Ames. "Some relative of my daughter's husband is— oh, my God! Pete, I forgot to tell you, Jemmy phoned again last night. That woman's coming in at twelve forty-two and we're supposed to meet her."

"It's 'way after eleven now," said Hannah Cadwall. "You'll never make it."

"That," Shandy replied, "remains to be seen. Come on, Tim."

"I'll get your coat," said Ben. "It's in the guest room."

"Don't bother, I can find it."

Shandy raced upstairs. His coat was somewhere in a heap on the bed, along with everybody else's including Hannah's own unmistakable red-and-green plaid and the ratty brown ulster Ben had worn for as long as anyone could remember. As the professor fished among the garments, something rolled to the floor and bounced under the bed. Muttering, he stooped to pick it up. The object was a yellow glass marble with brown streaks, oddly crackled inside. He'd have known it anywhere.

There was no telling whose cuff or pocket the marble had fallen out of, nor was there any sense in stopping to ask. He grabbed his overcoat, tucked the marble carefully into the inside pocket, and thrust his arms through the sleeves. When he got downstairs, Tim was already on the doorstep and Ben was ready to usher him out. They shouted words of thanks, wrung a few hands, and sped down to the garage.

Neither of the men spoke until they were safely in the rented car, headed for the turnpike. Then Timothy Ames heaved a long sigh and fumbled for his pipe.

"Thank God that's over. I'm just as well pleased the kids couldn't come. Lot of damn foolishness, but she'd no doubt have come back to haunt me if she didn't get a proper send-off."

He made loathsome noises with his pipestem and commenced stuffing tobacco into the burned-out bowl. "What the hell were they saying about you and some woman? I couldn't catch it."

"You didn't miss much. Another of my asinine jokes backfired."

Shandy explained his evil impulse and its embarrassing consequences. Ames was unsympathetic.

"Christ Almighty, Pete, when you set out to cook your own goose, you sure do it up brown. You know what's going to happen to you?"

"No, but I daresay I'll find out fast enough."

"Too right you will! They're probably back there tossing coins to see who gets first whack at warming your bed."

"What?" Shandy narrowly missed climbing up a Volvo. "You're out of your mind."

"Wait and see, old buddy. You're going to get propositioned at least six times between now and New Year's. As to what's going to happen when the holidays are over and the women have time to concentrate on tracking you down, all I can say is—" Ames gave way to unseemly mirth.

"I'm glad you're able to enjoy your own joke," said his friend austerely. "In all my eighteen years at Balaclava, I can assure you that none of those women has so much as—er—dropped her handkerchief in my direction."

"That's because they figured you for a sweet, innocent guy. From now on, they'll be dropping a damn sight more than handkerchiefs. Pete, you don't know what's in store for you. If you don't want to take warning, that's your funeral."

"Well, Tim, we won't argue. Time will settle the matter, one way or another."

"I just don't want to come back and find you a shattered hulk."

"On that, at any rate, we're in perfect agreement. Now if you can get your mind off—er—whatever it's on, I have something more important to tell you. I've found the marble."

"You've what? Where?"

"When I went upstairs to get my coat at the Cadwalls' just now. It rolled off the bed." He explained about the jumble of wraps.

"You couldn't tell whose it came out of?"

"Not possibly."

"At least I'm out of it," said Ames. "Now you see why it pays not to bother with an overcoat."

"Good Lord, Tim, I never thought of you."

"Why not? You can damn well bet Ottermole would have, if he could think. Anyway, it looks as though we've narrowed the field."

"That was my first thought. I only hope I can remember who was at the Cadwalls' till I get a chance to write down the names."

"What about the Cadwalls themselves? Are they out of it?"

"They're in. Ben and Hannah didn't hang up their coats, just tossed them with the rest. We all arrived in a bunch, you know, and I expect they were in a hurry to get the party rolling. Anyway, I've been rather wondering about that pair."

He told Ames why. The widower nodded.

"You may have something there, Pete. Ben must be hell on wheels to live with, and Hannah has plenty of chances to get at the cash. For one thing, she goes around and collects from the kids with the sleds.

They're not supposed to keep more than a couple of bucks in change on them, and you'd be surprised how much they pull in."

He grinned at his unintended pun and made more noises on the pipe. "Hannah also takes the money from the parking lot and those misbegotten gingerbread houses, which comes to a hell of a lot more than you might think. There's an elaborate system of cross-checking that's supposed to keep everybody honest, but Ben was the guy who drew it up. You know, old buddy, this is turning into quite an interesting problem. I sort of wish I weren't going away."

"Nonsense! Jemmy would be heartbroken."

Shandy stepped on the gas and concentrated on reaching the airport before Ames had a chance to talk himself out of the trip. They were going to be late for the incoming flight from California, as it was.

In fact, they were not. That plane was overdue. However, it turned out Tim hadn't heard Jemmy properly about his own time of departure. He had to be hustled madly past the reservation desk and down to the boarding gate, with loudspeakers blaring his name. Only when Ames was safely airborne did Shandy realize he'd forgotten to ask the name of the woman he was supposed to meet.

He was having wild thoughts about phoning Jemmy when more bleatings from the public address system sent impatient friends and relatives surging toward a gate far distant from the one they'd been told to wait at. Shandy surged with the rest, deciding he'd just have to hang around until only one person was left, then introduce himself and hope for the best.

It didn't work that smoothly. Outgoing passengers mingled with incomers. He had no way of knowing which was which. At last he drew a bow at a venture, choosing a middle-aged woman in a red wig and six-inch Wedgies as the likeliest prospect.

"Er—I'm Professor Shandy from Balaclava College."

"Whoopee for you. Beat it, Tyrone, I'm not open for business."

He was trying to get up nerve enough to make a second attempt when a gentle voice from somewhere around his left collarbone spoke.

"Excuse me. I believe I heard you say you're Professor Shandy?"

The speaker was a small woman of forty or so. Shandy's first reaction was that she seemed extremely well put together. Her pale blue coat sat on her compact figure as though it enjoyed being there. Her light blue hat showed just the right amount of fair, curling hair and made an agreeable frame for a peach-petal complexion. Her eyes were hidden behind dark glasses, but it stood to reason they would match her costume. Those features which he could see were in delicate harmony with the rounded oval of her face. He felt better for being able to look at her.

"I am," he said gratefully. "I'm supposed to be meeting a relative by marriage of the former Jemmy Ames. Dare I hope that you are she?"

"I'm Helen Marsh. I thought Professor Ames was coming. I expected to recognize him from pictures Jemmy showed me." She held out a small hand.

"You've missed Ames by about ten minutes," Shandy told her. "There was a mix-up in scheduling and his plane left before yours got in. We were in such a state of confusion that I forgot to ask him your name. Mine is Peter Shandy."

"Oh yes, the turnip man." Miss Marsh flushed, most becomingly. "I'm sorry. Jemmy has told me so much about you and her father and the giant turnip—"

"Actually it's a rutabaga, *Brassica napobrassica*, as opposed to the—er—common turnip, or *Brassica rapa*. The difference is rather interesting if you—er—happen to be interested in that sort of thing."

"I'm sure it is. Have you any idea where I'm supposed to pick up my luggage?"

"This way, I believe."

Shandy started down the apparently endless strip of light brown terrazzo, feeling exhausted and futile. Strangely, Helen Marsh seemed to sense his mood.

"I do hope you're going to tell me about the *Brassicae*."

He stopped in his tracks. "Did you say *Brassicae*?"

"Oh, dear, should it be *Brassicidiae* or something? I'm so stupid about botanical names."

"My dear madam, I was merely overwhelmed with joy at hearing a simple Latin noun pluralized correctly. It was like seeing a familiar face in a foreign land. You—er—wouldn't care for a bite of lunch, or a drink or something?"

"They served lunch on the plane, such as it was, but I wouldn't say no to a small glass of sherry, unless you're just being polite."

"There are those who will tell you I'm never polite. We have a long-ish drive ahead of us, and probably at least half an hour's wait before they finish jumping up and down on your suitcases. I thought we might spend the interval to better advantage in this—er—grotto than standing around the luggage counter."

"Grotto is a lovely word." Miss Marsh took off her sunglasses, confirming Shandy's hypothesis that her eyes would turn out to be a particularly attractive shade of blue, and accompanied him into the murky recesses with every appearance of pleasurable anticipation. A waitress loomed out of the smoky black-and-red like one of Persephone's handmaidens.

"You did say sherry?" he asked his guest. "Dry or—er—otherwise?"

"Amontillado, if they have it."

"Amontillado by all means. Two, please, miss. I suppose everybody drinks sherry in California."

"No, pink Chablis."

"Is that why you decided to come back East?"

"That among other things. I never adjusted. I can't do yoga and I blush terribly at the movies, and I think too much citrus fruit acidifies the system. At least something soured mine."

She ate five kernels of stale popcorn as Shandy counted them in silence, then laughed. She had a clear, small, gurgling laugh that went well with her smile.

"Did Jemmy tell you why I got fired?"

"I didn't talk with Jemmy myself. Tim only said you're a librarian, which was pleasant news to me, I may say. Er—why did you get fired?"

"The president of the college where I was working brought me in a manuscript and asked if I thought the university press ought to publish it. I sent it back with a note saying I'd found the work a lot of pompous nonsense, abominably written. It turned out he was the author. We had what might be called a confrontation scene, after which he said, 'Perhaps you may now wish to alter your opinion?' So I picked up the note and wrote, 'The author is an illiterate windbag,' and that's why I had to skip town."

They both laughed and drank their sherry in a pleasant glow of companionship.

Then Shandy said, "President Svenson is a remarkably intelligent man. I hope you won't make the mistake of—er—not thinking so."

"Am I likely to?"

"Probably not, but people have. The results are usually disastrous and sometimes fatal. Would you care for more sherry?"

"No, I think they must have got me unloaded by now."

She adjusted her scarf and picked up her gloves. Shandy paid the check and added a tip that would have brought a scolding from Ben Cadwall. He'd enjoyed standing Helen Marsh a drink. He even enjoyed shepherding her back along the terrazzo to where two matching blue suitcases were standing like orphans in the storm.

"Goodness, they were prompt," she said. "No, please, let me take one."

"Nonsense."

Shandy picked up both the bags, managing not to stagger. He was fully aware that he was showing off, and that such behavior was silly in a man of his age. Perhaps he might entertain Miss Marsh at a later time by swinging from tree to tree in his leopard skin. He pondered the notion and found it not wholly without merit.

NINE

"WE'LL HAVE TO walk the last bit," Shandy apologized. "Cars can't get up the Crescent during the—er—revels."

Helen Marsh knew all about the Grand Illumination. Jemmy had given her the highlights back in California, and Shandy had perforce filled in the blanks on their drive back, including as much about Jemima's alleged fatal accident as the neighbors knew. He thought it would be injudicious to tell her the truth.

He did confess his own part in precipitating the tragedy. To his unutterable relief, she laughed almost as heartily as Tim had done, though in a more seemly manner, and said she'd probably have done the same, if she'd been clever enough to think of it. By the time he opened the trunk to fish out her luggage, Shandy was in better spirits than he would have thought possible.

"Now, you're not going to carry both those heavy cases up that great, steep hill," she insisted, reaching for a handle.

"My dear lady, I have no intention of carrying either one, nor shall you. Here, Hanson!"

Shandy beckoned to a sophomore student who was lounging about the parking lot across the way. "Would you care to earn a surreptitious stipend?"

"If that means money, sure."

The strapping youth picked up the bags like a couple of pretzels, and was halfway up the hill before the others got fairly started.

"We have an unwritten law here at Balaclava," the professor explained. "Never do anything for yourself that you can wheedle a student into doing for you."

"How much is this particular wheedle going to cost?" asked Miss Marsh, opening her handbag.

"You must allow me, please. I don't get to play the gay gallant very often. Gay in the—er—formerly accepted sense, that is."

She laughed again, even more delightfully than before. "I can't imagine why not, when you do it so well. You've been awfully kind, Professor Shandy."

"Er—my given name is Peter."

"It suits you."

"Do you think so? Er—Helen has always been a favorite name of mine." He hadn't realized it until just then, however.

"Why?" she teased. "Did you have a Helen for your childhood sweetheart?"

"No, actually she was a Guernsey—" Shandy's voice died.

The student, making what was perhaps a natural mistake, had dumped the suitcases on the short walk in front of the brick house, and was studying the porch with gleeful interest. A few steps more, and Shandy could see why.

He had quite forgotten the plastic Santa Claus. One of the decorators' more perverted whimsies had been a life-size articulated mannequin of Old Saint Nick. The last time Shandy had seen the thing, on his way to catch the *Singapore Susie*, it had been standing beside the front door, as though about to climb up and feed the reindeer on the roof. Now the thing was back. Its back was turned to the passer-by, its hands were engaged at the front of the body, its red flannel trousers were down around its boot tops, and across the plastic buttocks somebody had printed with a Magic Marker: "Santa Claus is a dirty old man."

"Helen, I do apologize," he said stiffly. "Another of my—er—aesthetic sins has come back to haunt me. Hanson, would you happen to know anything about this?"

The student shrugged. Shandy pulled up the dummy's trousers and laid it on the porch floor.

"I'll put this abomination in the cellar as soon as we've got you settled, Helen. No doubt the students have been carting it all over the campus ever since I left. I should have known better than to have it around in the first place. Hanson, Miss Marsh is a relative of the Ameses and will be staying in their house."

"Oh. Hey, Professor, what happened to Mrs. Ames?"

"She is presumed to have fallen and fractured her skull while—er—checking on my Christmas trimmings while I was away on holiday. Chief Ottermole made that deduction from the available evidence, just as I deduce from that silly grin on your face that you know perfectly well who's been horsing around with my Santa Claus but don't intend to tell me."

Red-faced, Hanson picked up the bags. "Aw, you know how it is. The stiffs expect us guys to be doing crazy stuff all the time. It's part of the act. Somebody got the bright idea of kidnaping Santa Claus and holding him for ransom, but you weren't around so the gag fell kind of flat."

"And where has the dummy been all this time?"

"Oh, around."

"Last seen in the company of Till Eulenspiegel, I presume?"

"Who's she?"

Shandy sighed and drew a bill from his wallet. "Thank you, Hanson. We'll—er—take it from here."

"Okay, Professor. Enjoy your stay, Miss Marsh."

The student leaped off down the hill. Shandy fished out the bunch of keys that Timothy Ames, for a wonder, had remembered to leave with him.

"You'd better brace yourself for a shock, Helen. Jemima liked to think she had a soul above housekeeping."

"Jemmy warned me what to expect."

As they got inside she added with a brave little laugh, "My goodness, it was all true, wasn't it?"

"All and then some," said Shandy. "Wait till you see the kitchen. Look, Helen, if it's too awful, I have a reasonably comfortable guest room ready and waiting."

"Thank you, Peter. I'll remember that. However, I did come to house-sit this place, so I expect I ought to grit my teeth and give it a try. May I come over and borrow mops and things if I need them?"

"Anything you like. And—er—the college runs an excellent faculty dining room. Tim and Jemima generally ate there, and so do I. Perhaps you'd give me the pleasure of your company a bit later?"

"The pleasure would be mine, I assure you. When shall I be ready?"

"They serve dinner from half past five to half past seven. We keep farmers' hours here, you know."

"Then shall we make it half past six? That ought to give me time to blast a path 'twixt bed and bath. Heavens, I've made a rhyme."

"And a very neat one," he told her fatuously. "Then I'll—er—leave you to it."

With reluctance, he did. She was probably glad to get rid of so inept an escort. What madness had come over him, inviting that agreeable woman to stay in his house after that disgusting episode with the plastic

Santa Claus? The insult was a direct reference to the reputation he'd so recently and so undeservedly acquired, he had no doubt about that. If Helen spent a night under his roof, she'd be tarred with the same stick.

Halfway across the Crescent, Shandy stopped dead in his tracks. It was the students who'd kidnaped his dummy, but the faculty who were fabricating the gossip. How in Sam Hill had the story got from one group to the other so fast?

The college community had an unwritten law: What the students don't know can't hurt us. While gossip circulated freely around the Crescent and over the hill to the upper reaches where President Svenson and some of the other faculty and administrative people lived, it was understood that nobody ever passed on a word to the undergraduates. Since these young folk thought their seniors a dull lot anyway, the code was seldom broken and then only by gradual osmosis. There had been some unusually fast leakage here, and he wondered who was responsible.

Instead of going into the brick house as he'd intended, Shandy marched up to the Feldsters' front door and thumped the knocker. Mirelle came. He wasted no time on chitchat.

"Did you see who put that thing on my front porch this afternoon?"

"What thing?" Mirelle emitted a self-conscious titter. "Oh, you mean *that* thing. Honestly, Peter, I did think that was going a bit too far."

"So did I. That's why I'm asking you who's responsible. And also why you or somebody else didn't go over and do something about it."

"If you'll remember," said his neighbor nastily, "the last person who tried to do something about those ghastly decorations of yours got herself killed for her pains. Besides, how were we to know this wasn't just another of your quaint little whimsies?"

Shandy managed to control his temper. "All right, Mirelle. I deserved that. Now, since you've got it off your chest, perhaps you can answer my question. Who did it?"

"How am I supposed to know? Do you think I spend all my time gawking out the windows?"

The professor didn't answer. After a moment, Mirelle admitted, "I don't know who they were. They had on those knitted elf masks."

"Males or females?"

"Either or neither. You know as well as I do that all the students and half the faculty wear blue jeans and work boots and those padded, down parkas that make you completely shapeless. It could have been anybody."

"How did they get the dummy here?"

"Carried it between them, wrapped in a sheet of black plastic. Honestly, the thing looked just like a corpse. That's what attracted my attention." Mirelle was voluble now. "I had the impression they were simply going to dump it and run, but then one of them got a better idea."

"I'm intrigued that you think so."

"It's just an expression. I don't know what's got into you all of a sudden, Peter. You used to be such a quiet person. Now you're"—she paused, thought it over, and sidled a step closer—"interesting."

Mirelle's lips were slightly parted, her breath coming hard, her eyes hot and moist as a spaniel's at feeding time. "If I remember anything else," she murmured, "I might drop over later on and tell you. Jim has a lodge meeting, so I'll be alone and lonely."

Good God! This was worse than finding the body. Shandy backed hastily down the steps.

"I—er—expect to be out most of the evening. Thank you for the information, Mirelle."

"Any time, Peter."

In a cold sweat, he fled to his own place, only to be confronted by Mrs. Lomax in a state of righteous indignation.

"I must say, Professor, I didn't expect to come back here and find there'd been a death in the house."

"Neither did I," he retorted. "Do you have any idea how Mrs. Ames might have got hold of a key?"

"If you think she got it from me, you've got another think coming. I wouldn't have given that woman the time of day, always running the roads and laying down the law to everybody with dust on her furniture so thick you could write your name in it anywhere you'd a mind to. Not but what she was an upstanding, civic-minded woman," the housekeeper added hastily, mindful that it was rude to speak ill of the demised. "Did a lot for the college, you can't deny that."

"Ah," said the professor. "There you—er—strike at the heart of the matter. As you so rightly point out, Mrs. Ames was a woman of certain abilities, but she lacked your talents as a—er—homemaker. That fact has created a most unfortunate situation."

"Oh?" Mrs. Lomax perked up her ears.

"Young Jemmy—er—the daughter—"

"I know Jemmy Ames, for heaven's sake. She was in my Bluebirds."

"Well, then," Shandy beamed, "you're the very person to solve the problem. You see, Professor Ames has flown out to be with Jemmy during her—er—impending confinement and a lady who is a connection of Jemmy's husband has come to—er—help out. I brought her from the airport a while back," he added with a touch of complacency.

"Do tell! You mean she's traveled all the way from—"

"California. I was hoping to introduce you to Miss Marsh, but you—er—weren't around."

"You needn't rub it in. I know I'm late. Got home around noontime and found a busted pipe under my kitchen sink. Couldn't expect me to leave before the plumber got there, could you?"

"Er—no, of course not. And—er—plumbers being what they are—"

"I could tell you a thing or two about plumbers, Professor."

Mrs. Lomax seemed disposed to do so, but Shandy knew from experience that it was folly not to head her off.

"So, Mrs. Lomax, the lady is now over at the Ames place trying, as she puts it, to blast a channel. Perhaps you could go over and—er—lend a hand."

"You mean right now?"

"That was the general idea."

"What makes you think I want to take on another job?"

"That's for you to decide, of course. I was merely equating the need with your—er—exceptional qualifications. You might cut down on the time you spend here if you find the work load too heavy. But one cannot expect a woman like her to live in a mess like that."

"What's she like?" asked Mrs. Lomax abruptly.

"Miss Marsh seems pleasant enough," Shandy replied with due caution.

The housekeeper snorted. "You better watch your step, Professor. Those old maids are man-hungry, every one of 'em. Man-hungry," she repeated with a speculative gleam in her eye that her employer had never noticed before.

Shandy realized he was sweating again. "Good, then I'll—er—leave you to it. You needn't bother discussing salary with Miss Marsh. Let me know what's owed and we'll just add the amount to your usual weekly check. I can square up with Professor Ames when he returns."

Knowing he intended to do nothing of the sort, he fled to the bathroom and lurked there until Mrs. Lomax left the house. While waiting, he studied his face in the mirror. It was the same undistinguished, middle-aged countenance he'd seen yesterday, the same one he'd been shaving so meticulously for so long without untoward result. Why, all of a sudden, was it having this peculiar effect on the most unlikely women?

The sky was almost dark now, and had the weighted look that promised more snow. A storm would put no damper on the revels, unfortunately; but would only lead to joyous wallowings, snowball fights, and no doubt the erection of obscene snowmen on his front lawn. He must be sure to get up early and knock down any such artifact. He wouldn't want Helen offended again.

There was still a full hour to kill before he could drop over and pick her up. Actually there was an hour and three quarters, but he thought it might be a courteous gesture to arrive early with a bottle of amontillado and suggest a preprandial drink, since no liquor was served in the dining room. He ought to make sure Mrs. Lomax had left by then, however. Shandy was still feeling a bit nervous about that look she'd given him.

In the meantime, he supposed he ought to pop next door and find out whether they could give him any information either about the night of the murder or about the recent embarrassment. He didn't suppose they would. The Jackmans were a family with young children, so involved in their own manifold doings that they barely noticed what was happening around the neighborhood.

This was probably the worst possible time to burst in on them, but so was any other time. Groaning, for he was weary in body as well as in mind, Shandy bundled himself up and went out again.

TEN

THE JACKMANS WERE at home, no question about that. Even over the babble of the crowd and the peals of the college carillon, the sounds of "Sesame Street" and the shrieks of a child getting its hair pulled were only too audible. Shandy clutched the packet of gingerbread men he had procured from the convenient though ruinously expensive stand on the Common, and began a fusillade on the knocker. After a while, he succeeded in making himself heard.

"Mum! Mum, somebody's at the front door," shrilled infant voices.

"Well, answer it, Dickie," replied one tired adult. "You're door monitor today."

"No, I'm not. Wendy is."

"I am not!"

"You are, too!"

"Stop it, both of you!"

Mrs. Jackman came herself, looking determinedly bright and motherly, with a moppet clinging to each leg of her blue jeans. Mrs. Jackman always wore blue jeans. She had jeans of blue denim patchwork and jeans with her children's handprints embroidered on them and rhinestone-studded jeans for evening wear. Shandy tried to recall whether she had worn jeans edged in black to the funeral, but couldn't remember seeing her there at all. That was as good an opening gambit as any.

"Er—good evening, Sheila."

"Why, Peter Shandy, what a surprise! Wendy and Dickie, say good evening to Professor Shandy."

Dickie howled, "I don't want to," and Wendy began to sniffle. Shandy made the mistake of trying to placate them with gingerbread men. Their mother's firm "After dinner, darlings" brought wails of protestation.

At last she managed to herd the children back into the playroom and shut the door against the din.

"They're overtired," she apologized. "We only got home a little while ago. Do sit down, Peter. Where have you been keeping yourself? We haven't seen you in ages."

"I know. I was hoping we might—er—meet at the funeral this morning."

"Oh, heavens, was it today? I completely forgot. We'd planned this tobogganing trip, you see, and then Roger and the two older boys are sleeping out overnight at the shelter, which meant bundling up the sleeping bags and getting gas for the camp stove, and generally running around and back and forth like crazy. Then at the last minute we couldn't find the batteries for JoJo's electric socks, which meant a rush to the Sporte Shoppe. I couldn't disappoint the children by staying home, but I did mean to pop over and leave a note in Professor Ames's mailbox. Do explain for me when you see him."

"He's gone to California."

"How nice."

Sheila Jackman would have made the same response, Shandy thought, if he'd told her that Timothy Ames was being lowered inch by inch into a vat of boiling quicklime. She had one ear cocked toward the playroom and her mind on whatever was about to boil over on the kitchen stove. He might as well have saved the price of those controversial gingerbread men.

"I'm afraid I've come at a bad time," he ventured.

"Oh, not at all. I'm letting the children watch television an extra half hour as a special treat, so there's no rush about dinner. We're having things they specially like, baloneywoppers on French toast and cocoa with extra marshmallows. I don't suppose you'd care to stay?"

"Er—thank you, but I have another engagement."

"Then let me give you a drink. Just one second till I turn down the gas. I'm making mulligan stew to take up to the shelter tomorrow. The boys are having a cookeroo."

She went out before the professor could tell her he didn't want a drink, and returned with two very large and dark bourbon old-fashioneds.

"Hope you like the specialty of the house. Rog and I always keep a jug mixed in the fridge. We tell the kids it's Geritol."

She flopped into a modular arrangement of sofas and ottomans that bore the imprint of tiny feet on its cushions, and took a long, grateful swig.

"I suppose you think it's terrible to deceive a child, but honestly, sometimes you simply have to."

"Er—what might be called survival tactics," said Shandy.

"How nice of you to understand."

Sheila gulped some more of her vitamin compound and began giving the visitor her undivided attention. "You are nice, Peter. Come on over here where I can see you better."

She patted the squashy cushions, and the hairs on the back of his neck began to prickle.

"Thank you, but I'm afraid my—er—old bones require a straight chair."

"Don't be silly. You'll never be old."

This was getting worse by the second. He could swear she was batting her eyelashes at him. Shandy gulped and hastened to get on with his business.

"Sheila, I came to ask if you or Roger had seen anything unusual at my house on the night of the twenty-second."

" 'Way back then? How could I possibly remember?"

"That was the night of the Dysarts' party. And also the day I—er—had my decorations put up."

"Oh, now you're ringing my bell. Wendy came home with her eyes like saucers. She still hasn't stopped talking about those reindeer on your roof. She blows kisses to them every night. Like this."

Shandy flinched. "Did you go to the Dysarts'?"

"Yes," Sheila pouted, "but we couldn't stay long. We had a problem getting a sitter. Everybody was either off holidaying or working at the Illumination."

Shandy wasn't interested in sitters. "What time did you leave?" he prodded.

"About a quarter past nine."

"Then Jemima Ames was still there when you left?"

"I believe so. I know she came in right after we did, making a big entrance in that goofy purple cape of hers. Rog calls her the Batmobile. Oh, gosh, that doesn't sound so funny now, does it? Let me fix your drink, Peter."

"No, really, I have to be going. Just tell me one more thing, Sheila. Did you happen to see her after the party?"

"How could I? Wasn't it that same night she was killed?"

"I meant that same night, on her way to my house. She'd have come past your house, wouldn't she?"

"Probably." Sheila didn't sound very interested.

"And she left only a few minutes after you did. Adele Dysart says it was shortly before half past nine."

"Peter, that is odd." Young Mrs. Jackman bounced herself upright against the back of the sofa. "You see, we were stuck for a sitter, as I mentioned before. I was moaning to dear old Mary Enderble about missing the party, so she very sweetly offered to come over for a while. They never go to the Dysarts' for more than five minutes, you know. It's just not their kind of thing. But that's why we had to rush off, because it wouldn't have been very nice to keep her up past her bedtime. They sack in with the titmice, you know. Besides, she might not have been so ready to help me out another time. Survival tactics."

Mrs. Jackman chewed the orange peel from her drink. "So I started nagging Rog at nine o'clock sharp, and maybe fifteen minutes later I managed to pry him away. But by the time we'd stood chatting with Mary about the party and she'd told us this perfectly fantastic thing Dickie said—"

Shandy didn't want to know what Dickie said. Sheila went on with her tale. "Anyway, it must have been pretty close to half past when Roger started walking Mary home, and I stood right over there at the window watching to see if they made it. Frankly, I didn't think Rog could hold himself up, much less an elderly woman, but he managed somehow. He'd been drinking that God-awful punch Bob made. I swear it was radioactive. I took one sip and snuck out to the kitchen and fixed myself a bourbon when nobody was looking. Sure you won't have another?"

"Positive. But you say you stood there watching."

"For ten or fifteen minutes, anyway. They weren't making much headway against the crowd, then Rog had to stop in and say hi to John and pat the rabbit. He always gets silly when he's plastered. It must have been close to a quarter of ten by the time he got back in the house."

"And you didn't see Mrs. Ames at all?"

"Not for one itty-bitty teentsy-weentsy second. The first thing I said to Rog when we heard yesterday that she was dead was that we didn't even say good-by to her at the party and now we'd never see her again, which should be a lesson to us all," Sheila concluded somewhat owlishly.

"Yet according to the Dysarts, Jemima walked through the short cut straight into the Enderbles' yard. It seems most peculiar that she didn't meet Roger and Mary."

"Well, she didn't. Rog would have said so. You know Rog. Golly whiskers, it's going to be lonesome around here tonight. Peter, couldn't you possibly—"

At that moment the playroom door burst open and Wendy, pursued by Dickie with a rubber snake, hurled herself yowling into her mother's arms. Shandy took advantage of the incident to escape.

He was an extremely puzzled man. How was it possible neither of the Jackmans had spotted that magenta bulk in the Crescent? He must check with the Enderbles. Not now, though. It was getting close to six and the couple tended to be gently garrulous as no doubt he himself would when he was their age.

Why was he thinking so much about age all of a sudden? Annoyed with himself for no reason he could put his finger on, Shandy went back to the brick house, got a bottle of his best sherry, camouflaged it inside a folded newspaper, and battled his way over to the Ames house.

Already Tim's place, if not yet transformed, was beginning to resemble a human habitation. It was possible to walk through the vestibule without stumbling over fallen objects. The living room was almost tidy and the fire in the grate, for once, burned clear. Helen remained dissatisfied.

"I'm afraid everything's still in a terrible mess. Mrs. Lomax did wonders, but she couldn't stay long. She had to go home and feed her cat."

"The beast has a delicate stomach, I understand."

"So she told me. However, she's coming back tomorrow."

"Good."

Shandy unwrapped his present. "I thought you might like a drink before dinner. The college doesn't serve anything stronger than rose-hip tea."

"Peter, you are a kind man. I'll get us some glasses."

"Just a small one for me. I've already been dragooned into having a cocktail with one of the neighbors."

"Yes, Mrs. Lomax saw you going into the house next door to yours. She mentioned ever so casually that the husband's away."

"Good Lord."

"I gather there's not much around here she doesn't know."

"She often knows a good deal more than the facts warrant," said Shandy crossly. "Can I help with the wine?"

"No, sit still. You must be exhausted."

"So must you."

"I suppose I am, but I don't feel it yet."

Miss Marsh handed him a glass and sat down on the other side of the fireplace. "It's too late for Merry Christmas and a bit soon for Happy New Year. And Cheers doesn't sound particularly appropriate under the circumstances, does it? Poor Jemmy was dreadfully cut up about losing her mother. I'm so glad Professor Ames decided to go."

"So am I," said Shandy. "To your good health, then. That seems decorous enough, don't you think? I hope you're going to like Balaclava, Helen."

"So do I. I'm getting too old to keep moving. California was the worst mistake I ever made. I used to have nightmares about standing smack on top of the San Andreas Fault when it finally made up its mind to let go."

"It's just too bad you had to find chaos in this house and a carnival on your doorstep."

"But the chaos isn't permanent, I hope, and compared to what goes on out there, the Grand Illumination could pass for tranquillity. Peter, I don't want to rush you, but do you think we might go to dinner pretty soon? I've worked up a ravenous appetite and there's not one solitary thing to eat in this house except a box of Triscuits the mice have been at."

"Whenever you like," he replied, making no move to rise. "I'll take you grocery shopping afterward."

"If you're sure it won't be putting you out."

"Not at all. I'm down to three stale doughnuts myself."

"Poor Peter."

Helen picked up the empty glasses and carried them out to the kitchen. "I'll get my coat."

Shandy rather wished they didn't have to rush off. He was comfortable here in the tidied room beside the bright fire. It was the first time he'd ever been inside the Ames house and not wanted to leave.

Still, the anticipation of taking Helen Marsh to dinner was pleasing, too. Perhaps she'd invite him back afterward. He caught himself wondering if she'd pat the sofa cushions.

No such luck. Helen wasn't that sort of person. But then, he hadn't thought the others were either. Life was full of surprises lately. Surely one of them must turn out to his liking.

ELEVEN

"WATCH IT, PROFESSOR!"

"Drat it, I told you to keep that sled off the walkway!"

Needless to say, the girl charged on unheeding. Helen Marsh turned to look after her.

"What a gorgeous creature! Who is she?"

"A student named Heidi Hayhoe."

"Peter, you're making that up."

"Not I."

"Well, I suppose anything is possible. I went to school with a girl named Ethel Gasse. Is Heidi in any of your classes?"

"I wish she were," snarled Shandy. "I'd take great pleasure in flunking her out."

"Really? I should think you'd prefer to keep her after school."

"What for? My reputation as a—er—dirty old man is, I assure you, newly acquired and totally unfounded. In any event, President Svenson has strong views on the subject of—er—extracurricular fraternization between faculty and students."

"I'll bet Heidi Hayhoe hasn't. Somehow, I hadn't expected to find a girl of that type at an agricultural college. I don't know why. They're common enough. Sorry about that. I don't know if it's your sherry or my empty stomach. How far is the dining room?"

"First building on the right at the top of the Crescent. Think you can hold out that far?"

"I'll try. I do feel like a lady salmon at spawning time. Will it be as mobbed as this walkway?"

"Oh no. The public's not allowed and I don't expect many faculty people will be around. Monday's dinner is apt to be a warmed-over version of Sunday's, I'm afraid."

"It can't possibly be any worse than the lukewarm cardboard I had for lunch."

"As a matter of fact, we think the food is generally not bad. The dining room's operated as part of the course in restaurant management and the cooks get graded on their biscuits." He explained a bit of the college's unique work-study program as they topped the rise and entered the restaurant.

"I'm beginning to have a good deal of respect for this place," said Helen. "It doesn't sound like any institute of learning I've ever been at, but it certainly seems to fit students for the ways they're no doubt going to live."

"President Svenson would be pleased to hear you say so."

"I am pleased," boomed a voice in their ears. "Who is this perspicacious lady and why have I not met her?"

"She's only been in town since about half past three."

Shandy performed the introductions. "She's the relative of Timothy Ames's son-in-law who's come to—er—thrust a finger in the dike."

"Decent of you to come on such short notice. Mrs. Svenson's going to have you to tea some time or other."

"Thorkjeld, what a way to give an invitation," chided Sieglinde. "We shall expect you at half past four on Thursday afternoon, Miss Marsh, and you must bring this bad Peter Shandy with you to keep him out of mischief for a little while. Peter, I did not find your latest decoration amusing."

"Neither did I," he replied grimly. "I'm trying to find out who was responsible."

"Thorkjeld, don't you know?"

"I do not," snapped the president. "There seem to be quite a few things around here I don't know."

"How very remarkable."

Mrs. Svenson's handsome face actually lost its serenity for an instant. "Well, shall we find our tables? At least we shall learn who is responsible for giving us a good dinner tonight. *Smaklig måltid, Fröken Marsh.*"

"*Tack, Fru Svenson,*" Helen replied without batting an eye.

Shandy was impressed. "Are you Swedish, too, Helen?"

"No, but I worked for a while in South Dakota."

"What did you get fired from there for?"

"Peter, that's unkind."

Helen settled herself in the same chair Timothy Ames had occupied the day before and studied the menu for a moment. "Actually, it was on account of an irreconcilable difference between myself and the head of the English Department."

"On what subject did you differ?"

"I'd prefer not to say," she replied demurely. "Would I be safe in ordering the turkey divan?"

"There's only one way to find out. Two turkey divans, please, miss."

"Yes, Professor. Will you have the cranberry mousse suprême with it?"

"Who made the mousse?"

"I did. We're shorthanded on account of the Illumination."

"Then we must have some, by all means."

The girl flushed with pleasure. "I'll bring your soup right away."

She was back in no time flat with an armload of salads, hot breads, and two steaming bowls of, inevitably, turkey soup. The Svensons, who still had not been served, looked somewhat taken aback. Shandy noticed, and gave Helen a wry smile.

"As if I weren't in enough trouble with the boss already."

"What are you in trouble about?"

"Partly those idiotic Christmas trimmings, of course. Mrs. Svenson is not amused. Neither was poor Jemima."

"Peter, you mustn't dwell on that. You don't honestly hold yourself responsible for her death, do you?"

"I think we'd better discuss that later," Shandy murmured with an eye to the other tables. Leftovers notwithstanding, the dining room was doing a fair business.

Helen looked surprised, but changed the subject. "You were right about the food, Peter, it's excellent. And you say the whole operation is run by students?"

"Under supervision, of course."

He went on explaining the college's innovative curriculum. His companion began viewing President Svenson with such an approving eye that the great man motioned them over to his own table for coffee.

"Miss Marsh thinks you're fascinating," Shandy told him.

"So does Mrs. Svenson," said the president. "Don't you, Sieglinde."

"Yes, Thorkjeld. Eat your good rice pudding. Is it his looks or his mind you admire, Miss Marsh?"

"I think it's his common sense," Helen replied. "I've worked at colleges all over the country, but this is the first I've struck where everybody seems to know what he's doing, and why."

"Ah. Now that, Thorkjeld, is a compliment worth having. You are right, Miss Marsh, my husband is a sensible man. Some would think that makes him a dull man, but never in twenty-seven years have I found him so. No, Thorkjeld, no cream in your coffee. You had cream on your pudding. And what is it you work at, Miss Marsh?"

"I'm a librarian."

"*Ja*? Then you will be able to take over the position that Mrs. Ames did not leave. I say did not leave because she never began."

Mrs. Svenson playfully slapped the president's hand away from the sugar bowl. "She was a good worker only if she was minding somebody else's business. What you should have done with her, Thorkjeld, was appoint somebody else assistant for the Buggins Collection. Then she would have stolen the job out from under his nose and it would be done in no time. You will remember that if you ever strike another like her. My husband is like an elephant, Miss Marsh. He never forgets. He would also look like an elephant if I let him. No, Thorkjeld, you must not have more coffee. It gives you bad dreams. Explain to Miss Marsh what she ought to do and come home."

"Show up tomorrow morning at the library and ask for the key to the Buggins Room. I'll tell Porble you're coming."

"But don't you want to know about my background or training?" Helen gasped.

President Svenson rose and pulled out the chair for his wife. "I'll find out fast enough. Peter, you take her over. And remember, I've got my eye on you."

"They're quite a pair," said Helen when the Svensons were out of earshot.

"They're all that and then some. You watch your step, young woman. Is this coat really warm enough for you?"

"No, but I have my South Dakota woollies on underneath. Where are we going?"

"I think we'd better stop in and break the news to Porble that he has a new assistant before somebody else gets to him. Porble's inclined to be touchy."

"But Dr. Svenson is going to let him know."

"The tom-toms will be beating long before the president gets round to it."

Shandy took Helen's elbow and steered her toward the door. They didn't get far before somebody said, "Who's your friend, Peter?"

"Oh, hello, ladies. Pam Waggoner and Shirley Wrenne, this is Helen Marsh, who's just been made an assistant librarian."

"So we heard," replied Ms. Waggoner, a thin, dark assistant in Animal Husbandry. "You're Jemmy Ames's mother-in-law or something, aren't you?"

"Just a sort of courtesy aunt. Jemmy tossed me into the breach when she found out her father was going to need a housekeeper."

"He always did," said Ms. Wrenne, a long-faced blonde clad in a great deal of hand-weaving; she specialized in native crafts. "Are you a real librarian or another phony like Ames?"

"For God's sake, Wrenne," snapped her companion, "we all knew you hated Jemima's guts, but you needn't strew them around and stamp on them now that she's gone."

"Now that she's got what was coming to her for poking her nose in where it didn't belong, you mean," amended Ms. Wrenne, champing down hard on a radish.

"Oh, shove it," said Pam. "Enjoy your stay, Marsh, for however short it may be. I can't imagine you'll stand Balaclava long."

"I'm a qualified librarian," Helen replied, "and I think Balaclava is marvelous. Do come and see me at the library. If I find any Faith Baldwins in the Buggins Collection, I'll save them for you."

Before either of the women could form a reply, she moved on, a polite smile barely curving her rose-petal lips. Shandy bowed and went after her, wondering if Shirley Wrenne had in fact loathed Jemima as heartily as she claimed. If she did, it was stupid to keep saying so since Tim's wife was murdered.

But nobody but himself and Ames and President Svenson knew that. So her bitchiness ought to be a proof of innocence.

On the other hand, it could be a clever defense. Later on, when the facts leaked out as they surely must, she could say, "If I'd known it wasn't an accident, do you think I'd have been idiotic enough to talk about her the way I did?" President Svenson did not hire unintelligent instructors.

Pam Waggoner was no dimwit either. Shandy wondered, not for the first time, what precisely was the relationship between the two women. The fact that they shared a house and went about together a lot didn't necessarily mean they enjoyed each other's company, let alone any other close tie. Doubling up was probably a fiscal necessity on assistants' salaries, and unmarried females in this overwhelmingly uxorious society, denied any personal relationship with the male students, must often be hard put for companionship.

Pondering, he almost snubbed the Dysarts. Adele was having none of that.

"Peter, don't you speak to your friends any more? Aren't you going to introduce us?"

"Oh, sorry. Adele and Bob Dysart, this is Helen Marsh. Bob is the one with the mustache."

"Helen?" Mrs. Dysart laughed merrily. "I was sure you were going to say Susie."

"Miss Marsh is here from California," Shandy reminded her severely. "As you may recall, Timothy Ames and I spoke of her coming this morning after the funeral."

"Oh, of course. Do forgive me, Miss Marsh. It's just so difficult to keep up with Peter and his women. I hope you're going to enjoy your stay at Balaclava."

"We'll make damn sure she does," said Bob, pumping Helen's hand with unnecessary vigor for far too long a time. "Have to plan a little get-together as soon as we've recovered from the last one. Too bad you missed our Christmas party, Helen. Old Pete here did, too. You watch out for that guy. If he starts giving you a hard time, come and tell me."

"Thank you," said Helen, managing at last to extricate her fingers from his grasp. "I'm sure he won't. Good evening."

She was out the door before Shandy could effect any more introductions. He didn't blame her for wanting to escape.

"Perhaps you'd rather put off meeting Porble until tomorrow?"

"Oh no. People do run in types, don't they? Who's Susie?"

"Another of the petards by which I've been hoist."

As they threaded their way among the wandering sight-seers, he confessed his latest awfulness and its appalling repercussions.

"So of course Adele started dropping hints right and left, with the result that I'm now regarded as a—er—wolf."

"Oh, Peter! I shouldn't laugh because I'm sure you're in hot water up to the eyebrows already, but you must admit it's funny."

"I'm glad you think so. Tim would, if he were here. He predicted—er—dire consequences."

"Have they begun to happen, and is it really all that dire?"

"Yes to the first question. As to the second, not yet but I expect it soon will be. I suppose I ought to have warned you, Helen. Being seen in public with me is probably going to—er—"

"Blacken my honest name? I'll just have to take that chance, won't I? Which is the Porbles' house?"

"Right down there. First on the Crescent, as you see. Porble doesn't care to walk any farther than he has to."

"Why? Is he handicapped or just lazy?"

"Neither. He doesn't believe in wasted motion. That's why he's let the Buggins Collection gather dust for so long. He says the books have no practical value."

"What are they?"

"Nobody knows. The books aren't even listed, much less catalogued. And because they're not, we mustn't go in and disturb them."

"You mustn't blame the librarian too much," said Helen. "He's probably overworked and underpaid, like the rest of us. Most libraries have a bunch of old books stuck away somewhere that they're afraid to dump and haven't time to bother about. They're always meaning to get around to cataloguing them but usually don't unless somebody pesters them into it. Who got on Mr. Porble's back? Mrs. Svenson?"

"No, me," said Shandy unhappily.

"What made you get interested in the Buggins Collection?"

"I just thought there might be some things I'd like to read. That's a concept Porble doesn't understand. Neither did Jemima. Svenson gave her the job for the sole purpose of shutting me up and she used it to keep me out."

"Was that easy to do?"

"Yes, very. You'll see. Watch your step here. He hasn't wasted any extra motion sanding the path."

Shandy rang the librarian's bell. A girl of about fourteen answered.

"Good evening, Lizanne. Is your father in?"

"He's just sitting down to dinner," said the child doubtfully.

"This won't take a moment. I merely want to introduce Miss Marsh, who's going to take Mrs. Ames's place at the library."

"Oh." Lizanne gave Helen a sort of frightened bob and ran off, calling, "Daddy! Professor Shandy wants you to meet a lady."

"What lady?"

Not the librarian but his wife appeared. "Well, Peter, this is a surprise. I was just putting the food on the table. I'm afraid I can't ask you to join us at such short notice."

"No, no, we ate up at the college. That's why we stopped at such an inconvenient time. The president was there and suggested Miss Marsh take over the Buggins Collection assistantship. I thought Phil ought to meet her before he heard about it on the grapevine, out of—er—respect for his position. Helen's come to hold the fort for Timothy Ames. You remember we spoke of it at the Cadwalls' this morning."

"Oh yes. I must say not many women could pick up stakes and fly across country at a moment's notice." She emitted a particularly nasty little laugh.

Helen refused to be annoyed. "Actually, I was all set to come back anyway. I've given Buck and Jemmy my plants and furniture and they're keeping my books and whatnot till I decide where I'm going to settle."

"Oh, then you won't stay with Tim indefinitely?"

"I have no idea. I'm only trying to be useful in an emergency. Jemmy's such a love and she was tearing herself to pieces with the baby coming and her mother dead, wanting her father and being afraid of what would happen if he left the house empty during the Illumination, that I just said I'd come and I did."

Mrs. Porble began to thaw. "I always say families should stick together in time of trouble. Jemima's death was a terrible shock to us all. I said to Phil—"

They never did get to hear what she'd said, as Phil himself came bustling into the hallway.

"Well, Peter. Nice of you to do my work for me. I understand I've hired a new assistant for the Buggins Collection. Miss Marsh, is it? Would it be rude to ask if you've had anything in the way of library experience? Or perhaps a library card? You have at least been inside a library?"

"Fairly often," Helen replied calmly. "I got my doctorate in library science from Simmons College in Boston." She mentioned a few of the positions she'd held and Porble's sneer changed to awe.

"My God," he gulped. "I feel as if I've swallowed an oyster and choked on a pearl. And Svenson hired you to work on the Buggins Collection? The Buggins Collection!"

For the first time in their eighteen years' acquaintance, Shandy saw Porble crack up. "The Buggins Collection! Grace, did you hear that? The president's got me a DLS for the Buggins Collection."

His wife managed a dutiful giggle, though she was obviously more puzzled than amused. "But, Miss Marsh, since you're so well qualified, whatever possessed you to take such a ridiculous job?"

"I didn't exactly take it, I was given it. You know Dr. Svenson better than I. His wife asked me what I do and I said I was a librarian, and there we were. I might as well fill in until you can get someone else, if you want me. I'm supposed to see you tomorrow morning, but Peter thought we should just stop in and say hello. Now I think we ought to run along before your dinner gets cold."

They were back in the Crescent before Porble could recover from his paroxysm. Shandy was chuckling, too.

"You've brightened their evening."

"His, not hers," Helen corrected. "Mrs. Porble's probably feeling threatened just now. She's a nice woman, don't you think?"

"I thought she went out of her way to be nasty to you."

"I might be, too, if somebody barged into my house just at dinnertime waving a strange woman in my husband's face. As soon as she's got over the shock, she's going to arrange a little dinner for us. It will be a buffet with two different casseroles, a molded salad, and a fancy dessert she got out of *Better Homes and Gardens*. She'll wear a long plaid skirt and a black nylon blouse because it's dressy and doesn't show the dirt. They'll invite three other couples. We'll have a much pleasanter time than we expect."

"Tell me more."

"No, I won't. You're being snide. But you just wait and see."

"With pleasure." He liked the sound of that "three other couples."

"Where do we go next?"

"Groceries. There's a sort of general store down on Main Street that keeps open all hours. You can do your shopping, then invite me over for breakfast."

"Peter Shandy, you fox! Don't tell me that fish-eyed blonde was right about you, after all?"

"Adele is never right. She only thinks she is."

"She's the one with the money, I suppose?"

"Have you ever considered getting yourself burned as a witch? How do you know these things about people you've barely met?"

"I meet them everywhere. He's the sort who marries money and she's the sort who falls for men like him because she doesn't really know anything about people except that one needs them for an audience. I expect nobody cares much for either one of them, but everybody pretends to because they play so hard for notice that they make you feel guilty."

Shandy laughed ruefully. "I'd never thought of that. I always leave their parties wondering why everybody else is having so much more fun than I. Perhaps the others wonder, too."

"I know. Lots of noise, loaded drinks, and Adele wearing a jellaba she picked up on a guided tour of Morocco. I am being bitchy. What do you eat for breakfast?"

"Whatever you choose to give me."

A latter-day Antaeus, renewing his strength with every rib he elbowed, Shandy plowed a path for himself and Helen through the crowd.

TWELVE

THEY THREADED THEIR way back up the hill carrying brown paper bags. Shandy had tried to take her groceries along with his own, but she wouldn't let him.

"No, really, Peter. I'd feel like an old woman."

"Not possible. I suspect you're just trying to keep me from feeling like an old man. Speaking of longevity, would you mind if we dropped in for a few minutes on an elderly couple who are your neighbors, the Enderbles? He's professor emeritus of local fauna. Quite a distinguished scholar in his field."

"Not the Enderble who wrote *How to Live with the Burrowing Mammals* and *Never Dam a Beaver*? I'd be thrilled!"

"He has a new one coming called *Socializing Among the Snakes*. Mrs. Enderble believes it the crowning achievement of a long and distinguished career. She is—er—perhaps more broad-minded on the subject of reptiles than most ladies."

"I love the way you say ladies, Peter. You're so Victorian. You ought to wear lavender spats and carry a cane to twirl."

"Whatever you say. A cane would be a fine idea, actually. I could lay about me savagely when these confounded—Miss Hayhoe, if I catch you in the Crescent with that disgusting vehicle one more time—"

"Don't sweat it, Professor."

With a jolly laugh, the Amazon charged on.

"Drat the wench! She flouts me."

Shandy pulled off his glove and scratched his nose. "That's rather odd, come to think of it."

"Why? Have you never been flouted before?"

"I wasn't referring to any—er—personal chagrin, but to the young woman's flagrant indifference to a sensible rule. She could run over a gawker and lose the Illumination some business. I'm surprised the other students haven't cracked down on her."

"She's the type who gets away with things," said Helen. "With a name like Heidi Hayhoe, the girl's a natural for the role of campus cutup. She's here for laughs and men, and she doesn't make any bones about it."

"Then why in heaven's name did she choose Balaclava?"

"Oh, I expect she has some relative who's a rich and generous alumnus. Isn't there a Hayhoe who makes threshing machines?"

"Hayhoe Harvesters! Good Lord, of course. They donated one a while back. The school raises a lot of grain, you know. Tim and I have been working on a strain of super drought-resistant millet. Millet is a very underappreciated crop in this country. Except by canaries."

"But much of the world lives on millet. Peter, that's breathtaking! May I see what you're doing sometime?"

"Of course, not that there's much to see. Agrostology is not the most—er—flamboyant of professions. That's my proper field."

"I see. Rutabagas are just a sideline. But think of all the cows you've made happy. Poor things, eating's about all they have to look forward to nowadays. I'll bet Professor Dysart's field is artificial insemination. He looks like a male chauvinist pig. Probably a terror among the undergraduate women."

"Wrong this time, madam. Dysart's an engineer and Dr. Svenson is very strict about the student-teacher relationship."

"Dr. Svenson says himself that there's a lot going on around here he doesn't know about."

"That's only what he said. What he meant was that there is one particular thing he doesn't know about and God help me if I don't provide him with an answer."

"What will he do?"

"I don't know."

"Is it about Jemmy's mother?"

"Yes."

"But surely he's not blaming you?"

"Helen, could we talk in a less public place?"

"I'm sorry, Peter. Is this where the Enderbles live? I thought he'd have a hobbit-hole."

"Perhaps John would prefer that, but I doubt Mary would. I can't visualize Mrs. Enderble living anywhere but here. She's like the little woman in the weather house, never far from her own front door."

His description was apt. Mrs. Enderble did pop out on signal. She did look like a quaint folk figure, hair in a bun, face round and rosy, eyes rounded in perpetual wonderment, and lips curved in a merry smile. Even the maroon wool skirt and hand-knitted pink cardigan she wore contrived somehow to look like a peasant costume.

"Peter Shandy! I hadn't expected to see you again so soon. That was a lovely funeral, wasn't it? Exactly as Jemima would have wanted, though I daresay she'd as soon have put it off a few years, like the rest of us. Come in, both of you. John's in the study, wondering where he put something or other as usual."

"I've brought an admirer of his. This is Helen Marsh."

"Oh, you're the lady from California. How nice! I saw you and Mrs. Lomax out shaking rugs this afternoon. Jemima had many enthusiasms, but she always used to say housekeeping wasn't one of them. She was always scolding me for spending so much time puttering around the house when so many worthwhile things were happening outside. But I've never been one for committees and such. You have to let a place know you love it so it will love you back, don't you?"

"I expect so," said Helen. "I've never had a house of my own."

"Ah, but you're a nest builder at heart, like me," said Mrs. Enderble. "I can tell by the way you shake a rug. John, we have company. Here, let me put those bundles down for you, right here on the settle so you won't forget them when you go. What a pretty coat, Miss Marsh! Is that what they're wearing in California? I had a notion they didn't wear much of anything, from what you see in the papers. Come into the study, if you can stand the clutter."

The clutter consisted of a scattering of papers on a flat-topped golden oak desk and a basketful of pine cones spilled over the hearth. Two tiger-striped kittens were batting the cones around while the mother cat, a large dog of indeterminate breed, a vast white Belgian hare, and a man not much bigger than the hare observed their frolickings with benign indulgence.

"Peter, my boy, good to see you. What do you think of these little rascals, eh?"

One kitten abandoned its pine cone and started up Shandy's trouser leg. He reached down and gently disengaged needle-sharp claws from his left shin.

"That will do, young sir or madam. I am not a tree. I'm sure, John, that the error was due to youthful inexperience rather than perversity of nature. No, puss, don't eat my necktie."

"Animals always go straight to Peter," Mary Enderble explained to Helen. "They even like the way he tastes. Oh, John, this is Helen Marsh from California. Peter says she's a fan of yours."

"Glad to hear it." Enderble shook hands not without difficulty, as he was now in possession of the other kitten. "Mary, do we have anything to give these nice people?"

"Never mind us," said Shandy, who was trying to count the first kitten's whiskers while it sucked on his tie. "You'd better get a nursing bottle for this deluded infant. It thinks I'm its mother."

"Oh, dear, he's getting that lovely silk all wet. Go to mummy, Eugene."

Mrs. Enderble placed the tiny creature under his dam's stomach and waited until he was blissfully kneading fur before she nodded and started toward the kitchen.

"You two sit and warm yourselves. The Dysarts brought over some kind of fancy cordial and we've been wondering what it tastes like, but it didn't seem right to open the bottle just for ourselves."

She was back in the speed of light, bearing thimble-sized glasses, a small decanter, and a plateful of sugar cookies.

"Ouzo, they call it. Smells like paregoric to me."

"Good," said Helen. "I was raised on paregoric."

"So was I, my dear. Now you can't buy any without a prescription. I don't know what we're coming to. Well, happy days, though I suppose that's not a very kind thing to say considering what brought you here."

"What did bring her here?" asked Dr. Enderble.

"Why, she's that relative of the Ameses', come to keep house for Tim."

"How can she keep house for Tim when he's out with Jemmy?"

"Oh, John, you'll be a tease to your dying day. You know what I mean. I expect it must have been an awful shock to you, Helen. You don't mind my calling you Helen? I haven't got over it myself, Jemima here one day and gone the next and nobody the wiser. That was the awful part, nobody missing her for so long. We were so used to her being here, there, and everywhere that everybody just thought she must be somewhere else. Do try one of these cookies, dear, though I'm afraid I got in a speck too much vanilla."

"Not a bit. They're perfect. I'd love to have you call me Helen, but I don't deserve your sympathy. I'm only a cousin of Jemmy's husband's mother, and I'd never even met either of the Ameses."

"Then that makes it all the nicer of you to come and help out," said Mrs. Enderble. "Don't you think so, Peter?"

"Indeed I do. Er—speaking of Jemima's habit of not being where you thought she was, I've run into a bit of a puzzle."

"Tell John. He's good at puzzles."

Mary took the daintiest possible sip from her minuscule glass. "There, I knew it would taste like paregoric."

"What's this about Jemima, Peter?" John Enderble broke in.

"She doesn't seem to have come out where she went in. According to the Dysarts, she left their party just a couple of minutes before half past nine and walked down the path to the shrubbery. Several of the guests watched her out the window. However, Sheila Jackman claims her husband was walking Mary home at that same time, and that she herself stood looking out the window the whole time he was gone, which was perhaps ten or fifteen minutes because he stopped to say hello to you, John. And she insists Jemima never came out of the shrubbery."

"You don't suppose she stopped to listen for the screech owl?"

"Oh, John," his wife protested. "With all the yelling and hollering and carryings-on up and down the Crescent, she couldn't have heard a calliope under full steam, let alone a poor little bird too scared to open its beak. Anyway, Jemima never stopped for anything, you know that as well as I do. You always said Jemima didn't know whether she was coming or going half the time, but at least she never loitered along the way."

"Did I? Wasn't very charitable of me, was it?"

"It was the truth," said Shandy. "Jemima was not the woman to hang around in a cold, dark shrubbery when she had something on her mind. She'd been telling everybody at the party she was going over to rip down those—er—ill-chosen decorations of mine. She was found in my living room with one of the things beside her, but how did she get from here to there without being seen?"

"Blessed if I know," said Professor Enderble, "unless the Dysarts got the time wrong. I'm sure Sheila didn't because young Jackman did bring Mary home right about half past nine. I'd been watching out the window myself, worrying that they might keep her out late and wondering if I should go over there, when I saw them coming across the Crescent. I don't recall seeing Jemima go by during that time either. She'd be wearing that purple cape, wouldn't she?"

"So far as anybody knows. She had it on when she left the Dysarts' and was still wearing it when I found her."

"Well, all I can say is, if she'd come through our yard then, I'd have seen her," said Mrs. Enderble, "and so would John. We both have good eyesight, and we're both trained observers and we're neither of us afflicted with softening of the brain, though you might think so from the way we let these critters boss us around. Peter, I'm afraid Algernon is eating your shoelaces."

Shandy lifted his foot away from the nibbling hare. "I hope he doesn't choke on the tips."

"No fear. He may be naughty, but he isn't stupid. Here they are."

Mrs. Enderble pounced on the tiny cylinders, though they must have been almost invisible against the dark rug in the flickering firelight. She did have exceptional eyesight.

"Perhaps she went by while you were in here talking to Mr. Jackman," Helen suggested.

"Mercy on us, child, we know better than to ask Roger Jackman in when he's been celebrating. Roger's a lovely boy, but he gets to showing you how to throw forward passes with your best china vase. We just stood around the door till it got so cold we had an excuse to shut it and get rid of him. Jemima wouldn't have passed without at least saying hello."

"Oh. Well, that does leave one possibility, though I'm shy of mentioning it in mixed company."

John Enderble chuckled. "You mean that she got taken short? I thought of that myself, but I'd say it's hardly likely. She could have gone back to the Dysarts' or knocked and asked to use our bathroom. It's not as though we were strangers. She was only a couple of minutes from her own house, for that matter. I hardly think Jemima would take a chance on being surprised in an undignified position unless she couldn't help it. And then she'd have left sign in the snow and I'd have noticed. Mary and I visit the shrubbery every day to fill the bird feeders, and we're always on the lookout for animal tracks and owl casts."

"What about human footprints?"

"None in the deep snow. The path is well trodden, of course."

"Speaking of treading," said Helen, "don't you think we ought to, Peter? I don't want to wear out my welcome on my first visit."

"No fear of that," Mary Enderble assured her. "You drop over any time you take the notion. John and I don't go out much, and we're always glad of pleasant company. You won't mind sleeping over there all alone?"

"Oh no. I've been sleeping alone for more years than I care to count."

"Then you lock your doors and windows. This is a peaceable village ordinarily, but you never know who might be hanging around during the Illumination. Lately I've had a sort of feeling, like you get in the woods when there's an animal watching you. John knows what I mean."

"Yes, I do," said her husband, "and while I haven't felt it myself, I don't discount it. Mary's more intuitive than I. We're not trying to scare you, Helen, but you just remember there are neighbors handy and a spare room if you get edgy."

"Thank you. I won't try to be brave."

"We'd lend you old Rex here, but he's deaf as a post and no earthly use for a watchdog. Besides, he'd probably keep you awake all night fussing about Imogene and the kittens."

Mary Enderble bundled them into their wraps, reminded them about their groceries, and was still waving from the doorstep when Shandy saw Helen to her new abode.

THIRTEEN

"PETER, THAT'S BIZARRE! More coffee?"

"Thank you, Helen, I couldn't. That was a superb breakfast. Then you don't think Tim and I are deluding ourselves about Jemima's having been murdered?"

"I don't see how you could think anything else, especially since that marble turned up at the Cadwalls'."

Miss Marsh began stacking dishes. "Is there any chance they might be involved themselves?"

"At the moment, I can't think of anybody more likely."

Shandy told her why. "Of course the motive is pure conjecture."

"Yes, but it makes sense, and they did have the best opportunity. The obvious answer is most apt to be the right one. Where do they live?"

"Right there." He pointed out the window at the house next door.

"Then that could be why nobody saw Jemima come out of the shrubbery. Mrs. Cadwall was waiting for her at home. They'd planned to go over to your house together. To avoid the crowds on the Crescent, Jemima cut through the back yards."

"Wallowing in snowdrifts all the way? I'm not much up on ladies' finery, but I shouldn't think even Jemima would show that much disregard for her party clothes."

"Even when she was on a cloak-and-dagger mission?"

"Which she'd announced at the top of her voice all over the Dysarts' living room. Anyway, she'd have left a trail like a herd of elephants."

"It could have snowed and covered her tracks."

"It could have, but apparently it didn't. I can still see the tracks the workmen made putting up those accursed lights on my spruce trees, and that happened on the afternoon before she was killed."

"Oh, Peter, you do make things difficult. I'll have to think up a different theory. Right now, I suppose I'd better go brighten Dr. Porble's day. Are you going to walk me up to the library, or have you something else on tap?"

"Yes to both. I'll leave you to your job, and collect you for lunch about half past twelve, if that's agreeable?"

"Are you sure you want to?"

"Of course." He'd never been surer of anything in his life. "Why, would you rather not?"

"I'd adore to have lunch with you, but people might begin to think things."

"That would be a refreshing novelty, which we as educators have a duty to encourage. If you mean they might begin to talk scandal about us, I expect they already have, so we might as well be hanged for sheep as for lambs. Is this the coat you're going to wear? I do wish you had something warmer."

Helen gave him a wicked smile. "Go shopping with me. That should rattle a few eyeballs."

"It should, indeed. We must add that to our list of things to do."

"Don't you love making lists? It always gives me such a self-righteous glow to scratch things off."

Shandy hoped she wasn't planning to scratch him off, once she got the urge to move on again as she apparently was wont to do, but he didn't dare ask. He must make do with what he could get. The walk to the library was far too short, and Porble altogether too eager in welcoming his new assistant.

"Well, Helen. Don't mind if I call you Helen? We're one happy family here. I've been thinking how we might best use you."

"But I'm supposed to catalogue the Buggins Collection."

"Balderdash! Can't waste a person with your qualifications on that old junk. Now, I thought we'd start by—"

"Couldn't I at least see where the books are kept?" she pleaded. "I'm invited to tea with the Svensons on Thursday afternoon, and they'll be sure to ask for a progress report. The president seemed insistent that I get started on the collection right away. Didn't you think so, Professor Shandy?"

"Very insistent," Shandy replied.

Porble scowled. "Then I suppose you'll have to make some show of effort. It's a complete waste of time, but we don't want to get Svenson roaring in here chucking the desks around."

He fished in his top middle drawer for a key that had got tangled up in a wad of elastic bands and paper clips.

"This way." He opened a door that led into a rear corridor lined with doors, one to the mop room, one to the staff toilet, one to the basement, and finally to a room at the very end. This one, he attempted to unlock but couldn't.

"Drat! I seem to have brought the wrong key. Funny, I thought that was the only key I kept in that drawer. Usually I'm pretty careful about leaving them around, but this one wasn't worth—well, I'll have to go back and look again."

"Wait a second," said Helen. "I have Mrs. Ames's key ring. Maybe there's one on here."

After a couple of tries, they found it. The door opened on a smallish room that looked to be one solid jumble of books.

"God, what a mess!" said the librarian. "As you can see, Helen, your predecessor didn't get much done. She might at least have stacked the books in piles, instead of pawing them into one big mess. I can't imagine how the room got into this state."

"Neatness wasn't Mrs. Ames's thing," Miss Marsh agreed. "Are you sure a few freshmen haven't been in here having a book fight?"

"Not possible. Nobody except staff and cleaners is allowed into this corridor. As a rule, we keep that door out of the main reading room locked. You need a key to get to the bathroom. No doubt you'll find that on Mrs. Ames's key ring, too. She was big on prerogatives, though short on performance. I believe that's a desk over there among the debris."

"I'll fight my way to it in time," said Helen. "First, I'm going to need some more shelving and an armload of dustrags."

"We've got some old bookcases in the basement. I'll assign a couple of student helpers to move them up here and start tidying, in case the president should take a notion to check on you. He prides himself on running a tight ship. His grandfather was third mate of a New Bedford whaler or something. I suspect his grandmother was one of the whales."

"Balaena mysticetus?"

"Grampus orca, I should say," Porble replied gloomily. "They say it doesn't kill for sport, but we take no chances. Right, Shandy?"

"Entirely so, Porble. I think you're showing great acumen in—er—ordering full speed ahead on the Buggins Collection just now. Mrs. Ames's death is bound to raise questions at the next general meeting. I know you don't play campus politics, but it can't hurt to have the jump on those who do."

Having tossed his golden apple, Shandy judged it was time to leave, and did so. He looked into the Germination Laboratory, smiled fondly at the flats of vermiculite under whose misted plastic roofs lay the promise of Portulaca Purple Passion, then went to call on the security chief.

Grimble was in his office, yelling through the telephone about some matter that sounded remarkably trivial in proportion to the fuss he was making about it. Shandy learned a good deal about the fine art of fulmination before he got to state his business.

"I've been wondering how Mrs. Ames got into my house."

Grimble stared. "Through the door, I s'pose. How else?"

"That's precisely my point. To get in, she'd need a key. To lock the door after her, she'd also need a key. The doors were locked when I got home, but no key was found on or near her body. Where did it go?"

The security chief puffed out his cheeks and scratched his head. After a while, he replied, "So? Somebody else must have unlocked the door for her and taken the key away."

"Yes, but who?"

"How the hell do I know? Whoever had a key."

"Nobody had a key except myself and you and Mrs. Lomax, my housekeeper. Mrs. Lomax was visiting her daughter in Portland and took her key along with her."

"What for?"

"I suppose because it was in her pocketbook and she didn't bother to take it out."

"How they lug them trunks along is beyond me. And they claim women are the weaker sex."

Grimble showed an inclination to expand on this outmoded theme, but Shandy was having none of that.

"Grimble, I'm not a careless man by nature, neither am I a forgetful one. You told Ottermole that people around the Crescent are always leaving keys with their neighbors, and I daresay some of them do. I myself have never once, in all the eighteen years I've lived here, done so. I have no pets to feed or valuables to guard, so there's no need for somebody to keep running in. Mrs Lomax is paid to take care of the place and she's always been willing to adjust her holiday plans to mine. This was the first instance I can recall when we've both been out of town at the same time. As far as I can see, that key had to come from here."

"Well, it damn sure didn't," yelled Grimble. "Look here, Professor, I know my job. Nobody gets at those keys except me personally. Come in here."

He led Shandy to his private sanctum, a tiny office whose main feature was in fact a huge keyboard that ran all around the room. One wall was given over to faculty residences, with each hook marked by a neat sticker bearing one family's name and address. Each key on the hook bore a tag stating whose it was and what door it fit.

"See that?" Grimble pointed at the board with totally justifiable pride.

"Nobody takes a key off there but me. Anybody wants their own, they have to come to the outer office and ask for it. Anybody wants somebody else's, they have to give me a damn good reason or they don't get it. I can tell at a glance who's in and who's out. That board gets checked every day and if your key was missing, I'd damn well know it. And see this?"

He dragged out an immense ledger and dumped it on the desk. "Everybody's listed here. Every time the key gets taken out it has to be entered on the right page with the time written down, and when they bring it back I enter that time, too. Look, here's your page. One key, front door. Not one damn entry on it since the day you turned it over to this office. So the key didn't get taken. See, there it is, right where it's hung for the past eighteen years."

Shandy glanced at the tarnished bit of brass and shook his head. "That's not my key."

"The hell it ain't! It's got your name on it."

"That doesn't mean anything. Look here."

Shandy fished his key ring out of his pocket. "This is my front door, this is the back, and this is the cellar. The key on your board doesn't match any one of them."

"Could you have changed a lock, maybe?"

The professor didn't answer right away. He was busy counting keys. "Sixty-seven. And how many are listed in your book?"

"I never thought to count 'em," Grimble mumbled.

Shandy thumbed pages like a hound on the scent. "Sixty-eight. There's your answer. Somebody just lifted my key, switched tags, and put another in its place."

"Whose, for instance?"

"How should I know? Check your list and find out which hook is a key short."

The security chief was a shaken man. "But how could it happen? Nobody gets to these keys but me. Nobody."

"Are you sure of that?"

"Of course I am! My guys know the rules. They wouldn't dare set foot in here without me saying it was okay."

"But you have visitors coming and going all the time, don't you? Students getting keys to the labs, faculty people who've locked themselves out and whatnot?"

"Sure, that's what we're here for. But nobody gets past the outer office."

"What happens when you go on vacation?"

"I give Sam, my head assistant, a set of master keys that unlocks all

the doors in the college, and I make damn sure nobody gets it away from
him because I lock it on a chain around his waist. Cripes, his wife is
glad to see me come back! Then I send around a notice that campus
residents have to make their own arrangements about spare keys. You
ought to know that. You get one, same as everybody else."

"I suppose I do. I've never paid much attention, since I make my
own arrangements in any case. Then what it boils down to is that my key
could have been stolen any time these past eighteen years."

"No, it couldn't! I keep telling you." Grimble was thoroughly de-
moralized now, scarlet-faced and bellowing. "Nobody touches these keys
but me."

"Don't be a jackass," Shandy snapped back. "The damned key's
gone, therefore somebody took it. Since nobody's ever broken into my
house before, it's probably safe to assume either Mrs. Ames or somebody
who let her in stole the key for that specific purpose. If you'd stop yelling
and use your head, we might be able to determine how it happened. Who
cleans up in here, for instance?"

"I do, damn you!"

"All right. Now, when you say nobody ever comes into this office,
precisely how literally do you mean that? Suppose, for instance, that
President Svenson was locked out and came to get his house key. If he
happened to follow you, chatting as people do, would you slam the door
in his face?"

"Well, no, but—"

"Or Mrs. Svenson, or one of the trustees, or anybody in a position
to make things hot for you if you gave him or her a hard time?"

"I suppose not," the security chief mumbled, "but—"

"Of course you wouldn't. Neither would I. Let's take it a step further.
Suppose this person asked for a key that was on the opposite board. Since
the hooks are so admirably well marked, how long would it take him
to lift my key and put another in its place? The name tags would have
to be switched, but these clever little clip things you use don't seem to
present much difficulty. Time me."

Shandy plucked two keys from different hooks, whipped the tags off,
put one on its opposite, and hung that key back on the board.

"How long?"

" 'Bout a second and a half. Okay, Professor, have it your way."

"I'm not trying to score off you, man, I'm trying to make some sense
of what happened. It's a great deal more important than you seem to
realize. Who was in here late on the afternoon of the twenty-second?
Have you some way of knowing that?"

"Of course I know," said Grimble sulkily. "It's in the daybook."

He led the professor back to the outer office and pointed to a dog-eared binder lying open on the counter that barred entrance to his private office. "See, everybody that takes a key has to sign out when they take it and in when they bring it back, no matter if it's college or residence. If it's college keys, I make damn sure they bring 'em in by the end of the day, even if one of my boys has to track 'em down in the girls' shower rooms. If it's residential, there's not much I can do but call up and remind 'em. That's why I keep a special ledger for the house keys, so if somebody comes in here wantin' a key some other member of the family took out and didn't return, I've got a comeback. We don't run into that kind of trouble very often, I must say. Got 'em pretty well trained. It's a good system. At least I thought it was."

"Nothing is perfect," Shandy mumbled absent-mindedly. He was running his finger down the list of entries for the twenty-second. "Seventy-two. Good Lord, this place must have been a madhouse."

"It's like that sometimes. Then some days you don't get hardly anybody for hours at a time. Comes in bunches."

"Mrs. Jackman locked herself out, I see."

"She generally does. Sends the kids to get the key and we have a big fight about whose turn it is to sign the book."

"This time she seems to have signed it herself."

"Christmas shopping. Went by herself so the kids wouldn't see her dragging home the loot."

"Half past four," Shandy mused. "I rather had the impression she'd been at home with her children that afternoon, watching the men put up my decorations. Probably I misunderstood. Did she happen to follow you into the private office, do you remember?"

The security chief's eye became a thought less fishlike. "Can't say I'd mind if she did, them tight pants she wears."

"What ought I to infer from that?"

"Oh hell, I was only kiddin'. You know the rules around here, same as me."

Shandy also knew equivocation when he met it. Yesterday, he would never have entertained the possibility that pretty young Mrs. Jackman might look twice at a randy old goat with a paunch. Still, her name was only one among many.

"Who are all these people I don't know? Students, I suppose. You wouldn't let any of them past the counter?"

"Damn right I wouldn't."

"What's this name?"

Shandy pointed at a scrawl that spread itself across four spaces. Grimble hitched up his eyeglasses.

"Looks like Heidi somethin'. Oh, I know. Big blond kid. Took the key to the sled shed."

"Heidi Hayhoe? It would be, with a handwriting like that. But she's put down the time as a quarter past five. I should have thought the sleds would all be out by then."

The security chief smirked. "Maybe that's why she wanted the key."

"I see. You certainly are a stickler for morality on campus."

"What the hell am I expected to do, follow every damn kid on campus around to make sure nobody don't get screwed but the bunny rabbits in the animal lab? She brought the key back, see? That's all I have to know."

The man was starting to yell again. Shandy changed the subject.

"Why do you suppose Dr. Cadwall wanted the key to the weaving shop at two minutes before six? Why should he want it at any time, for that matter?"

"Because he's a goddamned Nosy Parker is why! Comes in here just when I'm ready to shut up an' go out to supper, follows me into my office chewin' my ear about—"

Grimble stopped short. "Followed me into my office, sure enough. And I was so damned mad I turned my back on him and took my own sweet time pickin' out the key."

"That key being on the board opposite the residential keys?"

"You bet your life it was. I ain't accusin' nobody of nothin', you understand. I'm just tellin' you what happened."

"Then do me a favor and don't tell anybody else. I'll take it from here."

Shandy left the security office. He didn't particularly want to confront Ben Cadwall right away. He ought first to think out a line of approach. Nevertheless, he found himself climbing the broad granite stairs of the yellow brick building that had housed the administrative offices since Balaclava College was hardly more than a few clapboard sheds and one small herd of Guernseys.

There was hardly anybody in the building today, not a telephone nor a typewriter to be heard. Those few secretaries who hadn't called in sick must be taking late coffee breaks or early lunches, or both combined. It was an unwritten rule that while the wheels of administration must be kept turning during the Illumination, nobody was to push any harder than necessary. Most of the bosses, including President Svenson, would be off skiing or otherwise holidaying. Cadwall, however, would probably be holding the fort. Shandy pushed open the golden oak door with "Comptroller" stenciled in black on its frosted glass panel, and went in.

Sure enough, Cadwall was at his desk. His mouth hung open. His eyes were staring, the pupils dilated. Nobody could look like that, and be alive.

FOURTEEN

VERY CAREFULLY AND deliberately, Shandy backed out of the comptroller's office and shut the door behind him. There was a telephone in the outside cubbyhole where Cadwall's secretary ought to have been sitting, but he did not use it. Instead, he walked down the corridor to Registrations, where Miss Tibbett was also absent from her post. He sat down at her desk because he suddenly realized his knees were wobbling, and reached for the local directory.

"Police station. Officer Dorkin speaking."

Shandy recognized the voice. A few years back, Budge Dorkin had been the guiding force behind his lawn mower.

"Hello, Budge," he said. "This is Peter Shandy. Is Chief Ottermole there?"

"Oh, hi, Professor. Gee, no, there's nobody here but me. Some guy in a sixty-six blue Stingray held up the liquor store, ran the red light on Main Street and totaled Mrs. Guptill's Dodge, fled the scene of the accident and skidded off the Cat Creek bridge. The chief's down at the scene, waiting for the fire department to fish the guy out so's he can throw the book at him."

"Well, you'll have to get hold of your chief somehow and tell him to come up to the college fast. I've just found Dr. Cadwall dead in his office."

"What from?"

"I don't know. That's why I want Ottermole. Hurry him along, will you, Budge?"

"I'll do my best, Professor. I'd go myself, only we can't leave the office unmanned. Say, doesn't it strike you sort of funny, Dr. Cadwall dying right after Mrs. Ames, them being next-door neighbors and all?"

"Funny is hardly the word," said Shandy grimly.

"Hey, I tell you what. If the chief doesn't show pretty soon, how about if I get on to the state police? They take over when something comes up we can't handle."

"That would be an excellent thing to do. Good thinking, Budge."

He hung up and searched the phone book again. The president would have to know, not that Shandy relished the prospect of telling him. After many rings had produced no result, he concluded the Svensons must have gone off on one of their family cross-country ski treks, no doubt toting knapsacks crammed with smorgasbord and extra socks. They'd be lost in the frozen wastes until sunset.

Who else? Melchett. The doctor could do nothing for Ben now, but he must be called anyway. Doctor was on his way back from the hospital and couldn't be reached at this time, but would be given Professor Shandy's message the second he walked through the front door. In a pig's eye he would. Shandy slammed down the receiver, sat brooding a moment, then switched to the interoffice line and rang Security.

"Grimble, this is Shandy. I'm over at Administration. Dr. Cadwall's dead."

"He's what?"

"Dead. Deceased. Defunct. I walked into his office a few minutes ago and found him. You'd better get over here. No, I won't touch anything."

Having done his best to sound the alarm, Shandy decided he'd better look for any sign of life in the building. At last a babble of voices led him to the mail room, where four or five secretaries and assistants were gathered around the sorting table sharing a spread of Christmas pastries. They were only mildly abashed at being caught.

"Come in, Professor. Care for some coffee?"

"Er—yes, thank you. Black. I've—er—" he stalled, wondering what line to take. Direct questioning might be less productive than shock tactics.

"Ladies and gentlemen, something terrible has happened. Dr. Cadwall—"

Kindly Miss Tibbett spoiled the effect he was trying to make by thrusting a paper cup full of boiling hot coffee at him. "Here, drink this right up. It's good for shock."

"Miss Tibbett, I am not in shock." Nevertheless, he took a sip of the scalding liquid. "Dr. Cadwall—"

"What's wrong? Is it his heart? Did he fall on the ice? Don't tell me he—" they were all talking at once. Shandy had to raise his voice to make himself heard.

"Dr. Cadwall has died. He is in his office. Just—sitting there." Shandy drank more coffee. "I've notified Security and Grimble is on his way over. Perhaps I shouldn't have left him alone, but the building seemed strangely empty, and I was wondering if any of you—"

"Bumped him off?" the mail boy suggested.

"That's not funny, Charles," snapped Miss Tibbett. "Professor Shandy means did we see him looking ill or—or anything?"

From a further confusion of tongues, Shandy gleaned that the comptroller's secretary was out with a cold, that nobody had seen Dr. Cadwall enter the building, and that in truth those present had spent most of the morning doing precisely what they were doing now. He finished his coffee and went back to the main corridor, with the lot of them tiptoeing after him like the chorus in an operetta. Nobody was putting on much show of grief. Cadwall had not been a liked man. Still, he was one of their own. As they neared his office, the chatter died and the faces turned somber.

"Who's going to tell his wife?" whispered one of the clerks.

"I'm sure I don't want to," sighed the professor. "Twice in three days would be a bit much."

"Oh, that's right! You're the one who found Mrs. Ames. What a strange coincidence. I wonder who's going to be next. These things always go in threes, my mother used to say."

"Thank you for those words of cheer and comfort, Miss Baxter."

"Professor, I didn't mean—"

Miss Baxter's protestation was cut off by the arrival of the security chief. He was not happy.

"For Christ's sake, Professor, what have you done now?"

"I haven't done anything," Shandy snarled back, "except to open the comptroller's office door and close it again."

"You didn't touch nothing?"

"Only the doorknob."

"Why the hell not? I'd have thought you'd take his pulse or something. Maybe he's just havin' a fit."

"He is not having a fit. Dr. Cadwall is dead. Go and look for yourself."

Grimble showed a not surprising inclination to stall. "What did he die of?"

"How should I know? I'm no doctor."

"Doctor. That's what we got to do, call the doctor."

"I've already called him," said Shandy.

Grimble sighed and decided he ought to look in on the corpse to make sure there really was one.

"I guess we better not get any more fingerprints on this doorknob. Anybody got a clean handkerchief?"

"There's a box of Kleenex on Charlene's desk," somebody suggested.

Grimble took a couple of tissues and made a great performance of wrapping them around the handle. "Don't none of you come in here. Is that how you left him, Professor?"

"Exactly."

The man was making an ass of himself, of course, but to call him one in front of office personnel would be an act of gratuitous cruelty. Two corpses in three days, as Shandy himself had remarked only a few minutes before, were a bit much for anybody. Perhaps this was harder on the security chief since he had to at least put on a show of coping, while Shandy need only dither on the sidelines.

Except, of course, that President Svenson had dumped the responsibility flat on his shoulders. That Cadwall's sudden death could be unrelated to Jemima Ames's was just not possible.

Now that he was mercifully numbed by shock, the professor found he could study the body quite objectively. There was no sign of a wound or a weapon. The color of the skin was bad, but Ben had always had an unhealthy complexion. There was a pen lying on the desk, and a pile of checks were scattered around, as though he'd been in the act of signing them when the final spasm occurred.

"Just—sitting there working." Miss Tibbett, whose thoughts must have been running parallel to Shandy's, craned her neck through the door. "I'll bet he never knew what hit him. Was it his heart, I wonder?"

"It was an embolism," pronounced another. "My aunt had one. Popped off in the midst of peeling potatoes."

"Ugh, stop it! You're giving me the creeps," cried the youngest of the group. "Professor Shandy, what do you think?"

"I think we ought to abandon futile speculation and wait for the doctor," he said. "In the meantime, perhaps it would be wise for you people to—er—resume your customary functions. Don't you agree, Grimble?"

"Yeah, that's right. You folks get back to work. Don't nobody leave the building till we find out what the doctor says."

"But what about lunch?" protested the boy from the mail room. "It's almost noontime."

"If I know you, buster, you been eatin' ever since you got here. Don't worry, you ain't goin' to starve. When did he say he was comin', Professor?"

"His wife said she'd give him the message as soon as he gets in, for what that's worth. He's alleged to be on his way home from the hospital."

"Means he's goin' to eat his lunch and take a nap, most likely," Grimble moaned. "We won't see him for another hour. I don't s'pose there's a spare cup o' coffee around anywheres?"

"I'll bring you some," said Miss Tibbett. "Cream and three sugars, isn't it?"

She headed back toward the mail room. The others straggled after her, some looking relieved, some disappointed.

"At any rate, the police should be here soon," Shandy said hopefully.

"You called them, too?"

"Of course."

"What the hell for? Look, Professor, I don't bust into your lab an' tell you how to grow your turnips, do I? I already caught hell for bringin' Ottermole up to the Crescent when we found Mrs. Ames. Dr. Svenson says he don't want no police called in for anything short of murder."

"What makes you think this isn't one?"

"Oh, Jesus! Why should anybody want to kill the comptroller? He's the guy who signs the checks."

"Very funny. Then why did you go through that performance about not touching anything?"

"Oh hell, that was just part o' the act. Got to show I'm on my toes, ain't I?"

They sat scowling silently for a moment. Then Shandy remarked, "It's interesting that you mentioned Mrs. Ames."

"You tryin' to make out there's some connection here?"

"We have to look at the facts."

"What facts? Mrs. Ames falls off a stool an' busts her head. Dr. Cadwall takes a fit or somethin'."

Miss Tibbett appeared with coffee and cake. Shandy gave up the struggle. Grimble would admit to nothing he didn't have to. They'd just sit here glaring at one another until somebody came to take over the responsibility. He might as well call Helen and cancel their luncheon. Sighing, he got up and moved toward the door.

"Hey, Professor, you ain't leavin'?"

"I'm going down the hall to use Miss Tibbett's phone. I was supposed to meet someone for lunch."

"Come to think of it, with all that telephonin' you been doin', you got hold of Mrs. Cadwall yet?"

"No, I haven't," Shandy was forced to admit.

"Should o' thought you'd call her first off the bat. Better do it now, hadn't you?"

"Grimble, why can't you tell her? I got stuck the last time."

"What the hell, we takin' turns? I wouldn't know what to say. Anyway, you found him."

"God, yes! After this, people will run when they see me coming."

Like it or not, he couldn't decently postpone the task any longer. To his intense relief, Hannah Cadwall didn't answer her phone. She was probably out hectoring somebody, in her new role as Jemima's successor. How would she react when she found out she was a widow? Ben had not seemed a lovable man, but one never knew.

Shandy made a couple more calls, to the commissary and other places where she might possibly show up, leaving messages for her to get in touch with her husband's office. Then he called Mary Enderble, who sensibly didn't waste his time asking questions he couldn't answer but said she'd look for Hannah around the Crescent and down at the supermarket.

Lastly, with extreme reluctance, he dialed the library and asked for Miss Marsh.

"Helen, you'd better go along to lunch without me. I'm in another mess."

"Poor Peter! What is it this time?"

Grimble appeared at his elbow all of a sudden, mouthing, "Is that her? What's she sayin'?"

Shandy fought down an urge to belt him over the head with the telephone.

"I regret having to break our appointment, Miss Marsh," he said severely, "but unforeseen circumstances have—er—circumstanced. I'll look for you in the faculty dining room if I manage to get out of here any time soon. If not, I'll get back to you when I can."

He hung up and turned around to scowl at Grimble. "No, I haven't been able to reach Mrs. Cadwall. Mrs. Enderble's out looking for her. Why don't you send one of your men to help?"

"Who, for instance? They're all on their lunch break but Ned an' he can't leave the office. She'll show up sooner or later."

They wandered back into the dead man's office, hideously fascinated by that waxwork figure in the high-backed leather swivel chair.

"Don't look much different dead than alive," the security chief grunted. "Old Smiley, that's what the kids called him. Don't expect he'll be much missed."

"I think he will, you know," Shandy contradicted. "He was an able and hard-working administrator. I only wish—"

"Wish what?"

"If you want the truth, I wish I knew whether he was also honest."

"Why shouldn't he be?"

"Why should he be dead?"

"Will you quit harpin' on that? He died, that's all. He just died!"

"Grimble, for God's sake, I'm not deaf. What's the matter with you?"

Well might Shandy ask. The man's face was purple, his hands trembled, his eyes were staring wider than the corpse's. Still he insisted, "Nothin's the matter with me! It's just—oh, what the hell? Havin' my routine upset, hangin' around here with a dead body while the work piles up—Svenson on my ear about one damn thing after another—now you tryin' to make out—oh, the hell with it! I'm goin' down the hall to see if they got any more coffee. If the doctor shows up, tell him I'll be right back."

Shandy didn't care. Being alone with Cadwall was less disagreeable than having Grimble there with him. Besides, it gave him a chance to look around. He knew he ought not to touch anything, but surely there was no harm in using his eyes.

He was sure Cadwall had been poisoned. As an agriculturist, the professor knew altogether too much about pesticides and their effects. Though he and Tim had for years been waging a ferocious battle against such toxins, there was still no dearth of lethal substances around Balaclava. But what poison would kill in just that way, and how was it got into the victim?

There was nothing on the desk to give a clue, only a clean blotter, the pile of checks, a few pens on a tray, and two baskets marked "in" and "out," both of them empty. There was no disarrangement of the victim's garments. Ben had always dressed like Calvin Coolidge, with starched collars and tightly knotted neckties and a buttoned-up vest under a buttoned-up suit coat. Even in summer, his only concession to the thermometer was to shed his vest. Presumably somebody could have sneaked up behind him and thrust a hypodermic needle through those several layers of clothing, but Shandy could see no indication that anybody had.

A person entering this office on evil intent during Illumination Week would be taking a special risk, simply because the normally busy Administration Building was so quiet. Should any of the staff happen by chance to be at his or her rightful post, the chance of being both observed and remembered was extremely high. It would make far greater sense to administer a slow-acting substance like arsenic and be far away when the stuff began to work.

Arsenic, being tasteless, was easy to give but Shandy didn't think it had been used in this case. He couldn't force himself to sniff at those slack lips but thought he could detect the disagreeable odor of gastric upset. Vomiting would be consistent with arsenic poisoning, but wouldn't it keep on until the victim died in agony, since nobody had been around to get help? Shouldn't Ben have been found on the floor in the men's room, not sitting here at his desk? It looked more as if the comptroller had got hold of something that made him sick, then put him permanently to sleep.

Ben wouldn't necessarily be alarmed at a sudden attack of nausea. He always welcomed a new symptom. If it took the form of cramps and diarrhea, he'd credit the laxative he'd no doubt dosed himself with the night before. If he vomited, he'd assume he was coming down with one of the viral bugs that were always around. Anticipating a stay in bed, he'd make a valiant stab at finishing up his work before he went home.

What sort of poison might give you a bellyache, then make you helpless and comatose before you realized how sick you were? Since plants were his business, Shandy's thoughts naturally turned to vegetable poisons. Why not? Why should a killer stick his neck out to buy or steal a lethal compound when plenty of local window sills offered death for the picking, even in midwinter?

Poinsettias and mistletoe, for instance, were far less innocent than most people supposed, but Shandy wasn't sure how they'd act. For guaranteed results, a murderer would be wiser to stick with the alkaloids. Trusty old *Conium maculatum* would leave Ben's mind clear enough to keep signing checks while his lungs were gradually paralyzed, but where could one find poison hemlock in December?

Solanine produced narcosis and paralysis. All you needed for that was a green potato, or the eyes of one that had begun to sprout. Then there were the simple heart depressants such as *Cannabis sativa*. A concentrated dose of pot could take a person so high he'd never come back. People weren't supposed to grow the stuff around campus, but there were always a few who thought it cute to do so.

All at once, Shandy could stand the sight of the dead man no longer. He went out and stood by the window in the corridor, hoping to catch sight of Dr. Melchett's car. However, nothing was to be seen but trodden snow and leaden sky and trees with bare branches moving in the raw December wind: maples silvery and slim-looking even when their trunks could hardly be spanned with outstretched arms, oaks rugged and stubborn as Thorkjeld Svenson with brown leaves still clinging to their boughs, a few graceful streaks of white bark where the birch-leaf miner hadn't yet managed to complete its dirty work; all silhouetted against the welcome emerald of pine and the deeper green of yews grown tall and knock-kneed in the many years since they were planted. There was a lot of yew around Balaclava. It made a goodly show at small expense and could be counted on to come safely through hard New England winters, though new students always had to be cautioned against eating the translucent red berries and animals kept from grazing on the foliage.

In fact, a decoction of taxine distilled from those omnipresent yew needles could also function as a heart depressant, working unfelt in the system until it brought just such a death as Ben's, if he remembered correctly. Shandy was pondering the various possibilities, wishing he could get hold of Professor Muencher's book on plant poisons or some other reliable text, when a four-year-old maroon Oldsmobile pulled up in front of the building and a shortish man in a dapper camel's hair car coat got out, pulling a pigskin satchel off the seat. Shandy hurried to open the door for him.

"Dr. Melchett, I'm relieved to see you. You got the message about Dr. Cadwall?"

"Only that I was supposed to get over here as fast as possible. I haven't even eaten lunch yet. Where is he? Why haven't you taken him to the hospital? Or the infirmary? What's the matter with him?"

"Er—he's dead. I called in on a—er—matter of business and found him sitting in his chair, exactly as he is now."

"Well, well."

Melchett set down his satchel on the comptroller's desk and hung his coat very carefully over the back of a wooden chair. "You never know, do you? I'd have said Ben was good for another fifty. Told him so at his last check-up. He didn't believe me, of course. Ben always liked to think he was on his last leg. Apparently he was right and I was wrong. Just goes to show we doctors aren't infallible, much as we'd like to think we are."

He bent over and rolled back one of the dead man's eyelids. "Where's Hannah?"

"We've been trying to get hold of her."

"Ah. Gone shopping, no doubt. It's amazing the amount of time women can spend in stores. I'd like to ask her what Ben's been dosing himself with."

"I've been wondering about the vegetable alkaloids," Shandy ventured.

"Why?"

"Because they're so easy to get hold of, I suppose, and because I've seen farm animals poisoned by feeding on them. They may remain in the body for some time with no symptoms, you know, then cramp and coma—"

"You don't have to teach me my profession," Melchett snapped. He studied the corpse a moment longer, then asked in a less belligerent tone, "Did you have anything particular in mind?"

"Coniine, cannabinine, solanine, taxine. I could give you a complete list, I expect, if I sat down and thought awhile. Toxicity in plants is something we agrologists have to concern ourselves with, you know."

"But how would the poison get into his system? Nobody with a grain of sense would ingest that muck."

"Not on purpose, certainly."

Melchett looked startled and began rubbing his chin. "Still, Ben was one of those health food freaks. Sprinkled wheat germ on his corn flakes, that sort of thing."

"I grant you that, but don't you think he'd make sure it was in fact wheat germ he sprinkled? Unless someone—er—switched the boxes."

The doctor quit rubbing his chin. "Shandy," he said primly, "that strikes me as a somewhat irresponsible statement. In view of your recent peculiar behavior, don't you think you'd better tone down your remarks?"

"In view of the present circumstances, don't you think you'd be well advised to request an autopsy?"

"I suppose so," the doctor sighed. "Damn it, my wife's nagged me for months about taking her to Florida over the holidays. This is what I get for staying home. Where's Grimble?"

"He said to tell you he'd be right back. That was about half an hour ago. I'd better go see if he's—er—finished interrogating the staff."

"He's probably interrogating some stenographer in the broom closet, if I know that old goat. Tell him to get the hell out here and call the county coroner's office. I'm not writing a certificate on this one."

There was a little stress on "this one" that prompted Shandy to retort, "Then you weren't entirely satisfied with the way Mrs. Ames died either."

Dr. Melchett stared. He opened his mouth, then snapped it shut, which was probably a wise thing to do under the circumstances. Shandy, knowing there was no use in pressing the issue, went to fetch the security chief. He found Grimble engaged in no more lascivious pastime than eating fruitcake.

The man rose with a fair show of alacrity, cramming the last bite into his mouth. "Thanks, folks. See you later."

"You will let us know what happened to poor Dr. Cadwall, won't you?" begged Miss Tippett.

"Yeah, and when we can split for lunch," added the mail boy.

"I think they'd better have some sandwiches brought in," said Shandy when the two men were out in the corridor. "Dr. Melchett isn't going to sign a death certificate."

"Huh?" Grimble sprayed fruitcake crumbs. "Why not?"

"I expect he'll explain that to you himself. He says you're to phone the county coroner."

"Oh, Christ on a crutch!"

Grimble managed to get rid of his mouthful in order to vent his feelings. "Professor, if you talked him into this, I'll—"

"He didn't talk me into anything," snapped the doctor, who had got tired of waiting and come to meet them. "The evidence speaks for itself. Where have you been, man? Get on that telephone and make it fast. In my professional opinion, you people have one sweet mess on your hands here, and I want no part of it."

Although he still had on his overcoat and galoshes, Professor Shandy began to feel cold. He walked over to one of the big old-fashioned steam radiators that ran the length of the corridor and pressed his hands against the grids. They were hot to the touch, almost too hot for flesh to bear, but they didn't convey any warmth to his body.

"I'm in shock," he thought dispassionately. "I ought to get some coffee."

He didn't go back to the mail room. Grimble had probably emptied the pot. Miss Tippett would be glad to make him some more, but he didn't want to stand waiting among that gabbling crew. He wanted to go get Helen Marsh and take her someplace where nobody had ever heard of Balaclava College.

Dr. Melchett was talking to the coroner's office. Shandy didn't bother trying to understand what he was saying. It was what the doctor had not said, that little flicker of his eyelid when Jemima Ames was mentioned, that told the most. Something must have struck him wrong the morning she was found, but since Ottermole and Grimble were so determined to call her death an accident, that same caution which was causing him to pass the buck now had prompted him to sign the death certificate without which Harry the Ghoul wouldn't have dared commence his gruesome rites.

One couldn't blame him, Shandy supposed. Murder, at least this kind of murder, just didn't happen in respectable little college towns. Even if a country GP did suspect there was something fishy about a sudden death, he'd think a long, long time before he risked his practice by starting a scandal.

If someone other than Shandy had happened to find Dr. Cadwall dead in his office, the normal reaction would be to call Security, just as he himself had done when he discovered Jemima Ames's body behind his sofa. Grimble would not have got the police, he'd have sent for Dr. Melchett. It was entirely possible that the pair of them would have managed to convince each other there was no need for further investigation, not because they were either wicked or incompetent but because anything other than natural death would be outside their customary frame of reference.

And also because they knew Thorkjeld Svenson would tear them apart if they raised a stink and couldn't produce a villain. As the affair now stood, if Miss Baxter's prediction ever came true, the third body found on campus might well be Peter Shandy's.

FIFTEEN

WAS THERE ANY outside possibility that Melchett could have wanted a cover-up for more urgent personal reasons? But doctors didn't kill people, at least not on purpose. Shocked by this outlandish idea, Shandy studied the man at the telephone more closely than he ever had before. The adjective that came to mind was "respectable."

Dr. Melchett had been part of the background ever since Shandy came to Balaclava. As official physician-on-call, he showed up at most of the bigger social affairs with his wife, a woman who, as Shirley Wrenne once remarked, had a new dress and an old cliché for every occasion.

The Melchetts' brand of respectability must cost them a pretty penny. Had the doctor found income not up to outgo, and started padding his bills to the college? If so, Cadwall would surely have found him out; but would that be sufficient motive for murder, and where would Jemima Ames come in?

What, in fact, did she and Ben Cadwall have in common, other than being faculty folk and next-door neighbors? They were both on intimate terms with Hannah, and they'd both had a hobby of finding out other people's business. Whether or not they ever got together and compared gossip was beside the point, since Hannah would surely pass along to her husband any tidbit Jemima let fall.

Jemima would tell, there was no doubt about that. Shandy had never once been able to visit Tim in her presence without having to listen to some story he'd far rather not hear. He couldn't imagine her getting hold of any piece of news and not confiding it to her best friend's ear.

During these past several weeks, Jemima had been closely involved with many of the students. What if she'd got wind that Melchett could be bribed to perform an abortion without going through channels and disturbing Balaclava's high moral tone, or that he was supplying drugs to undergraduates? Neither she nor Ben would be shy about confronting him with the rumor, or about cooking his goose in short order if he failed to convince them of his innocence. The moral tone at Balaclava being what it was, even a hint of malpractice could finish him with the Svensons, hence with the college, the town, and perhaps with Mrs. Melchett and all else he presumably held dear.

Poisoning a dedicated hypochondriac like Ben should be no hard task for the physician who for years had been hearing his complaints and doling out his placebos. Choosing taxine as the vehicle would be a clever touch indeed, since the stuff was not in the pharmacopoeia but available for the plucking to anybody who knew how to prepare a simple decoction; and Shandy could think of nobody on campus who didn't.

The fact that Melchett was at present engaged in passing the buck meant nothing one way or the other. No respectable doctor would care to be mixed up in a murder case. Shandy wasn't even thinking about that. He was thinking that if Melchett had in fact killed both Ben and Jemima, he'd be a fool not to kill Hannah, too.

Maybe he already had. Maybe that was why Mrs. Cadwall wasn't responding to any of the messages that had been left for her. Maybe she and her husband had shared a lethal breakfast and she was still sitting back in their house on the Crescent with an empty coffee cup in front of her, staring into infinity. Shandy found a chair, pulled it close to the radiator, and sat down, drawing his overcoat tight around him.

Melchett got through talking to the coroner's office, fetched his natty car coat from the comptroller's office, and came over to Shandy, satchel in hand.

"No sense in my hanging around here any longer. My wife's got lunch waiting. You and Grimble can hold the fort until the police get here."

"Are they sending another unmarked van?"

The doctor didn't seem to catch the allusion. "Are you feeling all right, Shandy?"

"No. I think I've caught a chill."

"Take some aspirin and go to bed."

"How can I, if I'm supposed to sit tending a corpse while you weasel out?"

Shandy was talking to the air. Melchett was already out the door. Grimble stared morosely at the departing Oldsmobile.

"The president sure ain't goin' to like this."

"The president will have to lump it," Shandy snarled.

He was sick of the lot of them. Two people murdered, and all they could think about was filling their guts and keeping their noses clean. He stayed huddled inside his good gray tweed, not responding to any of Grimble's observations, until a small procession drove up, headed by Ottermole in the village's one police car, then a state police vehicle and an ambulance.

"Here they are." Grimble swallowed noisily. "What are you goin' to tell 'em?"

"The truth, of course. I came to see Dr. Cadwall and found him dead at his desk."

"Yeah, but what about the key an'—an' the rest of it?"

"I don't know."

"Jesus, Professor, watch it, will you? Svenson's goin' to be—"

He shut up fast as the door opened and the law arrived. Shandy, realizing that the security chief was having an attack of mental paralysis, stood up.

"Thank you for coming, gentlemen."

Ottermole, who might have been expected to make the introductions, wasn't saying anything either, so Shandy took them upon himself.

"My name is Shandy. I'm a member of the faculty. This is Mr. Grimble, head of campus security. The—er—deceased, Dr. Cadwall, our comptroller, is in his office, through that door."

Grimble suddenly found his voice. "Yeah, see, Professor Shandy here was in my office and he says, 'I'm goin' over to see the comptroller,' an' the next thing I know, he's on the intercom tellin' me—"

"Whoa, back up," said the state policeman. "Ottermole, do you want to take notes, or shall I?"

"You better," mumbled Balaclava's chief.

"Right. My name's Olivetti. Now, Professor Shandy, suppose you do the talking."

He whipped out a small black notebook and a dashing gold pen just like Cadwall's. "When did you get here?"

"Well, as Grimble told you, I left the security office about half past eleven."

"Eleven thirty-two," Grimble put in. "It's right on the record."

"My God! I had no idea you were so thorough."

"Sure. Everybody gets checked in an' out, even if they only stop by to use the john."

Olivetti cleared his throat. "So you came straight here?"

"Yes, I did."

"Why?"

"I wanted to speak to Dr. Cadwall."

"What about?"

Now was the moment of truth. Shandy was pondering what to say when he felt a small, involuntary tightening of his body muscles. It was the same instinctive drawing-away that had kept him from dousing the embryo Balaclava Buster with an improperly mixed solution of liquid fertilizer which would surely have cremated the infant sprouts.

"A key," he replied cautiously. "I thought he might have—er—taken one that belonged to me."

"Happens all the time," Grimble butted in. "Not that I'm makin' cracks about absent-minded professors or nothin'—"

"Sure," said Olivetti. "So you came in and then what? Did you speak to his secretary?"

"She was not at her desk. I subsequently learned that she called in sick this morning. We always have some kind of mysterious epidemic among the administrative staff during the holiday season."

"Sure. Did you knock, or what?"

"I believe I merely opened his door and poked my head in. That's the—er—accepted custom around here. One asks, 'Are you busy?' or something of the sort, then either enters or goes away."

"Kind of dangerous, isn't it?" asked a cheeky youngster in whites who was carrying a folding aluminum stretcher. "What if he was taking a little time out with his secretary?"

"At Balaclava? That would seem a remote contingency. Although," Shandy added nastily, "no doubt Grimble would know better than I."

"Could we stick to the point?" asked Olivetti patiently. "How did you find him?"

"Do you mean in what position?"

"I do."

"Exactly as he is now. I realized at once that he was dead, so I shut the door and called for help."

"Where from? The secretary's phone?"

"No, I came back down the hall and used Miss Tibbett's. In the registrations office, right over there."

"Why?"

"I'm sure I can't tell you. Instinct, I suppose."

"Okay, so then what?"

"I started wondering where everyone had got to. The building appeared empty as a tomb, if you'll forgive the ill-chosen simile. I went along the corridor until the sound of voices attracted me to the mail room. There I found several staff members having their—er—coffee break."

"Probably been having it ever since they got in," said the young stretcher-bearer.

"That was my impression," Shandy conceded. "They looked—er—comfortably entrenched. All expressed surprise and dismay at my news. Miss Tibbett suggested that I drink some coffee, which I accepted most gratefully, I must say, then they accompanied me *en masse* back here."

"Did any of them go into the office?"

"No. Grimble arrived just about at that same moment. He and I went in together. The rest remained outside—er—looking through the door."

"No doubt," said Olivetti. "All right, Grimble, you take it from there."

"Well, I took a look at him an' decided the first thing to do was call the doctor an' find out what he died of. Looked to me as if he'd had a heart attack or somethin'. He was just sittin' there. See for yourself."

He marched them all into the comptroller's domain, took a tissue from the secretary's desk, and used it to protect the doorknob.

"This is what I done before. Bein' careful about fingerprints, see."

"Must have wiped them all off, if there were any," grunted Olivetti.

"Mine would be there," said Shandy.

"Right. Did you touch anything else?"

"No, I'm quite sure I didn't. Not on this—er—visit, at any rate," the professor amended. "Of course I've been in Cadwall's office on various other occasions. Most of us have, for one reason or another. Cadwall paid all the bills, you know, signed the salary checks, made the bank deposits, handled our insurance and tax deductions and so forth, took in the proceeds from the Grand Illumination—"

"You mean he was like the business manager?"

"Exactly."

"Then what does the treasurer do?"

"Very little, in my opinion. He would negotiate large bank loans or head fund-raising drives, say, if money were ever needed. But at Balaclava, money never is needed."

"You've got to be kidding. How come?"

"President Svenson runs a taut ship. Read our catalogue. Copies are available at the registration office, and I'm sure Miss Tibbett will be able to explain the fine points if you can—er—coax her back to her desk."

"I'll talk to the staff soon as we get squared away here," said Olivetti. "Okay, guys, let's take some pictures. What did you say his name was, Professor?"

"Benjamin Cadwall."

"Address?"

"Balaclava Crescent. We never bother with house numbers. It's that brown shingled house with the light tan trimming, next to the last on the right as you're coming up toward College Row."

"Married?"

"Yes. His wife's name is Hannah. We've been trying to reach her. She's apparently out somewhere."

"Shopping, most likely. They always are. Okay, Professor, I guess we don't need you any more at the moment. Weren't planning to leave town, by any chance?"

"Oh no. I'll be around. Grimble will know where to find me."

Shandy grabbed his hat and sped from the building. It was probably too late to catch Helen at the dining room, but he might as well try.

SIXTEEN

LUCK OF A sort was with him. He met Helen just outside the dining room door. However, she was on her way back to the library.

"I don't dare go back in with you, Peter. I got a stiff little lecture on punctuality. Dr. Porble expects me to set an example."

She studied his face. "It's something bad, isn't it?"

"Very bad. I went to accuse Ben Cadwall of pinching the key to my house from the security office, and found him dead at his desk."

"Oh no! Was it—?"

"I believe so. So does Dr. Melchett, although I have a hunch he wouldn't have refused to sign a death certificate if I hadn't forced his hand. My personal guess is taxine poisoning."

"Taxine? That's from yew, isn't it?" Helen instinctively drew the skirt of her light blue coat away from the shrubs that flanked the path. "How does it work?"

"Ben would think he was coming down with an intestinal bug. He might have to go to the men's room and vomit. Then, being Ben, he'd crawl back to clean up his desk before he went home. By the time he realized how sick he was, he'd be too weak and short of breath to call for help. Then he'd go into coma and that would be that."

"You do have a tidy way of putting things." She shivered and tried to bundle the thin coat more closely around her body. "What's happening now?"

"They've got the state police in, thank God. They're taking pictures. Hannah Cadwall's off shopping or something. At least, I hope to God she is. We haven't been able to reach her."

"I shouldn't worry. She's probably doing the after-Christmas sales.

You'd better go have some hot soup or something." Helen hesitated. "Peter, would you know the taste of taxine?"

"In case somebody laced my soup with it, you mean?" He tried to smile. "Oh yes, I think so. It's very bitter, I believe. Not the sort of thing you or I would swallow willingly."

"Then how did this Cadwall man get it?"

"Ben was a dedicated hypochondriac. He was always dosing himself with one thing or another. He'd assume that if something tasted ghastly, it must be good for him."

"I suppose everybody around here knew that."

"Oh yes. The neighborly aspect does rather intrude itself."

Shandy rubbed at his eyes. Helen put a hand on his coat sleeve.

"Go get some food now, Peter. Come over and have some of your sherry after I get through work, if you feel like it."

"I shall feel like it. How are you getting on?"

"Awful. He's got two kids slamming things around in the Buggins Room and me lashed to the reference desk copying out statistics on hog production. I'm so frustrated I could spit."

"Make sure you spit in Porble's direction, then. Will you be out by five, do you think?"

"Make it a quarter past. I'd hate to have you standing out in the cold, after all you've been through."

Feeling somewhat better than he had a few minutes ago, Shandy went in to lunch. It was late for Balaclava faculty people to be lunching. Hardly anybody was in the dining room except Professor Stott, the pig expert for whom Helen must be performing her distasteful task, and a somewhat boisterous gathering at one of the big round tables in the center of the room, made up of engineering teachers and aides from the power plant. Dysart was among them and, as usual, was doing most of the talking in a technical jargon that might as well have been Choctaw as far as anybody outside the group was concerned, and gave Shandy a legitimate excuse not to join them.

Stott was no threat to anybody's privacy. He was an agreeable man in his way, but wrapped heart, soul, and mind in swine culture. He even looked like a pig, with a large, pale face, turned-up snout, and small eyes set in deep circles of firm, healthy fat. He was eating a great deal, slowly and with concentration, and was doubtless unaware that a colleague had entered the room. Shandy was about to slide gratefully into a chair near him when Dysart happened to notice a chance to increase his audience.

"Hey, Pete, why so unsociable? Come over here and park the carcass. What's new among the rutabagas?"

"I haven't had time to notice."

Perforce, the agrologist joined the engineers. He debated whether to refrain from mentioning Cadwall's death, then decided there was no use in trying to keep it quiet. Dysart would be mortally offended, for one thing, and he'd already done enough to antagonize his neighbors.

"Actually, Bob," he began, "I've had quite a morning. I dropped in to see Ben Cadwall and found him sitting at his desk, stiff as a poker."

Dysart was startled, but not silenced. "Jesus, Pete, what are you, some kind of Typhoid Mary?"

"I'm beginning to wonder."

"You mean Dr. Cadwall's dead?" exclaimed one of the teaching fellows. "What happened to him?"

"That I'm afraid I can't tell you. Nothing—er—spectacular, at any rate. He was just sitting there."

"Didn't you call the doctor or something?"

"Oh yes. I called Dr. Melchett, who in turn called the county coroner, who sent over a delegation from the state police."

"The police? What for?"

"I suppose because that's the way it's done. I'll have the soup, miss."

"Tomato bisque or corn chowder?"

"Er—chowder."

"And something to drink? Coffee?"

"Tea," said Shandy firmly.

"Hey, coffee." Dysart slammed down his own almost-empty cup with a strange expression on his face. "That reminds me. Ned, you were here this morning, when Cadwall spilled his coffee."

"Was I?"

"Sure, you were."

"If you say so. Why, do you think he'd begun to feel faint or something?"

"Faint, hell! He was strong as a horse. You know what a health freak he was. Took better care of himself than Sieglinde does of Thorkjeld."

At this *lèse-majesté*, some of the younger men looked alarmed, but nobody contradicted Professor Dysart.

"Exactly what happened, Bob?" Shandy prodded.

"Well, Pete, you know what it's like around here in the mornings. People wait on themselves cafeteria-style, and there's apt to be a lot of confusion. Tom stops to talk with Dick while Harry's trying to get at the cheese buns or whatever. It's a nuisance, but they will do it."

Shandy nodded. The one who did it most often was Dysart.

"Anyway," the engineer went on, "I was at my usual table here with a few of the guys. Ned here needed a second cup of coffee to wake him up, obviously since he can't even remember what happened, so he took his mug and went back to the counter. I decided maybe that wasn't such a bad idea, so I yelled after him, 'Get me one, too.' Got that? In the meantime, Cadwall had collected his all-bran and prune juice or whatever he was currently poisoning his guts with, and headed for a table. Somebody joggled his elbow, and his coffee went flying. Ben was plenty teed off, as you might expect. So to make a long story tedious, I told Ned to give him mine. Had to keep in with the bloke who signs the checks, you know."

"Sure, Bob, we know all about it," said one of his satellites. "Did you get those cuff links in a Cracker Jack box?"

Dysart flashed the massive new gold jewelry with more than a touch of smugness. "Adele gave them to me for Christmas."

"Nice of her," snapped Professor Shandy. "So what it boils down to is that Cadwall drank a cup of coffee meant for you."

"That's the kernel in the filbert, Pete. Does it make you wonder a bit?"

"Yes." Shandy took a spoonful of chowder and chewed thoughtfully. "Yes, it does."

"Say, Ned," Dysart went on with a half-laugh to demonstrate that he wasn't really taking the matter seriously, "I suppose it's useless to ask if you remember who was standing next to you when you poured the coffee?"

"Oddly enough, I do, now that you mention it. It was Shirley Wrenne. I was trying to decide whether to be a gentleman and let her go first, thus risking a poke in the eye for sexist discrimination, or stay where I was and be a chauvinist pig. I opted for piggery, with all due respect to our learned colleague," he added with a dutiful bow toward the oblivious Professor Stott.

"Anybody else?"

"Professor Feldster annoyed me by grabbing over my shoulder for the cream. You know that boardinghouse reach of his. I'm sure there were others close by, because there always are, but I couldn't tell you who."

"Did anybody say anything to you, distract your attention in any way?"

"I suppose so. Somebody always does. Asks for the sugar or whatever. Honestly, Bob, I just can't remember. You know I'm never what you'd call brisk first thing in the morning."

"Yes, I know it, and I shouldn't be surprised if other people did, too. Pete, am I making something of nothing?"

The young assistant broke in. "Bob, you can't think there was something in that coffee I poured for you?"

"I'm not thinking anything, Ned. I'm only stating certain facts. Cadwall's dead all of a sudden for no apparent reason. I gave him my coffee. Or rather, you did."

"Are you accusing me?"

"God, no! That's the last thing I'd ever think. If you'd meant to kill me, thus scuttling your chances for promotion as well you know, you sure as hell would have managed to drop that cup rather than give it to Cadwall. And you couldn't have intended it for him because you didn't know you were going to be asked to leave it at his table until you were heading back here with both hands full. But think it out, Ned. There was a crush at the coffee urn. People were reaching for things. Everybody was either half asleep or talking to his neighbor. Who the hell would notice if something was dropped into a cup? I'm not saying it happened. I'm just saying it's possible."

"But what if they got the wrong cup? My God, I could have drunk the stuff myself!"

"Use your head. Yours was stained around the rim. Naturally the clean one had to be for me. It was foolproof, and damned clever." Dysart scribbled on the check, threw money on the table, and stood up. "Only of course it's all damned nonsense. See you, Pete."

Left alone, Shandy went on eating chowder for which he had no appetite. Was there any validity to Dysart's theory? It was typical of the man to grab any chance of putting himself in the limelight. Nevertheless, it was not an impossible supposition.

Most of the college people, even those like Jackman who made a point of breakfasting with their families, were in the habit of dropping in at the faculty dining room on their way to work. From half past seven until almost nine, the place was sure to be crowded, especially during this holiday season when those who might otherwise be rushing to early classes had a chance to linger and chat. This was where all the news and much of the gossip got circulated. Cadwall the busybody and Dysart the social lion never missed a morning. If somebody wanted to feed either one of them a slow-acting poison, this was as likely a place as any.

Shandy didn't know whether strong black coffee could mask the bitter taste of taxine. It might, he supposed, if the coffee was worse than usual, and that also could have happened with waitresses doing double duty as cooks during the Illumination. If he hadn't breakfasted with Helen, he'd know. A conscientious investigator ought, perhaps, to feel regret.

Had somebody in fact gone to the dining room with poison in his or her pocket, spilled Cadwall's coffee on purpose, and snatched at a fortuitous chance to dose the cup Ned had poured for Dysart after it had been rerouted to the comptroller? Preposterous as it sounded, the scenario was yet less inconceivable than that somebody had meant to poison Dysart, then sat and watched another man drink the lethal potion. Could any of their colleagues be so inhuman?

Possibly, Shandy supposed, if the murderer could see no way to take the substitute cup from Cadwall without attracting undue notice to himself. If he'd already killed Mrs. Ames, he might have suffered a dulling of the moral sensibilities, to the point where one corpse more or less wouldn't seem to matter.

On what grounds could Dysart be associated with Jemima's death? She'd been at his party and he'd watched her leave. Was that all? There was still the unexplained circumstance of her going into the shrubbery and not being seen to come out. Might Bob in fact have noticed something odd about her departure, and kept quiet about it?

Shandy couldn't imagine the engineer's ever keeping quiet about anything. It must be borne in mind, however, that none of the Crescent folk except himself and Timothy Ames and now Helen Marsh knew Jemima had died by design instead of accident. Maybe Bob wasn't talking simply because he didn't yet realize he had something to tell. That, from the murderer's point of view, would make him a walking time bomb.

By Professor Dysart's own account, though, he'd been too drunk to make a reliable witness by the time Jemima started her fatal walk. Ben Cadwall, who'd boycotted the Dysart punch bowl and was probably snooping as usual, would be far more apt to observe and remember.

Hannah wasn't at the party either. She was making her rounds of the Crescent. What if Ben had caught her where she wasn't supposed to be, doing something not even the most devoted husband could condone?

Hannah knew, of course, that her husband always got something to eat at the dining room on his way to the office. If she were to feed him a slow-acting poison before he left the house, show reasonable intelligence about getting rid of the evidence, and stick to her guns on questioning that she'd done nothing of the sort, attention would have to focus on the possibility that he'd got it here. By the time he died, whatever dishes he'd used must have been passed through the kitchen's efficient sterilizers and stacked with dozens just like them. Dysart's grandstand play would be an extra stroke of luck for her, but she really wouldn't need it. Any good lawyer could get her off on the ground of legitimate doubt, assuming she was ever brought to trial.

Did Hannah really have the brains or the enterprise to commit a double murder and not get caught? People tended to write her off as negligible because she was always in the shadow of two domineering personalities. Yet Jemima and Ben were both dead now, and Hannah had at least shown no lack of confidence stepping into Mrs. Ames's shoes.

Thinking of the Buggins Collection and the house Helen was still trying to make habitable, Shandy wondered. Could a woman who left her private affairs in total chaos have been, in fact, the great organizer she was cracked up to be? Might not the faithful henchwoman have done most of the real work on those many public projects for which Jemima snatched credit?

Ben couldn't have been any picnic to live with either, with his complaints and crotchets and his personal vendettas and his smarmy, know-it-all air. Maybe Hannah was plain sick and tired of being bullied.

Still, it did seem that an apparently sane and sensible woman could find some way of getting her friend and her husband off her back without having to kill them both.

SEVENTEEN

SHANDY WAS STILL brooding over half a bowlful of corn chowder when, to his intense astonishment, Hannah Cadwall entered the dining room alone and looking frazzled but not upset.

"Hannah, what are you doing here? Didn't Mary Enderble find you?"

"She was yoo-hooing to me across the Crescent, but I just waved and came on. I'm famished. Jackie, bring me a bowl of whatever Professor Shandy's eating and make it snappy, will you? If I don't get something inside me pronto, I'm going to faint."

She plumped herself down opposite Peter, snatched a stick of celery from his untouched hors d'oeuvre tray, and began to chomp. "Been over to the shopping mall," she told him with her mouth full. "What a madhouse! Had to fight my way every step. Thanks, Jackie. That was quick."

She picked up the spoon and began to bail chowder into her mouth at an incredible rate. Shandy watched, stupefied. Obviously Mrs. Cadwall still didn't know she was a widow, but how was a man to tell her while she was stuffing herself like a starved wolverine? When she paused to slap butter on a roll, he plucked up his nerve.

"Er—Hannah?"

"What, Peter? Why are you goggling at me like a fish out of water? Honestly, you're getting more peculiar every day of your life. What did Mary Enderble want?"

"To tell you that the police are looking for you."

"About that stupid permit for the extra parking facilities, I suppose. Why I ever let myself get sucked into taking over Jemima's job—"

"It's about Ben," Shandy fairly shouted.

"Well, what about him?" She took a giant bite of her roll. "Has he robbed a bank, or kidnaped the president?"

"He's dead, Hannah."

Incredibly, she kept on eating her roll. Then the impact of his words reached her. She gulped and shoved her plate away.

"Peter, is this another of your little games?"

"It's the truth, Hannah. I found him myself. I went over to see him a while back and found him sitting at his desk. He was just—gone. It must have happened quite suddenly, with no pain."

"But Ben wouldn't die! He's so darned careful of himself, he'll—I always thought he'd live to be a hundred."

"Hadn't you better drink your tea?"

"I don't want tea! I want my husband." Burying her face in a paper napkin, Hannah began to sob.

The young waitress ran over to the table. "What's the matter? Did you choke? Mrs. Cadwall, are you all right?"

"My husband's dead!"

"I'm sorry," Shandy told the bewildered girl. "The comptroller died suddenly this morning in his office, while Mrs. Cadwall was out shopping. This is the first chance anyone's had to tell her. I ought to have managed it more tactfully."

"How could you be tactful about a thing like that? My gosh, Dr. Cadwall, of all people! Shall I bring some more hot tea?"

"I don't know."

Shandy was experiencing the normal discomfiture of a man in the company of a hysterical woman. "Hannah, would you like more tea?"

"No."

"Shall I take you home?"

The widow blew her nose into the soggy napkin. "I suppose so."

"I'll get her coat," offered the waitress.

"You'd better give me the check first," said Shandy.

"Oh no! I couldn't make you pay, at a time like this."

"My dear young woman, you're going to make a fine wife and mother."

"Professor Shandy!"

Nevertheless, the girl helped him on with his overcoat and gave him a friendly pat on the arm. "You take good care of her, now. See if you can get a neighbor to come in. I'd go with you myself, but we're so shorthanded on account of the Illumination."

"Thank you. I daresay we'll manage."

At the moment, Shandy didn't see how. Hannah was a dead weight on his arm, not seeming to notice where she put her feet. If he managed to get her down that perilous walk without at least one sprained ankle between them, it would be an agreeable surprise.

"Peter, what am I going to do?" Hannah wailed.

He took a firmer grip on her arm. "The best you can, Hannah. You'll manage."

"But I'm alone. I've never been alone, not once in my life. First I lived with my folks, then I went away to school and lived in a dorm, then I moved to the sorority house, then I got married right after graduation and had the two children and now they're gone and Ben's gone, too. Peter, I don't think I can stand it."

"Of course you can." Dear God, this was awful. "Your friends will stand by you."

"What friends? Jemima was the only one who ever gave a hoot about me, and she's gone like the rest."

For a wonder, she didn't start to cry again. Realizing her complete bereavement seemed to have a calming effect.

"I'm on my own. On my own."

Hannah didn't say another word until they were inside the house she had shared with Ben Cadwall for so many years. Shandy got her coat off and led her to the biggest armchair in the neat, characterless, somewhat bleak parlor.

"This was Ben's chair. The kids got it for him one Father's Day. They had them on special down at the Emporium. Now it's mine, I guess."

She rubbed her hands over the slick brown vinyl arms, as though to make sure the furniture was there.

"Ben left everything to me, you know, for as long as I live. I can keep it or sell it, just as I please. That's one thing you have to give him credit for. He could be hell on wheels to live with, but he never went back on a promise. He said he'd take care of me, and he did. I get the insurance and the savings accounts and the securities and the money from the house. I'll sell as soon as I can. I couldn't go on living here by myself, even if the college would allow it. Anyway, I'm sick of Balaclava and everybody in it. Turn up the thermostat, Peter. Ben always insisted on keeping it down to sixty-two. I'm going some place where I won't have to freeze to death all winter long. How much will I get out of the pension fund? There'll be something, won't there, even if it's not as if he'd lived to sixty-five? But who's going to give it to me? Ben was always the one to sign the pension checks, and he's gone. Peter, you'll have to stick up for my rights."

"I'm sure there won't be any problem, Hannah. The treasurer will simply take over until a new comptroller can be found."

"Oh, that old fool. Ben always said he was about as much good as an old wet hen, though he'd kill me if he ever knew I repeated it. Ben always thought the post should have gone to him, though he wouldn't have been happy in it. Ben was a detail man. He liked having a finger in all the pies, and he got a kick out of knowing everything that went on. Not much got by my Bennie, I can tell you."

"That was my impression," said Shandy cautiously. "Tell me, Hannah, was Ben in the habit of discussing these—er—goings-on with you?"

She shrugged. "Yes and no. Of course we discussed things. What do you think? We couldn't sit around staring at each other like a couple of dummies. The trouble was, he always cautioned me against repeating anything and of course I wouldn't dare because it would surely get straight back to him. Then when gossip did get started, as it always does sooner or later, which you well know, he'd blame me when I hadn't said a word to anybody."

"Not even to Jemima?"

"She'd be the last person. I'm not one to talk against my own dead friend, but if they'd ever run a contest for the biggest mouth in Balaclava Junction, she'd have won hands down. Ben wasn't like her. He could talk your hind leg off, but he never said anything he didn't want you to know. Even with me, he'd clam up sometimes and get that mysterious smirk on his face. He'd be sitting right here in this chair, hugging some new secret to himself and I swear to God, Peter, there were times when I could have taken that poker and wrapped it around his neck. He did that with everybody. In a way, I'm surprised he got to die a natural death."

Hannah blinked. "Come to think of it, you still haven't told me what he died of. Was it a heart attack? Peter, why are you goggling at me like that? What was it?"

"I can't tell you, Hannah. There were no—er—external indications."

"Didn't you call the doctor?"

"Of course. Dr. Melchett was unable to form an opinion."

"What's that supposed to mean? Wouldn't he sign the death certificate? Dr. Melchett, of all people? Peter Shandy, you quit beating around the bush and tell me what happened to my husband."

"Hannah, I do not know. My personal opinion, for what it's worth, is that he may somehow have been poisoned."

"Oh, my God! They'll say I did it for the money."

Ashen-faced, Mrs. Cadwall cowered back into the vinyl armchair. "Peter, what am I going to do?"

Damn it, woman, how should I know? was the retort that sprang to his lips. Mercifully, he managed not to say it.

"Now, Hannah, there's no sense in borrowing trouble. Wait and see what they find."

"What who find?"

"They—er—took him to the county coroner's, I believe. It's a routine procedure in cases of sudden death. Oh, Lord, that reminds me. I must get in touch with Grimble and let him know you're here."

"Peter, don't! I'm scared."

"Why? You didn't poison Ben, did you?"

"Jemima said you had a rotten, vicious streak in you. She said you put up those awful lights and things on purpose to get back at us. I didn't believe her then, but I do now."

"Never mind that. Tell me what you gave Ben for breakfast. I know he stopped at the college dining room, but did he eat anything before he left the house? You'll have to tell the police, you know."

"I'll tell anybody who asks me. I have nothing to be ashamed of, which is more than you can say."

"All right, Hannah. What did Ben eat?"

"We each had a cup of rose-hip tea for the vitamin C, and a little all-bran for our bowels. And we used the same tea bag and the same bran out of the same box and the same milk out of the same carton. Then we had a piece of coffeecake that Sheila Jackman sent over by one of the kids. I suppose she meant well. Anyway, it was a change from all-bran."

"Ben ate some of the cake?"

"A little. He growled about the empty calories, but he ate it, so he wouldn't have to lie and tell Sheila it was good when he hadn't tasted it. Ben was honest, you know. Too damned honest, sometimes."

"Is there any of the cake left?"

"No, I finished it after he'd gone. I made myself some coffee. I always do."

"What was the cake like? I was thinking that if the children made it, they might have gone in for some—er—fancy touches."

"Like putting rat poison on top? You don't have to beat around the bush with me, Peter Shandy. In my opinion, the cake came straight out of a Betty Crocker box, and if there'd been anything wrong with it, I'd be dead instead of Ben because I ate about three times as much as he did. I can ask Sheila for the recipe, if you want."

"Let the police do that if they want. It will give them something to think about. I do think I ought to put in that call, Hannah. If you don't come forward, somebody might start wondering why."

"Oh, go ahead," she sighed. "What difference does it make? I'll have to get word to Benita and Frank, too."

"Yes, your children ought to be with you as soon as possible. Why don't you call them as soon as I've got hold of Grimble?"

"Not now! We always wait till evening, when the rates go down."

Shandy shrugged. "Where's the phone?"

"Right out in the front hall. Oh, Peter, do you have to?"

As it happened, he didn't. Shandy was looking about him for the instrument when Grimble and Olivetti came up the walk. He opened the door for them.

"I was just about to call you. I found Mrs. Cadwall in the faculty dining room and brought her home."

"We know you did," snarled Grimble. "Why the hell didn't you get in touch with me right away?"

"Because she was upset and wanted to come home. I believe you'll find her able to talk now."

"You been tellin' her what to say, huh?"

"Grimble, have you ever thought of getting yourself stuffed and mounted? What can she say, except the truth?"

"You'd be surprised, Professor," said Olivetti. "Where is she?"

"In here."

Shandy motioned them into the parlor, where Hannah still hunched in the brown vinyl armchair. She looked up at the men, but made no effort to rise, or even to speak.

Grimble lost his truculence. "Well, Miz Cadwall," he began awkwardly, "we kind of hate to bother you at a time like this. Sure was an awful shock, us findin' the comptroller like we did. Gosh, it was only yesterday afternoon he dropped in at my office, friendly as you please. We had a high old time."

At last Hannah broke her silence. "You surprise me, Grimble. Dr. Cadwall told me he was going over to tear your hide off. He said you'd been playing games with your expense account again and he was pretty fed up with trying to keep you honest. I'm glad you took the criticism in such a cordial spirit, though I daresay you have reason to feel you got off more lightly than you deserve. I believe he did put it to you straight that if you ever pulled one more stunt like the last time, he was going to take the evidence to President Svenson and you'd be out on your ear before you knew what struck you. I wasn't supposed to breathe a word to a soul, but I don't suppose it matters now. They can't fire him for breach of confidence, can they?"

Shandy blinked in admiration. The comptroller's widow was going to manage all right. Olivetti was gazing at the security chief with an interested glint in his steel-gray eyes. Grimble was squirming.

"Aw, nothin' like that ever happened. He must o' been jokin'."

"My husband never joked about money."

She made the statement in a flat, uninterested tone that was the ultimate in credibility. "Officer, have they found out what he died of?"

"I don't know, Mrs. Cadwall. I'll check with the lab again right now, if you don't mind my using your phone."

"Not at all. Peter, would you show him, please? I seem to be dreadfully tired all of a sudden. Shopping always exhausts me. Ben said I ought to wait for the final markdowns, but everything gets so picked over."

She started to cry again without sound or stirring, letting the tears run down her face and dampen the front of her sensible tan polyester dress. It was unbearable to watch.

Shandy got up. "Hannah, can I bring you a drink or something?"

She realized what was happening, and snuffled. "There's a box of Kleenex on the kitchen counter, and some of the sherry from Jemima's funeral in the underneath cupboard to the right of the sink. You might bring me a little of that. Maybe it will warm me up. I feel so cold, as if it were myself and not Ben who—"

"Yes, of course. That's perfectly natural."

He hustled out of the room to get away from the sight of those coursing tears. Olivetti was hanging on the phone when he passed through on his way to the kitchen, still waiting when he got back. He paused to ask, "Any news?"

"They're checking now. We can't expect results this fast. They've hardly had time to—yeah? You did? Well, what do you know about that? Sure, I understand. Thanks."

The state policeman hung up. "That doctor of yours is one smart man, Professor, in case you didn't know it. He told the coroner's office to test for the commoner vegetable alkaloids first, and they think they may be on to something already."

"Most interesting," said Shandy demurely. He was betting on taxine himself, but he deemed it prudent not to appear too knowledgeable. "May I pass on the information to Mrs. Cadwall?"

"Thanks, I'll tell her myself, when there's anything to tell. Say, Professor, haven't you got some papers to correct?"

"Or peddle? Certainly, if you'd rather I left. For what it's worth, Lieutenant, I really don't think Mrs. Cadwall poisoned her husband."

"Am I supposed to take that as an expert opinion?"

"Anybody who's been monitoring exams for a great many years tends to develop a certain sensitivity as to who has the answers taped inside his socks."

"So who's got the answers this time?"

"I don't know yet, but there's a chap named Dysart who has a story you might care to hear. Grimble can track him down for you."

"Thanks. And where do I track you down, just in case?"

"My house is directly across the way, the small red brick one with the—er—reindeer on the roof. Then I'll just give Mrs. Cadwall her drink and explain that I have to leave."

Hannah accepted the sherry, the tissues, and the good-by without comment. Shandy went out feeling guilty for no definable reason. He'd always thought of Ben's wife, when he thought of her at all, as one of life's minor nuisances. Now she was a person in trouble. How much of this trouble had been precipitated by his vicious reaction against her and Jemima's annual pestering?

His cousin's wife Elizabeth, who was a religious woman, would no doubt say that this horrible turn of events was a judgment upon him for losing his temper. He would not have believed himself capable of entertaining the possibility that Elizabeth could be right.

EIGHTEEN

OF ALL THE black thoughts surging through Shandy's mind, the blackest was that Helen wouldn't be free for at least another hour and a half. Next most dire was the fact that, although its presiding genius was dead and its acting chairman perhaps even now being arrested for a murder she almost certainly didn't commit, business at the Illumination was brisk as usual.

The master switch for the lights—his own, alas, among them—had already been thrown. The Gingerbread Houses had dropped their plywood fronts. Red-and-green elves cavorted about wearing sandwich boards that announced a Giant Marshmallow Roast with music by the Eskimo Pie-men, whoever they might be, to start at half past seven on the lower playing field, admission one dollar. One of them stopped the professor and tried to sell him a ticket. Shuddering, he turned downhill and sought refuge in the Enderbles' shrubbery.

It was curious how the dense growth, caked with hardened-on snow, created a sense of isolation. Even the hubbub he'd found intolerable on the Crescent so few steps away penetrated here only as a blending of happy sounds.

There were plenty of yews here. That didn't mean anything, of course; Balaclava was overgrown with yew. Still, if one wanted to gather the needles in total privacy, this would be a safer place than most. Shandy pottered along, trying to discern in the fading light whether any of the branches showed signs of being stripped. He went too far along the path, and Adele Dysart spied him.

"Peter!" she shrieked from a window. "Thank God you've come. I'm stuck in the house with a lousy cold and ready to climb the walls. Just a second, I'll open the door."

Shandy wanted neither Adele's cold nor her company, but she'd got him trapped and herded into what the Dysarts insisted on calling their family room before he could think up a tactful way to tell her so.

"Now you sit there and don't move. I'm going to fix you a slug of my special cough medicine."

"No, please don't. I'm due at a cocktail party pretty soon," he lied. He should have known better. She pounced.

"Who's giving it, and how come I wasn't invited?"

"Er—it isn't actually a party, just drinks with a—er—friend."

"Who, for instance?"

"Helen Marsh," he replied unhappily.

"You mean that washed-out old maid librarian you dragged over to the dining room last night? What is she, some poor relation of the Ameses'? Honestly, Peter, can't you do a little better than that? What happened to Susie?"

"Susie who? Oh—er—Susie. She—er—floated out of my life, so to speak."

It would be ludicrous as well as futile to try explaining why Helen was so much the more attractive of the two. Adele was looking, to use a trenchant simile often employed by Mrs. Lomax, like something the cat dragged in. Her hair-do had come unstuck and she'd made no attempt to sort out the resultant tangle of wiry elflocks. The make-up she was wearing must have been applied at least one day ago. Her housecoat could have done with a washing, and so could her neck. She dabbed at her scarlet nose with a wad of tissues and took a swig of her own prescription.

"And what brings you to these parts in the midst of your busy social life?"

An explanation came into his mind, and he uttered it. "I've been trying to figure out how Jemima got through that shrubbery after she left your party without being seen."

She wiped her nose again. "For God's sake, why?"

"I think it's curious. Mary Enderble and Roger Jackman must have been walking straight toward the entrance in one direction at the same time she entered the path from here, yet they didn't meet. Sheila was watching for about fifteen minutes out their front window and says she never saw her come out. Are you positive she didn't change her mind and go around by the street?"

Adele stared at him over her Kleenex. "Why would she do a thing like that? Look, she went out that same door you just came in, right? There's a path shoveled from the door into the short cut, right? And there's no path from that path to any other path, right? The only way she could get from the back to the front would be to come back through the house, which she didn't because a whole bunch of people watched her go down the path, right? Unless she went wallowing through the snow up to her eyeballs which nobody in her right mind would do when she had a path to walk in. Christ, if we ever get out of this lousy climate—" she sneezed again and sought solace in her tumbler.

"Then I suppose the only logical explanation is that somebody mistook the time."

"I don't see how. Sheila Jackman knew what time it was, all right. She'd been eying the clock and making noises at Roger for at least half an hour before they left. Needless to say, she had one hell of a time dragging him away. Rog has the hots for me, in case you hadn't noticed."

Shandy found that a highly improbable statement. It occurred to him that Adele must be roughly twice Roger's age.

"I see, so that made you aware of the time."

"Me and everybody else. That's what got Jemima fussing about having to go and be the boy on the burning deck some more."

"I see. And you had some—er—refreshment of sorts in the oven, I believe."

"Squid puffs. You know me, I have to be different. All they know around here is onion soup dip and potato chips."

That was a flagrant lie. Thanks to Mrs. Mouzouka's gourmet cooking courses, most faculty parties tended to be journeys into the unknown. Adele and her pretensions were a pathetic combination.

"And then of course my loving husband made this big scene about watching Jemima leave and my timer went off and there I was, rushing back and forth like a whirlwind."

"Did you personally see Jemima going down the path?"

"Well, of course. Who could miss that purple burnous? I suppose I oughtn't to talk that way now she's dead."

"But in fact you do know for certain that she left by the short cut almost immediately after the Jackmans."

"Not immediately, because she had to put on a big thing about how she had to rush off and all that garbage. Maybe five or ten minutes. Not longer. I know, because it's always scary when people start leaving one right after the other. Gives the rest ideas, and before you know it your party's died on you. I have a hunch that's why Bob started this big deal about Jemima. After the way he made fun of her, nobody else would dare bug out for fear he'd do the same to them."

She chuckled. "Bob's clever, you know. Plays dirty pool sometimes, but what the hell? You do the best you can with what you've got, right?"

"Er—within legal limits, at any rate."

"Peter, you're a one-man panic. Come on over here so I won't have to strain my throat hollering at you. Unless you're afraid of catching my cold," Mrs. Dysart added with a laugh he could swear was meant to be provocative.

"One can't be too careful this time of year," he replied caddishly. "Miss Tibbett says these things go in threes."

"What things?"

"Good Lord, do you mean to say you haven't heard about Ben Cadwall? Hasn't Bob told you?"

"Soon as he found out I was out of commission, Bob developed urgent business at the power plant. I haven't seen him since some ungodly hour this morning. What happened to Ben? Peter, you don't mean—not Ben?"

"I'm afraid so, Adele."

Shandy was surprised to see the woman looking genuinely disturbed. "I found him myself, in his office. It's getting to be an unpleasant habit of mine."

"My, God, two in a row! If I'd known that, I wouldn't have let you in. But Ben, of all people. Look, be a pal and get me some more bourbon. Never mind the ice. I think I'm having a chill."

"Here, put this shawl thing around you."

The professor snatched up a Mexican serape that had been thrown across the top of a sofa, and draped it over her thin shoulders. He was slightly worried lest she take the courtesy for a come-on, but Adele didn't even seem to notice. She was staring into the unlighted fireplace with a look on her face that might almost have been awe. Considering that the Dysarts had barely been on speaking terms with the Cadwalls until Jemima's funeral, her reaction seemed excessive, yet he didn't think she was play-acting this time.

He got her the drink, not without difficulty. The house was a tricky one. A narrow hallway that should logically have led to the kitchen took a sudden turn and wound up at the foot of the back stairs. He wondered if Jemima had come down that way. Bob would remember, perhaps, not that it meant anything one way or the other.

After blundering around awhile, Shandy did in fact locate the kitchen, which was in an unholy mess. The cleaning woman must be off for the holidays. The bourbon was sitting on the counter top, along with a repellent collection of unscraped plates. He slopped a couple of fingers into the glass and got out of there as fast as he could, which still wasn't fast enough for Adele.

"What took you so long?"

"I got lost."

"I wish I could, sometimes. What did Ben die of?"

Shandy had a sudden urge to play his hunch, and see how she reacted.

"Taxine poisoning," he said firmly.

"I don't believe you."

"Then wait for the official autopsy report."

"Peter, how could it be that? Taxine isn't something a grown-up takes by accident. It comes from yew. We had a lecture at the garden club. I remembered that one, because the name sounds like taxi."

Shandy had got roped into speaking at the Balaclava Garden Club once or twice. He knew many faculty ladies belonged. It was one of the few places where town and gown met on an equal footing, though no doubt some were more equal than others. If Adele knew about taxine, probably every woman in town did.

"No," he replied, "I'm sure Ben wouldn't ingest the stuff knowingly unless for some reason he decided to commit suicide."

"Ben kill himself? Never!"

"That's my personal opinion, but I must say I'm surprised to hear you being so definite. I had no idea you were that well acquainted with him."

Adele made a sound that could have been a laugh. She was quite drunk by now.

"There's one hell of a lot you don't know about me, Peter Shandy. I knew Ben Cadwall long before I ever met Bob. We were almost engaged once. Of course he was years and years too old for me," she added hastily.

"I'm sorry," Shandy replied. "I had no idea. Er—where did you know Ben?"

She set her glass down on the sticky coffee table. "Look, do me a favor and don't mention this to Bob. It was all over years ago, but he doesn't like to be reminded. That's why he and Ben always sort of had it in for one another."

"Does Hannah know?"

"I don't suppose so. Ben always got a kick out of keeping secrets. I must say it was a jolt when we moved here and found them on our doorstep. I might have known Ben would wind up in a place like Balaclava."

"I've often wondered what brought you and Bob here," Shandy ventured. "I'd have thought you'd prefer a more—er—urban atmosphere."

Adele shrugged. "Variety's the spice of life, they say. How about it, Pete. Care for a little variety?"

To Shandy's overwhelming relief, Bob Dysart chose that moment to barge in, shouting.

"Dell? Dell? Where the—oh, hi, Pete. Entertaining the little woman while the old man's out hustling a buck, eh? Nice work if you can get it. How're you feeling, gorgeous?"

"A fat lot you care," sniffled his wife. "Why didn't you tell me Ben Cadwall's dead?"

"Give me time. I just got here."

"You could have come home earlier."

"I was busy."

"Oh yeah? Who with?"

"You mean with whom. What are you drinking, Pete?"

"He's saving his thirst for later," said Adele with a savage laugh. "He has a heavy date with the lady librarian."

"Ah, so? I must check her out. Pause for laugh. Nobody laughs. How about you, pussycat?"

Without waiting for an answer, Dysart went and got what looked to Shandy like a great deal of whiskey.

"Thanks, pal, I needed that. Christ, what a day this has been! Pete, did you tell Adele how somebody tried to murder me this morning?"

"No, I—er—hadn't got to it yet."

"Jesus! Just because you don't give a damn, didn't it occur to you that somebody else might?"

Dysart was furious. He must actually have worked himself around to believing his own story.

"Bob, what are you talking about?" demanded his wife. "Peter says Ben was poisoned with taxine."

"Yes, and it was meant for me."

Dysart went on about the incident in the dining room. "And what would any intelligent person make of that?" he finished.

A great deal less than you're making of it, Shandy thought.

The second hearing was no more plausible than the first, to his mind. Why choose so risky a way of getting at a man who left himself vulnerable in so many other ways? And what could be the motive? Adele asked that question. Her husband had his answer ready.

"I can't say for sure, but I have a hunch it's something to do with the plant."

"The Skunk Works?" Shandy injudiciously exclaimed, using the inevitable student nickname.

"If you want to call it that," Dysart replied stiffly. "It just happens that we have some very interesting research going on there. I don't want to talk about it, and I don't want to toot my own horn, but just among us three, there's a potential for commercial development that will make your Balaclava Buster look like a worm-eaten radish, and I'm the guy who's pushing it. And if we do what I have in mind, it's going to be a real kick in the guts for the oil companies and the gas companies and the coal mines. I know this sounds like cloak-and-dagger stuff, but I'm talking straight fact, and I'm the only one who sees it. The rest of them down there are dragging their feet and piddling around, while I've been trying to line up ways to exploit the potential. And it's beginning to look as though somebody wants to stop me. Looks as if I'd better make sure my insurance is paid up. Got to keep the little woman in bourbon. Jesus, on second thought, I'd better not. I might be worth more to Dell dead than alive."

"Oh, stop talking like a fool!" his wife exploded. "I never know whether to believe you or not. You can be so damned convincing, then it turns out you're just building up for another of your funnies. Peter, could he possibly be telling the truth?"

Shandy hunched his shoulders. "I trust Bob won't take offense if I say that for his own sake, as well as yours, I sincerely hope he isn't. I don't mean that you're consciously trying to deceive either of us, Bob," he added hastily. "It does seem to me, though, that if somebody were—er—out to get you, he might choose a less chancy method. I can understand that with this—er—tremendous responsibility preying on your mind, you might make the interpretation you did. Being a simple-minded person myself, I'm more inclined to believe that since Ben Cadwall got the poison, it was Ben somebody meant to kill."

Dysart scratched his chin. "I don't know if you're trying to deflate my ego, Pete, or get my mind off my troubles. What the hell would anybody murder Ben Cadwall for?"

"Well, for one thing, he handled all the money around here, which meant that he had a great deal of power. For another, he was a busybody. Let's assume, by way of hypothesis, that somebody was actually plotting to sabotage your research, or your—er—merchandising efforts. Don't you think Ben would get wind of that fact even before you did?"

"My God, Pete, you've hit it! So that's why whoever poisoned my coffee this morning made no effort to get it away from Ben. It didn't matter which of us got killed first, since we'd both have to go anyway."

"Will you stop talking like that?" shrieked Adele. "Why did you drag me here in the first place? I can't stand it any more! We've got to get away."

"I'm not running, Dell."

Shandy reached for his hat. "I am," he said firmly. "I hope your cold is better soon, Adele. And, Bob, I shouldn't dwell on this matter if I were you. The comptroller's death probably has a very prosaic explanation."

He spoke more bravely than he felt. The likelihood that Ben had been killed for some reason less exotic than sabotage didn't preclude the possibility that Dysart was also on the murderer's list, and that the episode of the coffee cups didn't in fact mean exactly what Bob thought it did.

NINETEEN

"HELEN CAN WE skip the faculty dining room tonight?"

"Certainly, Peter, if you're tired."

"I'm not tired, I'm fed up. If I don't get away from here for a while, I'll start to climb the walls and gibber. There's a place about twelve miles out on the Dallow road that serves fairly decent roast beef."

"That sounds delightful. Shall we take the Ameses' car? I presume I have the keys."

"Thank you, no. Can you imagine what shape any vehicle Jemima drove would be in? I'll phone down to Charlie's garage and rent one. That will at least give us a fighting chance of coming back alive."

"Peter, you poor man! You're having a ghastly time, aren't you? Shall we talk now, or wait till we get some food?"

"Food first if you don't mind. Go get your things while I talk to Charlie."

He ought to think about buying a car of his own. Until now, it had never seemed worth the bother. Shandy poured another tiny puddle of sherry into the bottom of his glass, and went to the Ameses' telephone.

After he'd made his arrangements with the garage, he phoned to see how Hannah Cadwall was doing.

"She's asleep," Mary Enderble told him. "Dr. Melchett phoned in a prescription to the drugstore, and John went down to pick it up. Oh, and the police just called. They say it was taxine that killed Ben, of all things! Can you imagine?"

So Shandy's guess had been right. The knowledge gave him no satisfaction.

Helen was upstairs about ten minutes. She came down wearing a long-sleeved, long-skirted dress of flaming scarlet.

"I bought this thing ages ago and have been itching for a chance to wear it. In California, it always looked out of place."

"It's very nice," said Shandy awkwardly. It was a great deal more than that, but he didn't quite know how to tell her so.

"There's a heavy black cape hanging in the closet," Helen went on. "I don't suppose Professor Ames would mind if I wore it."

"Oh, no, I'm sure he'd be delighted. Jemima rather went in for capes."

"So I understand. One of the girls was telling me how she used to come swooping in with yards and yards of purple hand weaving swirling around her, knocking things off the desk and creating general confusion. They used to keep book on how many times a week she'd rush into the place, tell everybody how much she had to do, and rush out again without lifting a finger. They must find me horribly dull by comparison."

"I don't see how they could," said Shandy. "Jemima was a tiresome woman. Speaking of tiresome, how did you manage this afternoon? I hope Porble didn't keep you at hog statistics all day long."

"Not quite. I managed to sneak into the Buggins Room about half past four. The kids had got most of the mess up off the floor. Everything will have to be reshelved eventually, but at least it's possible to read the titles of those few that got put in right side up, or would be if they'd give me more than one forty-watt bulb for that entire room."

"Oh, I expect you won't have any trouble there. We have no energy shortage at Balaclava just now, though we may at any moment. Dysart thinks there's a plot afoot to sabotage the power plant."

"My stars and garters! Never a dull moment around here, is there? Could he possibly be right?"

"Only if you accept the premise that Standard Oil and Exxon are likely to feel threatened by a system that runs on animal droppings. We turn left at the foot of the hill."

"I know. We came this way when you brought me from the airport. Good heavens, was that only yesterday afternoon? It seems a lifetime ago."

"Yes, it does."

Shandy suddenly realized with a sort of horror that he could no longer imagine Balaclava Junction without Helen in it. Would he ever get up courage enough to tell her so? For the moment he must be satisfied to pilot her safely through the jostle of climbing visitors, many of whom stopped them to ask the way to the Giant Marshmallow Roast. At last they got the car and started threading their way through the traffic.

"Good God," he panted when they were clear of the mob and out on the Dallow road, "I hope the prime ribs are worth the struggle."

"I'm sure they will be," said Helen. "You're a very good driver, Peter."

"Do you think so? I learned on a John Deere tractor when I was five years old. Then I worked a lot at farms and field stations where one was always running a bulldozer or combine or something of the sort. I don't believe I've ever quite grasped the concept that a vehicle can be operated solely for pleasure."

"Probably not many of them will be, unless something can be done about the fuel shortage. Too bad your power plant people can't invent one that runs on cowflaps. You don't suppose that's why Professor Dysart's talking about sabotage, do you?"

"Oh, I hardly think so. The project would have to be discussed at faculty meetings before any work got started. Dr. Svenson believes in coordinated efforts toward shared goals."

"Do you share?"

"Fairly often. There's always a certain amount of jockeying as to whose project takes precedence, but in general I'd say the *esprit de corps* is maintained at a tolerable level. At least, I've always thought so."

Helen caught the doubt and despair in his voice.

"I know. It's like having a nail in your shoe, isn't it? No matter where you try to step, you keep landing on that same nasty little sore spot. I am sorry, Peter. Let's really talk about something else for a while. Tell me what you did when you worked at the field stations."

"It's so long ago, I can't remember."

Once started, however, Shandy recalled a great deal, some of it funny enough to set them both laughing. By the time they got to the restaurant, he felt ready to enjoy his meal.

The place was quieter than he'd ever seen it before. Everybody was broke from paying for Christmas presents, the waitress explained, or home eating leftovers or over at the Illumination. She piloted them to a corner booth Shandy had often coveted but never before got to sit in. They had soup that wasn't bad, or at least wasn't turkey. They had salad and baked potatoes and medium-rare prime ribs and a California Beaujolais that made Helen feel more kindly toward the San Andreas Fault. When he ran out of stories about life among the combines, the professor discovered that he didn't mind telling Helen about Ben Cadwall.

"Don't you think it's logical to assume," he concluded, "that Ben and Jemima were killed by the same person, for the same reason?"

"I think it's lots more logical than to believe there could be two unrelated murders within such a closed community in the space of three days," she replied. "Then there are so many possible connections. That marble you found in the Cadwalls' bedroom, for one thing. You don't know whose coat it fell out of."

"Good Lord, no, I don't. I was thinking of Ben or Hannah, but it could have been anybody. Ben might have seen the thing drop when he was taking someone's coat and not bothered about it because others were crowding in at the same time. Then later downstairs, when I told my little tale about slipping on the marbles—"

"Did you actually tell that?"

"I did. They wanted all the details, you know, about how I found Jemima's body. Somebody asked why I looked behind the sofa, so I explained about finding the marbles scattered over the floor and realizing that somebody must have been in the house."

"There you are! The marble falls. Maybe Dr. Cadwall actually sees what it is. Anyway, he says, 'Oh, you've dropped something,' and the other person says, 'No, I haven't,' because he doesn't know he has the marble on him."

"Or her."

"Of course. Then after you've told your story, he—I do wish somebody would think up a new collective pronoun—realizes it must have been the marble that fell, and sneaks back to hunt for it."

"But it's gone, because I took it. Tim and I rushed out before anybody else because he suddenly remembered we were supposed to meet your plane."

"So the murderer thinks Dr. Cadwall has the marble and will remember his having said he didn't drop anything when he obviously had. But then why hasn't he killed Mrs. Cadwall, too? Wouldn't he be afraid Dr. Cadwall had told his wife?"

"Maybe he tried. The taxine might have been meant for both of them and somehow she missed getting any. Or he might have known Ben's penchant for keeping secrets and gambled on her not knowing."

"Or she might have been the one who dropped the marble," Helen finished.

"She was my first suspect," Shandy admitted. "I figured she'd have had the best chance of killing Jemima because she wasn't at the party and might logically have gone along with Jemima when she broke into my house. I had some notion that Hannah might have been embezzling the Illumination money and was afraid Jemima would expose her. Jemima would do that, you know, even to her best friend. She was great on principle."

"She must really have been a rather awful woman. No wonder Jemmy went to California and her brother to the South Pole. I'm surprised it wasn't Dr. Ames who killed her."

"He might have, I daresay, except that Tim's deaf as a haddock and pretty much wrapped up in his work. In any event, I can assure you he didn't. And I'm fairly well convinced Hannah didn't kill Ben, either. His death came as a total surprise to her, I'll swear. I had the happy task of breaking the news in both instances, you know. However, as you say, I don't know anything about women."

"Poor Peter."

Helen touched his hand lightly. "Do you think we ought to start back? You've had a rough day."

"At least it began and ended pleasantly."

"Cross your fingers. It's not over yet." Helen shrugged Jemima's old black cape around her shoulders and slid out of the booth. "That was a lovely dinner."

"I'm glad you enjoyed it. We must come again soon."

"I'd like to."

After that, they didn't say much. Helen must have been feeling the effects of adjusting to a different climate and her first day on a new job. Shandy had to concentrate on his driving. The snow that had been threatening all day was now beginning to fall, spreading a slippery film over the road. They were almost back to Balaclava Junction before he broke silence.

"I think we'd better go around by the back road. The marshmallow roast must be breaking up about now, and Main Street will be total disaster. At least this will give you a panoramic view of the Skunk Works."

"I'm all anticipation. All but my left foot, at any rate. That's gone to sleep."

Helen slid her foot out of her shoe and rubbed at her toes, gazing out through the now thickening snow.

"How many marshmallows did they roast, for goodness' sake? I can see the bonfire from here."

"You couldn't possibly," said Shandy. "The playing field's in a deep hollow on the far side of the college buildings. What you're seeing—my God!"

He scrambled for the snowbanks as fire engines whooped down the icy road.

"Well, Helen, I guess I owe Dysart an apology. That's the power plant."

TWENTY

"WE'LL JUST HAVE to keep going."

Shandy found that he was sweating. Holding a car to this narrow, snaking road was tricky enough in broad daylight under decent conditions. On a night like this, with the snow falling thicker every moment and fire engines crowding past in astonishing numbers, he'd be lucky not to wrap them around a tree, or slide into one of the deep gullies he couldn't see but knew were far too close.

"Where are all these fire engines coming from?"

Helen sounded nervous, as well she might.

"They must have sent out a general alarm to the neighboring towns. Balaclava Junction only has one old ladder truck and a couple of pumpers for grass fires."

"That wouldn't happen unless it's really bad, would it?"

"I don't know, Helen. We've never had a fire before at the college. And why the bloody, flaming hell did it have to be tonight?" he snarled as another siren almost sent them into a bad skid.

"I shouldn't be surprised if Professor Dysart set it himself, just to prove his point."

Shandy grunted, then, to his own relief, began to chuckle.

"Neither should I. He's probably lashed himself to a turbine and vowed to go down with the ship."

"Not unless there's a television news crew around," said Helen. "Why does it make me feel better to be catty, do you suppose?"

"The natural perversity of humankind. If we succeed in getting out of this mess alive, I shall be glad you were with me."

"Peter, that's sweet. I'd give your hand a friendly squeeze, only I don't want to distract you from your driving."

"A wise but regrettable decision. I hope I can get you to reconsider at a more auspicious time."

"Are you flirting with me?"

"Flirtation implies a lack of serious purpose. Good Lord, look at that!"

They had rounded a hairpin turn that brought them out on a rise almost directly above the power plant. Even with snow blurring their view, the spectacle was awesome. From one of the methane storage tanks, a tongue of flame was shooting almost to the level of the ledge they were on. Nearby, a shed was being reduced to crimson embers by crisscrossing streams from fire hoses. Red searchlights cast an eerie glow over the snow, revealing swarms of black-clad figures rushing among the imperiled buildings.

The temptation to stay and watch was almost irresistible, but this was too dangerous a place. Shandy kept going until an auxiliary policeman barred his way.

"You can't go down there, mister!"

"It's Professor Shandy," he shouted back through the rolled-down window. "I'm trying to get home. I live on the Crescent."

"You'll have to ditch the car and walk."

"But this lady has no boots on."

"Oh, Jeez. Wait a second."

The snow-caked vigilante fumbled in a pocket of his parka and hauled out two enormous slabs of gray fuzz. "Always carry spare socks. Never know when you're going to need 'em. If you pull 'em over your shoes, they'll at least keep the snow out."

"What a marvelous idea! You're a lifesaver."

Shandy pulled the car off the road as best he could. Helen pulled on the policeman's socks. They reached to her knees and made her feet look as though they'd got tangled in a bath mat, but the rough knitting would give traction on the slippery road.

"What's happening down there?" Shandy asked the man while Helen was still struggling to coax the clinging wool over her already soggy shoes.

"Darned if I know, Professor. I heard the general alarm and came running. Ottermole sent me up here to direct the engines and stop anybody else from going down. Cripes, there's fire apparatus stretched from hell to breakfast. We thought for a while the whole place would go, but they seem to be making headway now."

"When did it start?"

"Maybe half an hour ago. One of the gas tanks blew first. Then that barn caught fire."

"What caused it? Does anybody know?"

"No, but I can make a mighty shrewd guess. See for yourself. There's the gas tank bang in front of us, and there's the barn 'way the hell and gone over behind the main turbine building. How's a flame supposed to jump that far and not hit anything in between? If you ask me, Fred Ottermole better start looking for a guy with a good pitching arm and a couple of beer bottles full of gasoline."

The man's attention was diverted by a carload of misguided sightseers. Shandy took Helen by the arm and started the downward trek.

At eye level, the fire was less impressive than it had appeared from above. The two separate blazes were well under control and everything around them encased in protective layers of ice from the fire hoses. Nevertheless, the fire fighters were taking no chances. They had the area so widely cordoned off that spectators were strung out into a thin, straggling line. Most of these seemed to think that the near-disaster, like the marshmallow roast, had been laid on for their entertainment. The only glum faces in the crowd belonged to college folk. Shandy and Miss Marsh had hardly begun to skirt the fire lines when they were hailed by a bundle of fake mink that proved to be Mirelle Feldster.

"Peter! Peter, where have you been? I went looking for you as soon as the sirens started."

"Why?"

"Oh, I don't know. I just did." She giggled self-consciously. "You know me, just being neighborly. Actually, it wasn't quite that soon. Jim and I were over at the Dysarts' playing Scrabble. Adele's got this awful cold, so Bob called and asked us to come over and cheer her up. We couldn't very well say no, though personally I'd rather have—oh, I didn't notice you've got somebody with you." Her voice, like the buildings around them, was abruptly encased in ice.

"This is Helen Marsh," said Shandy. "Mirelle Feldster is one of your new neighbors, Helen."

"Oh, then you must be the woman who's come to stay at the Ameses'. You travel fast, don't you, Miss Marsh?" Mirelle turned her back on Helen and resumed her narrative.

"As I started to say, we were playing Scrabble and having drinks— you know Bob—when the chapel bell started banging away like mad. At first we thought it was some of the students putting on a show. Then we heard fire sirens and thought the marshmallow roast must have got out of hand, but we kept hearing more and all of a sudden Bob jumped up and yelled, 'Christ! It's the power plant.' So then he grabbed his coat and ran. Jim ran straight after him, leaving me in the lurch as usual, but I wasn't about to get stuck alone with Adele and her germs. I said I'd better come along and see if I was needed because I'm in the Civil Defense auxiliary—at least I used to be when we had one—so anyway, here I am."

"Where's Dysart?"

"Around somewhere. I saw him up by the main turbine building a while back, waving his arms and yelling. I think he was trying to make the fire chief let him through the lines, but he didn't make it. I don't see why they should myself. Bob doesn't even have tenure. Honestly, the fuss he's been making, you'd think he owned the plant. Between you and me, he's about half sloshed."

It occurred to Shandy that Mirelle was, too. He tried to break away, but she had no intention of letting him go.

"Were you surprised when they arrested Hannah Cadwall?"

"Good Lord! When did this happen?"

"Around six o'clock. Of course they'd had her under house arrest all afternoon, ever since Grimble found Ben's body. Wasn't that a ghastly thing? Can you imagine just walking into somebody's office and seeing a dead man staring at you?"

"Er—yes," said Shandy.

Mirelle paid no attention. "So they started searching the house and found the poison, as I knew they would. As soon as I heard Ben was murdered I said to Jim, 'You mark my words, she's the one.' Did it for the money, of course. Ben would never let her spend a cent and they say he was absolutely rolling. Much good it's going to do her where she's going. I wonder who the man is."

"What man?"

"Oh, Peter, use your common sense. A woman wouldn't kill one husband unless she thought she had another one lined up. Would she?"

"I wouldn't know, Mirelle. Come on, Helen, we've got to get you home. I don't suppose those socks are doing much good."

"N-not much."

Her teeth were chattering. Shandy looked around, saw a hand sled which one of the elves had injudiciously abandoned, and snatched up the rope.

"Get on."

"Peter, should you—"

"Go ahead. Better to look silly than freeze to death."

Helen was in no shape to argue. She sat down on the sled and drew its plastic protective sheet around her shaking body. Shandy set off at a trot, heedless of amused glances. When they got to the steep incline that led down into the Crescent, he hopped on behind and shoved off, forgetting that these sleds were not made to be steered by the rider. In order to stop, he had to spill them in a snowdrift.

"Sorry about that," he panted, brushing Helen off and helping her to her feet. "If we'd kept going, we'd have been out in the middle of Main Street by now."

"I don't mind. It was fun, once I began to thaw. Are you coming in?"

"Only to see you safe inside. I expect you'll want a hot bath as soon as possible."

"If there is one. The fire may have done something to the power plant."

"Can't have. The lights are still on. Including mine, unfortunately."

"Peter, I do want to thank you for this evening."

"Even though it didn't turn out as I'd hoped."

"What were you hoping for?"

He hadn't kissed a woman for years, but he managed fairly well, all things considered. "Now go get your feet dry."

"If you say so."

Helen turned the key in the Ameses' lock, let them in, and started to hang up the wet cape. Suddenly she burst out laughing.

"Oh, Peter, what a spectacle I must have cut on that sled, with my feet in bags and that silly cape flapping out behind me."

"The sled got you here, didn't it?" Shandy's jaw dropped. "Good Lord, of course it did. How could I be so dense?" He planted one more fast kiss on Helen's startled face, and hurtled back out into the storm.

TWENTY-ONE

THE JACKMANS HAD not gone to the fire. Through the unshaded window, Shandy could see the young parents, their offspring presumably tucked away, sprawled on that overstuffed passion pit he'd so narrowly escaped having to share with Sheila. Fatigue was etched on their faces. Each clutched a large tumblerful of grown-up vitamins. It was cruel to get them up, but Shandy kept his finger on the doorbell until, after a short but vicious quarrel, the husband came to let him in.

"Peter Shandy! What brings you here?"

"An ill wind. Why aren't you at the fire with everybody else?"

"Listen, Peter, last night I slept, if you want to call it that, in a lean-to on Old Bareface with the wind howling up my pant legs and damn near freezing my—"

"It better hadn't," Sheila called from the sofa. "Come and have a drink, Peter."

"No, thanks. I just want to ask you one question. And believe me, it's important. Did either of you, or any of your children, see one of those elves dragging a passenger on a sled around my house the night I went away?"

Both Jackmans stared at him, as well they might. "For gosh sake," said Roger, "those kids are around all the time. How should we notice?"

"That's right," said Sheila. "They're supposed to keep the sleds up off the Crescent, but they come just the same."

"I know that. I don't mean on the walkway, I mean actually in my yard. Very late, when they ought to have quit."

"They never quit. Nor rain nor snow nor dark of night. Are you sure you won't join us in a little general anesthetic?" said Roger. "I'll get it.

Sheila brought Dickie and Wendy up to the shelter for a cookeroo this morning. She's even more whacked out than I am, or so she claims."

"I know all about the cookeroo and I don't give a damn," snapped the professor. "For God's sake rack your brains. Did you or did you not see anybody with a sled around my house late on the night of the twenty-second?"

"Honestly, Peter, I think you've lost your tiddleywinks," Sheila protested. "With all the pandemonium that's been going on around here over the holidays, how can you expect us to remember one stupid little—"

"Wait a second," her husband interrupted. "Shut up and let me think. Last night at the lean-to, while we were having our man-to-man talk, JoJo was giving me some kind of song and dance about the elves stealing Santa Claus and taking him for a ride."

"Get him up."

"Peter, no," Sheila wailed. "He's overstimulated already."

"So am I. Where does he sleep?"

Shandy headed for the staircase. Young Jackman leaped off the sofa.

"For God's sake, have mercy! You'll wake the whole damned pack of them. All right, if you insist, I'll get him. I'm sorry I opened my mouth."

He took a last pull at his grown-up vitamins and slogged upstairs. He was back in less time than Shandy could have hoped, preceded by a nine-year-old a good deal wider awake than his father.

"Pop says you want to see me, Professor Shandy."

"Yes, JoJo. I want you to tell me about the night you watched the elves kidnap my Santa Claus. Can you describe exactly what happened?"

The youngster wiggled and scratched. "Well, see, it wasn't elves. I mean it was only this one elf and I didn't really see him steal it. He just had it."

"You mean the Santa Claus dummy was on the sled when you first caught sight of it?"

"That's right. See, what happened was, we had the Sunday School party that afternoon. It was a real drag, so me and Tommy Hoggins got to kidding around about who could drink the most punch. They had this goofy punch, right, one bowl red and one bowl green. It was prob'ly just Kool-Aid or something, but anyway me and Tommy started mixing the two kinds together—"

"Like father, like son," Sheila murmured. "Never mind all that, JoJo. Professor Shandy doesn't want to hear about your tummyache."

"But if I hadn't drunk all that punch, I wouldn't have had to keep getting up and going to the bathroom," the boy pointed out reasonably. "That's how I saw the sled."

"Have you any idea what time it was?" Shandy asked.

"All I know is it must have been real late, because the Christmas lights were out and there was nobody around except this one elf, see, giving Santa Claus a ride on the sled. It was dumb. I mean, what's the sense of doing some oddball thing like that when there's nobody around to watch? I was going to yell down at him but then I thought I better not because I didn't want to wake up Mum and Pop and the brats," JoJo said virtuously.

"Did you put on the light in the bathroom?"

"I didn't have to. There's a little night light that's always on."

"That's right," Sheila put in. "We've had it ever since JoJo was a baby. Roger was always stubbing his toe on something when he had to get up in the night."

"That's because you always made me do the feedings when it was your turn."

Apparently Dickie and Wendy came naturally by their bickering. Shandy nipped the squabble in the bud.

"Then the elf never knew you were watching, JoJo?"

"How could he? I was upstairs and he was down on the ground. Anyway, he didn't look up."

"How could you tell where he was looking, if all the lights were out?"

"It's never pitch-dark when there's snow on the ground. You ought to know that," the child replied loftily. "Anyway, I'm good at seeing in the dark. Ask Pop."

"That's right," said Jackman. "JoJo has exceptionally keen night vision. It comes in handy, considering the times and places Sheila chooses to drop the car keys."

Before the wife could get in her retort, Shandy asked, "How long did you watch the elf?"

Jojo shrugged. "I don't know. A couple of minutes, I guess. There wasn't much to see. He just came across—"

"Across from where?"

"Across the walkway. Like as if he was coming from the Enderbles', only he wasn't."

"How do you know?"

"Because the sleds aren't allowed to go in the shubbery. Professor Enderble won't let 'em."

"But what if this elf disobeyed?"

"Then I guess Professor Enderble would get sore."

"So in fact all you can say for sure is that the sled was in the road

when you first saw it, and it came to my house. Did it come to the front
or the back door?"

JoJo hesitated. "I don't know. I thought it must be going to the front
because I figured the elf was going to put Santa Claus back on the porch
like you had it, but I couldn't tell because the spruce trees were in the
way. Anyway, I guess maybe he never went to either door because I
looked the next morning to see if the Santa Claus was back and it wasn't
and I never saw it again."

"You didn't notice where the elf went after that?"

"No, I went back to bed."

JoJo squirmed a bit inside his new Christmas-present bathrobe, then
blurted out, "I was sort of scared, if you want to know."

"Why, son? You didn't tell me that last night. Hey, come on. Get it
out and you'll feel better." Jackman was, after all, a concerned father.

"Well, like I said, there was something funny about the whole scene.
Like—I mean, I knew it had to be Professor Shandy's dummy on the
sled but it—it didn't feel like a dummy. It was as if it was real but not
alive. I don't know what I mean!"

He looked from one to the other, then said abruptly, "Can I go back
to bed now?"

"Of course," Shandy answered. "Thank you, JoJo. You've been very
helpful. You may be interested to know that the elves brought back my
Santa Claus yesterday, while you were camping. I put it in the cellar.
And—er—it's still a dummy. Come and see it tomorrow, if you like."

"We're going to a hockey game," said Roger Jackman. "You run on
upstairs, JoJo. Mum and I will be up soon. Very soon," he added with a
meaning look at their uninvited guest.

Shandy took the hint. "I'll be off. Sorry to butt in on you like this,
but I had to know."

"Aren't you going to tell us why?" Sheila pouted.

"Later, perhaps. Right now, I wouldn't know what to say."

Shandy let himself out and stood for a moment on the doorstep,
wondering what to do next. His own house stood next door, serene and
inviting in spite of its gaudy bedizenments, and he was extremely tired.
The snow was falling yet faster, caking on his overcoat sleeves and shoulders. There must be one hell of a traffic jam on Main Street by now.
Perhaps visitors would be stranded and the college would have to put
them up in the dorms. The gawkers would get their fill of Balaclava
before this night was over. He'd about had it, too.

Nevertheless, Shandy turned his coat collar as high as it would go,
jammed his gray felt hat down over his eyes, and trudged past his snug
front door, up toward the glow of searchlights that still showed through

the gathering whiteness to the northeast. Even as he walked, the lights dimmed and the noise of departing fire apparatus filtered down over the campus. The show was over.

But the trouble might hardly have begun. First it was a bludgeoning faked to look like an accident, now open murder and arson in one day. What was next on the agenda?

Arresting Hannah Cadwall wasn't going to solve anything. Only a nitwit like Mirelle Feldster could believe that. True, the police seemed to believe it, too, but he supposed they had to, once a jug of taxine turned up in her medicine cabinet and a whopping motive in Ben's bankbooks.

There was no such blatant evidence in Jemima's case. He was going to have one hell of a time convincing anybody that her body had been brought to his house on a sled, disguised by a Santa Claus mask.

Still, that had to be how it happened. The murderer, having somehow managed to pinch one of those all-concealing elf costumes, waited in the shrubbery knowing she'd make a production of leaving the party early to go on her self-appointed rounds, because she always did. If anybody else happened along the path in the meantime, it didn't matter. The elf was just another trespassing student. The worst he could get was a scolding.

Perhaps she'd been offered a ride on the sled. That would explain why there was no sign of a struggle in the snow. Jemima would fall for a silly caper like that. She loved being involved with the students' pranks and, like Helen, she'd been wearing her party shoes instead of sensible boots.

Excited now, Shandy walked faster, manufacturing dialogue. "Come on, Mrs. Ames, I'll ride you to your door so you can change."

Then a whack on the head in the dark—Jemima never bothered with a hat, so it would be easy enough to land a killing blow—and that was that. The plastic cover designed to protect the riders' clothing would hide her telltale purple cloak, the Santa Claus mask would cover her face and head. The dummy, no doubt, had already been kidnaped and taken sleigh riding around the Crescent. Nobody would notice it wasn't a dummy any more.

Still, the murderer wouldn't dare hang around in public for long. The sled must have been dragged off somewhere, probably up on campus where it ought to be anyway, and hidden somewhere until the coast was clear. If the body did happen to be discovered any time during the evening, the plan to pass off the death as accident would have been spoiled, but how critical was that? Suspicion would no doubt fall on the student sled-pullers, but there was no great likelihood the bogus elf would ever be caught.

According to JoJo, the killer was still in costume when he brought the body back. Then how did Alice's fried marble get into the Cadwalls' bedroom? It couldn't have got caught up in a trouser cuff or pocket as Shandy had supposed—unless Ben himself had been the one to carry it back.

Was it possible the comptroller had tracked the murderer into the brick house and actually been standing close by when the dish was overturned? Would he have had nerve enough to confront a killer in the act of dumping a corpse?

No, but he might very well have tried to nail a student who was carrying a joke too far, and that was what the whole scene had been staged to look like. He could have got into the situation without knowing he was risking anything other than his dignity. He could have hidden behind the whatnot and spilled the marbles himself trying to get at the elf, or more likely trying to get away. It would be like him to keep quiet afterward and play a lone hand, especially if he didn't know who was under the disguise but thought he had a good chance of finding out. It was also typical of Cadwall to believe he could pin down the culprit before the killer got to him.

Did that mean Ben had got hold of a tangible clue to the elf's identity? Shandy began to walk faster. If he had, the evidence must have been kept in his desk at the office, that *sanctum sanctorum* where not even his secretary would dream of meddling. Since the office had been locked up right after the body was found, there was a chance it might still be there.

Normally, Grimble would be off duty by now and his minions would never dare pass out a key in his absence. Because of the fire, however, there was a good chance he might still be around. Shandy only hoped he could get the man to open the comptroller's office without insisting on tagging along and wanting to know what the professor was hunting for when Shandy hadn't the least idea and probably wouldn't find it in any case. This was a stupid wild-goose chase and he'd probably catch nothing but flu out of it, if he hadn't picked up the bug already. Nevertheless, Shandy wallowed on.

He wished to heaven he knew where that dummy Santa Claus had been kept after it was taken, and whether the elves who brought it back were the same ones who'd staged the original kidnaping. There was another point he hadn't considered. Mirelle had seen two on Monday, but JoJo had seen only one the night Jemima was killed. Was there a second hiding somewhere then? Jemima was a big woman. Getting her off the sled and up into the living room must have taken plenty of muscle. Why had he been so ready to assume one person could manage the job alone?

Shandy gave up trying to think straight and concentrated on fighting his way uphill. It was a sticky, wet snow that clung to his galoshes like fresh cement. By the time he caught sight of the security office, he was thinking only of getting in out of the snow and sitting down. His heart sank when he saw the small building was in darkness, but he tried the door anyway and for a wonder it opened.

For a moment, he was too preoccupied with catching his breath and beating the snow off his coat to realize that he was not alone. From behind the closed door of Grimble's inner sanctum, voices were audible. Though he could catch no words, he deduced from the low-pitched grunts and the high-pitched squeals that one was a man and one was a woman. The man was certainly Grimble, but who was the woman and what were they up to?

It didn't sound like conversation. It sounded like—Shandy suddenly realized what it sounded like and, being a man of delicacy, decided this was no time to come looking for keys. The decent thing would be to go straight away. But he was very tired and cold, and the office was warm. He felt for one of the wooden chairs that ought to be ranged along the wall, and found it. There was something hanging over the back, some-thing soft and thick but wet, as though it had been out in the snow, a cap or muffler or some such thing. He fingered the knitted wool curiously. It was a cap, he decided, a long stockinet cap with three biggish openings knitted into one end. In fact, it was an elf mask.

Grimble.

Grimble, the one person who stuck out so far he couldn't be seen. Grimble, who'd managed to get Jemima's death passed off as an accident, who'd played the buffoon while Ben Cadwall was sitting dead at his desk, who had access to every house, every building, every room on Bala-clava's campus, Grimble who could go where he chose and apparently take whom he pleased, judging from the sounds beyond the door. Grim-ble, who'd probably flummoxed his own keyboard in case some wiseacre like Shandy came nosing about wondering how somebody could get hold of a key without authorization. Grimble with the soul of a ferret and the morals of a buck rabbit. Who was more likely to get caught *flagrante delicto* by a pair of snoops like Jemima and Ben, and who was better equipped to get rid of them both before they could make out a provable case against him?

A provable case. That was the rub. What proof had Shandy now but a soggy head covering identical to twenty or thirty others? Grimble could always say he'd found the mask outside somewhere, and who was to convince the police that he hadn't?

As to having a woman in his office, that was a misdemeanor, not a crime. Shandy might carry the tale to President Svenson and Grimble might get fired, but that would solve nothing. Shandy wasn't a vengeful man, he was merely a good farmer. Once a dog started killing sheep, you had to get him away from the lambs. But you didn't shoot the dog unless you knew for sure he was guilty.

Not liking the job at all, Shandy tiptoed over to the inner office door and pressed his ear against the crack. It was no good. There was weather stripping around the edges to keep out drafts from the constantly opening outside door, and also perhaps to muffle sounds from within, since the place seemed warm enough where Shandy was. He started to loosen his overcoat, then buttoned it up again. If the outer office was this temperate, the inner chamber must be a pretty hot spot, all things considered. Maybe they'd opened a window at the back. Wearily, he went out again to face the elements. Something landed hard on his head, and he knew no more.

TWENTY-TWO

"YOU'RE UNDER ARREST."

Shandy opened one eye, got a snowflake smack in the cornea, and shut it again. "What the hell are you talking about?" He had difficulty speaking, and this seemed due to the fact that somebody was sitting on his chest.

"I'm performing a citizen's arrest. Lie still or I'll clobber you." The voice was identifiable now. It was Shirley Wrenne's.

"Shirley," he began testily, "have you—"

"Why, Peter Shandy! I must say you're almost the last person I'd expect to find skulking around the security office."

"I wasn't skulking, damn it!"

He had been, but that was beside the point. "Get off me, you wanton hussy."

"I will not. I'm going to sit here till Grimble comes."

"Grimble's not coming. He's busy."

"Then you're in trouble, Shandy."

"What have you been drinking, for God's sake?"

Shandy struggled to get out from under the not inconsiderable weight, narrowly escaped being clobbered as promised, and at last managed to dump his irate colleague into a snowbank. Miss Wrenne fastened on his left ankle and had all but managed to divest him of his trousers when the lights in the security office went on and Grimble did in fact appear.

"What's going on here?"

"She's trying to arrest me."

"I am arresting him."

"What the hell for?"

"He was skulking."

"She's drunk."

"Wait a second. One at a time, damn it. Okay, Miz Wrenne, what's the scoop?"

"I caught him trying to break into the security office and bopped him one. He's a saboteur."

"I am not a saboteur," said the professor with what little dignity he had left, "nor was I trying to break into the security office."

"Tell that to the fuzz, buster."

"Now, just a minute," said Grimble. "Let's not get hasty. Professor, what was you doing?"

"I was looking for you," Shandy replied truthfully.

Miss Wrenne snorted. "The door's around the other side, in case you hadn't noticed."

Shandy realized his best defense was attack. "For that matter, what were you yourself doing here, Shirley?"

"Looking for saboteurs."

"Well, while you're horsing around out here bopping and clobbering innocent fellow faculty members, the saboteurs are probably up setting fire to President Svenson's pajamas," he snapped. "If you must play cops and robbers in the snow, why don't you go where the action is?"

"Yeah, that's right," said Grimble. "No hard feelings, Miss Wrenne, but we got security officers all over the place tonight. Why don't you go on home and get some sleep? Nice of you to take an interest," he added politely.

She was in no mood for courtesies. "Aren't you at least going to grill him?"

"Yeah, I'll do that. Professor, you go on into the office. I'll be back as soon as I walk Miss Wrenne up the hill."

"Don't bother," snarled the woman. "I can take care of myself, thank you."

She vanished into the storm, and Shandy passed gratefully back into the security office. He looked for the elf mask, but it was not to be seen. He sat down on the chair where it had been, and began digging snow out of his pant legs. The security chief took the chair beside him.

"Okay, Professor, what did you want to see me about?"

"For one thing, I'd like to know what happened to that elf mask that was hanging on this chair a few minutes ago."

"Huh?"

"I was in here, Grimble, listening to you conduct your nocturnal revels. You forgot to lock the outer door."

"Jeez! How could I—" The security chief caught himself. "Look, Professor, you don't understand."

"Yes, I do. Who was she?"

For a long moment, Grimble said nothing. Then a sly grin stole over his beefy countenance.

"Hell, Professor, do I have to answer that? What do you think she was so steamed up about?"

"You are referring to Miss Wrenne?"

"Well, like they taught us back at the police academy, you got to consider the evidence. It's tough on them single dames in a place like this," he went on in a voice of compassion. "Hot to trot and no place to go. I was just bein' neighborly, as you might say."

"Damned decent of you," grunted Shandy. "Miss Wrenne must be a remarkably fast dresser. I trust President Svenson will be able to view the incident in its humanitarian aspect."

"Hey, look, you wouldn't rat on a guy?"

"Why hide your light under a bushel? Your motives were pure, weren't they?"

"Oh, cripes, you know what he's like."

"Yes, I do. That's why I believe you're in no position to be uncooperative."

Grimble made a remark. Shandy chose to ignore it.

"Are you going to tell me what happened to that elf mask?"

"What elf mask?"

"The one that was hanging on this chair, soaking wet, about five minutes ago."

"I never seen no elf mask," the man muttered. "She must o' brought it in with her an' took it out again."

"Why?"

"How the hell do I know? I tell you I never seen no elf mask."

"I don't believe you," said Shandy, "nor do I believe it was Miss Wrenne you were canoodling with just now. However, I'm too tired to argue. What I want from you are the keys to the Administration Building and the comptroller's office."

"You can't go in there. They got it sealed up."

"We'll unseal it. Get the keys and let's go."

"Do I have to come, too?"

"Yes. If we run into any more self-appointed vigilantes, I'd rather they clobbered you than me."

Dragging the man who might be Ben Cadwall's murderer along on a search of the place where he'd died probably wasn't a brilliant thing to do, but Shandy wasn't operating by reason just now. Anyway, killer dogs weren't killers so long as the shepherd kept his eye on them. It didn't make much sense to leave him running loose in the dark either.

Shandy repeated his order. Grimble made another remark and fetched the keys. Together but not talking, the two men ploughed through the storm to that square of old red brick from which Dr. Cadwall's rigid body had been taken just about twelve hours before. It wasn't until he was actually unlocking the office that Grimble asked the inevitable question.

"What do you want in here, anyway?"

"Evidence," said Shandy.

"What kind of evidence? They've already caught Miz Cadwall with the poison. She's goin' to be arraigned tomorrow."

"I know. That's why I have to get in here tonight."

"Oh, Christ on a crutch!"

"Look, Grimble, why don't you stay out here? Then you won't be able to see what I'm up to and your conscience won't bother you."

The security chief grunted and flung himself into the secretary's chair. Shandy flipped the light switch, shut the comptroller's door behind him, and stood wondering. Now that he'd gained entrance, his brain felt as numb as his overtaxed body. The point Grimble had raised was valid. What did he want in here?

Mostly, he wanted to flop down in Ben's comfortably padded swivel chair and take a nap. On second thought, he didn't. That yellow waxwork face, those half-open staring eyes, were still too clear in his mind's eye. He shoved the chair out of the way and knelt in front of the desk.

The police had locked the drawers and presumably taken the key, but Shandy had locked himself out of his own desk often enough to have learned a few useful tricks. In a matter of moments, he was peering into the comptroller's most secret place.

It was a terrible disappointment. If Ben had found any clues, he certainly hadn't kept them here. He hadn't kept much of anything except the tools of his trade and one drawer amply stocked with patent medicines.

Shandy poked through the assortment. This could be a convenient way to poison a dedicated hypochondriac, but how had the deed been managed? Antacids, each in its sealed packet. Aspirins smooth and unmarred, Band-Aids, a clinical thermometer, foot powder, antibiotic salve, cough drops wrapped in silver paper, sunburn lotion, heaven knew why, a box of tissues, and a half-empty bottle of nose drops. Now he knew what he'd come for.

"Grimble! Grimble, come in here a minute."

"What? What for?"

The security chief, who'd evidently been taking a nap in the secretary's chair, stumbled into Cadwall's office. "What's the matter now?"

"You're going to be a witness," the professor told him, watching his face carefully. "I'm going to take this bottle of nose drops out of the drawer, holding it very carefully inside this tissue in case there might be any fingerprints on it other than Dr. Cadwall's, which I don't expect there are, and drop it into this envelope."

"What the hell for?" Grimble didn't look anything but sleepy and truculent.

"Because you and I are going to take it over to the organic chemistry lab. You're going to unlock the place for me, and I'm going to analyze what's in the bottle."

"Oh yeah?"

"Yeah. Get moving, Grimble."

TWENTY-THREE

GRIMBLE SNORED. HE had been snoring for hours, while Professor Shandy kept himself awake by counting every bottle, flask, pipette, test tube, and assorted whatnot in the laboratory. On the plastic laminated counter before him, Hannah Cadwall's fate hung in the balance.

No, by gad, it didn't! He shoved a cork into the vial that had just told him what he needed to know, packed it and the bottle of nose drops with scrupulous care into a small box he found, and pounded the security chief back to consciousness.

"Oh, Christ," moaned the man, "what now?"

"We're going to wake up the president."

"He'll kill us."

"That's a risk we have to take. Get your coat on."

The snowstorm wasn't going to amount to much. Already the flakes were falling few and far between, forming huge lumps as they collided in the air. But the cold was awful. Slopping along in his wet overcoat, Shandy wondered why he couldn't have waited till morning to show Svenson what he'd found. Then he caught sight of the chapel clock through a gray haze and realized it was morning. Almost half past five and he still hadn't managed to grab a wink of sleep. He'd begun to feel a personal hatred for the clever fiend who'd thought of putting taxine in Ben Cadwall's nose drops. He thought of punching Grimble in the mouth on the chance that he might be the right man, but hadn't the strength to do an adequate job.

The Svensons always claimed they kept farmers' hours, and apparently they did. By the time Shandy and his unwilling companion hove in sight of the immense white house on the highest part of the hill behind the campus, a light was burning in the kitchen. Sieglinde herself came to the door, more Valkyrie-like than usual in a long pale blue robe, with thick flaxen braids down over her shoulders.

"Peter Shandy! What do you here? Thorkjeld is still in bed."

"You'll have to get him up."

That was almost certainly the first direct order Mrs. Svenson had ever received from a faculty member. She gave Shandy a long, thoughtful look, then said, "Come in. Stand please on the mat while you drip."

Incredibly, the president came down. Thorkjeld Svenson was awesome enough in ordinary garb; swathed in acres of brown wool bathrobe, unshaven and red-eyed, hair twisted up into iron-gray horns at either side of his thunderous forehead, he was terrifying.

"What do you want?" he roared.

Grimble cowered behind Shandy and tried to pretend he wasn't there. The professor quailed, but stood his ground.

"I want you to get Mrs. Cadwall out of jail. She didn't kill her husband."

"Ungh."

The president hurled himself into a vast wooden chair and held out one hand. Sieglinde put a cup of coffee the size of a washbasin into it. Shandy winced in envy and longing. At his back, Grimble whimpered.

"Grimble and I," he began, because in spite of everything he felt a twinge of compassion for the security chief, "have been working all night."

"Ungh."

"Realizing that the police case rests only on the thin evidence of taxine somebody planted in Mrs. Cadwall's effects—"

"Ungh?"

"Thorkjeld, listen to him," said Mrs. Svenson. "No woman would be fool enough to keep such stuff after she had poisoned her husband with it. I certainly would not."

"Ungh!"

"Anyway," Shandy went on hastily, "we went looking for clues in the comptroller's office and found a bottle of nose drops."

"Yeah, that's right."

Seeing that the sky was not going to fall, Grimble decided to claim his share of the limelight. Shandy trod firmly on his toe and kept talking.

"This seemed a reasonable vehicle for a soluble poison with a nasty taste. The medication would disguise the flavor of the taxine, and by the time it trickled down the nasal passages into the throat, the victim would be almost certain to ingest a fatal dose."

"Ungh."

"So we took the bottle over to the organic chemistry lab and tested it and it's bung-full of taxine. You'd better take it down to the jail right away and tell them to let Mrs. Cadwall out."

At last the great man uttered what for him was a long sentence. "Why me?"

"Because you're more impressive than I am."

Sieglinde nodded. "That is true. Thorkjeld is impressive. You, Peter Shandy, are not. I will give you coffee."

"No, thank you. I'm going home to bed. Come on, Grimble."

"We might o' waited for the coffee," the security chief grumbled when they got outside.

"Don't be a jackass, man. Could you honestly sit down at that table and drink coffee with the president glowering at you from behind his whiskers?"

"No, I guess not," the man conceded. "Say, I guess I ought to thank you for—" he conquered his better feelings and turned off toward the security office.

Shandy wended his lone way downhill to the brick house, took a hot shower and three fingers of brandy, and climbed into bed. He did not wake until noon. His first conscious act was to telephone the library.

"Helen, can you meet me at the dining room?"

"I'd love to, Peter. Half past twelve?"

"Fine."

That barely gave him time to shave and dress, but he managed. His overcoat was still sodden, so he grabbed the old plaid mackinaw in which he'd knocked about the turnip fields for more years than he cared to count. This was no time to fret over trivia.

He'd just snaffled the table least vulnerable to intrusion when Helen entered the dining room, wearing high boots and a brand-new bright red storm coat.

"I nipped down to the village first thing this morning and got myself some heavy-weather gear," she said. "Now I can give that nice man back his socks. How are you, Peter?"

"Ask me later. I haven't had time to think about it yet. Beef pot pie seems to be the *pièce de résistance*."

"Fine, if the beef isn't too resistant. My jaws are tired from arguing with Mr. Porble about the Buggins Collection. Peter, would you believe I actually got him to let me spend a little time there this morning, and he says I can go back after lunch?"

"Splendid. Would you mind sitting here beside me so I won't have to shout?"

As soon as they'd got their orders in, he began telling her in a low voice all that had happened after he'd left her the night before.

"My personal conviction, appearances to the contrary notwithstanding, is that it could not have been Shirley Wrenne who was—er—closeted with Grimble."

"Of course it wasn't," said Helen. "If it were, she wouldn't have come bashing away at the first man she met. She'd have made herself scarce, which I'm sure is what the other woman did while you were having your rumpus outside, not because women are ashamed of having sex these days, or say they aren't, but because she'd hate to have you know she was doing it with Grimble. He's not exactly love's young dream."

"I've been trying to think who around college would—er—succumb to a man like him. She'd have to be hard up for company."

"Or else the original I-don't-care girl," said Helen. "I'll get cosy with some of the secretaries, if you want. They're always the ones who really know what's going on."

"I'd be grateful," said Shandy. "Every fresh discovery I make seems to put me one step farther back."

"Nonsense, Peter. You're the only one who's doing anything constructive. Here, let me pour you some more coffee."

For a blissful second, Shandy was Thorkjeld Svenson, reaching out for the cup he knew Sieglinde would have ready. It wasn't the coffee that mattered, it was the caring. Helen was only showing common courtesy but a man could dream, even a man fifty-six years old who was almost certainly coming down with a rotten cold. He drank the coffee.

"After all your adventures," said Helen, "I feel silly telling you about my own little mystery. I thought it might possibly mean something, but—"

"Tell me anyway," Shandy urged.

"Well, it's just that—Peter, I have to confess to you that I have this ridiculous habit of counting things. I simply can't be left alone with more than three related objects for two minutes before I find myself totting them up. It's awful."

"I've always found it a source of innocent pleasure and sometimes of illumination," said Shandy.

"Peter, you don't!"

"I do. On that necklace you wore last night, there are seventy-four pearls."

"Seventy-five. There's a little one set in the clasp. It's always flipping over so you probably couldn't see it. Oh, Peter!"

Surely not even Thorkjeld and Sieglinde had experienced such a moment. When the stars quit reeling in the firmament, Shandy spoke again.

"You were saying—"

"Oh yes. As I believe I mentioned last evening, Dr. Porble let me go into the Buggins Room for just a short while late yesterday afternoon. There wasn't much I could do in those few minutes anyway, so I stood there like a ninny—sorry, comrade—and counted them. And it was such fun that this morning when I got in there again, I—"

"Counted them over, as any reasonable person would do. How many?"

"That's my mystery. Yesterday, there were two thousand, six hundred and thirty-eight. Today there are two thousand, six hundred and thirty-three. And the room was locked and nobody's been in there except me."

"That is odd."

The professor consumed a forkful of beef pie thoughtfully. "There's no chance you—er—"

"Got mixed up in my count? Would you?"

"Perish the thought!"

"There, see, you're outraged at the mere suggestion. We compulsive counters do not lose count. Even if I did happen to skip one, I couldn't be out by five whole, great, fat books, could I?"

"Not possibly."

"Then where did they go?"

"You're suggesting that somebody obtained entrance by some method as yet undetermined, and snitched them? Considering that nobody in all these years has ever willingly set foot in the place, much less taken away any books—"

"How do we know that?"

Shandy put down his fork. "We don't, do we?"

"Would Jemima have known?"

"She ought to, if anybody did. Do you think there's the remotest possibility any of those books is worth anything?"

"I'm wondering. The collection is old, Peter, much older than I'd been led to believe. I thought it would be all Warwick Deeping and Gene Stratton Porter, but Ulysses S. Grant's memoirs seem to be among the more recent publications. I happened to pick up a copy of *Vanity Fair* that I thought might be a first edition, and—and I think I'm going to get in touch with an old friend in Boston who knows a great deal more than is legal about the rare book market. Do you mind if I leave you?"

"Yes," said Shandy.

He bolted the last of his lunch and flung money on the table. "Come on, you'd better use the phone at my house. No sense in running up toll calls on Tim."

"Oh, I completely forgot to tell you, he called last night shortly after I'd got in the house. Jemmy has a baby boy. I'm shaky on the details because neither of us could make much sense of what the other was saying, but he sounded positively ecstatic."

"I'm glad."

Shandy was in truth happy for his old friend, but more immediately concerned with the question of whether Helen's call was going to turn up anything. It didn't take long to find out. After an exchange of pleasantries, she stated her problem and got her answer. He thought she was going to faint.

"Oh no! That's just not possible. Yes, I know you—but I simply cannot believe—and have you any idea how much—oh, my God!"

Shandy thought he'd better fetch the brandy.

TWENTY-FOUR

WHEN HE GOT back, she'd hung up the phone and was staring into space, her face as white as the snow outside the window.

"Good Lord, Helen, what did you find out?"

She drank some of the brandy. "Thank you, Peter."

She set down the glass with great care. "During the past several months, there's been a strange little trickle of rare books coming into the market through a dealer whom my friend refuses to name, which means he's a fence. They all have had the same odd-shaped bookplate steamed out of them. Two weeks ago, the dealer got hold of the poems of Currer, Ellis, and Acton B-B—"

"Here, take more brandy. Helen, that can't be true?"

"It is if my informant says it is. He claims the book is in mint condition and the dealer got it for five thousand dollars because who ever heard of Currer, Ellis, and Acton Bell?" Her voice was shaking.

"Currer, Ellis, and Acton Bell," Shandy repeated in a stunned tone. "Charlotte, Emily, and Anne. Their one joint publishing venture, paid for out of their own thin pockets and a complete financial bust. Ten copies sold, or something like that?"

"Six, I believe," said Helen. "The rest were used to line trunks. Peter, I think I'm going to be sick. It's—it's like finding out Sir Parsifal had gone and hocked the Holy Grail."

The librarian wrung her hands in anguish. Shandy felt it only common courtesy to cover them with his own. The gesture led to further courtesies.

At last Helen murmured into his collarbone, "Peter, you're such a blessed comfort. I wish I didn't have to go."

"You don't."

"But Dr. Porble will be furious."

"To hell with Porble. How do we know he isn't a crook?"

"He'd never sell the Brontë sisters for a lousy five thousand dollars."

"He wouldn't know the Brontë sisters if they walked up and hit him over the head with their reticules."

"Then he wouldn't know enough to steal the book, would he? Peter, I really must go. Professor Stott will be coming in for his hog statistics and they're still not finished. I can't afford to get fired."

"Yes, you can. I should point out that what with having tenure in the rank of full professor, in addition to my royalties from the Balaclava Buster, et al., I am a man of not inconsiderable fortune."

"Whatever do you mean?"

"Lawful wedlock was what I had in mind."

"But you've only known me since Monday afternoon. Peter, you've been a bachelor—"

"Quite long enough. Nothing is more powerful than an idea whose time is come. You, as a woman of literary attainments, should know that. I'm not trying to rush you, Helen. I'm just—er—doing the preliminary spadework. A natural first step for a farmer to take."

"Then I may have time to think it over?"

"Of course. You—er—won't mind if I count the days?"

"I'd be disappointed if you didn't. I think I'd better go now. Thank you, Peter."

At least it wasn't a flat turndown. Shandy refrained from offering to walk her back up the hill, and sat down at his desk. He needed to collect his thoughts. Taking paper and pen, he started making a list.

Perhaps because his mind was running in that general direction, the first query he wrote down was, "Why would any woman in her right mind afflict herself with Grimble?" He could see but two possible explanations: either she was indeed damned hard up, or else she wanted something from him that she couldn't get any other way.

The one thing Grimble had that nobody else did was that keyboard in his private office. Was it actually possible one of the ladies Shandy knew—for she must somehow be connected with the Crescent as well as the college—could bring herself to commit such an act?

For five thousand dollars? Plenty of women had done it for less, and God alone knew how many books had been peddled out of the Buggins Collection by now. Even at cutthroat prices, the take must be impressive. Had the looting gone on over a long period of time, or was it the threatened fruition of his own long campaign to get the books into circulation that had inspired somebody to weed out the treasures first?

He wished he didn't keep coming back to the likelihood that he himself was responsible for the whole rotten chain of events. Doggedly, Shandy turned to another question. He was writing, "Who stole my Santa Claus?" when the doorbell rang.

It was a woman, and for one delirious moment he thought Helen might have returned to say yes. She proved, however, to be Hannah Cadwall.

"Peter, I came to thank you for getting me out of jail. The president says you stayed up all night hunting for taxine in Ben's nose drops."

"It had to be somewhere."

"But to think you'd do that for me! Peter, I didn't realize."

Oh, God, there was that look again, and this one's husband not even buried yet. Shandy backed away a step.

"Not at all," he replied stiffly. "Ben was a colleague, and I felt I owed you something in return for the capable way in which you managed Jemima's funeral."

"Oh, that."

Hannah strove not to appear deflated. "I'd forgotten poor Jemima. Well, I daresay the experience will come in handy now that I've got to do it over again for Ben. Harry the Ghoul ought to give me a cut rate."

She started to laugh, somewhat hysterically. Shandy remembered the brandy and she quieted down.

"Yes, I believe I would. Maybe it will take away the taste of that jail food. Peter, I simply can't tell you what it was like."

She proceeded to do so, however. It took Shandy some while to switch her off on a different track.

"Hannah, do you have any faintest glimmering of a notion who may have killed your husband?"

"Now, don't you start. Seventeen different policemen asked me that this morning, as soon as Dr. Svenson came roaring in like the Bull of Bashan and made them unlock the cell. Of course I don't. If I did, don't you think I'd have managed to talk my way out of being arrested in the first place?"

"But dash it, Hannah, you must know something? You lived with the man. Where did Ben get his nose drops?"

"Drugstore, I suppose, or at the Cut-Rate when we went shopping in the city. It's just a common brand you can buy anywhere. He always keeps—kept—I still can't get used to it—anyway, he'd always buy two, one for the house and one for the office. Ben had terrible trouble with his sinuses, you know. He claimed those nose drops were the only thing that ever helped him. Dr. Melchett tried to tell him it was the nose drops that caused the congestion, but of course he'd never get Ben to believe that."

"Would he have used them as soon as he got to the office?"

"I should think so, coming in out of the cold like that. He generally did."

Shandy had a thought. "Would he have done it that day after the funeral, when we all more or less arrived at your house in a bunch?"

"I suppose so. I had so many things on my mind just then, I wouldn't remember."

"Assuming he did, was he likely to go into the bathroom or somewhere and shut the door, or would he just bale the stuff into him wherever he happened to be?"

"Oh, you know Ben. He'd never miss a chance to perform in front of an audience. No misery ever loved company the way his did. That's the brandy talking, not me."

The professor nodded. "So undoubtedly at least some of the people there were treated to a discourse on nose drops. I daresay I'd have heard it, too, but I was preoccupied with Tim. That means anybody there could have got the idea of buying a bottle of that same brand, doctoring it with taxine, and planting it in Ben's desk with the virtual certainty that he'd pump poison down his throat the next morning."

"Why, yes, I suppose they could, if they could get in, but how could they do that? Ben was always so careful about locking up, even if he just stepped out to go to the men's room."

"What about his secretary?"

"Not Myrnette Woodruff," said Hannah flatly. "Anyway, she's been down with flu ever since Christmas night, because I called to let her know about Jemima's funeral and she was too sick to come. She felt terrible to miss it. And you needn't get any funny ideas about her and Ben either. Her husband's Master of the Grange and they celebrated their silver wedding anniversary this past October. Her daughter gave them a lovely party and Ben and I were invited. That's wonderful brandy, I must say."

She drained her glass and looked hopeful. Against his inclination, Shandy gave her a refill. This conversation was probably going to wind up as an exercise in futility. If she had anything of value to tell, that sharp state policeman would surely have got it out of her. All he himself would be likely to get was a hard time. Still, one never knew. He poured himself another modest tot and settled back in his chair.

"Hannah," he said abruptly, "did Jemima ever mention anything about books being taken from the Buggins Collection?"

"That's a crazy question, though, come to think of it, she did. She was stewing one day about making him bring it back."

"Making whom bring it back?"

"Oh, Peter, how can you expect me to remember a silly thing like that, with everything else that's happened? Jemima was always in a swivet about something."

"For God's sake, woman, try!"

"Don't yell at me like that! Ben never yelled. He could get pretty nasty sometimes, but he always kept his voice down."

"I'm sorry, Hannah, but you've got to remember! Damn it, the person who took that book is probably your husband's murderer."

"That's the stupidest thing I ever heard."

Mrs. Cadwall set down her twice-emptied glass and started gathering herself together. "I don't mean to be rude, Peter, I really do appreciate what you did for me, but I must say you're getting some awfully peculiar notions lately. Those plastic reindeer, for instance. Now, please don't take this the wrong way, but if I were you, I'd go and have a nice, quiet talk with Dr. Sidman."

She was out the door before Shandy could think of a way to convince her that he did not need a psychiatrist. Perhaps in fact he did, for a notion wilder than all the rest came surging through his brain. Quite forgetting what Mrs. Lomax was going to say when she found sticky glasses sitting on the walnut tables, he grabbed his ancient mackinaw and made a bee-line for the Administration Building.

Miss Tibbett was only too happy to make Professor Shandy free of her files, and intimated ever so gently that she'd be happier still to grant other freedoms. Shandy pretended not to know she wasn't talking about the files.

"No, no, Miss Tibbett, I mustn't take up any more of your valuable time. Just leave me here and go on with what you were doing. Er—there is just one more thing."

"Yes?" she responded eagerly.

"I expect it's been chucked out years ago, but is there the faintest chance you still have the *curriculum vitae* Dr. Cadwall submitted when he applied for the comptrollership?"

"We don't chuck things out, Professor."

Gracious even in disappointment, Miss Tibbett produced the document that had been lying dormant for over a quarter of a century. Shandy read it avidly and made careful notes. He asked for another more recent dossier and made further memoranda. He fought down an impulse to kiss Miss Tibbett, after all, and rushed from the building. Now that the preliminary research indicated a hopeful prognosis, his next step was obvious. He must find out where in Sam Hill Patsville, Ohio, might be, he must get there as fast as possible, and he must hunt up some long-time inhabitant with a good memory and a penchant for gossip.

When he stopped at the brick house for pajamas and toothbrush and the spare hundred-dollar bill he always kept hidden inside the stiff front of his only boiled shirt, he found Mrs. Lomax itching to state her views with regard to sticky tumblers on walnut tables. Shandy wasn't interested.

"Never mind that. When you've finished here, I want you to take this note across to Miss Marsh. If she isn't there, leave it where she'll be sure to see it."

"Why? Where are you going?"

"Away."

He put on his respectable overcoat, now only somewhat damp, grabbed his hat and muffler, and dashed for Harry's Garage, where a car was already being gassed up to take him to the airport. Mrs. Lomax gaped after the professor, then went to the kitchen and steamed open his note. It read:

Dearest Watson,
    The game's afoot. Stay in the roundhouse till I get back. They can't corner you there.

Devotedly,
Arsène Lupin

"Well," Mrs. Lomax remarked to the teakettle, "they've all been saying he's gone soft in the head. Now I'd believe anything."

TWENTY-FIVE

NOT UNTIL SHANDY was halfway back to Balaclava Junction did he remember that he'd been ordered by Mrs. Svenson to bring Helen to tea on Thursday afternoon. He checked with one of the airplane's stewardesses, who confirmed his suspicion that this was indeed Thursday. There was no way of finding out from here whether the engagement was still on in view of Cadwall's demise, but he'd damn well better show up, just in case. It was nip, tuck, and a costly speeding ticket, but he managed to reach the library in time to find Helen zipping up her new boots and casting worried glances at the clock.

"Young Lochinvar is come out of the west!" she exclaimed.

"Very funny. Is it still on?" he gasped.

"Yes, but don't you want to sit down a minute and catch your breath?"

"I'll breathe when we get there. Come on."

As it was already ten after four, Helen didn't ask the questions that were obviously burning on her lips. Together they toiled up to the crest where the president's house, white-painted and Palladian-columned in the tradition beloved of academe, rose in its majesty out of the snowdrifts. One of the several Misses Svenson, tall and fair as a young birch tree, let them in.

"Good afternoon, Professor Shandy, and this must be Miss Marsh. We're so glad you could come. I'm Ingeborg. Please come in. Mother is in the living room."

From the array of coats and boots in the front hall, they could see this was a party of no mean proportions instead of the intimate family tea they'd anticipated. In a way, Shandy was glad. It meant a stupendous smorgasbord after the chilly artifacts of plastic and cardboard that airlines and fast-food restaurants are pleased to call food. It meant tiny glasses of akvavit and large cups of hot tea to warm the cockles and cheer the spirit. It meant lots of people to cushion him from the full impact of President Svenson, but it also meant noise, confusion, a necessity to make small talk that would prevent his being able to mull over what he'd found out in Patsville, Ohio, and how it fitted in with the things he already knew. He decided to concentrate on the herring and postpone the mulling.

Helen Marsh, although no more prepared than he for the gala assemblage that met their eyes, was by no means out of countenance. Her well-made light blue dress and modest pearls were entirely appropriate, her smile unstrained, and her conversation ready. He was proud of her. He'd tell her so if he ever got a chance to speak to her again. They'd barely made their manners to Sieglinde when Professor Stott claimed her and led her to where the good things were piled highest, talking hog statistics with unwonted animation the while.

Shandy possessed himself of a plateful of sandwiches, a nip of akvavit, and a cup of tea, thinking to retire into some corner and refresh himself in peace. It was not to be so.

"Shandy, I want you."

"Certainly, President," he managed to articulate around a mouthful of rollmop, "if Mrs. Svenson doesn't mind."

Intimating that he didn't give a damn whether Mrs. Svenson minded or not, the great man led his victim into the library, and shut the door.

"Talk."

"What do you want me to say?"

"Don't be flip, Shandy. Damn it, I told you on Sunday to get this mess cleared up, and you've let it go from bad to worse. Now they've attacked my power plant."

"How bad was the damage?"

"Not bad," Svenson admitted. Then he roared, "Any is bad! Why, Shandy? Why?"

"I think I know why," the professor replied, "and also who and how. The trouble is, I have no stickable evidence yet."

"Horsefeathers! Get 'em in here. I'll make 'em talk."

"That would be one approach," said Shandy cautiously. "However, I—er—think I can manage something that would be more convincing in court than—er—confession under duress."

"I don't trust you."

Shandy slammed down his cup and sprang out of the chair. "I don't give two hoots in hell whether you trust me or not. I'm the one who's been victimized, I'm the one who got this mess shoved down his throat, and I'm the only one who's lifted a hand to straighten it out. I'm tired and I've got a rotten cold and I'm goddamned fed up with being badgered. If you want me to resign here and now, consider it done. If you want me to finish this job right, get the hell off my back and let me do it."

"By yumping yiminy!"

For a full thirty seconds, President Svenson stood snorting through his hairy nostrils like a bull about to charge. Then his lips curled skyward. He began to chuckle. It turned to a guffaw that brought Sieglinde hurrying into the room.

"Thorkjeld, what are you laughing at?"

"Shandy just told me to go to hell."

"Can you not go quietly? You frighten our guests."

"She's mad at me for leaving the party," said the president morosely. "It's Shandy's fault, Sieglinde. All right, Peter, I'll give you till tomorrow noon. Come and eat herring."

"Er—thank you, no. I seem to have lost my appetite."

"Eat herring!"

The professor ate and found it, after all, good. Nevertheless, the hollow feeling at the pit of his stomach remained even after he and Helen were settled back at the brick house and he was telling her what he'd found out and what he'd deduced and she was reacting altogether to his satisfaction.

"Peter, that's brilliant! I'm sure you're right."

"But how can I prove it? If I don't show up with the goods at twelve o'clock tomorrow, Svenson will be nailing my flayed pelt to the chapel door by a quarter to one."

"And Sieglinde will be right beside him, holding the hammer. I do like her so much."

"De gustibus non est disputandum."

"Oh, don't pull that professorial stuff on me. If you were nailing up President Svenson's hide, wouldn't you like having me caddy for you?"

"Yes, and it's a splendid suggestion. Helen, would you really?"

"That's a big commitment. I'll have to ponder the aspects."

"Don't pussyfoot, woman. Yes or no?"

"Peter, do you realize you could have any woman on this campus?"

"Dash it, I don't want any woman on this campus. I want you, to keep those she-wolves at bay."

"Is that all you want me for?"

"No. Helen, what in God's name am I going to do?"

Miss Marsh leaned back on the sofa, happening to encounter Shandy's arm. She did not draw away and he did not encourage her to do so. It was quite a while before they again addressed the problem under discussion. When Helen did speak again she sounded somewhat breathless, as well she might.

"Back in Victorian days, the gentry used to have beaters who'd flush the birds for them to shoot. What you need is a beater."

"Often as not, the hunter missed the bird and hit the beater."

"That's the chance we beaters have to take. Do you or do you not want me to hold the hammer for you?"

"Helen, if anything should happen to you—"

"Peter, nothing is going to happen to me. Let me do this for you and"—she planted one more light kiss on his glowing cheek—"maybe you can do something for me sometime."

"What are you going to do?"

"Just this."

She walked over to the telephone, studied the college directory, and dialed a number. She got her bird.

"Hello, this is Helen Marsh from the library. I'm the new assistant for the Buggins Collection, you know, and I've just happened on a note Mrs. Ames wrote to herself about a book you borrowed from the collection. She was apparently rather worried about getting it back. Oh, you did? Are you quite sure? You see, I've started the cataloguing, and I've run into some very disturbing problems. Some of the most valuable books in the collection are missing, and the one you took happens to be on the special list."

There was a noise on the other end of the line. Helen listened, then laughed merrily. "But of course we have! You don't think Dr. Porble would let such valuable acquisitions go unlisted, do you? The staff are making a careful check now and if we don't turn up the missing books, we're going to get special investigators—yes, of course. I understand perfectly. Perhaps if you took another careful look around—thank you so much. Then I'll expect to hear from you. Good-by."

She replaced the receiver. "Over to you, Arsène."

TWENTY-SIX

"HELEN, YOU'RE STUCK with the toughest job. You'll have to get on that phone and somehow convince Lieutenant Olivetti that we haven't both gone crazy. Explain who you are and make it sound impressive. Give him the facts and tell him to deploy his people on all roads leading out of Balaclava Junction, but not to interfere till I say so."

"Peter, you're not intending to face a two-time murderer alone?"

"No, not alone. Oh, Christ! Call the police. Hurry!"

He grabbed his jacket and rushed out of the house, downhill after an elf who was dragging an empty sled at a fast clip. The student was in complete costume with the elf mask pulled down over the face, but he'd suffered enough from this particular nuisance to recognize the form and gait beyond any doubt. Shandy put on a frantic burst of speed, took a flying leap, and landed on the sled.

"Turn around," he ordered.

"Huh?"

Taken aback, the sled-puller stopped short. "Hey, I can't take a passenger just now. I'm—doing an errand."

"For Grimble?"

Whatever else she might be, Heidi Hayhoe wasn't stupid. She picked up the sled rope again. "Where to, Professor?"

"President Svenson's house."

"All the way up there?"

"Yes, damn it, all the way up there. Get cracking!"

"There," said Mirelle Feldster from behind her parlor curtain. "He's gone loopy for sure. Just as well I didn't—"

"Didn't what?" asked her husband.

Mirelle's answer, if there was one, was drowned by yells from outside. Strolling gawkers, intrigued by the sight of Shandy, grim-faced as Scrooge, riding behind a straining, swearing, furiously sprinting elf. "Hi-yo, Santa Claus!" they shouted. A few tried to push or jump on the sled, but Shandy turned on them a face so savage that they fell back, staring and muttering.

The girl must be incredibly strong to keep up such a pace. The professor felt no remorse for what he was doing to her. Heidi couldn't be in such a desperate hurry unless she'd already got the tip-off, and Helen needed every minute he could gain to reach Olivetti and start the police moving. He stuck with the sled until they reached the end of Svenson's driveway.

"This far enough?" the student panted.

"It will do."

Shandy handed her a five-dollar bill. "Here. I know you always expect ample payment for your—er—services."

"Forget it."

Furious, she slammed her body down on the sled and began coasting downhill, trying to make up for lost time. Shandy hoped she'd come a cropper, but didn't wait to find out. He hurried up to the president's front door and thumped until another of the Svenson daughters let him in.

"Professor Shandy! But the party's over."

"That's what you think, young lady."

"Mother's gone to lie down," she stammered. "Daddy—"

He brushed past her and strode into the library, where Thorkjeld Svenson lay sprawled in a gigantic easy chair before a television set, watching John Wayne get his sombrero pierced by flying bullets. Shandy flicked the "off" switch.

"You want action, President. Get your coat and your car keys."

"Why?"

"Because I say so. Move!"

Incredibly, Svenson did.

"Daddy, where are you going?" called the daughter.

"Ask Shandy."

But Shandy had not waited to be asked. He was already behind the wheel of Svenson's beat-up Chevy.

"Is there any gas in this heap?"

"Who knows? Where are we going?"

"To head 'em off at the pass."

He crunched into first gear for the sharp pitch down to the road where he and Helen had got stopped the night before, then into high, casting worried glances at the gas gauge. It said "half," but there was no telling what that meant. Svenson's car, like its owner, was a law unto itself.

Shandy had counted on Helen's surprise attack to force their prey into doing something stupid, and it had. They picked up the trail with no difficulty at all. He didn't even have to work hard at keeping the other car in sight, since it was obvious where they were heading.

Once only, Svenson spoke. "There's a state trooper chasing us."

"Good," said Shandy. He blinked the lights a few times, and trod harder on the gas pedal. The engine coughed ominously. Cursing with great feeling and expression, he turned into a filling station. The police car started to follow him in, but he waved it on.

They lost minutes, but not too many. When they ran inside the airport terminal, two state policemen in uniform were standing near the door, trying to look nonchalant. Shandy rushed up to them and one murmured, "Boarding. Gate number six."

"Good. Come on."

Sure enough, there they were, clutching their boarding passes and the take-on luggage they must have kept packed and ready ever since they murdered Jemima. The man was tall and burly, clad in a rough dark overcoat and a black lambskin hat much like the garments President Svenson had on. The woman was almost as big as he. She wore a plain blue tweed coat, a blue Angora beret, woolly gray gloves, and enormous black leather boots. Under the beret showed a great knot of flaxen hair.

"Sieglinde!"

"President, no!"

Shandy flung himself upon the howling berserker and held back with all his might until the police could close in. "That's not your wife."

It was not Sieglinde. It was Heidi Hayhoe, mistress of disguise and, on the evidence, of Bob Dysart. Snarling, Svenson fought to get at her.

"Trollop!"

"Oh, hey, listen," cried the girl with a nervous giggle. "Anybody can happen to dress like somebody else. I've worn this outfit lots of times."

"She probably has, President," said Shandy. "I expect this pair of fun-loving pranksters have impersonated you and your wife on numerous occasions. At—er—motels and so forth."

"Arrgh!"

"Sure, what the hell?" Dysart, as always, was quick to see a chance. "You fellows know how it is. I'm a yang, she's a yin. Look, President, I know the rules about faculty-student relationships as well as you do, so let's just say I resign for reasons of moral turpitude as of here and now. I'll drop you a line and make it official, but right now my friend and I have a plane to catch, which we're going to miss if we don't run like crazy."

He was so plausible as a philanderer caught in the act that he might even have got himself and Heidi out the boarding gate, if Shandy hadn't reached over and wrenched open the tote bag he was carrying. In it were Cotton Mather's *Wonders of the Invisible World* and the original two-volume edition of Hamilton's *Federalist*, uncut. Dysart hadn't had time to steam out the Buggins Collection bookplates.

The pair were brought back to Balaclava Junction under heavy guard. Grimble was taken into custody and brought down to confront them. He lost his nerve and ratted. Then Heidi Hayhoe ratted, leaving Bob Dysart with nobody to rat on. In due time, the judge, showing a fine sense of what was appropriate, threw the book at him.

For Shandy the adventure ended where it began, in the brick house on the Crescent. He'd called Helen from the airport, and again from Otter-mole's office to say he was bringing company back. She had a fire going, sandwiches cut, coffee brewed, and sherry at the ready. Sieglinde Svenson, whom they'd collected when they dropped the president's car off, nodded her beautiful head.

"Now you have a home, Peter. Sherry, please. Also for Thorkjeld."

"And you, Porble?"

"Might as well."

The librarian was looking stunned and apprehensive. He still didn't know why they'd dragged him from his own fireside at this hour of the night, but it could be for no good reason.

"Take some yourself, Peter," Helen urged, "then for goodness' sake tell these people everything, from the beginning."

"Well," said Shandy, "I suppose you could say it started with the marbles."

He described once more how he'd found Jemima while hunting for his missing marble, how the errant sphere had turned up in Cadwall's bedroom and thus led him to discover the comptroller's body.

"I expect we'll find out somewhere along the line that either Dysart or Heidi tipped over the dish while they were staging the accident. They'd think it a clever touch, no doubt. Cleverness as opposed to intelligence was, you might say, the keynote of the whole operation. That ought to have made me think of Dysart right off the bat, though I'm ashamed to say it didn't."

"He took an awful risk," said Helen, "killing Mrs. Ames in his own house. At least, I suppose he must have."

"Oh yes. But he had a very pretty scheme worked out. He got her alone in the bedroom, whacked her on the head with a piece of two-by-four or some such thing, held edge-on so that it would leave the right kind of dent, and shoved her body under the bed. He then tossed that extremely noticeable and unmistakable purple cape out the window to Heidi, who was waiting below in her elf costume, having brought her sled to the house and stashed it out of sight. She covered her head and body with the cape and walked down the path in plain sight of the window, with Dysart making sure everybody noticed her going."

Porble winced. "I was one of them. My wife said, 'I'm afraid Jemima isn't quite herself tonight,' and Dysart laughed as though it was the funniest thing he'd ever heard."

"No doubt he was delighted to see his plan working so well," Shandy remarked. "Once she was well inside the shrubbery, the girl got rid of Jemima's cape. I expect she folded it as small as she could, then stuck it overhead among the branches, knowing the people going home from the party wouldn't be apt to look up. They'd tuck their chins into their collars and watch where they stepped on that slippery path. Then all Heidi had to do was step out and mingle with the crowd. Mary Enderble and Roger Jackman probably did see her, but paid no attention because the Crescent's always swarming with students in elf costume and Heidi's been taking particular pains to make herself noticed by barging about with her sled where she's not supposed to be."

"And getting away with it because she's a natural-born performer," said Helen. "People don't mind having the star take the stage."

"Especially not when they're related to wealthy alumni," Porble added nastily.

Shandy ignored the interruption. "I expect Dysart devoted the rest of the evening to getting his wife as drunk as possible while himself pretending to drink a great deal more than he did. He might even have given her a sedative, although," remembering Adele and her cough medicine, "that may not have been necessary. Anyway, once Adele was safely out of the picture and the Illumination over for the night, Heidi Hayhoe came back. Jemima was a big woman, but Heidi is an amazingly strong girl, as I found out earlier this evening. She and Dysart between them would have no trouble carrying the body downstairs and getting it on the sled, disguised in the Santa Claus mask off the dummy Heidi and no doubt some of her cohorts had pinched from my porch and—er—made sport with.

"Probably he then lay low for a few minutes while she dragged the sled over here. The Jackman child happened to catch her doing it, but of course all he actually saw was one of the elves riding Santa Claus around on a sled, as they'd been doing all evening. Interestingly enough, though, he seems to have got some kind of subliminal impression about the situation because he suddenly became frightened and scooted back to bed. If he'd stayed up, I daresay he'd have seen Professor Dysart taking a late-night stroll around the Crescent to sober up from his own party. When Dysart disappeared among my spruce trees, the child would think he'd sought shelter for—er—personal reasons."

"Not bad," said the president.

"No, actually, it was pretty good. If they hadn't overdone the cleverness by bringing in that unnecessary step stool and overturning the marbles that should have been safely out of the way, I might never have noticed anything fishy about the so-called accident. Except, of course, for the missing door key."

"That's where Grimble comes in, I suppose," said Porble.

"Exactly. Heidi got it from him using the same—er—methods Delilah used on Samson. I would not have believed an attractive young woman could be so—er—"

"I would," said Helen. "I told you what she was the minute I laid eyes on her, but you didn't listen."

"Good men never believe there are any bad women," said Sieglinde. "That is why good women have a duty to keep them from running loose and getting into trouble. These are excellent sandwiches, Miss Marsh."

"Thank you," said Helen, somewhat flustered. "Peter, what about the keys? She had one to the library, too, didn't she?"

"Dysart did. I expect she took them from the security office either with or without Grimble's knowledge, had them duplicated, then replaced the originals—er—next time around."

"My God," said Porble faintly.

"Why the Buggins Collection?" demanded the president. "Nobody else," he shot a javelin glance at the librarian, "thought it worth bothering about."

"And Peter," said Helen.

"And I," said Sieglinde. "Though I did not mean for Thorkjeld to appoint Mrs. Ames."

"I did it because you nagged me. It's all your fault."

"In any event, it was the Buggins Collection that killed her," said Shandy. "I suspect Dysart, having got hold of the keys, used to make his raids whenever he saw the chance. He could duck out into the corridor on the pretext of using the men's room and even if someone did happen to find him exploring the Buggins Room, there's nothing so very remarkable about an academic's showing a desultory interest in old books. However, Jemima, once she became assistant, also developed the habit of making whirlwind visits to the library. She happened to catch him in the act of taking one of the books. I suppose he told her Porble had said it was all right and, knowing what a slapdash sort of person she was, simply hoped she'd forget the incident. But Jemima didn't forget and kept nagging at him to return the book, which of course he couldn't do because he'd sold it. Furthermore, the fact that she knew he'd been in the room at all made him Suspect Number One if the thefts ever were discovered, and a stumbling block to a highly lucrative enterprise even if they weren't. He'd probably decided to get rid of her even before her— er—taking umbrage at my Illumination decorations suggested a method. I hope so, anyway."

"But what about Dr. Cadwall?" Sieglinde wanted to know. "Did he, too, know that Professor Dysart had taken the book?"

"Dysart probably thought he did because Ben was so inquisitive and his wife a close friend of Jemima, who was a great talker. However, he had another reason to be afraid of the comptroller. He knew that Ben had grown up in a small Ohio town with Adele, who's a good bit older than she would have us believe, and that in fact the two were once engaged."

"So?"

"So when Ben started taking public issue with the way Adele's money was being thrown around, Bob must have got worried. You see, Ben also knew that while Adele had, as advertised, come into her parents' fortune, being rich in Patsville, Ohio, doesn't necessarily mean quite the same thing as being rich in Dallas or Palm Beach. Since he'd almost married into the family, Ben had a pretty shrewd idea of how much she actually inherited, and of course he signed Bob's pay checks. It was obvious to him that the Dysarts' total income simply was not big enough to sustain their flamboyant life style for any extended time. The logical inferences were either that Bob was getting additional funds from some undisclosed source or that he intended to blow every cent he could milk from Adele's estate and then ditch her for somebody else. Since both surmises happened to be true, and since Ben was in a position of real power at the college, I expect Dysart considered him far the greater threat."

"Still, if Professor Dysart was planning to elope with Heidi Hayhoe, why did he not just go and not kill these good people?"

"Oh, I don't think he intended to clear out so soon. He'd spun that yarn about Ben's getting poisoned coffee intended for him, and then got his girl friend to torch the power plant in order to support the idea that he was being persecuted by saboteurs. I expect he thought he could keep it going until he'd finished plundering the Buggins Collection. He's an imaginative chap, you know. He must have enjoyed himself a great deal, ripping off a fortune from under Porble's nose and having an affair with a student in defiance of the college's strictest rule."

"You know," Helen mused, "it's conceivable that by forcing Professor Dysart's hand, we may have saved that girl's life. Do you think he ever really meant to take her with him?"

"That's a good question," said Shandy. "He wouldn't dare leave her behind alive, of course, and I'm not at all sure what he meant to do with her once they got away. The police found a ransom note in his pocket, that he'd evidently written in the car while she drove and meant to post from wherever they were going. I don't know if he actually thought he could get the college and Heidi's wealthy relatives to pay a large ransom to imaginary kidnapers, or if he was just setting the stage to kill the girl and do a vanishing act himself so he'd be presumed dead and left free to enjoy his loot. The man was absolutely dumbfounded when they arrested him, you know. I don't believe it had ever once entered his head that he couldn't outsmart the whole world."

"He outsmarted me, at any rate," Porble muttered. "I'm not going to offer any excuses, President. I was derelict in my duty, and I'm resigning here and now."

"You'll resign when I say so," roared Svenson.

"That is wise, Thorkjeld," his wife approved. "Dr. Porble was right to concentrate on the work that means most to the college. Miss Marsh will help us get back some of the stolen books, and as for the rest, why should we regret losing what we never knew we had? The money at least will not be lost."

"How?" demanded the president.

"There will be much publicity when the wicked Dysart and his young strumpet come to trial. This will be unpleasant for us, but we shall take a vigorous stand on the side of good and right and you will be dignified and majestic for the photographers and next year many more thousands of people will come to our Illumination and thus we gain back the money."

"Hoist with my own petard!" Shandy groaned.

"And you, Peter Shandy," Sieglinde went on unheeding, "will let the ladies of the committee select your decorations. You are not to be trusted. Thorkjeld, we must go."

Professor Shandy shook his head. "I can't believe this nightmare is over. I suppose as the last—er—item on the docket, one of us ought to go over and explain to Adele Dysart that her husband's spent all her money, killed two of her neighbors, and tried to elope with an oversexed undergraduate. President, you—"

"Not me! I delegated you to clean up this mess, Shandy, and by Yesus, you're still delegated. Go."

"Just one minute, Dr. Svenson," cried Helen Marsh. "If you think you're going to send this innocent man into that—that vampire's nest—"

"I do."

"Then," she sighed, "I suppose I'll have to go with him."

"To hold the hammer?" Shandy asked in the tone of a man who will brook no further shilly-shallying.

"Yes, Peter," she replied. "To hold the hammer."

"What the hell are they talking about?" demanded the president.

"Never mind," Sieglinde told him. "He knows and she knows. You do not need to know. Come, Thorkjeld, it is past your bedtime."

CORPUS CHRISTMAS

PROLOGUE

IN THE MID-1820s Erich Breul's grandfather parlayed three leaky river barges and the opening of the Erie Canal into a modest fortune. During the Civil War, Erich Breul's father added a second fortune running blockades. Erich Breul himself was the first of his family to be sent to Harvard—primarily to learn the art of managing money—and his postgraduate trip to Europe was meant to complete the family's transformation from flannel cap to silk hat in three generations.

Like many young scions whose lives were destined for the administration of settled wealth, Erich had developed a taste for fine art during his college years and Europe provided an ideal opportunity to pursue that interest.

To the elder Breul's dismay, young Erich's proposed year stretched to eight. Fortunately, Mr. Breul was healthy and vigorous at the time and he was prepared, within reason, to indulge his son's acquisition of culture. Times were changing and Mr. Breul was shrewd enough to change, too.

In Europe Erich immediately grasped what his freebooter father only dimly sensed: Culture could purify and legitimize the crude and occasionally bloody foundations that too often underlay even modest financial empires.

Yet it was more than that.

Young Erich Breul genuinely liked pictures and he made a substantial effort to cultivate an eye for adventurous art, especially since his allowance did not stretch to safely pedigreed old masters. He disdained the stuffy salon painters and also avoided the impressionists, thinking them too superficial. Instead, he was instinctively attracted by that mixture of dignity and daring found in the work of expatriate Americans like Whistler and Sargent. He had his portrait painted that first winter by the young

Italian virtuoso, Giovanni Boldini; and although a sympathy for noble sentiment drew him to intimist painters like Tranquillo Cremona and Arcangelo Guidini, his passion for bravura technique led him as far afield as Adolphe Monticelli.

In later years he liked to think he would have bought a Van Gogh had he seen that artist's work.

For eight years, crates of pictures arrived on the piers of New York with predictable regularity. A bewildered Mr. Breul paid the freight. He might not understand his son's preoccupation with collecting art but he continued to underwrite the expense since young Erich had, while collecting Ferdinand Hodler in Switzerland, also collected Fraulein Sophie Fürst, a distant cousin with a sizable dowry and trim ankles that flashed beneath her proper skirts.

When the newlyweds finally followed their treasures to America in 1887, Mr. Breul established them at 7 Sussex Square. Sophie decorated with late-Victorian opulence and Erich turned the cavernous ballroom into a personal art gallery.

As was the fashion in those days, pictures were hung in the salon style popular in Europe. In frames monumentally carved and gilded, they were stacked on the walls from chair rail to ceiling, one above the other, with little consideration for size or shape and with almost no space between each frame.

The collection spilled into the formal drawing room, leaped the great hall to the library and dining room, and still continued to grow: George Inness; Henry Creswell; William Carver Ewing; and Walter Sickert, a student of Whistler's with whom Erich had caroused in London before his marriage to Sophie. Almost by accident he acquired a decent Chandler Grooms and a better than average John La Farge.

Old Mr. Breul thought it a deplorable waste of money but he loved his son and for Christmas one year even gave him a set of Winslow Homer's marine drawings which had caught his eye and reminded him of his blocade-running days.

Despite Erich Breul's continued passion for pictures, he did not disappoint his father's hopes once he was home. He may have lacked his grandfather's gritty pioneer spirit and his father's ruthless zest and acumen but he eventually shaped himself into a dutiful businessman and, after the crash of 1893, even managed to recoup most of the losses.

Only one child was born of his happy union with Sophie Fürst. In due time Erich junior grew to manhood, attended Harvard like his father, and departed for his own *wander jahr* in Europe, where he was struck and killed by a team of runaway horses in a narrow Paris street two days before his twenty-second birthday.

Three months later, still dazed by his death, Sophie stumbled in front of the electric trolley that ran along the bottom of Sussex Square.

When his son's effects arrived from Europe, Erich Breul was touched to find a few crude pictures in his steamer trunks. It didn't matter that the pictures were dreadful—Erich could remember some mistakes he himself had made when he first began collecting—the tragedy was that the boy's life had been cut short before his eye could mature.

Heartbroken, he'd stored his son's possessions next to the trunk that held his memorial to Sophie: her nightdress, her autograph album, a lace handkerchief that still breathed the faint trace of her toilet water, along with a hundred other intimate bits and scraps that he couldn't bear to give away.

There was no question of another marriage for him, another child. He drew up a will that would turn 7 Sussex Square into a museum to house in perpetuity the pictures he'd collected; and although he continued to function—to work, to dine with friends at his club, to refine his collection—when the great influenza epidemic of 1918 struck, he succumbed almost gratefully.

"... *August and my cycling tour up the Rhône (along with that amusing adventure in Sorgues-sur-l'Ouvèze with those bohemian chaps) was, until now, my favorite month, although the autumn lectures at Lyons's Palais des Arts were as edifying as you had hoped, Papa, and my French is much improved. But now I am in Paris, the queen of cities! I still cannot believe I am here, here in the cultural center of the universe with my own snug rooms in Montparnasse. Notre-Dame! Montmartre!* Dites-moi, mes parents, *however did you force yourselves to leave? And yet, as the days shorten, shall I confess one small misgiving? Will you laugh at your grown-up son for his weakness? How I shall miss our jolly Christmas this year! Should I live to be a hundred, dear Papa and Mama, I shall never forget the roaring fires in every hearth, every room bedecked with garlands of holly and ivy, the smell of cinnamon and ginger and roasted goose wafting from the kitchen below to the nursery on high, and in the main hall, such a tree that to a little lad seemed to tower up to the heavens, each branch a-blaze with candles and bejeweled with Mama's glass angels. ...*"

LETTER FROM ERICH BREUL JR., DATED 11.5.1912
(FROM THE ERICH BREUL HOUSE COLLECTION)

ONE

Thursday, December 10

SNOW WAS PREDICTED by Sunday and a chill morning rain had drenched the city streets but it had stopped by ten A.M. when Rick Evans arrived at Sussex Square, that little gem of urban felicity down in the East Twenties. He paused a moment, propped his tripod on the wrought-iron fence which enclosed the tiny park, uncapped the lens of the camera slung around his neck, and slowly panned the area.

Unlike the broad avenues of commerce where New York's glamorous stores were bedizened with tinsel and glitter, Christmas down here approached in a resolutely nineteenth-century fashion that was less intimidating to someone born and reared in a small college town in Louisiana. The solid townhouses that ringed Sussex Square were built of stone, not wood; but most wore heavy wreaths of fresh evergreens, waxed fruits, and lacquered nuts that gleamed in the weak winter sunlight with a home-like familiarity.

Number 7 was twice as wide as any of its neighbors and bore a small brass plaque that informed passersby that this was the Erich Breul House, built in 1868 and open to the public since 1920.

Rick Evans focused carefully on the brass plaque, then retrieved his tripod and walked up the broad marble stoop to the recessed doorway, a doorway so imposing that he automatically wiped his boots on the outer mat before entering the marbled hall.

Black velvet ropes, looped through brass stanchions, formed a walk-way to a long Queen Anne tavern table where a middle-aged docent sat with a cash register on one side and a selection of brochures, books, and postcards on the other. The docent looked up from her knitting and peered at him in nearsighted hopefulness; but when the young man's camera case and folded tripod came into focus, her smile faltered with disappointment. Only that photographer she'd been told to expect; not a paying sightseer wishing a tour of the house.

From an alcove at the rear of the vaulted entrance hall, a young black woman saluted him with a friendly wave of her steno pad as her high-heeled boots clicked through a doorway that had once led to the butler's pantry but was now the director's office.

On the left, midway the depth of the hall, stood a bushy fir tree, at least ten feet tall, but dwarfed by the massive proportion of the carved marble fireplace. The tree was surrounded by open boxes of ornaments, a tall aluminum stepladder, tangles of candle-shaped tree lights, and three women dressed in urban-casual woolens. As Rick Evans approached them, the light floral scent of their perfumes mingled with the fir's woodsy aroma and for a moment he felt himself unaccountably, profoundly homesick for Louisiana and Christmas in his mother's house.

He propped his tripod against the opposite side of the fireplace and smiled diffidently at a kind-looking brunette whose graying hair was tied back with a red silk scarf. "Is Mrs. Beardsley here?" he asked.

"Is God in his heaven?" the woman replied in an unexpectedly deep voice.

"Oh Helen, you're awful!" giggled a shorter, round-faced woman.

"Shh!" a third woman warned.

Sensible leather heels tapped down the wide marble staircase at the right of the hall as Mrs. Gawthrop Wallace Beardsley, senior docent at the Breul House, descended triumphantly, followed by a man in dark green coveralls whose face was obscured by the boxes he carried.

"We found them," she said, bustling over to the group. "I *knew* we had more decorations than these." Her all-seeing gaze fell upon Rick Evans and she halted to consult the old-fashioned gold watch on her wrist. "Mr. Evans. Surely I told you the tree would not be ready to be photographed until *after* lunch?"

Rick fiddled with the lens cap on the camera still slung round his neck. "Yes, ma'am," he admitted, "but I had some free time and I thought maybe I could shoot some of the ornaments individually or something? I mean, aren't some of them pretty special?"

His voice trailed off in uncertainty.

The deep-voiced woman with the kind face took pity on him. "Yes, they certainly *are* special. Melissa, show him one of Mrs. Breul's glass angels."

Melissa, the widow of Dr. Higgins Highsmith Jr., whose many trusteeships had once included the Erich Breul House, plucked an ornament almost as delicate as she herself from its nest of tissue. From girlhood, Sophie Fürst Breul had collected dozens of fragile glass Christmas tree ornaments, charming souvenirs of carefree winter visits to relatives in Germany and Austria.

This particular angel had been blown from a pearly, opalescent glass and its features then hand-painted in soft pastels. Its robe was pale green and, incredible after so many years, fragile glass hands still held to those rosebud lips a gilt paper trumpet stamped with stars.

"Over a hundred years old!" marveled Melissa Highsmith. "And it's only frayed a bit here." Her wrinkled fingers sketched a circle around the trumpet's flare without actually touching the tattered edge.

"Do be careful," Mrs. Beardsley warned.

Her words were meant for the man, who was trying to set down his load of boxes without tipping them, but Mrs. Highsmith guiltily replaced the angel in its tissue as the deep-voiced woman stepped forward to help Pascal Grant.

Carefully, the workman straightened the boxes until each right corner was square with the one below, then turned to Mrs. Beardsley for approval with such innocent expectation that Rick automatically lifted his camera to his face to shield himself from so much physical beauty.

He knew that the Breul House contained basement quarters for a live-in handyman, but had not yet met him. In listing the people who worked there, his grandfather had hesitated at Pascal Grant's name and murmured something about a lamb of God, one of His poor unfortunates, which had led Rick to expect someone defeated or with an obvious physical handicap. A crippled alcoholic, perhaps.

Instead, now that the boxes no longer hid the man's face, Rick saw someone who looked like one of Sophie Breul's angels stepped down from a Christmas tree.

Pascal Grant was slender and finely built—even the coarse green coveralls he wore could not disguise that—with eyes as blue as the Virgin's robes and golden hair like spun glass. He had a thin, well-shaped nose, a rounded chin, and an upper lip so short that his mouth was seldom fully closed.

It must be those parted lips that made him look so innocent and young, thought Rick, twisting the barrel of his portrait lens until Grant's seraphic features filled the viewer. Too, the janitor seemed to keep his head tilted down so that when he spoke to anyone he had to look up from beneath level sandy brows like a child looking up at an adult.

He was looking now at Rick. "Hello," he said in a voice as light and sunny as his smile, and held out his right hand as if they were at a formal dinner. "You're Mr. Munson's grandson. You're going to take new pictures of everything. I'm Pascal Grant."

Puzzled, Rick lowered the camera and extended his own hand. "Rick Evans."

He was surprised by the unexpected strength of the janitor's grip, and noted that Grant's hand was calloused and that his fingertips were grease-stained beneath the ragged nails.

The women smiled approvingly at Rick. Even the patrician Mrs. Beardsley softened. "This is Helen Aldershott," she said, gesturing to the tall, deep-voiced woman. "And Melissa Highsmith, whom you've just met."

"So pleased," murmured Mrs. Highsmith, taking his hand between both of hers.

Her thin, arthritic fingers flashed with accumulated diamonds and he sensed that several of the rings were too loose, as if fashioned for younger, less gnarled hands. He wondered briefly how many generations of Highsmith fingers those rings had adorned.

The round-faced giggler and her shusher were Mrs. Dahl and Mrs. Quinones.

"Now then, Mr. Evans," Mrs. Beardsley said briskly. "Perhaps you can help Pascal bring down the last load? I don't possess quite the stamina I once had."

"You're amazing and you know it, Eloise," said Mrs. Aldershott. "You must have been from the basement to the attic a dozen times this morning. It's enough to tire anyone."

"I'll be glad to help," Rick said politely.

He hung his fleece jacket on the tripod, piled his camera and case next to them, then followed Pascal Grant up the broad marble staircase, which turned back on itself at a landing halfway up the height of the hall.

At the left of the stairs, eight thick red candles filled a freestanding fourteenth-century bronze candelabrum, and Mrs. Beardsley and her troops had garlanded the white stone balustrade in evergreen swags and tied them with red velvet ribbons.

On the wide landing, out of the way of passing traffic, stood the dummy figure of a woman, dressed in a ruffled, high-necked blouse and green serge skirt and buttoned shoes. Looking up at her from the curve of the balustrade on the floor below was her male counterpart, clothed as if on his way out for a stroll around Sussex Square on a December morning in 1905.

Thrifty Sophie Breul had seldom discarded anything, so the attic held trunks and boxes full of period clothes. When Gimbels closed its Broadway store, someone had salvaged several fashion mannequins for use at the Breul House.

It was almost like having a Ken and Barbie set for adults, and the docents enjoyed dressing the figures to suit the changing seasons.

Today, the gray-haired male figure wore a top hat, white silk muffler, and long black overcoat, and he carried a gold-headed cane.

The second floor was also open to the public, and it consisted of a wide central hall that was richly somber with a coved wooden ceiling and walls covered in dark burgundy silk. Two tall windows overlooked the park at one end and a carpeted mahogany staircase rose majestically at the other.

Narrow marble-topped tables hugged the walls beneath sumptuously framed oil paintings. The more important pieces of the Breul collection were displayed in the gallery downstairs. These were some of Erich Breul's less discerning purchases and the massive frames, each with its own small lamp, only mocked shrunken reputations. Here was a seascape by Henry Babbage, once praised as "the American Turner"; there, a landscape by Everett Winstanley, "our Constable"; plus a pair of heroic battle scenes with heavily muscled horses, plunging and rearing about with flared nostrils, the work of Genevieve Carlton, whom the late scholar, Riley Quinn, had called the Rosa Bonheur of central New Jersey.

Between the paintings, every door stood wide to reveal bedrooms and dressing rooms, Erich Breul's oak-paneled study and Sophie Breul's sitting room. The latter was elaborately carpeted, draped, and cluttered with fringed shawls, tasseled cushions, gilt mirrors, cut-glass lamps, and other ornate bric-a-brac that passed for tasteful decor in the late 1890's.

Halfway down the hall, they had to press themselves against the wall as a docent exited from the main bathroom with eight German tourists and their tour guide in tow. To judge by the laughter and bright chatter as they passed, the Victorian bathroom had been a great hit. Rick Evans had never seen a bathroom quite that large himself, nor one that lavish: walnut commode, a walnut-enclosed tub deep enough to float in, a wide marble lavatory, and all the brass fixtures fitted out with china knobs and handles.

At the end of the hall, the gloominess of the stair landing was relieved by an oval Tiffany window that Erich had ordered as a tenth anniversary present for Sophie. Even on this gray December day, its stained-glass leaves and flowers glowed with jewellike intensity.

Pascal Grant paused beneath it and smiled at Rick shyly.

"This is my second favorite window in the whole house," he said. "You should take a picture of it."

"I'm going to," Rick agreed. He had noticed it when Benjamin Peake, the director, had given him a hurried tour of the public rooms the previous week, but he planned to wait for a sunny day when the window would be more brilliantly backlighted.

"So," Rick said as they moved on up the steps to the third floor, "what's your first favorite window?"

"The front door downstairs," the other answered promptly over his shoulder. "Not the big door. *My* door."

Rick remembered seeing steps that apparently led down to a doorway recessed beneath the stoop of the main entrance. "The service entrance?"

Pascal Grant paused at the top of the stairs and nodded. "That's mine. I'm service. I have a key and everything." He pulled a tangle of keys from his coverall pocket. "See?"

Even though he stood a step or two higher than Rick, his head was tilted so low that he seemed to be looking up at someone taller as he returned the keys to his pocket.

The third floor was as solidly built as the second, but the hall was narrower and the ceiling was simple plaster except for the cast moldings. Benjamin Peake had made a point about them, but at the moment Rick couldn't remember if the director had said they were special because of the oak-leaf-and-acorn design or because of the process by which they had been cast. Whichever the reason, Rick decided he'd better borrow Grant's stepladder, rig some lights, and take a couple of close-ups.

The front rooms had belonged to Erich Jr. before he went off to France; but in 1948, an imaginative curator had removed the young man's personal effects to a bedroom on the second floor and restored these rooms to their original state as a nursery and playroom. Like so much else, Sophie had naturally saved everything her only child ever used, so the public now saw baby Erich's cradle, his crib, his nursemaid's narrow bed, and, in the connecting playroom, his horsehide rocking horse with its genuine mane and tail, the mane sadly reduced to stubble by much hard riding.

There were also wind-up toys, books, blocks, even a handful of wax crayons which were now scattered beside a childish drawing of stick figures labeled *Papa and Mama and Erich* in straggling letters across the picture. Another Gimbels mannequin, this one resembling a four-year-old boy, sat at the table with a crayon fastened in its hand. It was dressed in short pants and a jacket of gray serge, a white batiste shirt, a black silk bow, long black lisle stockings, and high-top, button-up shoes.

Here again were more visitors. Watched by a woman whose apprehensive air immediately identified her as a docent, seven young day-care kids and their teacher were getting a first hand look at how one privileged child had lived a hundred years earlier.

"Where's his television?" demanded a tot as Rick and Pascal Grant passed the doorway.

"*I* have a television," Pascal whispered to Rick. "Mrs. Beardsley and her ladies gave it to me. For my birthday."

"That's nice," Rick answered, a shade too heartily. Never before had he been required to interact with someone mentally handicapped and his natural compassion was jumbled with both embarrassment and uneasiness.

Physically, Pascal Grant could be any age from sixteen to twenty-six.

Mentally, he probably wasn't too much older than those children.

A damn shame, Rick thought soberly. The guy was so good-looking. Of course, there were no rules that said it had to be otherwise, but still—

They passed through an open set of frosted glass doors that bisected the third floor. At the far end of the hall stood a mannequin dressed as a housemaid in a long black cotton dress and white bib apron, with her hair neatly pinned up under a starched white cap.

On this half of the third floor lay bedrooms for the servants, their one small bath, and a back stairs that ran from the basement kitchen to the attic. In the old days, the glass doors were normally kept shut, but after touring the spacious quarters of the master and mistress, modern visitors always wanted to see where the live-in staff slept when they weren't cooking and cleaning or fetching and carrying for the Breul family.

The docents might loyally insist that the Breuls were enlightened and considerate employers, but most visitors gleefully picked up on how even the floor coverings defined class lines. On the nursery side of that translucent glass, the carpet was a thick wool Axminster; on the servants' side, woven hemp matting.

At the rear stairwell, black velvet ropes barred the public from further passage. From kitchen to attic, the steps were wide enough to accommodate wicker laundry baskets, cleaning equipment, or storage chests, but they rose much more steeply than the wider public staircases and they were uncarpeted. Pascal Grant unclipped one of the ropes from its brass wall hook, waited for Rick Evans to pass, then carefully clipped it back again before leading the way up to the fourth-floor attic.

The huge attic was warm and smelled almost like a hayloft—a clean, dry mustiness compounded of old cardboard, lavender, and mothballs. Odds and ends crowded the space in an orderly fashion: wooden wardrobe boxes, storage cartons of all sizes, trunks, spare furniture, and, to Rick's surprise, a makeshift office of sorts.

At the far end of the attic, extension cords had been strung for lights and a typewriter, and three old tables formed a U-shaped desk for a man who sat reading intently, half hidden from their view by tall metal file cabinets in which were stored a hundred years of Breul papers.

He did not look their way.

"Who's that?" Rick murmured.

"Dr. Shambley." Pascal put his finger to his lips. "Shh."

He pointed to the remaining boxes of Christmas decorations, gave half of them to Rick and started back down. Not until they were at the bottom of the attic steps did he speak again. "Dr. Shambley's new. Mrs. Beardsley doesn't like him."

Rick remembered that his grandfather had mentioned a new trustee who was an art historian or something. "Why doesn't she like him?"

"I don't know," answered the young handyman, but his manner was uneasy and Rick wondered if it were only Mrs. Beardsley who didn't like the new trustee.

On the third floor, they had to edge around the tourists who blocked the hall's frosted glass doors as flash cameras and video minicams recorded the turn-of-the-century housemaid from the toe of her lace-up boots to the tip of her starched cap.

There was no sign of the day-care group until the two men descended past the final turn on the stairs and saw the children being herded across the wide entry hall like a flock of pigeons. The teacher's voice echoed off the marble walls as she called, "Now who has to use the bathroom before we put our coats back on?"

"I do! I do!" they all cried and streamed for the cloakrooms on either side of the main entrance.

Mrs. Beardsley wore a determined smile on her face, a smile that became genuine as Pascal Grant set down his load of boxes and said, "We got them all, Mrs. Beardsley."

"Wonderful, Pascal. Now if you'll set up the ladder and if Mr. Evans will help you with the lights—though why we can't have real candles just once, I'll never understand," she fretted, half to herself. It was Mrs. Beardsley's annual regret that the insurance company and the New York City Fire Marshall were both so stuffy about using real candles on the tree.

Helen Aldershott rolled her eyes at the others and continued to untangle the tiny electric candles that would light the tree safely, if anachronistically.

It was a little past one and the docents were beginning to murmur of missed lunches before the last glass angel was fastened to the last bare twig. After one final inspection, Mrs. Beardsley nodded imperiously to

Miss Ruffton, who tapped on the director's door and summoned him to preside at the lighting ceremony.

Every hair was sleekly in place and a festive red tie was knotted beneath his pointed chin as Benjamin Peake emerged from his office, more urbanely than the butler who had once occupied that corner of the mansion. He acknowledged the hours the women had worked to transform the mansion's formality to a Dickensian festiveness, and he assured them that he spoke on behalf of the trustees when he expressed their appreciation—his, too, of course—for their artistry and dedication.

Benjamin Peake possessed a rolling baritone that filled the marbled hall and floated up the stairwell. Alerted by his formal tones, a small crowd soon gathered around the tree and even spread themselves along the staircase for a better view.

When he was sure of everyone's attention, the director drew his remarks to a close and smiled graciously at his audience. "A very merry Christmas to you all," he said and clicked the switch Pascal Grant had rigged.

"Ah!" everyone exclaimed, as the tree blazed forth in all its Victorian glory.

Fourteen senior suburbanites, in from Connecticut for the day and fresh from touring the Theodore Roosevelt birthplace a short walk away, had gathered in the entry hall for a guided tour. Several began taking pictures of each other in front of the Christmas tree.

"Your tree is much prettier than Teddy's," one of the women told Mrs. Beardsley.

Pascal Grant paused in the act of carting away the ladder and storage boxes. "Hey, Rick," he said. "Want to see my window now?"

Rick Evans made a show of looking at his watch. "Sorry, Pascal, but I'd better finish taking pictures of the tree."

Yet when he saw the open disappointment on the other's face, he relented. "Tell you what, though. Why don't I come a little early tomorrow, around four? You can show me then, okay?"

"Okay!" Grant nodded happily.

At the top of the house, Roger Shambley lifted his massive head from a letter that had been misfiled in a cabinet with some of Erich Breul's business papers.

"*Sorgues?*" he muttered to himself, remembering that name from a biography he'd once read. "August of 1912? Hmm . . . now wouldn't that be something?"

He looked past the circle of bright light in which he sat, out to the dim stretches of attic crammed with boxes and trunks, and wild surmises filled his head.

"*Silent, upon a peak in Darien,*" he jeered at himself.

And yet—!

In another attic several blocks southeast of the Breul House, a different discovery had just been made.

While renovating their old, but newly purchased, red brick row house in the East Village, Daniel and Gigi DeLucca had found a rusty tin footlocker pushed up under the eaves of the fourth-floor attic behind stacks of *National Geographics*.

"Old books?" he'd wondered.

"Old clothes," she'd guessed.

The hasp was rusted tight.

"Blackbeard's treasure," they decided and, lustily chanting, "Fifteen men on a dead man's chest, Yo-ho! Yo-ho!" they had hauled it downstairs and pried it open with a crowbar.

Inside they found an unpleasant musty odor and four little bundles wrapped in stained newspapers.

"Pigeon bones?" she asked as she finished unwrapping the first bundle.

"I don't think so," he said and carefully laid the second bundle back in the chest as if afraid it would explode.

It was a tiny mummified figure, entwined in what looked to the man like a shriveled grapevine but that the woman instantly recognized as an umbilical cord.

They left the last two bundles for the police.

Lieutenant Sigrid Harald arrived shortly after an assistant from the medical examiner's office. "I'm no Dr. Oliver when it comes to bones," said Cohen, referring to one of the country's leading experts on human skeletal remains, "but off the top of my head, I'd say all four are human and all died within hours of their births."

"When?" asked the tall, gray-eyed lieutenant.

"How the hell do I know?" Cohen answered testily.

They looked at the dates on the yellowed newspapers in which the four pathetic remains had been wrapped. The earliest was March 4, 1935; the latest was April 1, 1947.

"Look there, Lieutenant," said Detective Jim Lowry.

He showed her a flaking page of newsprint that headlined the allied invasion of North Africa. Overlaying a map with arrows pointing to Algiers were four faded brown ovals that looked very much like old fingerprints made by bloody adult fingers.

Their Christmas card that year depicted Father Christmas in his long red robes and furred hood as he warmed himself before a roaring fire. Inside was a verse from Sir Walter Scott, one of Mr. Breul's favorite authors:

Heap on more wood!—the wind is chill:
But let it whistle as it will,
We'll keep our Christmas merry still.

FROM *WELCOME TO THE BREUL HOUSE!—AN INFORMAL TOUR*, BY MRS. HAMILTON JOHNSTONE III, SENIOR DOCENT (COPYRIGHT 1956)

TWO

Friday, December 11

THANKS TO THE Sussex Square Preservation Society, which had success-
fully fought to retain them, six of the city's last original gas streetlights
survived in working order, and here in the early December twilight their
soft flickers gleamed upon polished brass door handles and kick plates.

A through street for cars and taxis passed along the bottom of the
square, but when vehicular traffic was banned from the northern three
sides around the small park, the original cobblestone carriageway was
repaved in smooth brick, a substitution Mrs. Beardsley regretted anew as
she stood in the doorway of number 7 and watched the last visitors descend the broad marble steps.

Mrs. Beardsley lived diagonally across the park at number 35. As
senior docent, however, she spent almost as much time at the Breul House
as she did in her own. She had hoped for the seat on the board of trustees
that had recently gone to Dr. Shambley, but until that prize dropped into
her lap, she would continue to conduct tours of the house, arrange seasonal decorations, and intimidate the reduced staff.

Mrs. Beardsley's officiousness might weary Benjamin Peake—especially when he was called upon to calm the ruffled waters she left in her
wake—but the director revenged himself with the secret knowledge that
the woman would never become a trustee as long as he had a say in the
matter. Otherwise, he had no intention of discouraging her interest in the
place. After all, she deferred to his position, she was capable of surprisingly shrewd promotional ideas, and she worked tirelessly without a salary, of itself no small consideration, given the Erich Breul House's
current financial difficulties.

Although a discreet sign inside the vestibule suggested donations of three dollars per person to view the house and its contents, at least a third of those who came either donated less or brazenly ignored the sign altogether. This wouldn't have mattered if hundreds daily thronged the house. Sadly, the two who had just departed were the forty-first and forty-second of the day.

An average day these days.

Mrs. Beardsley sighed and lingered for a moment in the chill twilight. She considered herself a closet romantic and the square was at its wintertime loveliest tonight. The very sight of it restored her good spirits because she could, she thought, take credit for its beauty—not only for the gaslights but even for the tiny colored lights that twinkled upon a tall evergreen at the center of the square's handkerchief-size park.

The tree represented compromise. Every year the question of decorative Christmas lights came before the Sussex Square Preservation Society and every year Mrs. Beardsley had managed to block their use. This year a younger, more vulgar contingent from numbers 9, 14, and 31 had rammed the motion through. Mrs. Beardsley had then rallied her forces and carried a vote that limited the lights to a single tree.

With predictable incompetence, the arrivistes had underestimated how many strings it would take to bedizen every twig, so the evergreen emerged more tasteful than Mrs. Beardsley had dared hope. In fact, it was even rather festive but Mrs. Beardsley had no intention of admitting that to a soul. Give them an inch and they'd string every bush next year.

One electrified tree was anachronism enough.

An icy gust of wind made the tall spruce dip and sway and Mrs. Beardsley shivered with a sudden chill that had nothing to do with the plummeting temperature.

"Somebody just walked over my grave," she thought and hurried inside.

Footsteps sounded on the marble stoop behind her and she held the tall door open a crack.

"I'm sorry but we're just closing and—oh! Mr. Munson. I didn't realize it was you. Do come in."

With a thin gray beard that hung down over his woolly muffler, Jacob Munson was small and spry enough to remind a more fanciful imagination than Mrs. Beardsley's of an elf escaped from Santa's workshop. Adding to the illusion was the perennial cloud of peppermint fumes in which he had moved ever since his doctors forbade cigarettes, and his eyes danced with merriment and goodwill beneath his wide-brimmed black fedora.

"Mrs. Beardsley, is it not?" A slight German accent underlay his friendly tone. "The others are here?"

"I believe so." She started to escort him toward the director's office at the far end of the vaulted marble hall where the others were gathered when she suddenly found her outstretched arm draped with Mr. Munson's muffler and overcoat. His hat and gloves followed in rapid order and he himself was speeding across the polished tiles before Mrs. Beardsley could make it clear that she was not some sort of resident butler or hat-check girl.

Miffed, she carried the art dealer's outer garments over to a bench near Miss Ruffton's desk and dumped them there, grateful that the secretary had not been required to attend tonight's informal meeting and had therefore missed this minor humiliation. Miss Ruffton was an enigmatic young black woman who never talked back or argued, yet Mrs. Beardsley suspected that she secretly enjoyed any affronts to the older woman's dignity.

As she put on her own coat and gloves to leave, Mrs. Beardsley subconsciously tried to fault Miss Ruffton but found nothing to seize upon. The secretary's gleaming desktop was bare except for an appointment calendar, a pot of red poinsettias in gold foil, and one of those stodgy brochures that outlined the history of the Erich Breul House.

And that reminded Mrs. Beardsley: Where was young Mr. Evans? Didn't Mr. Munson expect him to join them? She pushed back the cuff of her cashmere glove and glanced at her watch. Everyone else was there except him.

"Boys!" she murmured to herself. With her children hundreds of miles away and occupied by families of their own, she had unconsciously transferred her maternal interest to Pascal Grant, who would never completely grow up. And she'd be quite surprised if Rick Evans were a day past twenty. Now what sort of mischief, she wondered, could be keeping those two so long in the basement?

Officiously, Mrs. Beardsley opened a door concealed beneath the marble stairwell, passed along a short hall that led back to what was left of the butler's pantry, turned right, and descended the stairs to the basement.

An hour earlier, Rick Evans had followed Pascal Grant down those steps into the kitchen. It was enormous, but the stamped-tin ceiling was surprisingly low and the room's dry snugness made Rick think of *Wind in the Willows* and of Mr. Badger's home and Mole's cosy tunnels. Blue rag rugs were scattered over brown floor tiles, a massive cookstove resplendent with nickel-plate ornamentation dominated the room, and one wall was lined with shallow open shelves that held the blue willowware Sophie Breul had provided for her servants' daily use.

Rick had wanted to open the doors of the huge chestnut ice box, to lift the lids of painted tin canisters and peer into the built-in storage bins, but Pascal Grant had tugged at his sleeve.

"They're all empty. Come and see my window before it gets dark, okay?"

As he trailed Pascal through the cavernous basement passages, Rick was reminded of explorations he used to take with his best friend through abandoned barns and farm-houses back home in Louisiana's bayou country. There was that same sense of sadness, of human artifacts abandoned to their own devices.

On the other side of the scullery were empty coal bins, made redundant by an oil furnace that was itself in need of replacement. Beyond the kitchen lay rooms no longer needed for their original purposes: cold closets with sharp hooks for hanging meat and poultry, bins for food supplies, a laundry room, with deep stone sinks and tall drying racks. These were now lumbered with bulky storage crates, trunks, rolled-up carpets, and odds and ends too good to throw away, yet no longer needed for the day-to-day business of the museum. The hall wound past a room that held racks of pictures an earlier curator had weeded out of the main collection as too hopelessly banal; another room stored the folding chairs that were brought up whenever the main hall was used for lectures or recitals.

At the street end of the basement was a sturdy wooden service door that opened onto a shallow areaway beneath the grandeur of the high marble stoop with its elaborate railings. Echoing the rounded door top was one of those whimsicalities to which Victorians were so often given: a lacy wrought-iron spider web set into the upper third of the door, each interstice of the web fitted with clear beveled glass. At the center of the web was a tiny brass garden spider which Pascal kept polished till it shone like gold.

The window was uniquely decorative, yet city-smart as well. Callers could be identified without opening the door and the strong iron cobweb was fine enough that no burglar could smash a tiny pane of glass and reach through to unbolt the latch. Rick had no formal grounding in aesthetics but it occurred to him that Pascal's sense of beauty might be more sophisticated than he'd realized.

The young janitor was looking up at him through long golden lashes. "It's my first favorite window," he said shyly.

"It's beautiful," Rick told him. "I definitely want a picture of this." He tilted the strobe on his camera to bounce light off the ceiling and took a couple of experimental shots before switching lenses for a close-up of the spider.

As he worked, he began to consider the potentials the house offered. "My grandfather wants me to do a new brochure and perhaps some new souvenir postcards," he said, "and Dr. Peake wants me to photograph all the paintings, but I bet I could do a whole series of slides on just architectural details, another on furniture, perhaps one on Victorian clothes or dishes."

"*All* the paintings?" Pascal interrupted. "Dr. Peake said for you to take pictures of all of them?"

"Yeah, he said they've never done a photographic record of the whole collection." Rick finished with the window and recapped the lens.

"I've got some pictures in my room," Pascal said proudly. "Dr. Peake said I could. Come see."

He led Rick back down the passageway and through the kitchen. Beyond the service stairs was what had once been the downstairs butler's pantry, connected to the one above by a large dumbwaiter. This was where the Breul maids had put the finishing touches on meals before sending them aloft. Now the space was outfitted for the only live-in help left. On the counter beside the small sink was a new microwave oven, a coffee maker and a hot-air popcorn popper; below, a half-size refrigerator.

Although the kitchenette was for Pascal Grant's use, it was open to the stairs and kitchen and to the casual inspection of anyone passing through. Perhaps that was why it looked as impersonal as any laboratory, thought Rick.

As if he could read thoughts, Pascal paused before a closed door at the rear of the alcove and looked up at him with another of those seraphic smiles. "Mrs. Beardsley says everything has to be neat out here."

He opened the door and clicked on a wall switch. "I can do what I want to in here."

The room was astonishing. Everywhere Rick looked he saw patterns upon figures upon designs—paisleys and florals beside stripes and basketweave and geometrics. It was like a private retreat designed by some mad Victorian decorator and it should have overwhelmed Rick's visual senses; yet, the colors were so rich and dark that lamplight was soaked up until the whole room coalesced into a mellow warmth that made him think again of a small anthropomorphic animal's cosy den. A human hobbit hole.

Originally the servants' sitting room, the ceiling and windowless walls were papered in a faded turkey red and the floor was layered with odd-size throw rugs, all threadbare but of oriental design. A couple of shabby easy chairs stood on either side of an open hearth that sported a handsome overmantel of carved walnut. For sleeping, Pascal had pushed a double bed mattress and box springs up against a cluttered sideboard and covered it with embroidered shawls and thickly fringed pillows so that it looked more like a Persian divan than a bed.

The lower doors of the sideboard had been folded open to store his clock radio, tape player, and stacks of tapes within easy reach, while a nearby Moroccan brass coffee table held a miniature television.

Pascal unzipped his coverall and stepped out of it. Beneath, he wore jeans and a thin knitted jersey that molded every line of his slender torso. He hung the coverall inside a tall wooden wardrobe and pulled on a blue Fair Isle sweater, a castoff from one of Mrs. Beardsley's sons that echoed his clear blue eyes. Smoothing his tousled golden hair, he looked up at Rick happily.

"See my pictures?"

It was impossible not to since every wall was covered so closely that the red wallpaper beneath was almost hidden.

A large sentimental farmyard scene hung above the fireplace. It pictured baby ducks and chicks, rosy-cheeked children, and other young animals and was doubtless meant to inspire wholesome thoughts among the servants.

But that was the only properly framed picture in the room and the only one that clearly belonged to the nineteenth century. Everything else was thumbtacked to the walls and was vigorously modern: Kandinsky, Klee, Rothko, Pollock, Picasso, Dali, Ernst—all the twentieth-century icons. None were smaller than twenty-four by thirty-six inches and, looking closer, Rick saw that they all seemed to have begun as high-quality art posters. Some were so beautifully reproduced on such heavy stock that, with the subdued lighting, he had to touch the surface of a Dali dreamscape to reassure himself that it wasn't real.

"I cut off all that writing stuff," said Pascal.

"Writing stuff?"

"Museum names and numbers and stuff like that," the young handyman explained earnestly. "I don't read so good, but I know real pictures don't have that stuff on the bottom, so I cut it off."

"Where did you find so many posters, though?" asked Rick, curious.

"Dr. Kimmelshue—he was here before Dr. Peake. He died. He had a bunch of them in his office and lots more down here." He gestured in the direction of the storage rooms. "Dr. Peake told me to throw them all out and I told him I could take them if he didn't want them so he said I could have anything there I wanted."

Pascal paused and caught his short upper lip with his lower teeth. "Well, he didn't mean *anything* I wanted. There's some trunks with clothes and stuff. I didn't take those. He just meant the pictures. And you can take pictures of them, too."

There was such innocent generosity in his voice that Rick hesitated, looking for tactful words. "They're wonderful pictures, Pascal, but I think Dr. Peake's mainly interested in the real old stuff. Like that one over the fireplace. It's a terrific room, though, and you've fixed it up great."

To change the subject, he walked around the bed, sat down on the edge, and began reading the titles on the other youth's stack of cassette tapes. "Hey, what kind of music do you like, Pasc?"

Happiness suffused Grant's beautiful features. "Pasc. That's what my friend called me, my friend at the training center. That's where I learned how to fix things. Are you going to be my friend?"

"Sure," Rick said automatically.

"I'll get us some soda," Pascal decided. He fetched two cans from the kitchenette, and upon returning, stretched across the bed to hand one to his new friend.

Rick continued to read the titles of the tapes as he sipped from the can. "Basie, Lionel Hampton, Cootie Williams, Gene Krupa—you're really into classic jazz, aren't you?"

Pascal Grant sat down on the other side of the bed and began pulling out his favorite tapes. "I like it," he said simply. "It makes me feel good. Like the pictures do. Sometimes they—they get all mixed up together sometimes, the jazz and the pictures."

"You have Benny Goodman's Carnegie Hall concert?"

" 'Sing, Sing, Sing'!" Pascal exclaimed. "It's on the player. That's my very first favorite."

Balancing his soda, he pulled himself over the billowing cushions and punched buttons until Krupa's hypnotic drums filled the room.

"Hey, yeah!" breathed Rick. He pushed a couple of cushions into a stack and leaned back on them. Pascal did the same at the opposite end of the bed so that they sprawled heel to head, facing each other as they drank and listened to the pounding intensity of one of the greatest outpourings of spontaneous jazz ever recorded.

The music, the warmth, the rich reds and golds and purples of the room, the vibrant posters—Pasc was right, he thought, somehow they *did* look like jazz would look if you could paint jazz themes—everything about this moment combined to make him feel safe and unthreatened for the first time since coming to New York.

And there was Pasc himself, his angelic face in shadows, his tangled curls turned into a golden halo by the lamp behind him. A rush of love and pity welled up inside of Rick.

Then, as Jess Stacy's piano explored the outer reaches of the melody, he felt Pascal touch his shoe, heard his low voice say, "I'm glad you're going to be my friend, Rick," and was wrenched by something deeper and terrifyingly primal.

Startled, he sat upright and saw Mrs. Beardsley's disapproving face at the door.

"I knocked," she said in a stern voice, "but the music's so loud—"

Pascal Grant eeled across the end of the bed to lower the volume, then turned to smile at the woman. "I'm sorry, Mrs. Beardsley. I was showing Rick my tapes. He's going to be my friend."

"That's very nice, Pascal," said Mrs. Beardsley, "but right now, I think Mr. Evans is expected upstairs."

"Oh, gosh!" Rick groaned. Embarrassed and guilty, he left his soda on the sideboard and bolted past the stern-faced docent.

Benjamin Peake had, on his own initiative, called this special meeting to explore—informally, he assured them archly—various ways of stemming the Erich Breul House's rapidly growing deficit, and he was prepared to be gracious about Rick Evans' tardy entry for dear old Jacob's sake.

Not that Jacob had turned into a doting grandfather. A respected dealer and now senior partner at Kohn and Munson Gallery, Jacob Munson admitted to seventy although it was generally believed that he was much nearer eighty. His fierce, explosive temper had been tamed somewhat since the death of his son several years earlier, but his devotion to art and to the business of art remained strong, and his friendship had occasionally smoothed Peake's progress in the art world.

Beside him sat Hester Kohn, daughter of his late partner, a trim and smartly dressed brunette of thirty-four, with quizzical hazel eyes and a small mouth that smiled easily. She wore gray boots and slacks, a high-collared red silk shirt, and a wide flat necklace of gold enameled in colorful Chinese chrysanthemums. She was addicted to gardenias and her heady perfume fought Munson's cloud of peppermint to a draw.

Munson had been apprehensive when young Hester Kohn inherited her father's half interest in the gallery, but these past two years had gone smoothly. She handled the financial side of the business as efficiently as her father had and seemed equally content to leave final artistic judgments to him.

Jacob Munson considered himself less fortunate than Horace Kohn in his offspring. His only son, the son he'd groomed to come into the gallery, the son who painted like an angel, had been killed in a plane crash before the lad was twenty-five. His two older daughters, resentful because he'd never encouraged their participation until after the tragedy, resisted his tardy attempts to interest them in art. One was now a doctor in Seattle, the other taught economics at a small college in Louisiana. Although the doctor had remained willfully unmaternal, the professor had eventually managed one child, Richard.

Aware of his grandfather's reservations, Rick Evans found himself a chair just inside the director's door and now fiddled with his camera lens.

He focused on Munson's narrow foot, twisting the lens until his shoelaces came into sharp detail. Rick would have liked to point his camera directly at Munson's face but knew that would annoy. He wished that he pleased his grandfather better.

As Dr. Peake spoke of the Breul House's financial problems, Rick unobtrusively moved his camera toward Francesca Leeds. Lady Francesca had turned thirty-seven that year, but there was nothing in her clean-lined profile to suggest it. Her golden complexion was as clear as a girl's, her dark red hair glossy and natural, her slender body at the peak of its physical powers, with a lithe sensuousness that was the birthright of certain fortunate women.

Her companion was five years older and if one looked closely at his straw-colored hair one could see gray at his temples. He had an outdoorsman's face, yet it took expensive tailoring to disguise the fact that his muscular body had perhaps spent too much time behind a desk instead of at the helm of his racing yacht.

Søren Thorvaldsen was a Danish entrepreneur who had parlayed a boyhood romance with the sea into great wealth by refurbishing aging transatlantic liners into luxurious West Indian cruise ships. After years of hard work, he was ready to start playing again and Lady Francesca's proposal had amused him and appealed to both his financial and aesthetic appetites.

"Why don't you explain your idea to Mr. Munson and Miss Kohn?" Peake said smoothly, turning the floor over to Francesca Leeds.

She smiled. "It's really very simple. The Erich Breul House has a serious image problem. Is it a historical house or is it an art museum? Some of the pictures in this collection are first-rate. No one questions that. The others—"

A graceful half-humorous shrug of her shoulder indicated that she did not intend to speak uncharitably about the bulk of the founder's collection unless pressed.

"The Breul Collection is highly regarded by scholars world wide," said Jacob Munson, who chaired the board of trustees. "Even now, Dr. Roger Shambley is writing a new book using examples from the house."

"But is it the general public who'll be reading it?" There was a charming hint of Celtic lilt to the lady's British accent. Her father supposedly owed his title to one of those tumbledown Irish castles.

"Jacob, it's imperative that we find new sources of revenue," re-minded Benjamin Peake.

"*Ja, ja.* This is why we have lent you Richard." He unwrapped an-other piece of hard candy and popped it into his mouth. The fragrance of peppermint wafted through the office anew.

"And we appreciate the loan," said the director, smiling at young Evans, who looked back at him through the camera's range finder. "But there's no point in taking photographs for a new brochure or a larger collection of souvenir postcards if no one comes in to buy them."

"We think people have forgotten what serendipitous treasures the Breul House owns," Lady Francesca said coaxingly. "We must remind them—bring back not just the true art lovers but potential donors, too—the people who support what is chic to support."

Francesca Leeds described herself as a free-lance publicist but she was actually a matchmaker between money and the arts. She maintained a small one-room office in her suite at the Hotel Maintenon and new business came through personal recommendations of satisfied clients. As one of the four most highly regarded party planners in the city, she had a flair for matching corporate donors with charitable fundraising events.

An importer of Italian shoes, for example, could be persuaded to help support a fashion show to benefit a convent founded by a Sicilian nun. The importer's shoes would be featured throughout the show while the Santa Caterina Sisters of Charity would net several thousands to further their good works.

The parent company of an expensive line of camera equipment might sponsor a movie premiere to help fund further research in retinitis pig-mentosa.

For every worthy cause, Lady Francesca Leeds seemed to find a moneyed patron.

Her dark red hair glinted like polished mahogany as she tilted her head toward the heretofore silent Dane. "As a ship owner, Mr. Thorvald-sen recognizes a natural affinity for the Erich Breul House."

Rick Evans' camera followed her eyes, then swept the group as Hes-ter Kohn gave a muffled snort.

Hester was puzzled by her inclusion in this informal planning session. She was not a trustee and she was much less interested in Benjamin Peake's career than Jacob was.

She regarded her partner with fond uneasiness. He couldn't possibly last more than another year or two and then what would happen to the gallery? She had grown up speaking the specialized jargon of the art world and she was quite comfortable managing the gallery's finances. But Hester Kohn knew her limitations, knew that she was no judge of artistic merit. One could be cynical and say that given the current state of visual arts in this city artistic merit hardly mattered; yet ultimately, she knew, it *did* matter.

Although Jacob spoke halfheartedly of educating his slow-talking grandson, who had suddenly appeared full-blown from the Louisiana bayous this past September, Hester soon realized that the boy—he was only twenty—was even less intuitive about art than she herself. Her eyes lingered on him thoughtfully. Momentarily unshielded by his camera, he caught her gaze and turned away in self-conscious confusion. A tractable lad and willing enough to follow—she knew *that* better than anyone else in the room. Yet anything that couldn't be captured through a camera lens seemed difficult for him to grasp.

Jacob must see this, she thought, but would the ties of blood outweigh his devotion to Kohn and Munson's impeccable reputation? Or would he leave his share of the gallery to one of his protégés, someone like Benjamin Peake for instance?

She could keep Peake in line if she had to, she knew, shrewdly measuring his familiar, well-proportioned body with her hazel eyes. Despite his Ph.D. in modern art, she doubted that he was as sharp as Jacob wanted to believe, but allowances were made because Peake had been a close friend of Jacob's son. They had met as fellow students at one of Meyer Schapiro's seminars on modern art at Columbia, and after Paul Munson's plane crashed, Jacob had transferred his paternal interest to Peake's career. Indeed, Ben Peake owed his present position here at the Breul House to Jacob, who had persuaded the other trustees to hire him after that fiasco up at the Friedinger left him out on his ear. Jacob would not stand idly by and watch this place go down while under Ben Peake's direction if there was something he could do to help.

But what?

In accent-free English, Søren Thorvaldsen leaned forward to explain the similarities between his acquisition of a fleet of cruise ships and the first Breul's fleet of canal barges. They were kindred spirits, it would seem, and like called to like even after a century and a half.

"As I understand it, your endowment has been much eroded by inflation and maintenance," said Thorvaldsen, his keen eyes flicking from Benjamin Peake to Jacob Munson.

"*Und?*" asked the older man.

"*Und* I would like to help. If Dr. Peake and your board agree, I could underwrite the expense of mounting a major retrospective of an important artist."

"The Breul House doesn't do that sort of thing," Jacob Munson snapped, yet curiosity piqued him. "Who?"

"Oscar Nauman."

The old man smoothed his thin gray beard and shook his head. "He will not do it."

"He might if *you* asked him," said Lady Francesca.

"My dear lady, I *haf* asked him. Many times."

"Miss Kohn?"

"Don't look at me," said Hester Kohn. "I'd love to mount a comprehensive retrospective of Nauman's work, but Jacob's right. He won't even discuss it seriously."

"But why?" asked Thorvaldsen.

Munson gave a palms-out gesture.

"I think he's superstitious," said Hester Kohn. "Some artists are. They think a retrospective's the kiss of death, the beginning of the end, an official assumption that they have nothing more to say."

"Nothing more to say?" exclaimed Thorvaldsen. "But this is a man who has found a dozen new voices in his lifetime."

Hester Kohn uncrossed her trousered legs and sat more erectly in her chair. "Are you by any chance represented by Dansksambler in Copenhagen?"

Thorvaldsen hesitated, then nodded.

" 'Autumnal' and 'Topaz Two,' " she told her elderly partner.

"So, Mr. Thorvaldsen, you own two pictures by Nauman?" asked Jacob Munson.

"Actually, I own eleven of his works and I'm told there are things in his studio that have never been exhibited." It was not quite a question and there was a touch of wistfulness in the big Dane's voice.

"What do you think, Jacob?" asked Benjamin Peake and he, too, sounded wistful.

"Hester is right," Munson told them with Teutonic finality. "Oscar will not agree to this."

Lady Francesca stretched an appealing hand toward him and her soft brown eyes melted into his. "Dear Mr. Munson! Have you not been Oscar Nauman's dealer for over thirty years? And if you were to explain to him the situation here at the Breul House and entreat him for old time's sake—?"

Munson considered and Peake rushed into the lull. "If you approached him, too, Lady Francesca," he said gallantly. "I'm sure you could make him agree. I've always heard that Oscar Nauman responds to beautiful women, right, Jacob?"

Her smile did not falter, thought Jacob Munson, and the old man gave her full marks for self-control. Nauman tried to keep his personal life private, but the artist was a public figure and rumors did get around.

Jacob was under the impression that Oscar's affair with Lady Francesca Leeds had ended more than a year ago. He seemed to recall that there was a fresh rumor making the rounds now. A lady fireman, was it?

Or dog catcher?

Something unusual anyhow. Leave it to Oscar.

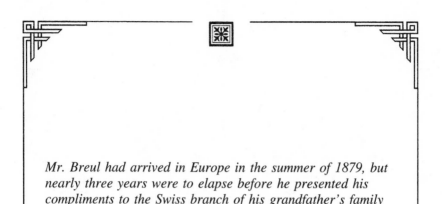

Mr. Breul had arrived in Europe in the summer of 1879, but nearly three years were to elapse before he presented his compliments to the Swiss branch of his grandfather's family in Zurich, where the Fürsts had been burghers since 1336.

In later years, Mr. Breul enjoyed to speak of that first encounter with his fair cousin, Sophie. Fresh snow had begun to fall as the young American crossed the park to the Fürst villa on the right bank of the lake. As he approached the gate, a small white dog darted through the railings, heedless of a girlish voice that called in vain. Though hardly dressed for the bitter weather, the impetuous girl had rushed from the house to rescue her wayward pet, undaunted by her thin shoes and indoor dress.

With the instant acumen that later marked his business dealings, Mr. Breul immediately grasped the situation and hastily captured the little dog by its collar before it could hurl itself beneath an oncoming carriage.

His quick action secured the young woman's gratitude, but when he insisted that she take his coat as protection against the falling snow, he won her heart from that moment forward.

ERICH BREUL — THE MAN AND HIS DREAM, PRIVATELY PUBLISHED 1924 BY THE FRIENDS AND TRUSTEES OF THE ERICH BREUL HOUSE

THREE

Sunday, December 13

EVEN BEFORE SHE was fully awake, Sigrid sensed a difference in the December morning light. And it wasn't just the difference between rural Connecticut and urban Manhattan either. She snuggled beneath a down comforter with her eyes half focused on one of Nauman's early oil paintings and drowsily noted a new clarity in the shifting planes of color, a new vibrancy.

A part of her brain cataloged the variance. The other part was still too drugged by sleep to care or analyze.

She yawned, turned over in the king-size bed, and abruptly caught her breath at what lay outside.

Oscar Nauman's house sprawled along the edge of a steep, thickly wooded hillside. With no near neighbors on that side, he had replaced his bedroom wall with sheets of clear glass so that nothing blocked her view of a tree-filled ravine that had transformed itself into a Currier and Ives print.

Yesterday's heavy gray sky was clear blue now and last night's thin flakes must have thickened sometime during the early morning hours because snow capped each twig and limb, softened the craggy rocks, and shone with such dazzling purity that sunlight was reflected inside to intensify Nauman's paintings and light up the room from unfamiliar angles.

A thoroughly urban creature, Lieutenant Sigrid Harald, NYPD, knew almost nothing about nature in the raw and, on the whole, rather mistrusted unpaved lanes and trackless forests. She cared little for wildflowers or for knowing the identity of birds hopping mindlessly around in treetops. An occasional *National Geographic* special on Channel 13 was her nearest link to wild animals.

Moreover, snow was usually an annoyance, dirty slushy stuff that got inside her boots or lay too long in messy heaps and, by alternately melting and refreezing, made city sidewalks treacherous for walking.

But to gaze out for the first time in years upon a virgin snowfall unsullied by any footsteps filled her with unexpected wonder.

She pushed herself upright in bed with Nauman's down comforter wrapped around her bare shoulders and watched a small black-capped bird try to perch on an ice-crusted twig just outside the window. It misjudged the ice's slickness and seemed startled when its feet slid out from under its first attempt at perching; but it recovered, settled onto the twig, and hunched into its gray feathers much as Sigrid hunched into the bedcovers.

Her breath puffed in visible little clouds and she felt a momentary twinge of solidarity with the bird. If it was cold in here, what must it be out there? And how did birds keep their unfeathered feet from freezing anyhow?

On the end wall opposite the bed, the stone hearth was black and lifeless. Nauman liked to sleep in an unheated room and last night's fire had already burned down to glowing embers before they fell asleep. She shivered and sank a bit deeper into the covers.

No sign of Nauman, of course. He was an early riser and had probably been up for hours.

According to the clock on the mantel, it was a quarter past eleven. Were she in her own apartment, Sigrid would have stretched contentedly and gone back to sleep. A weekends' greatest luxury was her freedom to drift in and out of sleep for several hours and she seldom rose before noon.

Nauman's Connecticut retreat offered better incentives to rise; nevertheless it took all the willpower she could muster to leave the warm bed and snatch up jeans and sweater.

Happily, the man's Spartan attitude toward cold bedrooms did not extend to his bath. The tiled floor felt pleasantly warm to her bare feet and the hot water was a benediction.

She showered, toweled the mirror free of fog, then ran a comb through her dark hair and pushed it into shape with her hands. Until October, her hair had been long and she'd worn it pulled straight back and pinned into a tight bun at the nape of her neck. Now ragged bangs swept over her strong forehead and the back was clipped short.

Smoothing moisturizer over her face, she hesitated over the other small bottles and tubes in her toiletry bag. Cosmetics were something else new in her life, and even though she enjoyed the sexual sizzle they sent through her body, she still lacked expertise with the intricacies of technique.

She would never be very pleased with her reflection—her face was too thin, her cheeks had never dimpled, her mouth was too wide—but she was starting to be satisfied with her eyes and the way her new bangs softened the former austerity. Cutting her hair seemed to have cut away some inhibitions as well, made her less reserved and awkward.

At least with Nauman.

Suddenly impatient to find him, she smudged on eye shadow and lip gloss and quickly dressed.

An aroma of coffee hung in the air and she followed it out to the kitchen, but that utilitarian room was empty save for the tantalizing smell of onions, herbs, and well-browned chicken now rising from the oven. Nauman cooked as instinctively as he painted and had evidently felt creative this morning. Sigrid poured herself a cup of strong dark liquid, pulled the plug on the coffee maker, and backtracked through the house to the end wing formed by the studio and its decks.

The lyrical intensity of a Martinu symphony was muffled by the double glass doors that led to Nauman's studio.

Essentially a huge sun porch, it was lined on both long walls with French windows that led to wide decks on either side. A high ceiling followed the pitch of the roof, accommodating two ten-foot easels; and with the snow outside today, the room was awash in brilliant natural light.

At the far end of the studio, beyond the thrift-shop of tables and cabinets that held his painting supplies, was a huge stone fireplace flanked by floor-to-ceiling bookcases. Oscar Nauman sat in one of the comfortable chairs pulled up before the blazing log fire and Sigrid paused to watch him relight his pipe.

He was half a head taller than she and a generation older with a lean hard body, piercing blue eyes, and thick silver hair that had finished turning white before he was thirty. They had sparred for six months, been lovers for six weeks, yet Sigrid was still unsure of her feelings for him— how much was sexual, how much emotional, and whether the two added up to that irrational state called love.

By nature and by training she was cool and analytical, but Oscar Nauman was the one element in her life that she consciously refused to analyze. Clearly he was too old, too quixotic, too opinionated, too self-centered. Why was she not heeding the logic of this?

Then Nauman's head came up, he smiled in her direction, and Sigrid's heart turned over. She smiled back and started to open the door before abruptly realizing that he was not alone, that his smile had been for a red-haired woman who now walked into Sigrid's view holding one of Nauman's pictures. Specific words were indistinct but her voice held a musical lilt.

With the snow reflecting so much dazzling sunlight into the studio, Sigrid knew she would not be seen if she retreated back down the shadowed hall and read the morning paper till the woman was gone. Two months ago, she might have done just that. She was still self-conscious with Nauman when around others but she was trying to overcome it. So she told herself that she lingered here only because she was uncertain if the woman had come for business or if her Sunday morning visit were purely social. Perhaps this was something neighbors did in the country?

There was only one way to find out.

Steadying the coffee cup in her left hand, she opened one of the glass doors. The others looked up as she entered.

This time, Nauman's smile *was* for her. "Come and meet Francesca," he said.

The visitor wore brown corduroy knickers crammed inside knee-length high-heeled brown boots and a loose pullover knitted in tones of russet and amber. Windswept auburn hair tangled itself around her fair face and her classic features appeared almost flawless as she put down the painting she'd been inspecting and came to Sigrid with her hand outstretched.

"I'm Francesca Leeds, and I'm so pleased to meet you at last," she said with a smile in her warm Irish voice. "Oscar's told me all about you."

"Has he?" Sigrid mumbled.

"Have I?" asked Nauman, frowning at a picture Lady Francesca had unearthed from earlier years.

"Well, somebody did, *acushla*. If not you, perhaps Hester Kohn or Doris Quinn." She turned back to Sigrid. "Anyhow, I know you're a police officer in the city. A detective, right?"

Sigrid nodded.

"And I'm an old friend of Oscar's come to talk him into saving one of New York's landmarks. You must help me persuade him."

There was something curiously familiar about the woman but Sigrid couldn't quite decide why. As Francesca Leeds described the Breul House's near destitution and the benefits an Oscar Nauman retrospective could provide, Sigrid had an opportunity to study her features more closely.

The bright glare of snowlight was not kind to the woman's skin. It washed out the golden tones and made her seem too pale. It also revealed tiny lines around her eyes and nose so that Sigrid revised her estimate of age upward. Instead of thirty, Francesca Leeds was probably closer to forty. Nevertheless, she remained a stunning creature with the sort of poised assurance that often destroyed Sigrid's.

Not this time, she told herself, making a conscious effort not to tighten up. But it was difficult. Despite the other woman's friendly smile and easy conversation, Sigrid knew that, she, too, was being studied and cataloged. She should have been used to it by now. Most of Nauman's friends fell into two camps: those who were amused by their relationship and those who were patently puzzled. Very few accepted her without question.

Lady Francesca appeared to have both amusement and curiosity well in hand and seemed bent on making Sigrid her ally as she pulled a small picture down from one of the racks.

"Think of it, Sigrid: Would you not love to see Oscar's whole career in one well-chosen show?"

"Pinned to the wall like a bunch of dead butterflies?" Nauman asked sardonically. "Forget it. Anyhow, you're talking to the wrong person. She doesn't like my work."

Francesca Leeds started to laugh, realized Oscar wasn't entirely joking, and looked at the thin brunette with fresh interest. "Really?"

Sigrid shrugged as she studied the small purple-and-black abstract Francesca had held out to her. "He exaggerates."

The implication not lost upon her ladyship, who knew something must exist before it can be exaggerated. How perfectly ironic that Oscar should be snared by someone indifferent to his artistic achievements, someone who could see him as a fallible man standing unclothed in fame and accomplishment. Francesca deliberately turned her mind away from the memory of Oscar's lean hard frame unclothed in anything, but there was veiled mirth in her brown eyes as she delicately probed, "Then your interests will be lying in music or literature, rather than the visual?"

"She's visual," Oscar said.

His rangy body continued to lounge in the deep chair, but his tone was sharper than necessary, defensive even?

Still holding the small oil from one of Oscar's middle periods, Sigrid glanced from one to the other, aware of a sudden tension in the air. She handed the violent abstract back to Francesca Leeds. "Even if I don't completely understand them, I do like some of Nauman's pictures."

Oscar abruptly leaned forward to poke the fire and add another log to the blaze. "Ask her anything about the late Gothic, though."

"Late Gothic? You mean Dürer? Baldung? Holbein?"

"And Lucas Cranach," Sigrid nodded. "Mabuse, too. And earlier, Jan van Eyck, of course."

"Ah," said Francesca, enlightened now. "The Flemish. Precision. Order." She waved her hand to encompass Oscar's cluttered studio, the vibrant abstractions, the large canvases slashed with color and free-flowing lines. "Anarchy repels you?"

"I *am* a police officer," Sigrid said lightly. "And I do know enough about modern art to know there's structure lurking in there somewhere."

Oscar laughed and stood up. "Stay for lunch, Francesca? I'm making my famous *coq au vin.*"

Francesca Leeds pushed back the heavy auburn hair from her face and turned her wrist to consult the small gold watch. "Can't, *acushla.* My hosts are expecting me back with their vehicle."

She smiled up at him as she reached for her brown suede jacket. "I'm not giving up, though. A retrospective's nothing like a ninth symphony, Oscar, and the Breul House really does need you."

She turned to Sigrid, who echoed the formulas of "so nice to meet you; perhaps we'll see each other again," and both were pleased to realize the formalities weren't totally insincere.

Exchanging comments on road conditions, icy patches, and the infrequency of snowplows through these back roads, Oscar and Sigrid followed Francesca out onto the deck. Oscar had cleared it earlier, as well as the steps leading down to the drive; but except for Francesca's single line of boot prints curving up from a borrowed van parked beside the road, the crusted snow around the house was unbroken.

"Driving's not bad," said Francesca. "The van has chains and four-wheel drive."

Even with all identifying landmarks blanketed by the snow, she seemed to know exactly how the drive curved, and walked confidently out to the van without tripping or putting a foot wrong. It was something Sigrid noted without actually considering as Francesca waved good-bye and called back, "At least you didn't say no."

"No!" Oscar grinned.

"Too late," she laughed and drove away in a flurry of snow.

Circling his studio to the rear deck, Oscar thoughtfully contemplated the ravine, where snow lay deep and crisp beneath pines and hardwoods so thickly branched that winter sunlight barely penetrated.

"The surface is too soft for conventional sleds," he observed.

Over the years, various visiting children had left plastic sliding sheets behind in the garage, and Oscar had discovered them while searching for a snow shovel.

His assertion that their appetites needed building sounded ridiculous to Sigrid, even as Nauman bundled her into a jacket and boots. Minutes later, she found herself alone upon a sheet of plastic, careening downhill on her stomach, half terrified and wholly exhilarated.

It was like being eight years old again—pushing off, oaring herself along with mittened hands, that slow gathering of speed, crashing through ice-coated grasses, dodging tree roots and low-lying branches, a belly-dropping sense of doom as she crested a small ridge and became briefly airborne before thudding back to cushioned earth again. Another straight shoot down the hillside and she hurtled toward a creek bank lined with dormant blackberry bushes and huge granite boulders, trying to judge exactly when she should come down hard with a braking foot to land in a laughing, tangled heap beside her companion.

Delighted by the sheer physicality of the experience, Sigrid unhooked her leg from Nauman's elbow and kissed him exuberantly.

By their fourth trip down, Oscar had a long briar scratch across his forehead and Sigrid had jammed her right index finger. Climbing back to the top of the ravine each time left them winded, wet, and red-cheeked, yet both were somehow reluctant to end this brief return to childhood pleasures and go inside.

On the other hand, warmth and the expectation of good food did offer certain inducements. Not to mention the adult pleasures of stripping off their wet clothes and rediscovering other physical joys.

"What are you smiling about?" Nauman asked suspiciously.

"I was thinking about raw clams on the half-shell."

"You want to eat first?"

"No." Her slender fingers touched the red scratch on his head, caressed his left ear, then slipped to his bare shoulder. "I was remembering my cousin Carl. One of my Southern cousins. He bought a cottage down on Harker's Island and it took him more than ten years before he'd even taste a raw clam. He's been trying to make up for lost time ever since."

"I don't know that I like being compared to raw clams," Nauman grumbled.

"But they're so delicious," she murmured wickedly, running her hand down his muscular flank.

Lunch was just as leisurely, and afterwards, Sigrid curled up in one of the large chairs before the fire in Nauman's studio and opened the *Times* to the puzzle page. The large crossword appeared to contain a humorous yuletide limerick, and she became so absorbed in penning in the answers that she didn't notice when Nauman, perched on a tall stool at his drawing table, began to sketch her, his pencil moving rapidly across the pages of his notebook.

He hadn't done a figurative portrait in years, not since his student days, probably, but there was something about her eyes, the line of her long neck, the angularity of the way she sat that intrigued him. If he could catch her on paper—

Sigrid glanced up. Nauman's eyes were a clear deep blue and the intelligence which usually blazed there had become remote and fathomless. She moved uneasily and saw the remoteness disappear as his eyes softened.

"What did Francesca Leeds mean when she said a retrospective isn't a ninth symphony?" she asked, abandoning her puzzle.

Nauman closed the notebook before she could become self-conscious and began to relight his pipe. "It's something that seemed to start with the composer Gustav Mahler."

He looked down at the elaborately carved pipe in his hand as if he'd never before seen it. Today's was shaped like a dragon's head and fragrant smoke curled from the bowl.

"Mahler noticed that Beethoven and Bruckner had both died after composing ninth symphonies, so he decided nine was a jinx. Tried to cheat—*Das Lied von der Erde* after his eighth. Said it wasn't a symphony—was, though. Decided he was being silly, wrote his ninth. Died before he finished his tenth. Dvořák and Vaughan Williams, too."

"But surely that's a coincidence?" From the way Nauman's speech had suddenly become telegraphic, Sigrid knew he was absorbed by parallel lines of thought. "By the time a composer reaches his ninth symphony, wouldn't he be old and near the end of his life anyhow?"

"Like an artist with a retrospective," Nauman said bleakly.

"Then you *are* superstitious?"

"And you're avoiding the issue. I'll be sixty goddamned years old next July, old enough to be your—"

"How many symphonies did Mozart compose?" she interrupted.

"Hell, I don't know. Forty or fifty."

"And he was thirty-five when he died. How many retrospectives do you think Picasso had before he kicked off at the tender age of—what was it? Ninety? Ninety-one?"

"Okay, okay." Nauman smiled, holding up his hands in surrender. "I'll do it."

"Only if you want to," Sigrid murmured demurely, and suddenly they were no longer talking about art exhibits.

BURRIS BROTHERS, DRY GOODS
806 Broadway

To Acct. of: Mr. Erich Breul   Aug. 25th, 1900
              7 Sussex Square
              New York City

Parasol, blue silk..$1.25
Hamburg edging, 2" wide
20 yds. @ $0.06 per yd...1.20
2 silk glove cases @ $0.55 ea...1.10
Linen napkins, 3 doz. @ $0.50 per doz. 1.50
                                                                    $5.05

                "We allow 3 per cent. discount for cash."

_____

May 6, 1901, from Wm. Fenton & Co.,
    Agents for Genevieve Carlton:
    "Maeve's Gallop"...$200.
    Frame 12.50
                                                                    $212.50

July 22, 1901, from Atwater & Sons:
    Babbage engr., "Running Sea" $22.
        Frame   6.
                                                                    $28.

_____

MISCELLANEOUS BILLS AND MEMORANDA
(FROM THE ERICH BREUL HOUSE COLLECTION)

FOUR

Tuesday, December 15

BENJAMIN PEAKE ARRIVED at the Erich Breul House shortly after ten to find his office invaded by Roger Shambley, Ph.D., scholar, newest trustee, and all-around bastard.

Shambley was shorter than his own five eleven by a good six inches and ugly as a mud fence with a dark, shaggy head that was two sizes too large for his small, stooped figure. As far as Benjamin Peake was concerned, expensive hairstyling and custom-tailored clothes were probably what kept children from throwing rocks whenever Shambley passed them in the street.

"Can I help you with something?" Peake asked sarcastically as Shambley ignored his arrival and continued to paw through the filing cabinets at the end of his long L-shaped office. He had to stand on tiptoe to read the files at the back of the top drawer.

"I doubt it." Shambley paused beside the open drawer and made a show of checking his watch against the clock over the director's beautiful mahogany desk. "I've only been here two weeks to your two years but I probably know more about what's in these files than you do."

"Now let me think," Peake responded urbanely as he hung his topcoat in a concealed closet and smoothed his brown hair. "I believe it was William Buckley who spoke of the scholar-squirrel mentality, busily gathering every little stray nut that's fallen from the tree of knowledge."

"Actually, it was Gore Vidal," said Shambley, "but don't let facts spoil your pleasure in someone else's well-turned phrases. I'm sure Buckley's said something equally clever about academic endeavor."

Annoyed, Benjamin Peake retreated through an inner door that led to the butler's pantry.

Hope Ruffton was pouring herself a cup of freshly brewed coffee and she greeted him with a pleasant smile.

When Peake took over the directorship and was introduced to her two years ago, he'd returned that first smile with condescending friendliness. "Hope, isn't it?"

"Only if it's Ben," she'd replied with equally friendly condescension.

"Oh. Well. Excuse *me*, Ms. Ruffton."

"Miss will do," she'd said pleasantly.

If he'd had the authority and if old Jacob Munson hadn't been standing by, twinkling and beaming at them like some sort of Munchkin matchmaker, Peake would have fired her then and there.

He still did not completely understand how foolish that would have been although there were times when he uneasily suspected it. But he did soon realize that professionalism was more than semantics to Miss Ruffton. She had ignored his sulks and, with cool efficiency and tact, had deflected him from stupid blunders as he settled into the directorship. The irony of being trained for his position by a nominal subordinate went right over Peake's head and Hope Ruffton was too subtle by far to let him see her own amusement.

These days, with Roger Shambley poking his nose into every cranny and making veiled allusions to certain lapses of competence, Miss Ruffton's efficiency gave Peake a sort of Dutch courage. He might not always have a clear grasp of details, but Miss Ruffton did; and without articulating it, not even to himself, Peake trusted her not to let him make a total ass of himself in front of Shambley.

So he smiled at her gratefully, accepted the coffee she poured for him, and said, "You look like a Christmas card this morning."

A Victorian card, he would have added, straightening his own red-and-green striped tie, except that he was afraid she might tartly remind him that most Victorian cards pictured only blond, blue-eyed Caucasian maidens. Her white silk blouse was tucked into a flowing skirt of dark green wool and it featured a high tight collar and cuffs, all daintily edged in lace. Her thick black hair was brushed into a smooth chignon and tied with a red grosgrain ribbon that echoed a red belt at her waist and clear red nails on her small brown fingers. She wore a simple gold locket and her drop earrings were old-fashioned garnets set in gold filigree that caught the light as she returned Peake's greeting.

"Too bad about the MacAndrews Foundation," she said.

"They turned us down *again?*"

Miss Ruffton nodded, her dark eyes sympathetic. "I left the letter on your desk."

"Oh well," he said, trying to make the best of it, "we weren't really counting on their support."

She gazed into her coffee cup with detachment. There was no way to break bad news gently. "But we *were* counting on Tybault Industries."

His thinly handsome face grew anxious. "They've withdrawn their annual donation?"

"Cut it," she said succinctly. "By a third. With a hint that it may be cut by another third next year."

"Oh, God!" Peake moaned, pacing back and forth from his office door on one side of the room to the dining room door on the far side. "Whatever happened to good old-fashioned altruism?"

"At least the projection figures look good on the Friends membership drive," she said, but Peake refused to be comforted.

"Penny-ante. We've got to find a way to raise more real money or the Erich Breul House is going right down the slop chute," he predicted gloomily.

He started back to his office and hesitated, remembering that Shambley was probably still there.

"What is Dr. Shambley really looking for?" asked Miss Ruffton, with that uncanny knack she had of reading his thoughts.

"God knows," he muttered drearily. "Fresh material for his new book on late nineteenth-century American artists, I suppose." And then, although Peake seldom consciously picked up on Miss Ruffton's subtle inflections, her last words sank in and triggered an automatic alert. "What did you mean 'really'?"

"We've allowed other historians access to the Breul papers," she said slowly. "Dr. Kimmelshue always granted permission. And not just artists or art historians. We've had antique dealers, students of interior design—"

"Well?" Peake asked impatiently.

Miss Ruffton looked at him coldly. "Perhaps it was only my imagination," she said and turned away.

"I'm sorry," he apologized. "Please go on."

But already she had opened the door to the service hall beneath the main stairs, the quickest route to her own desk, and she did not look back.

"*Merde!*" Peake muttered beneath his breath and charged back into his office.

"Listen, Shambley," he said to the historian's slender back, "what are you really looking for?"

"Mi scusi?" Whenever he wished to insult, obfuscate, or stall until he'd chosen his next words, Roger Shambley always affected Italian. He lifted his oversized shaggy head from a low file drawer. "Why should you think I'm looking for something special?"

"You've spent the last few days quartering this house like a bird dog," said Peake, abruptly realizing that this was true. "All the Breul papers are up in the attic. What do you expect to find in old Kimmelshue's files?"

"Merely fulfilling my duties as a trustee," Shambley said smoothly. "Familiarizing myself with past routine. And present. Which reminds me: Why are there no current inventory sheets? I find nothing later than 1972."

"The inventory hasn't changed enough to justify a new one," Peake snapped. "All the corrections have been noted on our master copy."

He strode over to the file cabinet nearest his desk and extracted the inventory folder. "I can have Miss Ruffton make you a copy, if you wish."

"You checked it thoroughly against the contents of the house when you took over?" asked Shambley.

"Well, no. I saw no need when—"

Shambley cut him off with a sneer. "You know what's wrong with you, Peake? You're lazy. Physically and intellectually. That's why you fouled up at the Friedinger." His eyes narrowed speculatively in his ugly face. "Or was it solely that?"

"What's that supposed to mean?" asked Peake, becoming cautious.

"I think it's time the board asked for a complete inventory. See if there's been any 'unauthorized deaccessioning' down here." He closed the file drawers he'd opened earlier and took the inventory folder from Peake's suddenly nerveless fingers.

"Listen," Benjamin Peake blustered, "if anything's missing, you can't blame me. Everyone knows Dr. Kimmelshue was senile the last three years before he died. Anything could have happened then."

Roger Shambley turned his huge head and haughtily waved Peake aside. *"Permésso,"* he said languidly and left the office.

Mrs. Beardsley was becoming heartily sick of Dr. Roger Shambley's *permésso.* In a house this size, one would think a body that small could find a clear space in which to pass without shooing people aside as if they were witless flocks of chickens. And she wasn't taken in by his air of haughty politeness. Mrs. Beardsley knew all there was to know about using manners as a stick to beat those one considered inferior to oneself. Not that she ever did, she told herself.

Well, not without provocation, she amended.

She would admit that she was disappointed when Dr. Shambley received the trusteeship she had sought. She might not have his degrees or his growing reputation as an art scholar, but certainly she knew more about the soul of this house itself than any outsider could hope to. And her income was several times his. She'd checked. Considering the Breul House's financial difficulties, a trustee willing to give generous support should have counted for something, shouldn't it? Nevertheless, she had swallowed her disappointment and welcomed him as graciously as possible and what did she get for her graciousness?

Permésso.

Uptown, in the business office of Kohn and Munson Gallery, Hester Kohn listened in growing alarm as Benjamin Peake screamed in her ear about Roger Shambley.

"For God's sake, Ben, get hold of yourself," she interrupted crisply. "*Have* you taken anything from the house?"

"Of course, I haven't!" he howled.

"Then you've nothing to worry about."

"Yes, I have and you do, too, Hester. You didn't hear the way he said 'unauthorized deaccessions.' That bastard! He picks things out of the air. You know what art historians are like."

"Give them a flake of blue plaster and they'll prove a Giotto fresco once covered the wall," the woman sighed. She looked up as her secretary entered with a letter that required her signature. "Hold on a minute, Ben," she said and tucked the phone between her shoulder and ear while she signed, then told the secretary, "I want to see those consignment sheets before you call the shippers, and don't forget to remind Mr. Munson about tomorrow night."

She waited until the secretary had closed the door behind her, then spoke into the receiver. "There's no way Roger Shambley will start speculating about what really happened unless you give him that first flake of plaster."

But for several long minutes after she'd hung up, her hazel eyes were lost in thought as she wondered if she'd made a mistake in encouraging Jacob to sponsor Shambley on the Breul House's board of trustees. She'd considered it a minor quid pro quo when Shambley approached her about the vacancy in October. She didn't know how Shambley had heard about her tutorial sessions with young Rick Evans or how he knew she'd prefer Jacob not to learn of them, but smoothing his way onto the board seemed a small price to pay for his silence.

Not that he'd been crass enough to threaten her. Open confrontation was not Shambley's way. The man was oblique indirection: a lifted eyebrow, a knowing twitch of his lips, a murmured phrase of ironic Italian. His victim's guilty conscience would do the rest.

Only . . . had she drastically mistaken which situation Shambley meant her to feel guilty about?

In the office across the hall, Jacob Munson unwrapped a peppermint drop from the bowl on his desk. He had not intended to eavesdrop on the conversation between Benjamin and Hester and had almost announced his presence on their line when something in Benjamin's voice kept him silent. A lover's quarrel, he'd thought at first.

When he'd realized last year that Hester and Benjamin were occasional lovers, he'd hoped that it might lead to marriage. Thirty-four, Hester was, and time was running out if she wanted children.

That would have made an appropriate solution to the gallery's uncertain future—Horace's daughter and the best friend of Jacob's only son. To his disappointment though, their relationship had never gotten out of bed. When dressed, they didn't even seem to like each other most of the time. So what was all this about plaster flakes?

He sighed and absently tucked the cellophane candy wrapper into his pocket. Maybe it was a sign. Maybe blood was best after all. Surely it was not too late to train young Richard to carry on the Munson heritage at Kohn and Munson?

By closing time, Rick Evans had shot the last roll of film that he'd brought with him to the Breul House. He climbed down from Pascal's tall aluminum stepladder and unplugged the floodlights he'd used to light the plaster moldings on the ceiling of the third floor hallway.

"I guess we'll call it a day," he told Pascal Grant, and began packing up his cases.

Pascal bent to help, his smooth face so near Rick could have touched it with his own. His beautiful eyes met Rick's trustingly. "Will you need my ladder anymore, Rick?"

"Not for now."

They collapsed the light stands and carried everything through the frosted glass doors, down to the end of the hall and the mannequin maid, where they loaded it all on the dumbwaiter—easier than carting everything up and down by hand. Together they carried the ladder down the back service steps and unloaded the dumbwaiter down in the basement next to Pascal's room.

"Want to go get a pizza?" Pascal asked hopefully when they had stowed Rick's equipment in an empty cabinet. "We can eat it in my room and listen to some more jazz."

Rick hesitated; then, with a fatalistic *que sera sera* shrug of his shoulders, he nodded.

"Dr. Shambley?"

The patrician voice floated through the marble hall, startling him as he descended the main staircase, now dimly lit. For a moment, he almost thought he'd been addressed by the elegant female mannequin on the landing. Then he realized it was that Beardsley woman speaking to him from the doorway of the darkened gallery beyond the massive fireplace.

"*Cretina!*" Roger Shambley mumbled under his breath. He thought everyone had left for the day and that he was alone except for the simple-minded janitor somewhere in the bowels of the house.

Mrs. Beardsley turned off the lights in the cloakroom, leaving only the security lights in the hall, then buttoned her red wool coat and pulled on her gloves. "You won't forget to let Pascal know when you're leaving tonight, will you, Dr. Shambley? The burglar alarm wasn't switched on till almost midnight last night because he thought you were still here."

"I'll remember," he said brusquely. "*Buona notte.*"

Dismissing her, he crossed the hall and entered the library, pettishly turning on the lights she had extinguished only moments before.

A slam of the front door restored the earlier silence. Already, the automatic thermostat had begun to lower the temperature here. For a moment, he contemplated finding the master control and turning it up again, then decided it was pointless.

He'd begun to despair of finding the letters he knew Erich Jr. must have written during his brief months in France. He had already leafed through all the personal papers still stored in Erich Breul's library. Except for that one tantalizing letter misfiled in the attic, there was nothing later than the spring of 1911 when young Breul wrote to say how pleased he was that both parents were coming to Harvard, that he'd reserved rooms for them at Cambridge's best hotel for graduation weekend, and that "although you will find her much altered since her father's death, Miss Norton trusts that her health will enable her to receive you at Shady-hill."

Charles Eliot Norton! Shambley had marveled when he read that. One of the patron saints of fine arts—an intimate of Ruskin, Carlyle, Lowell, and Longfellow—and the Breuls, *padre e figlio*, had been guests in his home!

Disconsolate, Shambley twirled Erich Breul's large globe in its teak stand. Those letters might as well be in Timbuktu for all the chance he had of finding them at this point.

Sophie Breul had saved her son's toys, his schoolwork, his best clothes. Surely she would have saved his letters as well. Yet he'd exhausted all the logical places and no more of Erich Jr.'s last letters were to be found.

He gave the globe a final twirl, switched off the lights, and crossed the hall to the cloakroom for his overcoat, the hollow sound of his footsteps on the marble floor echoing eerily from the walls all around him.

He started to leave, remembered Mrs. Beardsley's injunction, and descended the stairs to the basement, muttering to himself. As if he had nothing better to do than remind another cretin of his duties!

At the bottom of the steps, Roger Shambley paused, uncertain exactly where the janitor's room was. Lights were on along the passageway beyond the main kitchen and he followed them, noting the storerooms on either side. Late last week he had checked through the racks of pictures that Kimmelshue had consigned to the basement on the off chance that the old fart really had been as senile as Peake claimed. A waste of time. No silk purses hiding among those sows' ears.

No pictures stacked behind that pile of cast-off furniture, trunks, and rolled carpets, or—

He stopped, thunderstruck.

Trunks?

Slowly, almost holding his breath, he found the light switch, pulled a large brown steamer trunk into an open space, and opened it.

Inside were books, men's clothing, turn-of-the-century toilet articles, and a handful of—*Dio mio*, yes! Programs from Parisian theaters, a menu from a Montparnasse café, and catalogs from various art exhibits.

Excitedly, he pawed to the bottom. A few innocuous souvenirs, more clothing, nothing else. Erich Breul Jr.'s last effects didn't even fill one trunk.

Well, what did you really expect? he jeered at himself.

Retaining the catalogs, he shoved the large trunk back in place and lifted the lid of the smaller one to see yellowed feminine apparel, an autograph album from Sophie Breul's childhood, and what looked like an embroidered glove case. He almost pushed it aside without opening it, but scholarly habit was too strong and as soon as he looked, he knew he'd found treasure: fourteen fat envelopes, thick with European postage stamps. The top one was postmarked August 1911 and had been mailed from Southampton, England; the last from Lyons in *Octobre* 1912. And *si! si! SI!*—near the bottom was an envelope postmarked XXXI *Août 1912*.

His hand was shaking so that he could hardly read the faded city. Lyons?

If he remembered rightly from his one course in Post-Impressionism, Sorgues lay south of Lyons in the Rhône River valley.

In 1912, Pablo Picasso and Georges Braque, the co-founders of cubism, had spent the summer in Sorgues, where, in a burst of creativity, the two friends had invented the first collages.

For a moment, as he experienced a pure rush of excitement, Shambley's ugly face was almost attractive. Here was every scholar's dream: the discovery of primary documents, a chance to become a permanent footnote in history. He wanted to sit down and read them immediately; but innate, self-serving caution made him put the letters back in the glove case and slide it and the catalogs into his briefcase until he could be certain of no interruptions.

Leaving the storage room as he'd found it, he switched off the light and retraced his steps. Beyond the stairs, he noticed a door that was slightly ajar, and when he pushed it open, he realized he'd found the janitor's bedroom. No janitor, though.

In his state of excitement, the room's ornate sensuousness neither surprised nor interested him. All he cared about was scribbling the dummy a note—assuming the dummy could read—that he'd left the house for the evening.

He propped the note on the mantelpiece and, from force of habit, read the signature of the saccharine oil painting there. Idly, his eyes drifted over the posters with which the janitor had lined his walls and at the doorway, he paused, amused by the coincidence of seeing a reproduction of an early Braque collage when his head was so full of the possibility that Erich Breul had actually met Braque.

He hesitated, eyes on the poster. Braque or Picasso?

In later years even Picasso had trouble identifying which works were his and which were Braque's, so why should he be any more knowledgeable? The wood-grained paper overlapping a sketchy violin said Braque, but something about the lines of the head—a monkey's head?—said Picasso.

Curious, Shambley leaned closer, searching for a signature. There was none. Suddenly, a frisson of absolute incredulity shot through his very soul. This wasn't some poster issued by the Museum of Modern Art. That scrap of yellowed newsprint at the edge of the picture was real! He ran his hand ever so lightly across the surface of the picture and felt the irregularities where one piece of paper had been layered over another.

Very gently, he removed the bottom two thumbtacks by which the paper was held to the wall and lifted it up. With a minimum of contortion, he could read the words scrawled in charcoal on the back by two clearly different hands: "*A notre petit singe américain—Picasso et G. Braque.*"

Hardly daring to breathe, he carefully replaced the thumbtacks precisely as before and moved to the two pictures nearby. Even in this soft light, he could now see that they, too, were no mere reproductions but oil paintings unmistakably by Fernand Léger, another master of cubism. Indeed, the canvases still held faint crease marks from where they had been rolled and squashed.

The trunk, Shambley thought. The collage was small enough to lie flat on the bottom, but the pictures must have crossed the Atlantic rolled up in that trunk and there they'd stayed for the next seventy-five years because Kimmelshue had his ass stuck firmly in the nineteenth century and Peake was too damn lazy to get off his. A goddamned fortune thumbtacked to a janitor's bedroom wall.

"And little ol' *piccolo mio*'s the only one who knows," he gloated, wanting to kick up his heels and gambol around the room.

The distant sound of a closing door and young male voices raised in laughter alerted him. He quickly snatched up his note and stepped outside, pulling the door shut just as Rick Evans and Pascal Grant walked into the main kitchen carrying pizza and a bottle of Chianti.

Shambley was startled. Young Evans he'd met and had treated with courtesy because of his relationship to Jacob Munson, but he had never really looked at the janitor. The guy usually had his head down or his back turned when Shambley was around and he always wore rough green coveralls and mumbled when he spoke.

Tonight, Grant was dressed in tight Levi's and a beige suede jacket, his blond curls had been tossed by the icy December wind, his fair skin was flushed with cold, and his face, his beautiful face, was so animated with laughter that it was impossible to believe that he was the same slow-witted Quasimodo who had ducked in and out of his presence these last two weeks.

The two youths halted at the sight of him. Pascal Grant's laughter died and he lowered his head fearfully as they waited for the trustee to speak.

"A party?" Shambley asked. He'd meant to sound friendly, but it came out a sneer and for some reason, Munson's grandson flushed.

Instantly, Shambley knew why and was swept with a jealousy that he could hardly conceal. Deliberately, he walked over to Grant, put out his small hand, and lifted that soft round chin, but the handyman trembled and wouldn't meet his eyes.

"Take your nasty hand off him!" Rick Evans snarled, stepping toward him.

"Or you'll what?" asked Shambley. "Give me a proper thrashing?"

Without waiting for an answer, he released Grant and waved them both aside. "I'll let myself out this way. *Buona sera.* Enjoy your"—he let his voice turn lewd—"pizza. Or whatever."

As he passed through the shadowed passage to the front door, he almost forgot his first discoveries in the contemplation of this last: old Jacob Munson's grandson a *femminella.* Well, well, well.

Back in the warm security of his nest-like room, Pascal Grant rubbed his chin where Roger Shambley had touched him. "I don't like him, Rick."

"I don't either," Rick Evans said and his soft Louisiana voice was grim.

On any clear winter night, Søren Thorvaldsen could look upriver from his desk and see the distant George Washington Bridge strung across the Hudson like a Victorian dowager's diamond necklace, but it was not half so beautiful to him as the cruise ship docked almost directly below his office window. The *Sea Dancer* was lit from stem to stern by her own glittering lights and she would sail on Saturday with eighteen hundred winter-weary customers.

A soft trill drew him from the window back to his desk where a winking button on his telephone console signaled a call on his private line.

"Thorvaldsen here."

"*Velkommen hjem,* Thorvaldsen." A gurgle of Irish laughter warmed her golden voice as Lady Francesca Leeds stumbled over the word for home.

Her attempts at Danish amused him. "I tried to call you from the airport," he said.

"I know," she replied. "I'm sorry. I was tied up with a client tonight."

He looked at his watch. Nearly ten. "Is it too late for a nightcap?"

"I'm afraid so," she murmured regretfully. "But I have good news for you."

"Oscar Nauman's agreed?"

"Not exactly. But he hasn't said no, either, and this is the closest anyone's come yet. I've arranged a small cocktail party tomorrow evening at the Erich Breul House. Jacob Munson's going to bring Nauman to look at the space. You'll come?"

"*Helt sikkert!*" he assured her happily.

Her voice turned teasingly miffed. "I think you'd rather see Oscar Nauman than me."

He laughed as she said *godnat* and hung up, but her teasing held a shadow of truth. Francesca Leeds excited him more than any woman in years. It wasn't solely because she so outranked him in birth, although bedding a woman out of his class had always been an aphrodisiac. It was her special blend of sophistication and earthiness that was so irresistible to the self-made Dane, who had learned to hold his own in the drawing room without ever quite forgetting what went on out in the kitchen. She was capricious enough to keep him off balance, uncertain of victory.

Yet past successes, spiced with a tinge of cynicism, let him savor the chase. For the first time, he enjoyed prolonging the preliminaries. Inevitably, she must surely come to his bed.

In the meantime, Oscar Nauman was even less predictable and Thorvaldsen looked forward to meeting the artist whose pictures had given him so much pleasure, pictures that were as much a reward for his years of hard work as sex with a beautiful woman.

"A party?" Sigrid asked, dismayed. "I'm no good at parties, Nauman. You should know that by now."

"I want you to meet Munson. You don't have to dress up. Besides," he reminded her, "you're the one who thinks I ought to have this retrospective, so you might as well come along and see the place. Meet me there at seven and we'll have dinner afterwards."

Remembering that her housemate had mentioned something about a pickled boar's head in honor of the season, Sigrid decided that a party was probably the lesser of tomorrow's two evils.

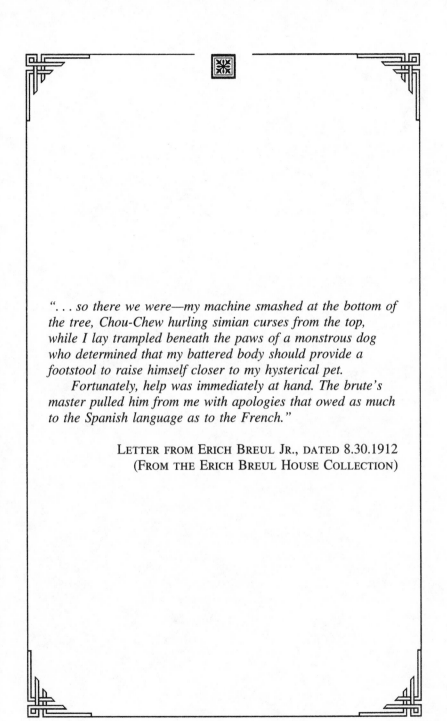

"... so there we were—my machine smashed at the bottom of the tree, Chou-Chew hurling simian curses from the top, while I lay trampled beneath the paws of a monstrous dog who determined that my battered body should provide a footstool to raise himself closer to my hysterical pet.

Fortunately, help was immediately at hand. The brute's master pulled him from me with apologies that owed as much to the Spanish language as to the French."

LETTER FROM ERICH BREUL JR., DATED 8.30.1912
(FROM THE ERICH BREUL HOUSE COLLECTION)

FIVE

Wednesday, December 16

THE CATERERS ARRIVED at the Erich Breul House shortly after six, and Mrs. Beardsley, delegated by Lady Francesca Leeds, was there to direct them through the door under the main stairs and into the butler's pantry.

In the dining room, the formal table was relieved of its extra leaves and draped in dark red linen with green plaid runners. The caterers had brought their own silver-plated canapé trays and their own chafing dish for the hot hors d'oeuvres, but the dozen or so sterling candelabra that would soon light the long room with tall white tapers belonged to the house.

An arrangement of cedar, red-berried holly, and shiny magnolia leaves had been delivered earlier, and as Mrs. Beardsley centered it between the candles, Pascal Grant paused with table leaves in his arms. "Do you want me to do anything else, Mrs. Beardsley? Bring up some more chairs?"

She glanced about the room. Sophie Breul's Sheraton dining table could be expanded to seat forty, but twenty chairs were its normal complement and Lady Francesca had said tonight's party was to be quite small.

"Just three or four of the trustees, Dr. Peake and his secretary, the art people, Mr. Thorvaldsen, and of course *you*, Mrs. Beardsley. When Oscar Nauman asks about the history of the Breul House, we must have someone who can tell him."

Mrs. Beardsley had known she was being buttered, but that didn't diminish her pleasure. It was such smooth butter. Now she smiled at Pascal Grant. "I think we have enough chairs for anyone who might wish to sit. You go ahead to your movie, Pascal, and you needn't worry about coming up later. We'll put everything back as it was first thing tomorrow. Just don't forget the alarm when you come back tonight."

"I won't, Mrs. Beardsley. Good night, Mrs. Beardsley."

"Good night, dear," she said absently, giving the room a final check.

Everything seemed quite under control. Gas logs blazed upon the open hearth next to the glittering Christmas tree and together, they lent the great marble hall an almost Dickensian warmth and cheer. Paneled pocket doors between the drawing room and gallery to the left of the hall had been pushed back to form one long open room and a hired pianist was familiarizing himself with the baby grand at the street end of the drawing room. The caterers had set up their bar in the pantry, appetizing odors were coming from the oven, and Miss Ruffton had returned from the cloakroom wearing a red skirt shot through with gold threads, a gold ribbon in her hair, and a party smile on her face. Even Dr. Peake had changed his tie before drifting in to lift the domed lid of the largest silver chafing dish and sample a hot savory.

"It's beginning to look a lot like Christmas," he said, licking his fingers like a mischievous boy.

Earlier in the afternoon, Mrs. Beardsley had slipped across the square and changed into her own holiday dress, a black wool sheath topped by a red Chanel jacket, her grandmother's three-strand pearl choker and earrings, and an emerald-and-ruby pin that seemed appropriate for the season. Now she decided it was time to complete her own costume, to exchange her sensible low pumps for the patent leather T-straps waiting for her in the cloakroom.

As she crossed the hall, the door swung open for Francesca Leeds, her windswept red hair swirling upon the collar of a dark mink coat, which she wore like a cloak over an evening suit of raw gold silk. "Show time!" she caroled.

Uptown, along the broad avenues, Salvation Army Santas were jostled for sidewalk space by three-card monte dealers and free-lance Santas who hawked "genuine Rolex watches, jus' twenny dollar—check it out" between nips from their hip flasks.

Skaters twirled and circled before the blazing tree at Rockefeller Center; a string quartet sheltered in the street-level jog of a huge skyscraper to play German carols, while an artist chalked the sidewalk in front of St. Thomas's Church with an ambitious choir of angels. Further up Fifth Avenue, wide-eyed toddlers, blissfully indifferent to the monetary worth of diamonds and rubies, were lifted up by their parents to watch Muppets romp among the gems in Tiffany's windows.

As customers streamed through the doorways of lavishly decorated stores, seasonal Muzak occasionally floated out to mingle with the Salvation Army bells. The vaguely religious music fell equally upon the warmly dressed and upon the shabby bundles of rags who tried to hunker deeper into the few dark corners. For many, the street people added just the right tinge of guilt to the general thank-God-*I'm*-making-it aura of self-satisfaction, a sort of memento mori that made modern yuletide hedonism all the more pleasurable.

In the art gallery just off Fifth Avenue, Oscar Nauman refilled his empty cup from the fat china pot on Jacob Munson's desk, leaned back in the comfortable leather chair, and smiled at his friend. "I must be getting old, Jacob, when I prefer your hot chocolate to your cold whiskey."

"*Ja*, sure," the old man jeered, unwrapping another of his perpetual peppermints. They were imported from France especially for him and were made with particularly pungent oils that bit the tongue and almost compensated for his forbidden cigarettes. "Wait till you are my age. At least you don't have doctors telling you what you can drink. I look at you, Oscar, and I see still the boy who first came through this door with those charcoal drawings of Lila under his arm."

"The hair," said Oscar.

It was true. That thick mane of hair had turned completely white before he was thirty. His height helped, as did the probing intelligence in his intensely blue eyes, but it was the white hair that gave him such an aura of timelessness. Munson tried to look at him objectively, to catalog the fine wrinkles around his eyes, the lines beneath his firm chin, but it was hard to perceive the softening of age in that strong face. He did recognize that inward-turning melancholy however. Lila's name still had that power.

If only the woman would die, he thought. Die or be cured. God knows she'd tried to kill herself often enough in the past twenty-five years. Jacob sipped his cocoa and refrained from looking at Oscar's left ear. He knew that the scars Lila's knife had left there were almost invisible. And the scars on Oscar's psyche should have faded as well, but how could they while the woman remained alive in that prison for the criminally insane?

"I'm sorry," he murmured. "I'm a stupid old man to mention her."

"It isn't just Lila." Nauman cradled the cup with the fingertips of both hands and gazed at it bleakly. "That's the worst of this retrospective business, Jacob. I'll have to look again at so many things I thought I was finished with. I don't think I want to do that."

"For a *real* retrospective, perhaps not," Munson agreed, stroking his wispy beard. "But the Breul House—this we will treat like a preview, *ja?*" he said coaxingly. "The space is small. Friendly. This you will do for your old friend?"

"Preview?" Nauman growled.

"*Ja*, sure. How much longer can I keep working, Oscar? I tell you alone: I am eighty-two. Most men my age are dead but I cannot retire before we do your retrospective." He tried to sound frail and pathetic, but his small body was still too wiry and agile and there was a jaunty glint in his black eyes. "You are killing me."

"*Ja*, sure," Oscar said sardonically.

The office door was ajar and Hester Kohn, vivid in red and purple, stuck her head in. The lush scent of her gardenia perfume floated in ahead of her.

"Car's here," she said, holding out Jacob's coat and muffler.

Munson beamed. "Good, good! Now we meet your lady fireman."

"Lady policeman," Oscar grinned.

Sigrid had intended to leave work early enough to allow herself plenty of time for a long hot shower and a leisurely hour to dress, but in the late afternoon, she'd been called to an unexpected meeting that ran past six-thirty.

If she hoped to make Sussex Square before the party was over, Sigrid knew she could forget about that shower, much less changing into something more glamorous than the shapeless black wool suit and white turtleneck sweater she'd pulled from her closet this morning.

She rummaged in her shoulder bag and found a tube of lipstick and some mascara. She'd been running late the day before yesterday and had planned to duck into the locker room here at work, then completely forgot about makeup as soon as she saw the papers that had accumulated on her desk over the weekend.

Well, mascara and lipstick were better than nothing, she thought, and headed for the locker room where she washed her face and hands, pushed her hair into place and started on her eyes.

It looked so simple when other women did it. And really, what was so difficult? A steady hand, a bit of bravura and *voilà!*

"Oh, damn!"

"Something wrong, Lieutenant?"

Sigrid whirled to see Detective Elaine Albee peering around the bank of lockers.

"No." She turned back to the mirror where she saw that the pretty blond officer was frankly staring at the smeared dark black rings around her eyes.

Sigrid was torn with frustration and embarrassment. "I'm supposed to be at a cocktail party in Sussex Square in exactly thirteen minutes and I look like a goddamned panda!"

"I was wondering if someone had given you a black eye," the younger woman ventured. This was the first time she'd ever known the lieutenant to worry about her looks and Elaine wasn't quite sure how to react. Lieutenant Harald could freeze a blast furnace with her tongue when annoyed.

"It's probably because the light's so bad in here," she said diplomatically.

"This is ridiculous," Sigrid said, grimly washing off the smeared mascara. "I'll just call and say I can't make it."

"Let me help," Albee offered. "I keep a few things in my locker for emergencies."

"You have emergencies like this?" Sigrid asked curiously. "You always look so put together."

"Come with me," Elaine grinned and Sigrid soon found herself seated on a bench in front of the other woman's locker.

Five minutes later, her eyes were expertly lined and shadowed, the planes of her cheeks subtly enhanced with blusher, her lips—

"My lip gloss is wrong for you," Elaine frowned. "I'm blond, you're brunette. You need something richer than anything I have here."

Sigrid brought out her own lipstick. "Will this do?"

Elaine uncapped it, examined it critically and handed it back with approval. "Perfect for you. How did you stumble—" She caught herself. "I mean—"

"I know what you meant," Sigrid said dryly as she leaned toward the mirror on the door of Albee's locker and applied the lipstick. "It was the woman who cut my hair last month. She picked it out. I've just tried to follow her directions."

She capped the lipstick and looked at the finished result as impersonally as if her face belonged to someone else.

"Uh, Lieutenant?"

"Yes?"

Elaine reached into her locker for a plastic bag with the name of a dress shop located on the next block. "I picked this up on my lunch hour today. It was on sale and looked like something that might come in handy during the holidays. You can borrow it, if you want."

It was a scoop-necked shell of gold sequins that glittered and sparkled like Christmas lights when Elaine lifted it from the bag.

Sigrid made one weak protest, then shucked off her jacket and sweater, remembering just in time not to smear her lipstick. The sequinned top fit fine. Albee was curvier, but she was taller, so it balanced. With her jacket left unbuttoned, she looked almost glamorous.

Elaine was getting into the sport of it now and pulled out some gold-colored costume jewelry: bracelets and a pair of earrings.

Sigrid accepted the bracelets but regretfully confessed, "My ears aren't pierced."

"You have to have earrings."

Another woman entered, greeted Albee by name, then gave Sigrid a formal nod and a curious glance.

"I'm late," Sigrid said, looking at the clock on the end wall, but Albee was lost in thought. "Quaranto!" she exclaimed suddenly. "In Records. She keeps a wad of costume jewelry in her desk."

"I have to go," Sigrid objected.

"Not without earrings," Albee told her firmly and neither woman noticed that in this area it was now Albee who commanded. "I'll meet you by the elevators on the first floor in two minutes."

She sprinted for the door. Sigrid folded her turtleneck and left it in her own locker, put on her heavy coat, then took an elevator downstairs.

True to her word, it wasn't much more than two minutes later that Elaine Albee raced down the stairs with a glittery dangling earring in each determined hand. Without a shred of self-consciousness, she stood on tiptoe to clip them on Sigrid's ears, then fluffed her hair and stepped back to look at what she'd wrought.

"Your coat!" she cried. "I think I know someone—"

"No!" Sigrid protested, clutching her camel hair topcoat protectively.

"Well—" said Elaine. "But take it off the minute you get there, okay?"

"Okay." Sigrid hesitated and awkwardly held out her hand. "Thanks, Albee."

"Any time, Lieutenant." Feeling almost maternal, the younger woman watched as her boss hurried out into the winter night, earrings swinging with each long stride.

"There you are," said Jim Lowry when she returned to the squad room. "What's funny, Lainey?"

"Nothing," she grinned. "Except that now I know how the fairy godmother felt when she sent Cinderella off to the ball."

"Huh?"

"Skip it. Didn't you want to make the early movie?"

The cabbie had bent the speed limit, and Sigrid, who normally hated fast driving, gratefully added a little extra to her tip as he let her out in Sussex

Square. It was only nineteen minutes past seven. Fashionably late, she told herself and hurried up the brick walk.

Remembering her promise to Elaine Albee, she slipped her coat off as soon as she entered the Erich Breul House. There she was greeted by a dignified gray-haired woman in a red jacket and beautiful pearls.

"Welcome to the Erich Breul House," said the woman, directing her to the cloakroom. "I'm Eloise Beardsley, senior docent."

"Sigrid Harald," she responded and handed her coat over to an attendant. "I think Oscar Nauman's expecting me?"

"Ah, yes." Mrs. Beardsley led her past an ornate Christmas tree and gestured toward the arched doorway near a wide marble staircase. "There he is now."

Suddenly all the silly panic over her clothes and makeup seemed worth it for the look in Nauman's eyes as he crossed the hall to her.

"Very nice," he said, handing her a bourbon-and-Coke. "I was afraid you might not come."

"Not come?" she asked. "Why would you think that?"

Seated at the desk in his makeshift office up on the fourth floor, Roger Shambley happily fingered the pack of letters. He had read them so many times since last night that he'd virtually memorized whole passages. For the most part they chronicled the usual unexceptional adventures of an earnest young man released from schoolbooks and given permission to play for a year or two before settling into adult responsibilities.

After graduation in the spring of 1911, young Erich Breul Jr. had spent the summer at the family's vacation "cottage," near Oswego on the eastern end of Lake Ontario. (Nowhere near as grand as the "cottages" at Newport, the Breuls roughed it each summer with a mere eighteen rooms and a live-in staff of only five.)

In August he sailed to England for a month in London, then entrained for Vienna by way of Antwerp, Cologne, and Frankfurt. Christmas and most of January were passed with his mother's people in Zurich. Spring found him in Rome. In each great art center, he dutifully visited the appropriate museums and churches, attended the expected concerts and operas, and afterwards, with filial rectitude, recorded his impressions of each for his "dear Mama and Papa" back home.

As spring turned to summer in those letters, Shambley could read between the lines and sense young Breul's growing saturation with the old masters, lofty music, and approved lectures in fusty rooms. June made him restless for open air and manly exercise. Accordingly, he had sent his luggage ahead to Lyons and, in company with several similarly minded youths, had hiked along the Mediterranean coast from Genoa to Marseilles.

At Marseilles, he had somehow acquired a pet monkey, Chou-Chew. The details of that acquisition were glossed over; Shambley suspected a rowdy night in one of those waterfront taverns frequented by seamen from all over the world.

In any event, Breul had parted from his friends, who were going on to Barcelona, purchased a bicycle, and, with the monkey in an open wicker basket on the front, had pedaled northward up the Rhone valley. He meandered through small villages where he bought bread and cheese or a night's lodging; and as he entered the fertile plains north of Avignon, he enjoyed both the blazing sun overhead and the cool shaded avenues of plane trees that lined the irrigation canals.

It was mid-August and the young vagabond was dawdling along a back road near the nondescript village of Sorgues-sur-l'Ouvèze when his innocent reveries were suddenly interrupted by an enormous white dog that bounded over the hedgerows, barking with such deceptive ferociousness that the startled young American promptly crashed his machine into the nearest tree.

Enter Picasso and Braque, thought Shambley, who had spent most of the night reading everything he could put his hands on concerning their summer of 1912.

The dog was Picasso's, a Great Pyrenees, one of those shaggy white creatures as big as a Newfoundland or Great Dane. His whole life long, Picasso had adored animals, from exotic zoo specimens to the most common domestic cat. How could he resist a monkey?

Braque, himself a cyclist, was more concerned about the damage done to Breul's new bicycle.

While Picasso quieted his dog and charmed the frightened monkey from the tree with his dark expressive eyes and coaxing voice, Braque hoisted the crumpled machine over his broad shoulder. Together, they led the youth to the nearest blacksmith's, left the bicycle for repairs, and insisted that he go with them for a glass of wine.

As so often happens—even with strictly reared young Lutherans— one glass of wine led to two and before long, the first bottle was empty and Picasso ordered a second in which to toast "*le grand Vilbure*," that great American whom he and Braque admired above all others and whose death that spring had so impoverished the world. The Spaniard spoke French with such a heavy accent that Erich Jr. had to ask him to repeat the name twice. Even then, Picasso had to spread his arms and make engine noises before Breul understood that they were toasting Wilbur Wright.

Eventually, the blacksmith's apprentice tracked them down and informed M'sieu Breul that it would be three days before his bicycle could be repaired. His master had sent to Orange for the necessary part. One must be patient.

"But I'm due in Lyons day after tomorrow!" said M'sieu Breul. "I'm to meet friends there. It's my birthday."

"*Tant pis*," shrugged the blacksmith's apprentice.

"Never mind," Braque and Picasso told him. "We will celebrate your natal day here."

Although this would be the last summer that Picasso had to worry about money, the two artists had deliberately chosen Sorgues for two reasons: it was cheap and no one knew them there. But perhaps they missed Apollinaire, Max Jacob, Derain, Manolo, Juan Gris, Havilland, and all the other friends with whom they socialized back in Paris. Or perhaps their kindness to the young American sprang from a combination of great personal and professional happiness just then. Not only did their work intoxicate them, so did their women.

Braque and his Marcelle still considered themselves newlyweds and Picasso had only that spring taken a new mistress, the lovely and delicate Eva, "*ma jolie*," who was to die so young.

In any event, Picasso volunteered to nursemaid Chou-Chew and Braque arranged for Breul to stay with him and his wife at Villa Bel Air, a rather dreary and commonplace house that was more beautiful in name than in fact.

Shambley wished Erich Jr. had written less about Braque's domestic arrangements and much more about Braque's studio, the pictures he saw there, or the conversations that must have passed between the two artists when Picasso arrived the next morning with the monkey on his shoulder.

Instead, after a brief reference to Braque's *trompe-l'oeil* technique and how he used combs and varnishes to duplicate the appearance of marble or grained wood on his canvases, Erich Jr. wrote that he did not think dear Papa would find the work of his new friends very meaningful. "I fear that you, with your deep love and knowledge of pure art, would scorn their *papier collé* and the strange analytical shapes of their designs, but their experiments interest me very much and when they explain what they are doing, their excitement infuses me as well."

Having seen the results, Shambley could use his imagination to fill in the details Erich Jr. so lightly touched upon. They made him sit in a chair all afternoon, gave him Braque's violin to play and, while the monkey clambered at will over sitter and artists alike, began to devise a birthday portrait, using their new techniques. In the evening Marcelle and Eva produced a special dinner and Breul gave them most of his pocket money for wine. By midnight, the portrait was declared finished (even though it had taken on certain simian details as more bottles were emptied) and both artists had signed it on the back before making a formal presentation to the birthday boy.

In return, Erich Jr. had risen to the occasion with a speech about Spanish-French-American friendship, in token of which he now gave his bicycle to Braque and his monkey to Picasso. Early the next day, with his portrait tied up in brown paper, a slightly queasy young American—"I think it must have been the sausages," he wrote his parents—caught the morning train to Lyons, where his *wander jahr* returned to its prescribed paths.

Except that it hadn't quite, thought Shambley, turning to the letters written after Breul settled in Paris for what was to be his final six months before sailing home. He was discreet about his sorties into bohemia, and his assurances of studious application to conventional art and culture were probably written in response to pointed questions from home. But the catalogs and Montparnasse menus, not to mention the two Légers hanging four floors down in that zoo of a janitor's room, gave ample evidence that the junior Breul had spent as much time among the avant-garde of Paris as in the venerable Louvre.

Shambley returned the last letter to its envelope and blocked them between his small hands like a deck of cards. At that moment, Dr. Roger Shambley was a deeply happy man. All his life he'd chased those capricious goddesses, Fame and Fortune.

Native intelligence and dogged hard work had made him a well-regarded expert in nineteenth-century American art. His first two books had gained him tenure; his third confirmed his reputation for good solid scholarship, which translated into speaking engagements, magazine articles, even an occasional spot on the *Today Show* when a feature story required an art historian's authoritative comment. If that art historian came across the tube as acerbic and witty, all the better.

Yet everyone dreams of immortality. No matter how competently and wittily written, few books survive their time if they only rehash previously known data; but the discoverer of new material will always be read simply because he was *first*. That's why every scholar dreams of new finds—that Greek statue only a shovelful of dirt away, that major missing piece of the puzzle. Discoveries automatically turn on the grant machines and roll out appointments and promotions.

With these letters and a description of how he found an unknown seminal work, Shambley knew he could write a monograph that would become a permanent appendage to the Picasso-Braque legend. Not only that, he would become a hero to everyone connected to the Breul House.

Once it was made public that this dead-in-the-water museum contained the only documented example in the entire world of a Picasso-Braque collaboration, they'd have to put in a conveyor belt to keep the crowds moving.

Which took care of fame.

As for fortune . . .

Those two Léger canvasses presented interesting possibilities, none of which involved the Breul House. Today, he had gone to the Museum of Modern Art and bought two Léger posters as nearly like the two on Pascal Grant's wall in size and composition as he could manage. He had already stashed them in one of the basement storage rooms. In the next day or so, as soon as he could substitute them for the real pictures, he would announce his discovery of the Picasso-Braque collage.

There would be such an instant uproar of excitement that even if the janitor noticed the difference between the posters and the authentic paintings, who would pay him any mind?

No one. He'd be home free with two Légers of his very own. Too bad he couldn't openly offer them for sale at, say, Sotheby's. Auctions always brought the highest prices. But Sotheby's required a legal history of the artwork it put on the block: documents, canceled checks, and bills of sale; and the only provenance he could offer would be the 1912 catalog he'd found in Erich Jr.'s effects.

No, he'd have to find someone with a love of modern art, a streak of larceny, and the resources to indulge expensive tastes.

He looked at his watch. Time to put in an appearance downstairs. He started to put the letters back in his briefcase, then hesitated. Maybe it would be safer to leave the letters here for now. There were a million hiding places in this cluttered attic but, as most scholars knew, a misfiled letter is a lost letter.

Shambley opened a drawer marked "Miscellaneous Business Correspondence: 1916/1917" and craftily filed the packet under "August 1916."

At that moment he felt positively gleeful, as if the ghost of Christmas Present had upended an enormous bag of toys at his feet. If the attic stairs had possessed a free-standing banister, he would have slid right down it, and it was all he could do to keep from chortling aloud. He stepped into the servants' lavatory on the third floor, smoothed his unruly hair, and put his pugnacious face into a semblance of professorial dignity.

But as he walked downstairs to join the party, it occurred to Roger Shambley that perhaps he wouldn't have to look very far for the buyer he needed.

The Breul dining room was the scene of many elaborate and festive dinners. Sophie Fürst Breul's mother was famous in Zurich for her brilliant dinner parties and her daughter brought the Fürst touch with her to New York. Although extravagant, perhaps, by our 1950's standards, Mrs. Breul's dinners were considered small and select in their day and the guest list never exceeded forty, the number which could be comfortably seated at her table. Like Scrooge after his conversion, it could be said that the Breuls "knew how to keep Christmas well, if any [couple] alive possessed the knowledge"; and it was their custom to invite a few friends for "supper" on Christmas night. The following is from Mrs. Breul's menu files and was dated "Christmas 1906."

Créme d'asperge
<hr>

Hûtres   Sardines   Dinde fumée
<hr>

Rôti de boeuf
<hr>

Haricots verts   Pommes

Sacher Torte   Noix glacée   Topfenstrudel
<hr>

Vermouth   Bordeaux   Champagne
<hr>

FROM *WELCOME TO THE BREUL HOUSE!—AN INFORMAL TOUR*, BY MRS. HAMILTON JOHNSTONE III, SENIOR DOCENT. (© 1956)

SIX

Wednesday Night (continued)

"SIGRID HARALD?" ASKED Søren Thorvaldsen. "*Er De dansk, frøken Harald?*"

"My father's father was from Denmark," Sigrid acknowledged, "but I'm afraid I know very few words of Danish."

And not much more than a few words of party talk either, she thought as she listened to a small white-haired woman quiz Thorvaldsen about the frivolous names he'd given his cruise ships.

"I think ships deserve more stately names," said the woman, whose own name Sigrid couldn't remember. "Something like *Empress of the Sea* or *Queen Margrethe.*"

"But those are for serious ships," Thorvaldsen answered her playfully. "My ships *are* frivolous, Mrs. Hyman."

Hyman, Sigrid told herself. Hyman. Wife of David Hyman, trustee. And next to Mrs. Hyman was Mr. Herzog. Albert. Husband of Lydia Herzog, another trustee, whom she hadn't yet met but of whom Mrs. Hyman had whispered, "Lydia was a Babcock, you know."

Sigrid did not know, but had dutifully placed a mental star next to Mrs. Herzog's name and attached a Babcock in parentheses since Mrs. Hyman seemed to think it was important. It was the sort of remark that reminded Sigrid of going through reception lines with her Southern grandmother. If Mrs. Lattimore's hierarchal memory of bloodlines and obscure degrees of kinship had ever failed her, Sigrid was unaware of it.

"I shouldn't have thought you'd find much profit in running Caribbean cruises out of New York," Mr. Herzog observed.

"Oh, you might be surprised how many people like the extra time in our casino," Thorvaldsen said with pleasant candor.

With a vague smile as Thorvaldsen elaborated on Caribbean fun ships, Sigrid detached herself from the group standing near the piano in the drawing room and wandered back to the gallery. So many pictures stacked on the walls like cordwood both fascinated and repelled her. As did everything else she'd seen of this house so far.

It was too full of *things*. How could anyone relax in a place so visually distracting? Even tonight, with the lights lowered and candles to soften the impact, the busyness of the decor made her edgy. She tried to imagine the walls stripped of the pictures Erich Breul had collected, the furniture surfaces cleared of vases, ornaments, and other bibelots. Even so, would these ornate rooms really make an appropriate exhibition space for Nauman's abstract pictures?

Evidently she wasn't the only one who wondered that, for immediately after her arrival, while still talking to Jacob Munson, whose old-world courtliness had charmed her, a tall storklike man in formal evening clothes strode into the Breul House, spotted Nauman, and immediately cried, "Oscar! What's all this crap about a retrospective *here?*"

"Behave yourself, Elliott," laughed Francesca Leeds, swooping down upon them, "or we shan't let you play, shall we, Jacob?"

The newcomer murmured appropriately as Sigrid was introduced to him, but his eyes were for Lady Francesca and Oscar Nauman. Arguably the hottest curator in town, Elliott Buntrock did not recall having met Sigrid at a Piers Leyden opening back in October. Nor did he seem to consider her someone with whom he need bother tonight.

Which suited Sigrid. As the other four began to discuss the possibilities of an exhibit here at the Breul House, she had followed the sound of a piano into the drawing room where Mrs. Beardsley had introduced her to Thorvaldsen and some of the trustees of the Breul House.

And now she had examined all the pictures hung one above the other on the gallery walls and, except for the Winslow Homer drawings, the only work that really captured her interest was a still life of bread and cheese. It reminded her empty stomach she'd eaten nothing since a push-cart hot dog around noon. Back at the far end of the drawing room, Thorvaldsen and the Hymans had been joined by Francesca Leeds and Jacob Munson; a young black woman entered the gallery in animated conversation with a vivacious middle-aged blond who exhibited a slight limp; and, as Sigrid crossed the great hall at the upper end, she saw Nauman and Elliott Buntrock walking slowly in her direction.

Both men were tall and lean, but while Nauman looked fit and moved easily, the curator seemed all joints. In his formal black-and-white evening clothes, he looked like some sort of long-legged water bird, a stilt or a crane, picking his way across a shallow lake, on the alert for any passing minnows. He had neglected to check his long white evening scarf and it hung down over his jacket. Occasionally he would forget and gather both ends in a large bony hand and pull his head forward while making sweeping uncoordinated gestures with his free arm. Nauman had an expression on his face that did not bode well for whatever Elliott Buntrock was propounding.

Sigrid prudently continued into the dining room.

"You're too important for this place," said Buntrock. "A Nauman retrospective's big business. Where's your head on this, Oscar?"

"*If* I do it—" Nauman began mildly.

"You're doing it!" the curator interrupted. "And high time, too."

"—it'll be for Jacob."

"Loyalty. How touching. But why here? With your reputation and my connections, we could easily have the Whitney. Or what about a triple header? Any three galleries you name, any part of the city. Uptown, downtown, Soho, the Village—you say it, you've got it. But for the love of God, Montresor, not here."

"Nobody's threatening to wall you up with a cask of Amontillado," Nauman grinned. "You don't have to get involved. It was Francesca's idea; I told her you wouldn't be interested."

"Francesca Leeds is the only one with any sense on this whole damn project. Of course I'm interested."

The art world was always a little crazy but Elliott Buntrock was beginning to feel as if he were caught in a comic opera version of "This Is the House that Jack Built." Francesca Leeds' wealthy shipowner wanted to sponsor a Nauman retrospective. Everyone knew Nauman refused to have one. Somehow Francesca had known that Munson was Nauman's Achilles' heel, so she'd gone looking for Munson's, and, of all the absurd people in the world, wouldn't you know it'd turn out to be that goof-up Benjamin Peake?

Buntrock wasn't quite sure *why* Peake's well-being was important to old Jacob Munson. Francesca thought it had something to do with Munson's only son who'd been killed years ago.

Anyhow, there they were: Peake's career was wobbling again, so once Jacob Munson was persuaded that a Nauman show would shore it up, he'd put the screws to Nauman, who was evidently unwilling to refuse his old friend.

Exasperated, Buntrock pulled harder on his silk scarf, which only hunched his angled head forward and increased his resemblance to a reluctant stork being pulled along to his doom. Only a fool would turn down the chance to curate a major Nauman exhibition, but *here*?

They had entered the gallery. It was the first time Buntrock had ever been here and he just stood shaking his head from side to side. "The most important abstract painter of our time in a shrine to nineteenth-century kitsch? You're crazy, Oscar."

Until their conversation, Nauman had not made up his mind but now the trendy curator's patent dismay roused the imp of perversion that lurked in his soul.

"The Breul House or no house, Buntrock. Take it or leave it."

"Done!" Elliott Buntrock groaned, already hearing the disbelieving jeers that would rise from his compatriots in the art world when they learned what he'd agreed to. He looked down the long space beyond the archway, to the drawing room, where the others were gathered around the piano. "Shall we tell them the wedding's on?"

"Be my guest," said Oscar. "I want another drink."

In the dining room, a waiter had taken Sigrid's empty glass, and promptly returned with a full one.

At the buffet table were a gray-haired man and woman who both smiled as she approached. "The pâté's good," said the man, gesturing to the platter with a hearty friendliness.

"So are the crab puffs," said the woman, who was so painfully gaunt beneath her diamonds and pearls that Sigrid couldn't believe anything more caloric than lettuce and water ever passed her lips.

Another couple at the end of the table broke apart from what seemed like an intense conversation. The dark-haired woman wore a vivid red-and-purple dress with panache and she turned with an equally vivid smile on her attractive face. "Miss Harald? I'm Hester Kohn, Jacob's partner. Have you met Benjamin Peake? He's director of the Breul House."

"So pleased," the director murmured and took her hand and looked into her eyes as if he'd waited all his life to meet her.

Unfortunately for the effect, he immediately turned that same look upon the thin woman beside them, "Mrs. Herzog! Have you met Miss Harald, Oscar Nauman's friend? Miss Harald, Mrs. Herzog. And this is Mrs. Reinicke. They're two of our most dedicated trustees, Miss Harald."

"Winston Reinicke," said the man. "Great admirer of Nauman's work. Fine painter. Fine."

"Thank you," Sigrid replied inanely as the man pumped her hand.

Mrs. Herzog continued to smile graciously, but Sigrid suddenly felt herself inventoried, cataloged and ready to be shelved. Mrs. Herzog ("She was a Babcock, you know") was not deceived by gold sequins and costume jewelry. "We at the Breul House would feel so honored if an artist of Oscar Nauman's standing should come to us."

"Is it quite settled then?" asked a languid voice behind them.

A man approached from the stairs beyond the arched doorway. Sigrid noted that he was several inches shorter than she with a slender, almost childlike body, and the head of someone much bigger. His thatched brown hair grew low on his forehead, almost meeting his thick shaggy eyebrows, and as he crossed to join them by the table, he carried his chin thrust upward at such an angle that Sigrid was reminded of a haughty ape.

"He hasn't definitely committed himself," said Benjamin Peake, "but Hester thinks Jacob may persuade him tonight. Perhaps Miss Harald knows?"

The newcomer looked at her curiously as Sigrid disavowed any insider knowledge of Oscar Nauman's ultimate decision.

"We haven't met," he said, offering her his hand. Its smallness and delicacy was surprising after the visual impact of his massive head, but the lack of physical vigor made the limpness of his clasp almost an insult. "I'm Roger Shambley."

"Dr. Shambley's our newest trustee, Miss Harald," boomed Mr. Reinicke. "A fine scholar. He's going to put the Breul collection on the map, eh, Dr. Shambley?"

For a moment, Shambley's ugly face was lit by sly glee. "You could say that," he drawled. "Yes, you could definitely say that."

Winston Reinicke beamed at him. "Spoken with the enthusiasm of a real scholar! A *catalogue raisonné* of the whole collection, eh?" His vigorous arm gesture took in all the pictures that lined this room as thickly as in the gallery across the hall.

"Not exactly," Shambley corrected him disdainfully. "My new book will merely cite some of these works as examples of general currents in the late nineteenth century. And it will probably sell fewer than five thousand copies nationwide, Reinicke, hardly enough to start a stampede for the Erich Breul House."

"Of course, of course," Winston Reinicke said heartily. "Still, one never knows what will further the cause, eh? Something for everyone."

"Speaking of which," said Shambley, "I'm told that Rockwells and Sharpes are rising in value. Have you considered them for your empty spaces?"

Sigrid sensed a sudden intake of silence around the buffet, almost as if everyone had stopped breathing.

Then Reinicke said, "Lydia, my dear, shall we take Albert and Marie some of these crab puffs? They must think we've gotten lost, eh?"

Murmuring polite phrases, the older couple arranged several hors d'oeuvres upon a plate and departed.

"Still pulling wings off flies, Roger?" Hester Kohn's tone was light but there was a wary look in her hazel eyes.

Shambley ignored the other woman's gibe. "Are you in the art world, too, Miss Harald?"

"No."

"Miss Harald's a police officer," Hester Kohn told him.

Shambley looked at Sigrid with the most animation he'd shown yet. "How appropriate. Robbery, may one hope?"

"No," Sigrid replied, wondering why Shambley had glanced so pointedly at Benjamin Peake. "If you don't expect your book to sell many copies, Dr. Shambley, what *are* you planning for the Breul House?"

"Publicity comes in many forms, Miss Harald," he said. And with a languid wave of his small hand, he parted a space between Sigrid and Hester Kohn. "*Permésso*," he said and drifted toward the door.

Hester Kohn exchanged a glance with Benjamin Peake, then flashed her professional smile at Sigrid. "Would you excuse us, please, Miss Harald?"

Sigrid barely had time to nod before the two followed Shambley from the room.

At the end of the table, a waiter lifted the lid on the silver chafing dish.

"Swedish meatballs?" he asked.

Sigrid nodded hungrily.

Jacob Munson hesitated in the doorway of the drawing room. Only a moment before he'd seen Hester out here in the hall, a flash of purple and red followed by Benjamin, and he had thought it would be pleasant to tell them of Buntrock's announcement. But when he reached the hall, there was no sign of them. He crossed the hall, peering into the cloakrooms, and finally heard voices from the library—Benjamin's voice raw with anger, Hester's intense and cold, and another voice that held a lazy sneer. He listened a moment and realized the third voice belonged to Dr. Roger Shambley.

"*Was ist los?*" he asked, peering around a bookcase at the three who stood there glaring at each other. In his agitation, he realized he'd spoken in German. "What's going on?" he repeated in English. "Hester? Ben?"

"A hypothetical question," Shambley said smoothly. "To which they gave a hypothetical answer. *Scusatemi, per favore.*" He smiled and walked past Munson into the great marble hall.

Before the inner woman was completely satisfied, Sigrid was joined by Nauman.

"Worked through lunch again, hmm?" he asked, eyeing her plate of appetizers.

"Have a stuffed mushroom," she advised. "I think they just came out of the oven."

"You'll spoil your appetite."

"Never."

He laughed. "You must be the only woman in the western world who doesn't worry about her figure."

A lot he knew, she thought, watching Francesca Leeds across the room on Søren Thorvaldsen's arm. Now there was a figure worth worrying about. There was no envy as she noted the way Lady Francesca's copper hair fell in artful tangles around her lovely face, the way the silky gold fabric enhanced her perfect figure. Yet, Sigrid did find herself wondering again why Francesca Leeds seemed so familiar, almost as if they'd met in another life or something.

There was a pleased expression on Thorvaldsen's rugged face and Francesca was smiling.

"Elliott said you've agreed, Oscar. That's grand of you." With a graceful gesture, she laid her cool fingers on his neck and pulled him down so she could kiss his cheek.

"How pretty!" said Roger Shambley, who had approached unnoticed. "Portrait of the artist with harem?"

Thorvaldsen frowned. "That's a tasteless remark, sir."

"Unlike your taste?" drawled Shambley. "But then you and Oscar Nauman have identical tastes, don't you?"

His eyes glittered beneath his heavy brows as they swept Francesca's body with an insulting deliberation that was like a physical pawing. Thorvaldsen's brawny hand shot out and grasped Shambley by the lapels and for a moment they could see the brawling stevedore he'd once been as his right hand drew back in a fist. Sigrid started forward, but Nauman had already caught his arm before it could throw the punch.

Immediately, Thorvaldsen released Shambley with a muttered apology.

Shambley straightened and drew himself up arrogantly. "I think you will pay for that," he told Thorvaldsen, then turned from the room and walked up the wide marble staircase.

The restaurant was intimate and candlelit, but dinner had become strained.

"Will you stop projecting your guilt feelings onto me?" Sigrid said tightly. "For the third time, I'm not angry and I am *not* jealous."

Her fork clattered sharply against her plate as she put it down and reached for her wine glass.

Nauman pushed a broiled scallop around his plate moodily, wishing all the hurtful words to come were already said so that he could touch her hand or make her gray eyes dance with laughter again.

"If you'd just let me explain—"

"Damn it, Nauman, there's nothing to explain." Her gold-colored earrings swung back and forth with each word. "There can't be many sixty-year-old virgins walking the land and what you did before we met is none of my business. Aren't you going to eat your scallops?"

He handed them over. He didn't know which annoyed him more: that she'd thrown his age in his face or that she could still be hungry after realizing he and Francesca had been lovers.

"You really *don't* give a damn, do you?" he asked disconsolately.

"It's illogical to be jealous about things that were over and done with before I knew you," she said, transferring his scallops to her plate. "I just mind that I was so stupid."

"Stupid?" he asked hopefully.

"Stupid. I knew she seemed familiar, but I thought it was my imagination. And all the time, there was that portrait of her in your apartment."

He paused in the act of signaling their waiter. "Portrait? I've never done a portrait of Francesca."

"Of course you have. It's hanging over that Spanish chest next to your door. I know it's not a literal representation, but still—"

Nauman shook his head and his white hair gleamed in the candlelight. "That painting is a purely abstract construction generated from sets of inverse Cassinian ovals. That's all there is to it."

"It's also—" She fell silent as their waiter approached.

"Everything all right?" he asked.

Nauman handed him their empty wine bottle. "Another one of these, please."

"It's also a portrait of Francesca Leeds," Sigrid said as the waiter left them. "The way her hair falls away from her face when she tilts her head back and laughs. All that orange and gold and brown. And those big canvasses in your studio up in Connecticut—the ones you said you painted year before last—most of those use the same colors, too. Francesca's colors."

He started to deny it, then looked at Sigrid with perplexed admiration. "I'll be damned, Siga. You're right."

Nauman never tried to analyze why he painted as he did. Let others theorize after the fact; when things were working, he only knew that they felt right. Nevertheless, it was interesting to catch his subconscious off guard. He had enjoyed Francesca, her beauty, her sophistication, her body. But she was more uptown than he, more interested in the right social circles. It had exasperated her that he wouldn't capitalize on his fame, so they had parted as amicably as they'd begun and he hadn't realized that she'd affected his palette.

Now he remembered that violent purple-and-black study Francesca had pulled from the back of his storage racks up in Connecticut last weekend. He fingered his left ear unconsciously. Blacks and purples that sloped into somber browns.

Lila.

His mind shied at the thought of Lila, locked away all these years; and he willed himself to consider instead the vivid, almost garish colors he'd used during those exuberant postwar years with Susan; or those serene pastels that had echoed Cassandra's quiet blond loveliness. Odd that he hadn't seen—hadn't let himself see?

Four women. All different.

And what would Sigrid bring?

"Don't!" she said sharply, and gold sequins shimmered like moonbeams on water as she flinched from his gaze.

"What?" he asked, bewildered.

"You look at me sometimes as if I'm a—I don't know. As if I were a thing, not a person."

The waiter arrived with more wine, filled their glasses, and departed.

Nauman lifted his glass in tribute. "Oh no, my dear. Never that," he said, and was glad to realize that their fight seemed to have ended before it ever began.

A clock was chiming nine-thirty when Roger Shambley came downstairs to use the telephone on Hope Ruffton's desk. The caterers had long since gone and the rooms were dark and silent. He called information for the number he wanted, dialed and, when an answering machine beeped at the other end of the wire, spoke the cryptic words he'd rehearsed, then hung up.

He crossed the echoing hall to unlock the front door and as he returned, a figure appeared in the doorway of the darkened library.

"*Gesù e Maria!*" he exclaimed. "You startled me. I thought you left hours ago."

In the warm snug hobbit-hole room, the last tape had come to an end and Rick Evans was enjoying the comfortable silence when he suddenly stiffened like a burrowing animal that hears the dogs above him.

"What's wrong, Rick?" Pascal Grant asked sleepily.

"Sh! I thought I heard a noise out there."

Pascal raised himself to a kneeling position beside Rick. The only light in the room was a small amber lamp shaped like an owl near the door and both held their breath, listening. Rick looked around for a weapon of some sort. "You have a stick or something, Pasc?"

"Like my softball bat? Sure."

Rick slipped off the mattress and pulled on his trousers. "Where is it?"

"Behind that chair." Then realizing what Evans meant to do, Pascal Grant clutched at his leg. "No, Rick. Don't go out there. Please!" His voice grew louder as he became more agitated. "I don't like Dr. Shambley. He scares me."

Of course, Rick thought, Shambley. That dirty little coward. What gives him the right to sneak around down here? Was he hoping to find Pasc alone? He thinks he knows what Pasc and I are, but we *know* what he is and he's not going to wreck things.

With angry, confused thoughts running through his head, Rick grasped the bat, unlocked the door, and stepped out into the kitchenette.

"Who's there?" he called, suddenly caught by conflicting emotions.

In the dim warmth behind the half-closed door, Pascal Grant huddled uneasily on the bed, wishing Rick would come back and lock the door and they could talk some more and listen to the old Louis Armstrong tape Rick had brought and forget about Dr. Shambley. Before yesterday was bad enough, Pascal thought unhappily, but ever since last night when he put his hand on my face— And today, he keeps looking at me and he makes me feel dirty, like Mr. Gere at the training center—

Pascal shivered and tried not to think of Mr. Gere and what Mr. Gere had wanted him to do.

There was a thump and clatter out in the main kitchen and Pascal sprang from the bed and ran to the door. "Rick?"

An icy draft of air met him at the kitchenette and he glanced across the dim stretches of the main kitchen to the passageway that wound out to his spiderweb door.

A forty-watt security light burned over the stairs off to his left and something dark lay crumpled at the bottom. Half whimpering with terror, Pascal edged closer. "Rick?"

A moment later, with the bat clutched in his hand, Rick emerged from the dark hallway into the main kitchen and found Pascal shivering over a twisted bundle at the foot of the stairs.

"Dr. Shambley," Pascal whispered.

Rick drew near. The ugly little man lay face up on the tiles, his eyes stared unblinkingly at the light, his lips were drawn back almost in a snarl.

"Is he dead?" asked Pascal.

It reminded Rick of finding a dead snake in the road. Neither wanted to touch him. Rick nudged Shambley's head with the bat. It flopped to one side and they saw that his shaggy brown hair was matted with blood. Rick knelt down then. There was no pulse in the man's lifeless wrist.

"Did you hit him?" asked Pascal. "I heard the bat."

"No," Rick said sharply. "Someone else was here, too—in the hallway. I ran after them but the bat banged into the wall and I dropped it. Whoever it was must have pushed him down the stairs and then run away."

"Why?"

"I don't know," Rick said grimly, "but we can't leave him here."

"Why, Rick?"

"Because they might think *you* pushed him. Or me."

"But we'll just tell them we didn't. I'll call Mrs. Beardsley. Or Dr. Peake. They'll know what to do."

"No!" Rick looked at Pascal's beautiful innocent face despairingly. "Look, if you call them, you'll have to tell them I was spending the night with you and they wouldn't understand."

"You're my friend."

"I know, but most people would think that was wrong."

"Wrong to have a friend?"

"Wrong to let him sleep over with you. They'd make something dirty out of it. They think everything is sex."

"Oh," said Pascal. He caught his lower lip between his teeth and nodded.

"We'll take him up to the third floor and leave him at the bottom of the attic stairs. Those steps are steeper. They'll think he tripped and fell up there."

Still shivering, Pascal reluctantly agreed to Rick's plan. Even though Shambley's body was small, neither youth was strong enough to carry him very far. Instead, they rolled him onto one of the blue rag scatter rugs, loaded him inside the dumbwaiter, and hoisted him aloft.

Up on the third floor, they carried him across the wide hall to the foot of the uncarpeted steps and Rick tried to arrange those limbs into a natural-looking sprawl.

When they were finished, they lowered the dumbwaiter and, as a precaution, Rick stopped it at the butler's pantry beside the dining room.

Back in the basement, they were left with a patch of sticky blood on the tiles where Shambley's head had lain. They swabbed up the worst with the blue rag rug since it already had blood smears on it. While Pascal got a mop and scrubbed away the rest of the blood, Rick bundled up the rug, stashed it in one of the storage rooms, then returned to Pascal's room to finish dressing.

"Aren't you going to stay?" asked Pascal. His large blue eyes were frightened.

"Listen, Pasc," Rick said seriously. "If you want to stay friends, you have to do exactly what I tell you, okay?"

"Okay."

It took almost a half-hour before Rick was certain the janitor had their story straight: they had gone to a movie, come back and listened to jazz for a while, then Rick had gone home at nine and Pascal had fallen asleep without remembering to set the burglar alarm.

"I could set it now," Pascal said.

"Better not," Rick said. "Otherwise they'll ask you if you checked to make sure Dr. Shambley was gone."

"Oh. Okay."

"You didn't see Dr. Shambley."

"I didn't," Pascal agreed. "Not till—"

"Not at all," Rick reminded him. "You didn't see him since before the party, okay?"

"Okay." Pascal looked up at his friend trustingly. "I wish you could sleep over, Rick."

"Another time," he said and clasped Pascal's shoulder as he stood. "I promise."

At the spiderweb door beneath the main stoop, he drew on his gloves, pulled his collar snugly around his neck, and stepped out into the freezing night as Pascal locked the door behind him.

Shortly after eleven, Rick let himself into the apartment on the upper West Side. His grandfather usually went to bed early, but he was a light sleeper. Tonight, a muffled snore was all Rick heard as he crept past Jacob Munson's closed door and gained the sanctuary of his own room. He expected to lie awake reliving the horror of the evening; yet no sooner did his head touch the pillow than he was instantly and deeply asleep.

Mrs. Beardsley awoke near midnight with a painful leg cramp. Groaning, she pushed aside the covers and made herself stand up and walk around the room until the spasms passed. Her bedroom faced Sussex Square and, though she told herself it was childish, she lingered at the window to watch the tall spruce tree turn off its lights. The automatic timer was set for midnight, and there was something magical about catching the precise moment.

There! The tree's blaze of colored lights vanished, leaving only the old-fashioned gaslights to illumine the square. Pleased, she started to turn from the window when a movement diagonally across the park caught her eye. Someone was coming down the front steps of the Breul House. She strained to see.

Dr. Shambley?

No, Dr. Shambley was shorter than she and this man—if it were a man—was taller.

The figure came down the steps, head hunched into the turned-up collar of the topcoat, and hurried along the brick walk. At the corner, the figure became recognizable as he passed beneath the electric streetlight there, turned west at the corner, and disappeared from her view.

Now why, wondered Mrs. Beardsley, had Mr. Thorvaldsen come back to the Breul House so late at night?

Sigrid turned in the night and found her bed empty. "Nauman?"

The room was quite dark but there was a movement by the door. "I didn't mean to wake you."

"What time is it?"

"Not quite five. Go back to sleep," he whispered.

She raised herself on one elbow and looked at the luminous clock dial in disbelief. "Five! Why are you up so early?"

"I couldn't sleep and there're things I need to do."

He came and sat on the edge of the bed and gathered her into his arms. She smoothed back his hair and felt the rough stubble along his chin line. "Come back to bed."

He kissed her then, a yearning, tender kiss that transcended carnal desire, and tucked the blanket around her body. "I'll call you tonight."

Too sleepy to argue, she snuggled deeper into the covers.

Zurich

My dearest husband,

    Mama's health is so much improved this week that I begin to think I may soon be released from sickroom duty and may truly begin to plan our return. You will be surprised at how our son has grown since you last saw him in April. He all but tops my shoulder now.

    In these three short months, his German has become quite fluent. He has made great friends with Papa's friend, Herrn Witt, one of the directors of the new art museum, and a visit to that magnificent institution is his dearest treat. Herr Witt asked him how he came by such a fine eye for art at so early an age and young Erich replied, "Es kommt von meinem Papa!"

    I will always regret, mein Lieber, *that God in His infinite wisdom did not see fit to bless us with a dozen children, yet I can never give thanks enough for the angel-child He did lend us . . .*

LETTER FROM SOPHIE FÜRST BREUL TO
ERICH BREUL SR., DATED 6.20.1899.
(FROM THE ERICH BREUL HOUSE COLLECTION)

SEVEN

Thursday, December 17

SIGRID HAD DROPPED Albee's sequin top at a dry cleaners near headquarters and waited to have the claim ticket stamped paid, so she was a
few minutes late for work. Jim Lowry, Matt Eberstadt, and Elaine Albee
were already in the staff room with coffee and doughnuts and the morning
papers. Sigrid had tucked the costume jewelry into a small plastic bag
and she handed it and the ticket to the young blonde with a quiet, "Thanks
again, Albee. And thank Quaranto for me, too."

Any other woman in the department and Elaine Albee would have
asked how the evening went. With the lieutenant, discretion was always
the better part of valor, so she smiled and said, "Any time, Lieutenant,"
and went back to reading aloud the *Daily News* follow-up story on the
"Babies in the Attic Case," as it called the discovery of the infant remains
found in that East Village row house.

They had reprinted earlier pictures, including one of Detectives Harald and Lowry as police officers who appealed to the public for any
information about former occupants from forty years earlier.

" 'Baby killer still stalking East Village?' " read Albee. " 'Area residents mum.' "

"*Are* area residents mum?" Sigrid asked, taking the last glazed doughnut in the box.

Matt Eberstadt regarded the empty box with mild sorrow. Now in his
late forties with a wiry, iron gray hairline that had receded to the top of
his head, he'd been put on a strict diet by his wife Frances—"You'll lose
six more pounds before Christmas or no strudel for you this year," she'd
threatened—but his heart wasn't in it.

"The problem may be finding any longtime residents, talky *or* mum," Lowry said pessimistically. "So far, the canvass hasn't turned up on anybody earlier than 1954. I think Bernie's over checking records this morning."

Eberstadt shifted his girth in the chair and slipped his thumb into his waistband. Not as snug as last month, but not nearly loose enough to satisfy Frances. He met Lieutenant Harald's gaze and hastily reported, "Those fingerprints we found on the newspaper have been on the wire almost a week. Nothing so far."

"And I don't suppose Cohen has anything more for us yet?" Sigrid asked. "No? Okay, on to other matters."

The next twenty minutes were devoted to cases still pending, then Albee and Lowry settled into paperwork while Eberstadt went off to review his testimony for a court hearing.

Bernie Peters returned with some names he'd dug out of public records. Now that his infant son was finally sleeping through the nights, he seemed to have more energy for work again.

"That block was mostly Polish and Ukrainian in the thirties," he said. "Still is, to some extent."

By cross-referencing real estate and tax records, he'd learned that the house was sold in 1934 to a Gregor Jurczyk, who'd converted it to an eight-unit tenement. Old telephone directories turned up a single telephone listed in Jurczyk's name, at that address, until he died in 1963 and left the house to his sisters, Angelika Jurczyk and Barbara Jurczyk Zajdowicz. Even after his death, the telephone continued to be listed in his name until 1971, which would lead one to believe at least one of his sisters was still in residence there until the property was sold to a developer who went bankrupt in 1972, at which time the house was taken over by a bank.

"And after that I didn't bother," said Peters. "I called a friend of mine in Vital Records. Angelika Jurczyk died in 1970, age sixty-seven. No death record for Barbara Zajdowicz."

Sigrid jotted the figures down on her pad. "That would have made her forty-four in 1947 when the last infant was put in that trunk. Any idea of the age of her sister?"

Before Peters could answer, they were abruptly interrupted. A patrol officer in Sussex Square had requested the assistance of investigators at the Erich Breul House where a dead male had been discovered.

"*Where?*" Sigrid asked, startled.

"Sussex Square," Elaine Albee repeated. "Wasn't that where you were last night?"

*   *   *

Patrol cars had driven up onto the bricked walk around Sussex Square and eight or ten uniformed officers clogged the doorway when Sigrid arrived with her team.

"Too many unnecessary personnel," Sigrid said crisply, as they entered the vaulted marble hall. "Clear them out, Cluett."

Detective Third Grade Michael Cluett was an old-timer from Brooklyn who'd been wished on her by Captain McKinnon. He didn't seem to resent taking orders from a woman, but he was too close to retirement to worry about impressing anyone. His only ambition seemed to be finishing out his forty years on the force without screwing up. He hitched his belt up around a belly that sagged worse than Eberstadt's and moved off to carry out the lieutenant's instructions.

Dr. Benjamin Peake was speaking to a uniformed officer at the rear of the hall and his handsome face grew bewildered at the sight of Sigrid.

"Miss Harald!" he exclaimed. "I'm afraid we're closed—"

"Lieutenant Harald," she said, pointing to her badge. She was almost as surprised to see him. They'd been told only that a man had been found dead under suspicious circumstances at the Breul House, not who the man was, and for no good reason she'd halfway expected it to be Peake. "Who—?" she asked him.

"Dr. Shambley. A dreadful accident. Dreadful. Fell down the stairs. I'll show you," Peake said.

"That won't be necessary," Sigrid told him.

Elaine Albee was beside her as she started up the wide marble staircase. "This is one of the places I keep meaning to come see," said the younger woman. She noticed the rich details of the dress worn by the female dummy on the landing. "How did Breul make his money? Railroads? Oil?"

"Canal barges, I think," Sigrid said, threading her way past the uniformed officers who loitered in the second-floor hallway frankly sightseeing at the moment. She could only hope they'd had the sense to keep their feet out of the actual crime scene.

"That's nice stained glass," Albee said, pausing beneath the oval Tiffany window where spring flowers blossomed on this December day.

Tiffany glass seldom appealed to Sigrid and she didn't break her stride as she continued up the last flight of steps to the third floor.

"Through there, Lieutenant," said a patrol officer, who was posted to limit access to the rear half of the third floor.

They passed through the frosted glass doors that were blocked open and at the end of the hall found Officer Paula Guidry already photographing the body, which lay sprawled on the bare floor at the base of some steep wooden steps. A frosted glass window high in the rear wall flooded the area with cold north light.

Across the wide landing, a mannequin dressed in the long bib apron and starched white cap of an old-fashioned maid smiled at them serenely.

Sigrid was glad to see that the end of the hall was roped off and that everyone seemed to be respecting the integrity of the crime scene. "Who was responding officer?" she asked.

A uniformed patrolman in his late twenties stepped forward. "Officer Dan Monte, ma'am."

Without being asked, he flipped open his notebook and described how he'd been dispatched to number 7 Sussex Square in response to a call placed by a Miss Hope Ruffton, the secretary here.

"This place opens at ten A.M. and a Mrs. Eloise Beardsley—I think she's a volunteer—came upstairs at approximately ten forty-five and discovered the body lying face down just as you see it. She said she tried to find a pulse, then realized the individual was dead."

Officer Monte had arrived at 10:57, observed certain inconsistencies, and immediately requested investigators.

"What inconsistencies?" asked Jim Lowry.

"Not enough blood," the patrol officer replied succinctly. "You can see from here—the back of his head's pretty messed up and blood's clotted in his hair, but it didn't run down his face and there's none on the floor beside his head. The stairs are bare wood and I guess he could have hit his head on one of the sharp edges coming down, but again, no blood."

Sigrid watched as Guidry indicated she'd taken enough pictures of the body and its immediate surroundings. While the photographer waited for someone from the medical examiner's office to turn it over, the crime scene unit began processing the area around the body.

"Who was in the house when you arrived?" Sigrid asked.

"Just the secretary, the Beardsley woman, the live-in janitor, and the director," answered Monte. "They're all downstairs. The ambulance crew got here at eleven oh-two and confirmed death."

For a moment, Sigrid almost forgot and looked around for Tillie, the officer on whom she most relied, the one who usually acted as her recorder and could be trusted to note every minute detail.

Unfortunately, Detective Tildon was still recovering from the bomb blast that had nearly killed him in October. He was home from the hospital now and healing nicely, but was not expected back at work till next month. Mick Cluett was certainly no substitute and Albee was already catching her share on other cases. Sigrid told Lowry he'd won recorder's job and the younger man gave a mock groan as he continued to measure distances for sketching the scene.

Bernie Peters, directing the application of fingerprint powder on the stair rail, grinned in sympathy.

Cohen arrived from the medical examiner's office and greeted her sardonically. "We gotta quit meeting like this, Lieutenant."

A few minutes later, he'd agreed with Officer Monte's suspicions. "Lividity's not much help if he was moved within a half-hour of death, but that wound bled like hell and there ought to be a puddle under his head. He didn't die face down though. And see this?"

Cohen pulled back the collar of Shambley's shirt and Sigrid saw that a thin trickle of blood had run down inside to his back.

She nodded thoughtfully. "So he was upright when he received the wound?"

Cohen shrugged. "He did most of his bleeding while lying supine; but yeah, I'd guess the blow came while he was sitting or standing."

"He didn't hurt himself in a fall?"

"Maybe. But I can't see him standing up again after getting this wound, so how'd blood run straight down his neck?"

They would keep it in mind, Sigrid told him as Guidry photographed the stain.

The dumbwaiter shaft had been discovered and a good set of prints were found on the enamelled wood molding that framed the hinged doors. Officer Monte had managed to keep everyone off the back stairs, so Albee started down to determine the dumbwaiter's current location, being careful to keep to the center of the treads and on the lookout for anything out of the ordinary.

Cohen finished his preliminary examination and stripped off thin latex gloves as he stood. "Funny-looking guy, isn't he? Little Ed with the big head. Something odd about that head."

"Besides its size?" asked Lowry, who had chalked an outline of the body's position before Cohen began.

"Not our old friend the blunt instrument?" queried Bernie Peters.

"I'll let you know after I've taken a look at that wound in the lab," Cohen told them.

Guidry stepped back in for more pictures now that Cohen had turned the body face up.

"Want to estimate a time of death?" Sigrid asked.

Cohen shrugged. "Rigor's complete, but there's still a little body warmth, so we're talking maybe twelve to fifteen hours, no more than sixteen hours max."

They looked at their watches. Between 7:15 and 11:15, always taking into account that the temperature in this hallway may have been measurably higher or lower than it was now, or that the dead man had some physical quirk that would quicken or retard rigor mortis.

"I saw him alive between eight and eight-thirty last night," Sigrid said.

Bernie Peters shot Lowry a telling glance. The lieutenant had a reputation for coldness, but she hadn't turned a hair upon seeing the body. Even Cohen looked at her curiously. "Friend of yours?"

"No," she answered distantly. "There was a party here last night and he came, too. We met briefly and he left early. Or rather he went upstairs early. I believe he was doing research on some papers in the attic."

Elaine Albee reappeared on the back stairs. "The dumbwaiter's on the first floor," she reported, slightly out of breath. "And there looks like a smear of blood inside."

"Probably turn out to be roast beef," Cohen grinned. "You guys ready for me to take him?"

Sigrid queried her people. Guidry was satisfied with the number of photographs she'd taken and Lowry and Peters had just finished with their inventory of Roger Shambley's pockets, so everyone stood back as Cohen's assistants lifted the body onto a collapsible gurney, covered it, and strapped it down. Rigor mortis made for a bulky shape and Sigrid was not the only one reminded of a grotesque and badly wrapped Christmas package.

"By the way, Lieutenant—" Cohen paused before following the body downstairs. "You'll get my official report late this afternoon, but I can put it in an eyedropper right now: On the bones last week, you can forget about actual age, sex, race—hell! I couldn't even swear they aren't monkey bones. All I can say is that they're consistent with what you'd find if a newborn baby was wrapped in newspapers and stuck in a trunk for thirty years, give or take a week."

"What about the mummified one?" Sigrid asked.

"Caucasian girl," he replied promptly. "And before you ask, yeah, she was born alive. I found lint in her breathing passages. Looks like she no sooner got herself born than she got herself smothered."

With a laconic "Ciao for now, *amici*," he trailed after the gurney, never realizing that he'd allowed Roger Shambley one final exit in Italian.

With the body removed from the landing, Sigrid went up the steep attic stairs to examine the makeshift office Roger Shambley had created amid file cabinets and storage boxes. Later, someone would go through the papers and folders so neatly stacked upon his work tables, but for now she simply wished to sit in the art historian's chair and try to get a better feel for the man she'd met so briefly last night, some sense of why he'd died.

The tabletop directly in front of his chair was bare, so she assumed he'd probably finished work for the night and cleared away his papers. Into one of those folders, perhaps. Or into his briefcase, which still sat beside the chair. A methodical man?

She rather thought there had been method in Shambley's calculated insults last night—to that trustee, Mr. Reinicke, to Søren Thorvaldsen and, by extension, to Nauman and Francesca Leeds—but she'd observed him too briefly to understand the motive for his rudeness. There had been a certain electricity in his manner, though; as if he were so wired about something that he hardly knew or cared what he was saying.

Or to whom.

Power, Sigrid thought. Shambley had acted like someone who'd just won a lottery or inherited a throne and suddenly felt free to ride rough-shod over everyone else.

"Lieutenant?" Jim Lowry's voice at the attic door drew her back to the present. "We think we've found where he died."

They went down the narrow back stairs, past the butler's pantry on the first floor where Officer Guidry had photographed the dumbwaiter before the crime scene technicians took a sample of its stains for the lab, and from the butler's pantry, on down the broader, more commodious stairway to the basement.

As they descended, Sigrid noted and carefully sidestepped three chalk-circled spots.

At the foot of the steps, a portable floodlamp lit up the area and made it quite apparent that the floor there had been recently—and inexpertly—mopped. They could clearly see a circular spot where dried streaks of water left dull swirls upon the shiny dark tiles.

"Bonded commercial cleaners come in every Monday," said Elaine Albee as they watched a technician fill small glass vials with samples of a brown sticky substance he'd scraped from the joints between the tiles. "According to the woman who found the body, the cleaners bring their own equipment and part of their routine is to wax and buff the floors down here."

A mop, still damp, had been found in the scullery, she told Sigrid. It, too, would be taken to the lab for analysis.

"And the blood on the stairs themselves?" Sigrid asked, referring to those chalk circles.

"Couple of small splashes up on the tenth and eleventh treads; a bigger one down here on the third," said Bernie Peters. "Nothing on the upper landing and, from the shape of the drops, he was moving down at the time."

It was consistent with what Cohen had told them. Until they uncovered data to disprove it, their working theory would be that Shambley had started down the basement steps when he was struck a tremendous blow on the head from behind. He had fallen here, bled copiously, then his body had been hauled up to the third floor soon afterwards.

"Why not leave him here in the basement where he fell?" Sigrid wondered aloud.

"The perpetrator wanted him found quickly?" speculated Lowry.

"Maybe he *didn't* want him found quickly," Albee countered. "There's a live-in janitor who has a room down here. Maybe the perp wanted time to get away and set up an alibi before the janitor stumbled over him."

"Or maybe it was an individual that just didn't want us taking too close a look at the basement," suggested Peters.

"In which case," said Sigrid.

The others tried not to groan as they looked across the crowded Victorian kitchen to the warren of storage rooms beyond.

"There's still a bunch of uniforms wandering around upstairs," Mick Cluett reminded her.

"Might as well put them to use," Sigrid agreed. "And start a canvass of the square, anyone seen entering or leaving these premises last night. In the meantime, Lowry, you and I will begin with the staff."

They commandeered the stately, book-lined library for questioning their witnesses and lunchtime came and went before the two police detectives had heard all that the Breul House staff were prepared to tell them.

With commendable initiative, the secretary, Hope Ruffton, had typed up a guest list from the previous evening, complete with addresses, which helped them track departures. Sigrid knew that the three trustees and their respective spouses had left shortly after eight, and that she and Nauman left at 8:20. After that, as best the others could reconstruct, the curator, Elliott Buntrock, said good-night at 8:30, followed soon by Søren Thorvaldsen and Lady Francesca Leeds, Hope Ruffton, Hester Kohn, and Jacob Munson, in that order.

Hope Ruffton had been collected by three friends for a musical comedy playing up in Harlem and she supplied the detectives with a separate list of her friends' names and addresses.

Benjamin Peake declared that he'd planned to wait until the caterer's men had gone, but Mrs. Beardsley, the senior docent, had volunteered to stay in the director's place since she had only to walk across the square after she'd locked up.

"Mr. Peake left about eight-forty," Mrs. Beardsley told them. "The caterers were finished shortly before nine; then I double-checked to make sure no candles were still burning, turned out the lights, and went home shortly after nine."

"All the lights?" Sigrid asked. "What about Dr. Shambley?"

"I refer, of course, to the main lights," Mrs. Beardsley replied, sitting so erectly in the maroon leather wing chair that Sigrid was reminded of one of Grandmother Lattimore's favorite dicta: a lady's spine never touches the back of her chair. "The security lights are on an automatic timer and they provide enough illumination for finding one's way through the house."

"And you didn't see Dr. Shambley after the party last night?"

"No. Dr. Shambley often worked late," said the docent with a slight air of disapproval.

"What about the janitor?"

"Pascal Grant had permission to attend a movie. I assume he hadn't yet returned by the time I left."

"Permission?"

"When you speak to Pascal, Lieutenant Harald, I think it will be evident why we give him more guidance and direction than an ordinary worker. This is his first job since he left the shelter and I do hope you'll be patient with him. He's really quite *capable* within clearly defined limits. You'll see."

"So as far as you know, Dr. Shambley was alone in the house when you left?"

"Y-es," she said, but something unspoken lingered indecisively on her face.

Pressed, Mrs. Beardsley described how she'd awakened at midnight and seen Mr. Thorvaldsen descending the front steps of the Breul House.

Sigrid went to the library window and asked Mrs. Beardsley to point out her house across the square. It was a windy gray day and the reporters who crowded around below to question the police guard outside had bright pink cheeks and blown hair. "You're positive it was Thorvaldsen?"

"Absolutely," the lady said firmly. "He's quite tall and when he passed under a streetlight at the corner, I saw his fair hair."

On his identity, Mrs. Beardsley could not be budged, although she was quick to admit that she hadn't actually seen the Dane exit from the house. "I thought perhaps he might have returned for something he lost or else forgot and left behind."

"Who has keys to this place?" asked Lowry from his place at the end of a polished wooden library table.

"All the trustees have keys." Mrs. Beardsley patted her purse with a proprietary air. "I, too, of course, as senior docent."

Seated across the table from her, Sigrid looked at the growing list of names on her notepad. "Thorvaldsen, as well?"

"Oh, no, he's not a trustee. But Lady Francesca might since she's going to be in and out a lot if Mr. Nauman's retrospective takes place." She gave Sigrid a friendly social smile and began to describe how surprised everyone was to discover that last night's Miss Harald was today's Lieutenant Harald.

Jim Lowry was diverted by these clues to the lieutenant's off-duty life. Odd to be taking down her testimony as background for a case. Oscar Nauman's name rang a vague bell, but he couldn't quite recall why. Besides, wasn't she supposed to be living with an oddball writer named Roman Tramegra? Maybe Lainey would know.

The lieutenant's cold gaze fell on him and he started guiltily. "Um— keys," he croaked. "Who else has them? The janitor?"

"Oh yes. Not to the main door, but to an outside door in the basement." The gray-haired woman hesitated. "And Miss Ruffton and Dr. Peake, of course."

"Of course."

Miss Ruffton shared with them her impression that Dr. Shambley had been up to something besides pure disinterested research, but did not suggest what that something might be.

Dr. Peake grew defensive, mistook their questions for innuendoes, and wound up revealing more animosity toward Dr. Shambley than he'd intended.

"A busybody and a snoop," declared Peake. "With delusions of mental superiority and the reverse snobbism of the proletariat."

"Really?" Sigrid asked, not having heard that epithet since her college days.

"Proletarian roots compounded by his shortness," Peake theorized. "He always insulted his superiors."

Sigrid thought of last night. "At the party, he was rude to Mr. Reinicke, Mr. Thorvaldsen, and Professor Nauman.

"Well, there you are." Peake nodded. "They're all much taller."

When it was his turn to be questioned, Pascal Grant sat in one of the heavy library chairs with his ankles crossed like a schoolboy and kept his head down when spoken to. The janitor was so uncommunicative that

Sigrid at first wondered if the young man fully understood what had happened to Shambley, and she and Lowry found themselves phrasing their questions in words of one syllable.

"I didn't see Dr. Shambley at all last night," he said, looking up through thick golden lashes as he answered. "Rick and me, we went to the movie."

"Rick?"

"Rick's my friend," Grant said softly.

"What time did you get back here?" asked Lowry.

"I don't know. We listened to tapes, Rick and me. Then Rick went home and I went to bed. I didn't hear anything."

Sigrid looked up from her notes. "Your friend Rick was here?"

"He went home," said Grant, darting quick glances at both of them. "He didn't hear anything either."

"Does your friend Rick have a last name?"

Pascal Grant concentrated a moment and then his face lit up with a beautiful smile. "Evans. His name is Rick Evans. He's Mr. Munson's grandson."

They could extract no further information. The young handyman continued to insist he and Evans had neither seen, heard, nor spoken to Roger Shambley the previous evening.

Unfortunately for him, Bernie Peters came up just then to announce that their search had turned up a bloody scatter rug hidden behind some boxes in one of the storerooms, and that a softball bat found beside Pascal Grant's bed seemed to have a suspicious stain at the business end.

"Is that how you killed him?" Sigrid asked gently.

Young Grant shook his head and tears pooled in his blue eyes. "No, I didn't. We didn't see him. We didn't do it."

Feeling rather like the schoolyard bully, Sigrid sighed. "Take him back to headquarters for further questioning," she told Peters. "And have Rick Evans picked up, too."

Mrs. Beardsley was so outraged by Pascal Grant's removal to headquarters that Sigrid was not overly surprised to reach her office and find the woman had gotten there before her. Nor to see that she had brought along her own lawyer, a thin dry man with tonsured hair and an ascetic manner. Harvey Pruitt might be more at home dealing with wills and deeds and other civil matters, but for Mrs. Gawthrop Wallace Beardsley's sake, he seemed prepared to represent Pascal Grant, should the young janitor be detained on criminal charges.

Rick Evans had been located at the Kohn and Munson Gallery, and an equally protective Hester Kohn had accompanied him downtown.

Three minutes after their arrival, they were joined by the gallery's attorney, a tall, brown-haired woman in what looked like Eskimo mukluks, a deerskin parka lined with fur, and gold-rimmed granny glasses. Ms. Caryn DiFranco.

The two lawyers immediately went into a huddle, then requested and were given a private room in which to confer with their respective clients.

It was long past lunchtime, so Sigrid and her team took advantage of the lull to send down for sandwiches. Mick Cluett had been sent off to check Shambley's apartment and to notify his next of kin; but Eberstadt, back from court, joined them with an enormous corned beef on rye.

"If Frances could see that," said Bernie Peters, shaking his head.

"Salads are for summertime," Eberstadt said defensively. "In December, a man needs something that'll stick to his ribs."

"Just what you need." Elaine Albee grinned. "More meat on those puny ribs."

Eberstadt laughed and as they ate, the others filled him in on Roger Shambley's death amid such Victorian surroundings.

They had taken a set of elimination prints from staff members at the house. "Just eyeballing it, I'd say the Grant kid's the one who left prints on the dumbwaiter," said Peters.

"You should see his bedroom down there in that basement," Jim Lowry told Eberstadt. "Looks like a Chinese whorehouse—red velvet and gold satin, snaky lights, and art posters or calendar pictures on every square inch of wall space."

"Calendar pictures?" Eberstadt leered. "Art posters?"

"Get your mind out of the gutter," Albee told him. She reached across the table to commandeer his kosher dill pickle. "He's talking abstract art, not *Playboy* art."

"Yeah, it's funny," said Peters. "You'd think a guy like him—not too swift on the uptake—would have pictures that looked like real things."

"Probably sees enough of those upstairs," said Albee. Between crunches of Eberstadt's pickle, she described for him the tiers of gilt-framed pictures that lined the walls of the main galleries at the Erich Breul House.

Matt Eberstadt savored the last morsel of corned beef and licked his fingertips. "Frances keeps saying we ought to go tour the place. She likes old things," he said, wiping his hands on a less than clean handkerchief.

"Like you?" gibed Peters.

Sigrid ate her own tuna sandwich swiftly and quietly, with one eye on some paperwork and only half an ear for their give and take. Casual camaraderie had never been easy for her, although now that Nauman had entered her life, she found these unofficial sessions a little easier than before.

She skimmed through one report a second time, then passed it down the table to Bernie Peters. "The neighborhood canvass turned up someone who remembers the Jurczyks."

The others looked at her blankly, trying to place the name.

"Oh, yeah," said Peters. "Those baby bones."

He read the highlights of the report aloud. "Mrs. Pauline Jaworski remembers the Jurczyk sisters from her childhood in the fifties. Thinks her mother may still be in touch with Barbara Zajdowicz. Mother's name, Mrs. Dorota Palka. Currently resides at Lantana Walk Nursing Home up in Queens."

Elaine Albee's head came up. She had briefly worked undercover there back in the spring. "Lantana Walk? Queens? I thought they put that place out of business last spring."

"The director testified against his partners and got off with a suspended sentence and a hefty fine," said Sigrid, who had followed the situation and been disappointed by its outcome.

As they wadded up foam cups and paper napkins from their impromptu lunch, word came that Pascal Grant and Richard Evans were ready to make their statements. Sigrid checked her watch. "Lowry, I want you and Albee to sit in on this, too. Peters, see if you can get a statement from that Palka woman."

"Just how I wanted to spend the afternoon," Bernie Peters grumbled to Eberstadt when the other three had gone. "Freezing my ass off on the F train to Queens."

"Better than surveillance," replied his partner, who had done his share of sitting in cold cars on icy winter streets.

Flanked by their lawyers, Pascal Grant and Rick Evans each appeared very young and very intimidated when they entered the interrogation room; but once all the legal formalities and stipulations were out of the way, their statements were quite straightforward.

They were questioned separately and then together. The second time around, Rick Evans did all the talking at first, in a soft voice full of southern inflections. Sigrid listened without questions as he described again the noises they had heard the night before, his impression that someone had left through the basement door, Pascal Grant's discovery of the body, and his own decision to move it to the third floor using the dumbwaiter.

When he finished, Sigrid said, "Do you have anything to add to that, Mr. Grant?"

Looking like a frightened Raphael angel, Pascal Grant darted a quick glance at her through thick sandy-blond lashes, then bit his lip and shook his head.

"You didn't set the burglar alarm; therefore anyone who had a key could have walked in without your knowing. Is that right?"

He nodded without lifting his eyes.

"What if that person *didn't* have a key?"

Puzzled, Pascal Grant looked at her. "He couldn't come in?" he guessed.

"No," Sigrid said patiently. "I meant what would happen if someone rang the bell? Would you hear?"

"Oh. Yes," he nodded vigorously. "It's right over the door in my room. Makes a real loud noise. Even if my tapes are on." He hesitated. "Or did you mean the bell board in the kitchen? It's nice. The bells jingle and a little flag comes up to show which one it is. Mrs. Sophie had a bell and Mr. Erich and—"

"No, I meant the doorbells," Sigrid said, interrupting his enthusiastic description of how Victorian employers had once summoned their servants to particular rooms of the house.

"The doorbells ring in the office and they buzz in my room," said Pascal Grant. "A big buzz means it's the upstairs door and a sort of littler one means it's the spiderweb door."

"And did you hear either buzzer last night?"

Pascal shook his head.

"You're sure of that?"

He nodded solemnly.

The two youths described how they had returned to the Breul House from an early showing of *Round Midnight*, entered through the basement door, and headed straight to Pascal Grant's room without going upstairs and without seeing anyone.

"So you were in your bedroom listening to jazz tapes," Sigrid said, "and you heard someone outside. What time was this?"

Pascal's smooth brow frowned in concentration. "Around ten-fifteen, I think. Maybe ten-thirty."

"Yet you didn't go out to investigate?"

"I thought it was Dr. Shambley," Pascal said slowly.

"Did Dr. Shambley often come down to the basement that late?"

"He was everywhere."

"Did you like Dr. Shambley?"

"No," said the golden-haired janitor before his lawyer could stop him.

"My client's personal feelings toward the deceased had nothing to do with his death," said Harvey Pruitt.

"Then you won't mind if he tells us why he disliked Dr. Shambley?" Sigrid asked.

"I'm afraid I can't allow that at this time," Mr. Pruitt said austerely.

"Very well. What about others at the house, Mr. Grant? Who else didn't like Dr. Shambley?"

"Mrs. Beardsley didn't like him."

"Why not?"

Mr. Pruitt started to object, then sat back.

"I don't know," said Grant. "She said he got her place or something."

Sigrid looked at the lawyer, but Pruitt shook his head. "This is sheer hearsay, you realize?"

"Of course."

She turned to Rick Evans. "You said you had an impression that someone else was there in the passageway when you came out of the bedroom. Who did you think it was?"

Rick shook his head. "I didn't think. I just heard—like footsteps or something. And then I felt a draft from the open door and heard it close."

"Did you go down and look through the door window?" asked Lowry.

"I didn't see anyone," Evans said.

They asked Pascal Grant to explain once more why there was blood on his softball bat if he hadn't hit Shambley with it.

"I didn't!" Pascal said.

"He's telling the pure truth," said Rick in his soft Southern voice. "I was the one carrying that bat. The whole time. I didn't want to touch Dr. Shambley at first. I thought he was dead. He *looked* dead and I just sort of poked him to make sure he really was."

The weakest part of their story was the reason they gave for moving the body and not calling the police. No matter how many times the police detectives returned to that point, the story remained that they were afraid to have Shambley's body found so close to Pascal Grant's door. Period.

While Jim Lowry and Elaine Albee pressed the two youths for stronger reasons, Sigrid leaned back in her chair trying to decide whether or not to charge one or the other or both with the murder. They'd had a weapon, an opportunity, and probably a motive if that lawyer's reluctance to let Grant discuss his distaste for Shambley meant anything.

On the other hand, Grant said he hadn't heard a doorbell, yet that Beardsley woman claimed she'd seen Thorvaldsen there at midnight.

And what was Rick Evans holding back? That he and Grant were sleeping together. Was that all?

She was almost grateful when a uniformed officer opened the door, peered in, and signaled that she had an important phone call.

"Sorry to interrupt, Lieutenant," he said when she came out into the hall and closed the door to the interrogation room, "but Dr. Cohen said you'd probably want to know right away."

The assistant medical examiner was as laid-back over the telephone as in person. "You know that softball bat you people just sent over? Forget it. Too big. You're looking for a rod, not a club."

"A rod?" Sigrid was surprised. "With a wound that messy?"

"I told you there was something odd about that head," Cohen reminded her. "He had a big skull, but it was paper thin. Want the Latin for it?"

"Put it in your report," she said. "What do you mean by a rod? Like a curtain rod?"

"One of those solid brass ones, maybe. Or a broom handle."

"What about that mop handle?"

"Not thin enough. We're talking something no thicker than my thumb. A cane, maybe, or a poker or the handle of an umbrella even. Anyhow, as thin as his skull was, it wouldn't have taken much force whatever they used."

Back in the interrogation room, Sigrid told the two lawyers that as soon as a statement could be typed up and signed, their clients would be free to leave.

Rick Evans gave an involuntary sigh of relief and smiled at Pascal Grant. His smile faded though when she added, "Of course, there will probably be further questions in the next few days, so we expect you not to leave town."

"I won't," Pascal Grant said earnestly.

"No easy solutions," Sigrid told Elaine Albee and Jim Lowry when Grant and Evans had signed their statements and departed. The younger officers were disappointed to learn that the blow that killed Shambley could have been delivered by either a man or a woman, or possibly even a determined child.

"Did any of those people last night carry a walking stick?" asked Albee.

"Not that I noticed," said Sigrid. "The wife of one of the trustees, Mrs. Reinicke, walked with a slight limp, but I didn't see her with a cane." She described the animosity she'd witnessed between Shambley and Reinicke, then checked the time. "I'll take Thorvaldsen and Lady

Francesca Leeds; you two can split the trustees—the Reinickes, the David Hymans, and Mr. and Mrs. Herzog."

Sigrid's voice was cool and her face perfectly serious as she told Lowry, "Mrs. Herzog was a Babcock, you know."

"Huh?" said Lowry.

Later, he and Albee stood on a chilly IRT platform, surrounded by Christmas shoppers with brightly wrapped packages, and debated whether or not the lieutenant's last remark was meant to be humorous.

As the Lexington Avenue train squealed to a stop, they decided it probably wasn't.

In a cab headed uptown, Hester Kohn and Caryn DiFranco discussed the pros and cons of contact lenses while Rick Evans sat sandwiched between them on the rear seat with his feet drawn up on the transmission hump.

The furry hood of Ms. DiFranco's parka brushed Rick's nose as the lawyer leaned over for a closer look at the lenses in Hester Kohn's eyes.

"I just can't wear mine," she sighed. "I looked absolutely gorgeous in them, but I can't see a damn thing. Besides, I've decided glasses are who I am. People expect me to look like this. *I* expect me to look like this."

The round gold frames of her granny glasses had slipped down on her little button nose and she pushed them up in a delicate gesture.

"I know what you mean," said Hester Kohn. "I wore glasses for almost twenty-five years. They were such a part of me I felt naked the first few times I went out without them."

Caryn DiFranco peered into Rick's brown eyes. "Do you wear contacts, Rick?"

"No, ma'am."

"*Ma'am?* Omigod! That makes me sound like I'm eighty years old."

Rick flushed. "Sorry. I keep forgetting people don't say that up here."

"It's okay, kid. You'll be as rude as the rest of us soon enough." She caught a glimpse of passing street signs and tapped the driver on the shoulder. "Let me out at Macy's, okay?"

The driver grunted.

"I've got to buy and mail presents to half of Michigan," she complained to Hester Kohn. "Be grateful you're Jewish."

"I frequently am," Hester said dryly.

As the taxi double-parked in a no-parking zone and Caryn DiFranco opened her door, Hester added, "Thanks for coming down, Caryn."

"Don't thank me. You'll get the bill. Speaking of which, do we bill that MCP partner of yours or the gallery?"

"The gallery."

"Right. Stay out of mischief, Rick, and don't talk to any strange cops."

"Thanks, Miss DiFranco," he said.

She rolled her eyes, slammed the door, and disappeared among the crowds of Christmas shoppers.

The cold air that rushed in when Caryn DiFranco got out had briefly dispersed Hester Kohn's gardenia perfume, but as the cab swerved back into the flow of traffic, the sweet scent again filled the space between them even though Rick had moved to the far side of the seat. For him, it was a disorienting smell, one connected with hot drowsy summer days, swinging on the porch of his mother's house, a porch surrounded by those glossy bushes heavy with waxy white blossoms. Somehow it seemed all wrong to be smelling his mother's gardenias here in this New York City taxicab on a cold December afternoon. Especially with the new associations the heavy scent of gardenias now held.

Dusk was falling and rush hour had begun in earnest. All lanes were clogged at Forty-second Street.

Forty-sixth, Forty-seventh, another snarl in front of Radio City Music Hall.

Hester Kohn smoothed her dark hair and loosened the top button of her red wool coat. "Want to tell me what's really bothering you?"

"Nothing." Without a camera to shield himself from her face, he unconsciously sank deeper into his corner and kept his eyes on the neon-lit stores and buildings they were now creeping past.

A complex blend of affection and irritation and a few stray tendrils of pity as well swept over Hester as she remembered Rick's first few weeks at the gallery.

Her own virginity had been lost so long ago that she had forgotten what terrors true sexual innocence could hold. Despite their age difference, she had dazzled him, made him want her, made him helpless to resist; yet, until they were well into the act, she hadn't even considered the possibility that it might be his first time. In that moment she had become tender and sentimental and had almost broken it off because she suddenly found herself panged by a conscience she didn't know she still possessed.

If I'd known, I would have made it more beautiful, she thought.

Too late. Already the sweet liquids of youth were spilling from his touchingly inept body.

With those first hot rushes of manhood, another boy might have become immediately cocky and boastful, a royal nuisance. Instead, Rick came to each subsequent session reluctantly and seemed miserable and guilty afterwards.

As he was now, in this overheated cab. It wasn't only his involvement in Roger Shambley's death that made him shrink into that corner, yet Hester knew that if she removed her glove and touched his bare, chapped hand with hers, he would be unable to resist. She considered testing her power, but they were now too close to the gallery.

Instead, she sank back into her own corner and wondered if young Rick had, after all, seen or done more last night than he was willing to admit.

Over in Queens, an artificial Christmas tree decorated the main lobby of the Lantana Walk Nursing Home and an electric menorah stood on the reception desk with two bulbs lit for this second day of Hanukkah. As Detective Bernie Peters soon discovered, he had arrived at the most restless hour of the day for ambulatory residents, and Mrs. Palka was not in her room.

"The dinner shift is promptly at five," explained the new resident-director, "but they begin gathering outside the door by four o'clock. No doubt that's where we'll find Mrs. Palka."

They walked through halls wide enough for two wheelchairs to pass each other, into a lounge decorated with more symbols of Hanukkah and Christmas. There they found a querulous elderly woman with thick glasses and a hearing aid struggling to understand what she could expect for dinner as her incurably cheerful friend read the menu aloud.

"Roast ham?" she sniffed. "We had ham for supper last night and dry, stringy fodder it was, too, with a smidgen of honey glaze or pineapple."

"Lamb!" her friend enunciated loudly. "Roast *lamb*, Maureen. And you know perfectly well the doctor said you can have sweet things."

"Wheat beans? What're wheat beans? Do speak up, Dora."

"There she is," said the director, gesturing toward the cheerful little dumpling of a woman, who leaned heavily upon her aluminum walker and watched their approach with lively curiosity.

The director introduced Detective Peters to Mrs. Palka, pointed them to a quiet corner of the lounge, and expertly vectored Mrs. Palka's hard-of-hearing friend toward another group of residents waiting for their dinner.

"My daughter told me someone from the police might be up," beamed Mrs. Palka. She lowered herself painfully into a chair, refusing Peters's help. "I had a hip replacement two years ago," she explained. "Eighty percent who get it can go dancing in six months. I'm part of the twenty percent who have to hang up their dancing shoes."

"I'm sorry," Bernie Peters said awkwardly. The infirmities of age made him uncomfortable. Even though he knew intellectually that everyone grows old, he was still young enough to believe he would somehow be exempted.

Mrs. Palka patted his hand. "Don't be sorry. I danced plenty in my lifetime, believe me." She sat erectly in her chair and cocked her small white head. "So! Dead babies in Gregor Jurczyk's attic. Whose babies were they?"

"Well, that's what we were hoping you could tell me Mrs. Palka. Your daughter thought you were friendly with the Jurczyk family and might remember some of the people who lived in that house."

"Pauline says between 1935 and 1947. That right?"

"Those were the dates on the newspapers we found them wrapped in," Peters nodded.

"Now let me think. The Depression was going strong then and then came the war. They couldn't have been Barbara's. She was very good, very religious and would never. Besides, she and Karol—that was her husband, lovely man—they couldn't have babies. And Angelika was a businesswoman, worked as a secretary in one of those big-shot investment places on Wall Street. She never married, so it couldn't have been her. There was a Mr. and Mrs. Rospochowski, but they had a new baby almost every year. When did she have time to slip in four more? Now there *was* a pretty little redheaded thing. What was her name? Anna? Anya?

"Ah, but what am I talking?" Mrs. Palka shook her head ruefully at what she considered a failing memory. "That one didn't come till after the war started."

"What about Mr. Jurczyk? Was he married?"

"Not that one. Too interested in the almighty dollar to spend a penny on a wife."

The dining room opened and residents began a modest surge through the doors. The smell of roast meat and steamed broccoli spread through the lounge and stirred those still seated to action. Even Mrs. Palka began to move her walker into a ready position.

"But really, Barbara's the one who could tell you better about the people who lived there," she said. She took a slip of paper with a Staten Island address from the pocket of her pink cardigan and gave it to Peters. "*If* she'll talk to you. We used to call each other up on the phone at least once a month, but she's gone downhill so much this year. Last time I talked to her—back in August that must have been—I don't believe she knew who I was. But then she *is* eighty-seven, four years older than me."

Getting up from a chair seemed almost as painful to Mrs. Palka as sitting down, but as she regained her feet and had her walker pointed toward the dining room, her querulous friend impatiently called to her, "Hurry up, Dora! Loretta says we're having colicky moose for dessert." A ridiculous mental image filled Peters's head, and plump little Mrs. Palka, her wrinkled face aglow with laughter, winked at him with such insouciant charm that he found himself laughing, too.

"That Maureen! She knows perfectly well that Loretta said chocolate mousse."

The Hymans lived on Central Park South, but the Herzogs and the Reinickes lived within three blocks of each other in the East Sixties, so Elaine Albee and Jim Lowry decided to interview them first.

Lydia Babcock Herzog was tall and gaunt in a high-necked tunic and slacks of ivory wool. The young policewoman admired her dramatic gold necklace, her diamond earrings, her beautifully furnished drawing room with its miniature gold Christmas tree set upon an intricately carved ebony stand, even her tall and dignified husband; but as far as Elaine was concerned, that old adage, "You can never be too rich or too thin," was only half right. Mrs. Herzog would have to gain ten pounds just to qualify for anorectic, never mind too thin.

Mr. Herzog was quietly handsome, like a fair-haired English film star of the forties, refined and reserved. He offered Jim and Elaine drinks and, when they refused, continued with the one he'd begun before they arrived.

Mrs. Herzog's drink remained untouched on the low table before her. She sat on a sofa of pale blue brocade, inclined her head graciously, and repeated how shocked they had been to learn of Dr. Shambley's untimely death. How utterly shocked, in fact.

Jim Lowry rather doubted that. Mrs. Herzog seemed too detached to have ever been shocked by anything, but he nodded. "We understand that he hadn't been there very long?"

"He was appointed at our semiannual meeting in September," said Mrs. Herzog. "Jacob Munson put his name forward. I wasn't quite sure he was right for the Breul House—he was on sabbatical from the New York Center for the Fine Arts, you see—but Jacob assured us his academic credentials were impeccable and we did lack a scholar on the board." She watched her husband refill his martini glass from a silver shaker on the antique Chinese sideboard. "I suppose we shall have to find ourselves another scholar."

"This time from the *Institute* of Fine Arts," her husband murmured as he sat down again in a pale blue chair by the sideboard.

"Yes." She lifted her own drink from the gleaming teak table and held the long-stemmed crystal cocktail glass with skeletal fingers while she stared at the small white object awash in clear liquid.

A Gibson, Elaine decided. Martinis had olives, Gibsons had pearl onions.

Of course.

Onions also had fewer calories than olives. Not that it actually mattered.

Without touching the glass to her lips, Mrs. Herzog returned it to the table.

"Were you aware of any animosity between Dr. Shambley and anyone else at the Breul House?" asked Jim Lowry.

"We hardly knew him, Detective Lowry. Marie Reinicke arranged a luncheon at the house for everyone to meet him, early last month. He was quite witty that day. A bit *too* witty for my taste, but then perhaps I—"

She hesitated as her husband stood and casually poured himself another drink, then looked at her inquiringly. "Another for you, my dear?"

"No, thank you," she replied. "I still seem to have some."

"We were told that he was witty at Mr. Reinicke's expense last night," said Elaine Albee.

"Precisely my point. Winston was devastated when he had to part with his Van Gogh drawing, and for that odious little man to make light of it—!"

Her voice lost its detachment and Mr. Herzog completed the thought for her in a dignified tone. "He was no gentleman."

"Was Mr. Reinicke angry last night?" asked Lowry.

"Winston Reinicke *is* a gentleman," said Mrs. Herzog. "If you're really asking if he remained behind last night and exacted revenge for Dr. Shambley's insults, he did not. The four of us left Erich Breul House together shortly after eight and shared a car uptown. We dropped the Reinickes at their own door well before eight-thirty."

"Are you quite sure I can't fix someone a drink?" Mr. Herzog asked courteously.

When they regained the street some twenty-seven floors below, Elaine Albee and Jim Lowry unconsciously paused to draw in several deep breaths of frigid night air.

Lowry laughed when he realized what they were doing. "That's how it must feel in a submarine or a spaceship," he said. "Every crack hermetically sealed and all the air recycled over and over until there's no oxygen left in it."

Rush hour traffic was still building and streams of headlights could be seen all the way down Park Avenue. The Reinickes lived in a building that fronted the park and as she and Jim walked over to Fifth, Elaine said, "Before we do the Hymans, let's stop in at F.A.O. Schwarz if we finish up with the Reinickes in time. I need to see some kids talking to Santa soon or I'm going to lose all my Christmas spirit."

The Reinicke apartment rose high above Central Park. The living room was furnished with an eclectic mix of beautiful antiques, modern couches, small collectibles, and a large, bushy Scotch pine squashed into a corner window; its colored lights overlay the lights of the park and were reflected back into the room. Despite the clutter, the place seemed warm and cozy after the airless precision of the Herzogs' home.

Mrs. Reinicke was a vivacious blonde of late middle-age and seemed totally unself-conscious about her limp.

"Polio," she said cheerfully when she noticed Jim Lowry's surreptitious glance at her rolling gait. "Jonas Salk was eight years too late with his vaccine for me. Even so, I was lucky. My baby sister died."

She tilted her blond head to them. "So much anxiety now with AIDS but we've forgotten the sheer terror of the polio epidemics, haven't we? I do hope there's a heaven. Dr. Salk and his colleagues so deserve one."

Winston Reinicke, bluff and hearty, patted her hand tenderly. "So they do, my love, so they do."

"Forgive my asking," said Elaine, "but do you ever use a cane?"

"Oh, no. Not for me. I tried once but such a nuisance you wouldn't believe! Getting in and out of cabs, and they always slide off your chair and trip up the waiters. I have an Irish shepherd's crook for tramping around our country place, but here in the city I simply can't be bothered. Winston, do fix these two young people something to drink."

She waved aside their demurrals. "It doesn't have to be alcoholic. We have juice, Perrier, or—I know! In honor of the season, what about some eggnog without the nog or mulled apple cider?"

The detectives had not wanted to accept drinks from the Herzogs, but somehow it seemed all right from the Reinickes and soon they were sipping hot cider, warmed inside and out by the spicy bouquet of cloves and cinnamon.

"I grew up on an apple farm in Pennsylvania," Lowry said contentedly, "and this smells like Christmas at home."

Both Reinickes looked as if they'd much rather discuss apple farms or Christmas customs or even Lowry's mother's recipe for mulled cider than Roger Shambley; but it was clear that someone had already given them all the news about the art historian's death. Once the initial awkwardness wore off, they freely answered questions about the previous evening as if the detectives were there solely to gather background material. Neither seemed to realize that Mr. Reinicke might be a suspect.

"It was an informal sort of get-together," explained Marie Reinicke. "Four or five of the trustees and their spouses, some art people, people from the Breul House. Organized by Lady Francesca Leeds with, I suppose, Mr. Thorvaldsen picking up the tab?" She looked doubtfully at her husband.

"Quite right, quite right," agreed Mr. Reinicke. "All their idea, and a tax write-off to boot, so it's only right, eh? Our funds are too low for impromptu parties, I'm afraid. And don't forget Oscar Nauman."

"Of course," Mrs. Reinicke nodded briskly. "He was the whole point of the party. You've been told that though?"

"He's a painter—going to exhibit some of his pictures there, isn't he?" Lowry asked hesitantly. "And that's supposed to help bring in more money?"

"And publicity." Mrs. Reinicke cocked her blond head at Lowry's uncertainty and charitably elucidated, "Yes, you might say Oscar Nauman's a painter. Like Donald Trump's a carpenter or Pavarotti sings a little. Nauman's never had a summary exhibition and to have his first at the Erich Breul House—! There'll be lines all around Sussex Square."

Jim and Elaine exchanged glances. Neither had realized that Lieutenant Harald was involved with someone of that stature.

"And the Kohn woman, Jacob Munson's colleague at the gallery," said Mr. Reinicke, who was still reconstructing last night's party, "and that quiet young woman with those extraordinary gray eyes. She came with Nauman. Did you meet her, Marie? A Miss Harald. Tall woman. Didn't say much, but had a nice smile."

"He never listens to a thing I tell him," Mrs. Reinicke confided to Elaine and Jim. "Now, Winston, don't you remember when Hope Ruffton called to tell us about Dr. Shambley? She said that the police officer in charge of the investigation turned out to be the same woman who was there last night with Oscar Nauman."

"Eh?" Mr. Reinicke drew himself up and looked at Lowry and Albee with the first signs of suspicion. "Well, then. You must already know everything that happened, eh?"

"Not really," Elaine Albee said smoothly. "Lieutenant Harald was there as a guest, like everyone else, and she was only one person. She couldn't have seen everything Dr. Shambley did."

"But she *did* hear his exchange with me, eh?" He glowered down at her.

"Now, Winston—"

"She said he seemed like a very rude man," Elaine answered diplomatically.

Mr. Reinicke flexed the tension from his shoulders and smoothed the lapels of his tweed jacket. It was like watching a farm dog lower its hackles and become good ol' Shep again, thought Lowry.

"Dr. Shambley was rude to you last night?" asked Mrs. Reinicke. "You didn't tell me, Winston."

"No need, my dear, no need at all," he said gruffly. "He'd heard about our Van Gogh and it amused him."

"*Amused* him?" Mrs. Reinicke began to grow indignant.

"And then he had the unmitigated gall to suggest I could upgrade my collection with a Norman Rockwell or a Pierson Sharpe."

"My dear!"

"Sharpe?" asked Jim Lowry, who rather liked Norman Rockwell's down-to-earth pictures and didn't see where the insult lay in Shambley's remarks.

"He's the man who draws those kids with the big sad eyes," Elaine told him. "The one my sister-in-law likes so much."

Lowry knew what Lainey thought of her sister-in-law's taste and began to understand the Reinickes' annoyance.

"No wonder you and Cheevy were gone so long last night," said Mrs. Reinicke sympathetically.

"You went out again last night?" asked Elaine.

"Needed a good long tramp," Winston Reinicke nodded. "Walked around the edge of the park to Columbus Circle, then up to Lincoln Center and back down Broadway to Times Square. Don't mind admitting the fellow got to me. Nobody likes to admit he's failed."

"Oh, for heaven's sake, Winston!" Mrs. Reinicke stood, plucked her husband's empty glass from his hand and stumped over to their liquor cabinet to pour him a fresh drink. "You had a temporary setback. And you were hardly alone. I never liked that Van Gogh anyhow."

"Well, *I* did!" he said testily, waving away the drink she offered him.

Mrs. Reinicke evidently knew her husband's moods quite well, for she continued to hold out the glass until he sighed and took it.

"Suppose that lieutenant woman wants to know what it was all about," he told Lowry and Albee. "Black Monday. Took a real bath on the Street. Overextended. More than I could raise to cover all my margin calls. Elliott Buntrock'd had his eye on my Van Gogh for years and he offered to help liquidate some of my collection in a hurry if I'd give him first shot at that drawing. Didn't try to fudge the prices either. Damned decent of him. Might've gotten a bit more if I'd put them up for a proper auction; but if I could've waited for an auction, wouldn't have had to sell out in the first place, eh?"

"And now you can have the fun of building a new collection," Marie Reinicke observed indulgently.

"Not the same," said her husband, taking another swallow of his drink. "Not as much fun having people to dinner any more either."

"It was a very gloomy drawing," Mrs. Reinicke told the young officers. "But some people were impressed to learn they were dining in the same room with a Van Gogh and Winston loved to show it off. Personally, I miss the Cassatt pastel more and no one ever paid it a shred of attention."

"After Dr. Shambley's remarks, though, it's certainly understandable that you'd want to walk off some steam," said Elaine Albee.

It all sounded very much like a tempest in a teapot to Jim Lowry, but he knew that murders were committed every day for even sillier reasons. It was lucky that Mr. Reinicke had an alibi.

"Did your friend come home with you?" he asked.

Mr. Reinicke looked blank. "Friend?"

Elaine realized that Jim was trying to avoid raising Mr. Reinicke's ire again. "You said that you and a Mr.—Cheever, was it?—took a long walk together," she said helpfully. "If you could give us his full name and address—"

"Cheevy?"

Mrs. Reinicke lay back in her chair and whooped with laughter. "*Mr. Cheevy!*"

"Cheevy's our dog," chuckled Mr. Reinicke, his good spirits partially restored. "A King Charles spaniel out of Scorned Lady of Winterset, so we had to name him Cheevy. First name"—he chuckled some more— "Miniver, of course."

Mrs. Reinicke took pity on the detectives' puzzled looks. "From the Edwin Arlington Robinson poem," she smiled. "You know: 'Miniver Cheevy, child of scorn'?"

Elaine looked at Jim, then sighed and took a deep breath. "I'm sorry, Mr. Reinicke, but we have to ask you exactly what time you left this apartment, when you returned and if you met anyone you recognized during that time?"

Traffic was beginning to thin out, and as they walked down Fifth Avenue to see if the famous toy store were keeping late Christmas hours, a sharp arctic wind swept across the park. With mittened hands, Elaine pulled her woolly blue knitted hat further down over her face and turned up her collar till only her eyes and her pink-tipped nose could be seen.

Jim Lowry had not worn a hat or cap since he was twelve and still under parental control, but he turned up his own collar and wrapped his wool scarf tighter so that his ears were somewhat protected. His breath blew out in white clouds before him as he said gloomily, "I don't think Lieutenant Harald's going to accept the testimony of a King Charles spaniel."

Elaine pulled him to a stop. "Look down there," she said, gesturing with her head. "Cohen said a rod or a stick, right? Do you suppose Mr. Reinicke has one?"

On the sidewalk a few yards ahead of them, a man was cleaning up after his poodle with a device that looked something like a long-handled dustpan.

Jim began to laugh. "You gotta promise I can be there when you ask the lieutenant if Shambley could have bought it with a pooper-scooper."

With a fuzzy hat pulled down over her ears and a long fur coat that swathed her tiny body like a djellaba, Søren Thorvaldsen's middle-aged secretary tripped up the gangplank and across the wide deck as if the frigid gusts whipping off the Hudson River were nothing more than spring zephyrs.

Probably one of those dauntless Nordic types that went from steaming saunas to splashing among ice floes, thought Sigrid as she shivered along behind in a utilitarian coat and hood of heavy black wool that had weathered nine winters. The usual river traffic seemed to be out on the choppy water tonight, but the wind made her eyes so teary that she could only distinguish blurred lights in the darkness.

When she called earlier to set up this meeting, Sigrid hadn't expected it would take a half-mile hike to find Thorvaldsen. But she'd arrived at his office overlooking the river to find a Danish pixie who, after a quick telephone conversation conducted in Danish, had immediately encased herself in an envelope of fur and led Sigrid through a maze of hallways and elevators and eventually across a bone-numbing expanse of wind-swept pier and up onto the deck of his cruise ship, the *Sea Dancer*.

"She's supposed to sail Saturday at noon," explained the pixie, a Miss Kristensen. Even in high-heeled leather boots, the woman barely came up to Sigrid's shoulder and her words were almost blown away as she trotted along ahead of the tall police officer. "—partial loss of power in one of the main generators."

She tugged open a heavy steel door and they were suddenly and mercifully out of the biting wind and into the silence of a glass-enclosed promenade. Through another door and this time they entered true warmth. Sigrid pushed back the hood of her coat and felt her face begin to thaw.

They were inside a spacious lobby decorated in tones of peach, melon, and sunshine yellow, but Sigrid was given no time to play tourist. Already, Miss Kristensen was halfway across the wide expanse of floral carpeting, heading for a bank of elevators. Sigrid almost expected to see her pull out a large turnip watch and murmur something about being late. She lengthened her own stride and caught up with the other woman just as the elevator arrived.

Instead of descending to the depths of the ship, or wherever they kept generators—Sigrid was weak on engineering details—the elevator rose. Soon she was once more following Miss Kristensen through a maze of confusing twists and turns, then down a wide, paneled hall carpeted in rich patterns of luscious tropical colors.

Abruptly, Miss Kristensen opened the door of a luxurious room with a sweeping view of the river. "Mr. Thorvaldsen's suite," she murmured. "If you'll wait here, Lieutenant Harald, he'll join you shortly." She flicked on a soft light over a fully equipped bar that gleamed and sparkled with chrome and crystal and cut-glass decanters like a tiny, perfect jewel box. "May I get you something to drink while you wait?"

"No, thank you," said Sigrid.

"Then I'll say *godnat*." Wrapping her furs tighter around her small form, the secretary hurried away.

Sigrid was drawn to the bank of windows at the end of the room where a wide couch had been built into the curve of the window. Upholstered in buttery soft leather of a tawny topaz color, it invited one to curl up and enjoy the view. She slipped off her coat and rested her strong chin on the back of the couch to stare through the glass.

The 180-degree night view was breathtaking. Across the water, a huge neon coffee cup dripped its good-to-the-last drop in front of New Jersey's lights; on the near shore, the skyscrapers of midtown Manhattan became towering tiers of cubed light; while upriver, the George Washington Bridge spanned the two shores with graceful, glittering loops.

The city's stately nighttime beauty, coupled with the ship's warmth and quiet, made Sigrid relax. It had been a long day and as the moments passed, relaxation turned to increasing lethargy. Just as she was beginning to think she ought to take a turn about the deck to wake herself up, the door opened and Søren Thorvaldsen entered.

He was casually dressed in dark wool slacks and a white hand-knit fisherman's sweater that had a fresh smear of grease on the left cuff, and he was followed by a waiter whose tray held a silver thermos jug of steaming hot drink and plates of cheese and crackers and smoked fish.

"Can't offer you much," Thorvaldsen said as the waiter spread the food on the blond oak table before her, then left. "The kitchen staff's off duty until tomorrow morning."

"This wasn't necessary," Sigrid told him, but she was suddenly conscious of hunger and took the plate he offered with no further protest.

The hot drinks were Tom and Jerries, not a concoction Sigrid cared for, although she could appreciate how fitting it was for the cold night and for the yuletide season.

"*Glaedelig ful,*" said Thorvaldsen, lifting his glass toward her.

"*Skål,*" she replied.

The spicy hot rum slid down easily and began to create its own inner warmth.

"I didn't realize you were such a hands-on shipowner," Sigrid said, watching Thorvaldsen dab with a linen napkin at the grease on his sweater. There was an unpretentious, raw vitality about the man that kept one subliminally reminded of the working-class roots even when he wasn't boasting of them.

"That generator could wind up costing me an extra eighteen hundred unnecessary meals if we're a half day late leaving port," the Dane said with a shrug. He finished his drink and poured another from the thermos. "Plus the extra time and labor to serve and clean up afterwards."

Sigrid cut herself a wedge of soft Havarti and spread it on a slice of dark bread. "All because it leaves in the evening instead of noon?"

"Everything that happens aboard ship, every detail, has a price tag. Leaving a half day late could mean getting into Bermuda long after lunch instead of well before. This is a very competitive business. Something goes over cost, it comes out of profits. When that happens, I want to know why."

The serious lines in his open rugged face crinkled as he grinned and added, "Eighteen hundred lunches would just about buy one Oscar Nauman painting."

Sigrid followed his eyes to a picture on the far wall, in a place of honor beyond the bar. Its colors and rhythms were arresting: very manly, very—now that she looked at it—Nauman. She was surprised to realize that she could recognize the painting as indisputably his. It was a large abstract in those topaz and rust tones that she now identified with Francesca Leeds.

In fact this whole room with its blond oak, its amber and russet-colored couches and chairs, its gold chrome and its touches of burnt orange might have been designed as a setting for Francesca Leeds.

"Which came first?" she asked, curious. "The picture or the decor?"

"The picture, of course," he answered, apparently surprised that she would need to ask.

Sigrid gave an inward sigh. It was awkward to be the only person in Nauman's world who wasn't particularly enthusiastic about his work. She didn't wonder that this self-made millionaire could respond so directly to the strength of Nauman's art. Intellectually, she, too, could appreciate the games Nauman played with color and mathematics, with subtle rhythms and thematic variations; and she wished she liked it more. But it was just too abstract to move her emotionally, unlike the old German painters whom she loved for their spare asceticism and because they *were* rooted in the particular.

"—and perhaps it appeals to me precisely because I have spent so many years in hard serious work, but there's always Nauman's playful quality," Thorvaldsen was saying.

Wasn't there just, Sigrid thought wryly, momentarily diverted from Thorvaldsen's enthusiasm by certain memories of Nauman's playfulness.

"—an artist of his own time and one who isn't afraid to leave the loose ends. The high purpose of art is to remind us that something is always left undone—to remind us that it's not human to expect too much from method and plan. Only third-rate artists paint perfect pictures. Real life isn't tidy," said Thorvaldsen. "Look at this ship—all a fantasy!"

Thorvaldsen tilted the nearly empty thermos jug inquiringly. "More?"

Sigrid shook her head and covered the top of her glass with her hand. "No."

She pulled a notepad from the outer pocket of her coat and placed it on the table. "You *do* realize this isn't a social visit?"

"Too bad." His voice was slightly slurred, but his eyes were wary.

He seemed to be drinking quite a lot, Sigrid noted. That was the trouble with mixing alcohol with eggs and spices. Those hot Tom and Jerries were like eggnog: if one hadn't eaten, it was too easy to treat them like food instead of drink.

Sigrid patted her other coat pockets and finally the pockets of her dark blue jacket and gray slacks without finding a pen.

Smiling, Thorvaldsen handed her his, a slim gold-filled object. His fingers brushed hers and lingered a moment before he released the pen.

Deliberately?

"Thank you," she said stiffly. "I gather you'd already heard about Dr. Roger Shambley when I called before."

"Yes. Someone told Francesca and she telephoned me." Thorvaldsen buttered a cracker, added a morsel of smoked fish, and popped the whole thing in his mouth.

"How long had you known Dr. Shambley?"

The shipowner swallowed. "I didn't. Heard his name, of course, and knew he was an art historian writing a book, but that's all."

"What did you think of him?"

Thorvaldsen gave a short explosive laugh and spoke a couple of one-syllable words in Danish that need no translation. "You were there, *frøken* Harald. You heard him threaten *me*."

"Yes. What did he mean?"

The big Dane shrugged. "Who knows what small men dream?"

"You weren't afraid of his threat?"

"Of course not."

"Would you describe, please, what happened at the Breul House after Nauman and I left?" asked Sigrid.

"After you and Nauman left, it became boring." Thorvaldsen leaned back in a creamy leather chair with his left ankle resting on his right knee and his brawny hands clasping his left shin. "I spoke with that curator chap, Buntrock, for a few minutes. Very knowledgeable about Nauman's work. Then I left with Lady Francesca Leeds. About eight-thirty, I think."

"Shambley didn't reappear?"

"He did not."

"And then?"

"And then?" he mimicked. "You wish to know what happened *after* we left the Breul House?"

"You had words with Dr. Shambley, laid hands on him, almost hit him," Sigrid said calmly. "A few hours later, he was dead. You may not want to answer without a lawyer—"

"*Lawyers!*" Thorvaldsen snorted scornfully.

"—but I have to ask you to account for those hours up until, say, one A.M."

"Eight-thirty till one A.M.," he repeated slowly.

"Yes."

"We had dinner reservations at Le Petit Coq," he said, naming an expensive French restaurant a few blocks west of Sussex Square. "After that I put Francesca into a taxi for the Maintenon and came back to my office to work."

His blue eyes were sardonic. "You have a most unprofessional look on your face, *frøken* Harald. You are surprised to hear that she went back to her hotel alone?"

"Not at all," Sigrid lied. "You and Lady Francesca parted at what time?"

"Ten-fifteen, ten-thirty. I didn't look at my watch."

"And then?"

"I worked until midnight, went to my apartment on the top floor, had a drink, and went to bed. Alone."

"Is there anyone who can confirm that? Miss Kristensen, perhaps?"

"Not even Miss Kristensen is that dedicated."

"What about a night watchman or a cleaning person?"

He shook his head and his fair hair was like old mellow gold in the lamplight of this golden stateroom. "Sorry. There's only my word."

"Your word?" Her eyes were skeptical chips of gray slate as she lifted them to his.

"You're an odd woman," he said, standing abruptly. He stretched out his hand to her. "Come, please."

Puzzled, Sigrid stood up.

He pointed toward the glass.

Out in the channel, a tugboat moved slowly past the *Sea Dancer*. Car lights passed in an intermittent stream along the expressway, and high above the Palisades could be seen the red and green flashes of airplane lights.

"In the glass," Thorvaldsen murmured and Sigrid saw themselves reflected as in a dark mirror.

"It did not surprise me that Oscar had taken Francesca," he said thickly. "But you—!"

He tried to pull her to him.

"Mr. Thorvaldsen—"

"Oscar Nauman is a man of fire. You can't be as cold as you look."

He put his arms around her as if to kiss her.

"Are you crazy? Stop it!" she cried and, when he didn't release her, kicked him in the shins. Hard.

As Thorvaldsen tightened his hold, Sigrid's police training shifted into automatic. She abruptly relaxed, leaned into him, and a moment later, sent the Dane crashing to the floor.

Instinctively, her hand went to the handle of the .38 holstered in a shoulder harness beneath her jacket as she waited to see how Thorvaldsen would react.

At that moment a voice behind her said, "Is this a private game or can anybody play?"

Sigrid released the gun handle, took a deep breath, and slowly turned. "Hello, Lady Francesca."

Francesca Leeds closed the door behind her and looked from Sigrid, breathing hard in the middle of the room, to Søren Thorvaldsen, now sitting on the floor and rubbing his left eye where it had banged against the low table. Her smile was tentative as she said, "I'm sure there's some perfectly rational explanation for what's happened here."

"Not really," said Sigrid. "Mr. Thorvaldsen was a bit uncertain about a woman's ability to defend herself and I'm afraid he goaded me into a demonstration. Quite unprofessional of me. I apologize, Mr. Thorvaldsen."

She had expected him to be sullen. Instead, he came to his feet with an easy smile and a shrug.

"No apologies, *frøken* Harald. You showed me what I wished to know." He greeted the elegant redhead with a kiss on her cool cheek. "You see, *Lsøde ven?* I'm still an Ålborg roughneck."

Not fully convinced, but willing to let it pass, Francesca threw her mink coat over a nearby chair, added her gloves to the heap, and headed for the bar. "I feel as if I'm two drinks behind. Fix anyone else something?"

"Not for me," Sigrid murmured.

"Just an ice cube," Thorvaldsen said ruefully, as his fingers examined the lump swelling beneath his eye. "You come in time to rescue me, Francesca. I'm being grilled about Dr. Shambley."

Francesca paused with a decanter of Irish whiskey in her graceful hands. "Should I be leaving then, Sigrid?"

"Why?" asked Thorvaldsen.

Sigrid stood. "Perhaps it would be better if you both came to my office tomorrow and made formal statements."

"Me?" Francesca seemed surprised. "Why on earth would you need a statement from me? I barely knew the man."

"But you have a key to the Breul House, don't you?" asked Sigrid.

"Well, yes, but— Oh, don't be daft, Sigrid! He was a grotty little man but you can't think I went back there last night and sneaked in and killed him?"

"Can you tell me where you were between eight-thirty and one A.M.?" Sigrid asked bluntly.

"To be sure, I can," she said in her Celtic lilt. She brought Thorvaldsen an ice cube wrapped in a napkin and sat down with her drink at the other end of the couch from Sigrid. "Søren and I finished dinner shortly before ten, then I took a cab to the Maintenon. Some friends of mine were just going into the lounge when I got in around ten-thirty— George and Bitsy Laufermann—and they insisted that I join them. We stayed for the midnight show. I'll give you their phone number, if you wish, and you can also ask the maître d'. He'll tell you I was there."

Sigrid jotted down the names and numbers, then asked, "What about your key to the Breul House? Do you carry it with you?"

"On my key ring, yes," said Francesca. "I suppose you'll be wanting to see it."

She moved so beautifully, Sigrid thought, watching as the other woman crossed to her fur coat. Tonight she wore a dark brown taffeta dress edged with a stiff, narrow self-ruffle at the neck and wrists, shot with gold threads that gleamed with every swing of the skirt. Her lustrous hair fell in copper tangles about the perfect oval of her face.

Even as Sigrid went through the formalities of this interview with one level of her mind, another level cataloged Francesca's almost flawless beauty. Thorvaldsen's advances had been clumsy and insulting and she should have decked him harder, but she could almost sympathize with his basic confusion. How could Oscar Nauman possibly be attracted to her when he'd had one of the most beautiful women in New York?

Last night she had meant it when she told Nauman she wasn't jealous of the women he'd known before her. Tonight, on this ship, she found herself wondering who had initiated their split—Francesca or Nauman?

Francesca Leeds dug into one of the deep pockets and came out with a handful of keys. She detached one and handed it to Sigrid. It was tagged *EBH*.

"I'd like to keep this for now," Sigrid said, wrapping it in a clean sheet of notepaper. She quickly wrote out a receipt for it. "One more question: do you know why Roger Shambley was killed?"

The copper-haired woman resumed her place on the couch and her brown eyes regarded Sigrid humorously. "Because he couldn't keep his mouth shut?"

Sigrid looked up inquiringly.

Francesca shrugged. "I only know what I've heard."

"Which is—?"

"Word around art circles is that Roger Shambley liked to know things. He listened and he heard and he was a bloody genius with insinuations. People often thought he knew more than he did, but by the time they realized he didn't, it was too late because they'd already let too much slip." She looked into her glass and laughed. "Does that make any sense?"

"He was a *røven af fjerde division*," Thorvaldsen growled, the ice cube still held to his eye.

"That, too, if it means what I think it does," Francesca nodded. "He liked to know unpleasant things about you and then rub your nose in it." She tilted her glass to her lips and drank the rest of her undiluted whiskey. "Or so I've been told."

More specific, she would not be; so Sigrid turned her gaze back to the man, who had taken Francesca's glass over to the bar for a refill.

"Would you prefer to finish your statement down at headquarters tomorrow, Mr. Thorvaldsen?"

"I thought I had finished already," he said, pouring Irish whiskey into two glasses.

Sigrid flipped back several pages in her notebook. "You told me you worked until midnight and then went to bed."

"*Ja.*"

"Yet we have a witness who saw you at the Breul House at midnight."

That finally got under the shell of amused condescension that he'd adopted since Francesca's arrival.

His blue eyes narrowed. "He must be mistaken."

"No," she answered flatly.

Francesca looked up at him as he returned with her new drink. "Søren?"

He ignored her. "And if I say he lies, it is my word against his. Then what happens?"

"Then your people here will be questioned. No matter what you think, if you returned after midnight, someone will have seen you. Lady Francesca's key to the Breul House will be analyzed. If the lab finds any waxy or soapy residue, that might indicate that it'd been duplicated without her knowledge. We would probably look more closely into your activities, see if Roger Shambley had learned something interesting about you—how you acquired all the pieces in your art collection, for instance. And then—"

"Enough, enough." He turned to Francesca. "I did *not* use your key."

"But you did go back to the Breul House," Sigrid prodded.

"*Ja,*" he sighed and walked over to the windows to stare out at the dark river.

Francesca's eyes met Sigrid's and both women waited silently.

With his back to them, Thorvaldsen said, "When I returned to my office last night, there was a message on my machine from Dr. Shambley. He apologized for what he'd said about Francesca and Nauman and said he wanted to make it up to me."

"Is the message still there?" Sigrid asked.

"No, I erased it." Thorvaldsen sank heavily into the tawny leather chair opposite the low oak-and-glass table, his full glass cradled in those strong hands. The red lump under his eye had begun to turn blue.

"Did he say what he planned to do?"

"Not in so many words. Francesca told you before: he could say one thing, but you knew he meant something else." He looked at his glass, then set it on the table without drinking.

"This you must understand, *frøken* Harald—I did not get here by following every rule."

He made a sweeping gesture of his hands that encompassed their luxurious surroundings here on the high deck of this ship and, by extension, all that it symbolized. "If I'd done that, I'd still be breaking my back under bales of smoked herring on a dock in Ålborg. Back then, *ja*, maybe I did sail too close to the wind. But that was then and this is now. Now, my money makes more money. All by itself and all legal. Now, I want things I never dreamed of when I was a kid in Denmark. Now, I have time to learn what these things mean, and money to pay for them."

He gestured toward the painting across the room. "Twenty-three years ago, I was walking along a street in København and I saw a picture in the window of a gallery. A little thing, so"—he sketched a small rectangle with his hands, approximately twelve by eighteen inches—"and it stopped me cold. I didn't know why, I just knew I had to own it. It took me two years to pay for it. My first Nauman picture. Now I own eleven Naumans and they form the heart of my collection. I've collected other artists, of course—two Picassos, a Léger, a wonderful Brancusi sculpture, and a number of works by lesser-known practitioners of what I call 'cerebral abstraction.' "

Francesca slipped off her brown high-heeled boots and tucked her legs up under her skirt with a rustle of taffeta, but Sigrid remained motionless as Thorvaldsen abruptly reached for his glass.

"And for all these works," he said, "I have documents, bills of sale, certificates." He drank deeply. "But every now and then, people come to me with very beautiful, very rare things and they don't always have documents and I don't always ask for receipts. Shambley knew this."

Thorvaldsen gave Francesca a crooked smile. "Or, as you said, *min dame*, he made me think he knew this."

"He offered to sell you a stolen painting?" Sigrid asked.

"Not in those words, but yes," Thorvaldsen admitted. "At the same time, he made me think that if I didn't come, questions would be raised by others. Just now—"

He broke off and gave a sardonic shrug of his broad shoulders. "Let's say that at this particular moment, I don't want controversy. *Any* controversy. Next month, okay. Now, no."

"So you went to the Breul House?"

"Not immediately. But the more I thought of this other matter, the more I decided I had to go, at least hear what he wanted to say. I walked over to Eleventh Avenue and caught a cab going downtown. Got out near Sussex Square. He said to come in without ringing; the front door would be unlocked."

"Was it?"

His affirmative grunt was halfway between a *ja* and a yeah.

"And the time?"

"A few minutes past eleven, I think. The great hall was dim inside. I called his name. No answer. A light was on in the library, so I went in there and sat until I almost fell asleep. Finally, I began to think it was some kind of stupid joke, so I left."

"What time was that?"

"Midnight." A more genuine smile flitted across his rugged features. "As I came down the steps, the lights on the Christmas tree in the middle of the park went off."

Sigrid found it hard to believe that a man like Søren Thorvaldsen would sit meekly in a library and wait almost an hour for someone like Shambley to jerk him around and she said as much.

Thorvaldsen finished off his drink and set the glass on the table between them with a decisive clink. "Think what you like. You wanted my statement. That's it."

The lump beneath his eye was nearly purple now and Sigrid saw that he winced when he touched it absentmindedly. It was probably pointless to continue with Thorvaldsen tonight, she thought. Better to wait and get him down to her office when he was less belligerent. Time enough then to ask if he'd had a look around for whatever shady art object Shambley may have planned to sell him.

She slipped on her coat, stowed the pad in one of its pockets, and pulled out her gloves.

"Did you leave a trail of bread crumbs coming in?" Francesca asked.

"No," Sigrid smiled, "but I think I can find my way out."

As she said good night and opened the door, Francesca suddenly slid on her boots and said, "Better let me point you toward the nearest gangplank. Back in a minute, Søren."

They walked down the wide passageway to the elevator. Sigrid said, "Do you suppose the ship's doctor is on board tonight? Someone ought to take a look at that eye."

Francesca was amused. "I'm sure Søren's had worse knocks than that. He made a pass at you, didn't he?"

"Not exactly."

They rang for an elevator and Sigrid felt the other woman's appraising eyes as they waited.

"He's really not like that," said Francesca. "You probably won't believe me, but I've been seeing him for two months now and underneath all that diamond-in-the-rough facade, he's been a perfect gentleman. *Too* perfect, in some respects."

The elevator arrived and they stepped inside. "In fact," she added, "I was beginning to wonder if he marched to a different drummer or if I was losing it."

"You?" Sigrid murmured, feeling like a drab country mouse next to Francesca's rich shimmer of brown-and-gold taffeta.

As the elevator doors opened for them, Francesca laid her hand on Sigrid's arm. "Does it make a difference to you, Sigrid? About Oscar and me, I mean? I saw your face last night when you realized what Roger Shambley meant."

Sigrid was silent. She rather doubted if Francesca Leeds had seen any more in her face than the redhead expected—or wanted?—to see; and she had never felt comfortable exchanging girlish confidences.

Evidently Francesca felt differently. "What Oscar and I had was wonderful while it lasted, but it's been over for more than a year."

And what, Sigrid wondered mutely, was the proper response to that? I'm sorry? I'm glad? Were you glad when it ended? Was Nauman?

"Ah! There's the door I came in," she said, pulling on her gloves and raising the hood of her coat. "I think I can find my way out from here."

And beat a coward's quick exit.

It was after nine when Sigrid got home. She'd stopped off at a bookstore along the way to begin her Christmas shopping. This was a young cousin's first Christmas and she couldn't decide whether to get him a traditional *Mother Goose* or a lavish pop-up book, so she bought both. Baby Lars had been named for her favorite great-uncle, but she couldn't neglect the other five in Hilda's brood, especially when one stop could take care of the whole Carmichael family so simply.

She had spent a happy hour browsing through *Wind in the Willows, The Secret Garden, Watership Down, Treasure Island,* and *Charlotte's Web,* leafing through dozens more before adding a newly published and beautifully illustrated book of fairy tales for Hilda, who collected them.

A book for Hilda's husband wasn't quite as simple. What does one give a CPA who has everything? Impulsively she chose a book on building Chinese kites. A man with six children might find that diverting.

Laden with bundles, she arrived at number 42½, a sturdy green wooden gate set into a high nondescript wall on an equally nondescript street full of rundown buildings at the western edge of Greenwich Village. She unlocked the gate and found Roman Tramegra stringing lights on the dogwood tree that stood in the center of their small garden. He was bundled against the icy December night in a bizarre white ski mask, multicolored scarves, and three layers of sweaters and he greeted her gaily in his deep booming voice as she piled her packages on a stone bench.

"Ah, *there* you are, dear Sigrid! Had I realized you'd be home so soon, I would have waited. No matter. I shall be the president and *you* can be the little child that leads us."

It had been almost a year since this late-blooming flower child, to use Nauman's phrase, had wandered into her life and, by an odd set of circumstances, wound up sharing with her an apartment he'd acquired through arcane family connections.

Although only a few years older than she, he had adopted an avuncular manner and by now felt free to comment on her clothes, her hair, her makeup, and whether or not she was eating properly and getting enough sleep. He was so easily deflected, however, that Sigrid, by nature a solitary person, found him less of an intrusion than she'd feared. She discovered that she enjoyed coming home to a well-lit apartment full of occasionally entrancing dinner aromas—Roman was an adventurous cook; not all his adventures had a happy ending—and his magpie curiosity and verbal flights of fancy kept her amused more often than not.

He was tall and portly and there was just enough light in their tiny courtyard to make him look like a cross between a Halloween ghost and Frosty the Snowman. The eye and mouth holes of his white ski mask were outlined in black and the dark toggles of his bulky white cardigan marched down his rounded torso like buttons of coal on a tubby snowman as he positioned the last light and held out to Sigrid the plug end of the tree lights and the receptacle end of an extension cord that he'd snaked from the house.

"Everything's ready," he caroled. "Come along, my dear. No speeches, though I really should hum something appropriate. What did the Marine Band play the other night when they lit the White House tree?"

In his deep basso profundo, he began to hum the national anthem.

Laughing, Sigrid stepped up to the tree and, in a Monty Python imitation of ribbon-cutting royalty, plugged the two electric cords together and said, "I now declare this Christmas season officially opened."

A blaze of colorful lights twinkled through the bare twigs of the dogwood.

"God bless us, every one!" said Roman.

Although Mr. Breul never summarily disregarded expert opinion, he had no use for pedantry. Being well-educated and well-informed, he preferred to trust his own eye to pick out the one good thing from a gallery full of old pictures and to leave the bad behind and he had no need to lean upon the advice of others in so doing. So secure was he in his own taste, that he was never disturbed when, as it occasionally happened, an attribution of his purchase was afterward discredited.

"It matters not who actually painted it. The picture still retains the lofty qualities for which I chose it," he would say as he continued to give it high place within the collection.

ERICH BREUL — THE MAN AND HIS DREAM,
PRIVATELY PUBLISHED 1924 BY THE FRIENDS AND TRUSTEES
OF THE ERICH BREUL HOUSE

EIGHT

Friday, December 18

SIGRID MOVED THE morning session briskly through the usual update on current cases. Matt Eberstadt brushed powdered sugar from his dark green shirt and maroon tie and reported a conviction in the drug-related homicide trial that finally went to the jury yesterday. "They were only out twenty minutes."

The neighborhood canvass around the house that held those infant remains had turned up no one else who could remember the Jurczyks or their tenants from the thirties, but Bernie Peters had already been on the phone to the nursing home in Staten Island, where a staff doctor confirmed Mrs. Palka's fears about her former East Village friend.

"Mrs. Barbara Jurczyk Zajdowicz has had a series of small strokes this past year," Peters said as he tore open a packet of dry creamer and added it to his coffee. "She's in a wheelchair now and the doctor says some days she's cogent, most days she's not. He suggests that we try her immediately after Saturday morning confession."

"Who's her next of kin?" asked Sigrid.

"None listed."

"Who pays the bills then?"

"I talked to an individual in their business office, and the way it works is that she paid into something like an annuity when she first went there back in 1971. Probably what she got for the house. On top of that, she signed over her husband's pension and social security and they're supposed to take care of her as long as she lives."

Elaine Albee shivered and pushed aside her jelly doughnut. She hated the whole idea of growing old, especially here in New York City, and tried not to think about it any more than she could help. It kept getting shoved in her face, though: bag ladies homeless on every street corner; women who once ran but now hobbled down subway platforms, fearfully clutching their lumpy shopping bags as they moved arthritically through doors that closed too fast; women like Barbara Zajdowicz, who'd outlived brothers and sisters and husbands and were now warehoused in nursing homes with no one to watchdog their interests or—

Lieutenant Harald's cool voice cut across her private nightmare. "Are you with us, Albee?"

"Ma'am?"

"Your interview with the Reinickes," the lieutenant prodded.

Feeling like a third-grade schoolkid caught goofing off by a strict teacher, a likeness subliminally underlined by the lieutenant's no-nonsense gray pantsuit and severe white blouse, Albee sat up straight and summarized what she and Lowry had learned from Winston and Marie Reinicke.

"So there's no alibi for Reinicke but his wife doesn't use a cane either," she finished, wadding up the scrap of paper Jim Lowry had slipped her under the table with *P—S??!!* scrawled on it in bold block letters.

"We did pick up something from the Hymans, though," said Lowry.

After looking at kids who were looking at toys in F.A.O. Schwarz, he and Lainy'd swung west to the Hymans' terraced apartment on Central Park South. David and Linda Hyman appeared to be in their midsixties. Mr. Hyman still looked like the rabbinical student he'd once been before he became an economist. His thick and curly beard was more pepper than salt and his dark eyes flashed with intensity as he spoke. A faint rusty glow through her soft white hair hinted that Mrs. Hyman had been a strawberry blonde in her youth. She was small and quiet, but her face had held an amused intelligence as her husband described the things they'd noticed last night.

"They said they saw Shambley come out of the library with a cat-that-ate-the-canary look on his face last night," Lowry reported. "He'd been in there with the director, what's his name? Peake? And the Kohn woman. The Hymans didn't hear what was said between them, but evidently old Jacob Munson came in on the tail end of the conversation and didn't much care for what he heard because he told Hyman that maybe he'd made a mistake when he recommended Shambley as a trustee last fall."

"After the Hymans left the Breul House, they went on to a dinner party in Brooklyn Heights so it looks like they're out of it," said Elaine Albee. "And Mrs. Herzog didn't like the way Shambley was riding Reinicke Wednesday night, but she and her husband alibi each other and their maid confirms it."

Sigrid reported the salient points of her interview with Søren Thorvaldsen and Lady Francesca Leeds and there was a brief discussion of how Thorvaldsen's movements fit into the timetable they were beginning to assemble.

Gray-haired Mick Cluett shifted his bulk in a squeaky swivel chair and phlegmatically reported that the Sussex Square canvass had drawn a blank. No convenient nosy neighbor with an insatiable curiosity about the comings and goings of the Breul House.

He had, however, found an address book in Roger Shambley's upper West Side apartment, which had helped him locate a brother in Michigan who would be flying in tonight. A cursory examination of the apartment revealed nothing unusual to Cluett's experienced eyes.

"Looked like standard stuff to me," he said. "Small one-bedroom apartment, nothing too fancy, but good stuff, you know? Lots of books and papers, nice pictures on the walls. The brother said he'd let us know if he finds anything odd when he goes through the stuff."

They batted it around some more, then Sigrid laid out the day's assignments: in addition to ongoing cases, there were alibis that needed checking, interviews still to come, a murder weapon yet to be discovered, and that interesting possibility that Shambley might have brokered art works of questionable provenance.

Someone with a knowledge of art had been specialed in from another division to go through the papers Shambley had left behind in the Breul House attic, and Eberstadt and Peters were given the task of backtracking on Shambley's last few days as well as taking a quick poll of how his colleagues at the New York Center for the Fine Arts had felt about him.

Leaving Mick Cluett with a stack of paperwork, Sigrid left with Albee and Lowry to do another sweep through the Erich Breul House.

Elliott Buntrock leaned on a chair beside the desk like a great blue heron with a potential mullet in view and cocked his head at Miss Ruffton, who was a peppermint cane this morning in red wool suit and white sweater.

"Looking for something?" he asked. "Looking for what, for God's sake? And how would he know if he'd found it, as much *stuff* as this house has crammed into it?"

Miss Ruffton shrugged imperturbably as the electronic typewriter continued to hum beneath her capable brown fingers. "You asked me why he was acting so smug Wednesday night. I've told you what I thought. Now do you want me to finish with these dimensions or don't you?"

"I do, I do!" he assured her. With a stilt-legged gait, he picked his way across the marbled hall and through the gallery arch to glare at a picture of dead swans and market vegetables which had caught his eye high on the far wall. A passionate proponent of the latest in art, he considered "preart" anything exhibited in America before the Armory Show of 1913.

Kitsch, kitsch, and more kitsch, he thought, contemptuously dismissing the Babbages and Vedders. And all this recent fuss over Sargent. One of the few silver linings to the gloom of curating a show in this place would be the sheer pleasure of dismantling these stiff rows of gilt-framed horrors and seeing them stacked somewhere else for the duration. And he wouldn't limit himself to stripping the walls either. Much of the furniture and all of the tacky gewgaws would have to go as well.

Dressed today in black jeans and a fuzzy black turtleneck, he stood in the exact center of the long gallery with his arms akimbo, the tip of his right boot *en pointe* while the heel lay flat against his inner left ankle, and his bony chin angled forward and up as he considered the size and shape of the long room. This was his favorite contemplative pose and one that a clever photographer had once captured in black and white for a whimsical *New York Today* article entitled "City Birds." To Buntrock's secret gratification, she'd captioned his portrait *Curatoris Hotissimus (Genus Arbiter Artem)*.

As he mentally cleared the gallery and the long drawing room beyond of their resident pictures and superfluous adornments, Elliott Buntrock had to admit that it was actually a rather lovely space, nicely proportioned, architecturally interesting. Maybe wrong for Nauman's work— the restrained sensuality of his middle period, in particular, would be killed by these ornate moldings and marble pilasters. But a Blinky Palermo or a Joseph Beuys, one of those early late-postmoderns—what a curatorial coup it would be to show *them* here!

It was hard, though, to keep his mind firmly fixed on an exhibition some twelve to fourteen months in the future when murder had occurred less than forty-eight hours in the past. He had barely known Shambley. Rumor tagged him a ravenous careerist, all the more dangerous for the depth of his expertise and the thoroughness of his scholarship.

Zig-zags of fashion being what they were these days, Dr. Roger Shambley would probably have had his fifteen minutes of fame, would have found a way to titillate the gliterati's gadfly interest in turn-of-the-century American art, perhaps even, Buntrock thought with a twist of the self-deprecation that made him so attractive to his friends, have been featured in a whimsical *New York Today* photograph of his own.

The telephone out on the secretary's desk trilled softly. He was too far away to hear her words, but Buntrock saw her answer, listen briefly, then hang up.

Hope Ruffton thought Shambley had spent the last couple of weeks looking for something specific and that his cocky arrogance Wednesday night meant that he'd found it. "He wanted the inventory sheets and he was rude about Dr. Peake's ability to recognize authentic work," Miss Ruffton had said.

Buntrock had cocked his bony head at that statement, wondering how much Peake's present secretary knew about the Friedinger brouhaha when Peake wrongly deaccessioned some pieces that later turned out to be authentic after all. And not only authentic, but valuable. No malfeasance had been charged, merely simple stupidity, which, in the art world, could be almost as damaging as a suspended jail sentence.

Innocent though Miss Ruffton's interpretation of Shambley's insinuations might be, Peake and several volunteer docents were even now up in the attic with the same set of inventory sheets that Shambley had used, trying to duplicate the dead man's discovery, if discovery it had been. They were aided by the strong back of that simple-minded janitor as they shifted trunks and furniture around the big attic.

"Taking that list and checking it twice," Buntrock whistled half under his breath as he ambled from the gallery into the drawing room, and from the drawing room back out into the great hall with its opulent Christmas tree. "Gonna find out if naughty Shambley took something nice."

Fully indulging his momentary mood of postmodern grand funk, he ignored the disapproving glance of an elderly docent who guarded the entrance against casual visitors. The Breul House was unofficially closed today except for a group of art students, who had booked a tour for this date several weeks ago and were due in this afternoon from a women's college in Raleigh. Buntrock looked around for Hope Ruffton and found her desk unexpectedly vacant.

"Miss Ruffton went up to tell Dr. Peake that the police are coming back this morning," said the guardian of the gate.

"Very good," said Buntrock. "I'll just carry on."

Continuing his casual whistling, he circled the mannequin that stood below the curve of the marble balustrade. That masculine figure was still dressed in heavy winter garment's suitable for a brisk morning constitutional and his blank face still tilted up toward the female figure on the landing as if he were being instructed to pick up a quart of milk and a pound of lard on his way home. Smiling at his own drollery, Buntrock ducked through the doorway under the main stairs.

Let Peake explore the high pikes, he thought; surely there was a reason Shambley had died down in the basement. He remembered that when he and Francesca Leeds discussed logistics Wednesday night, she'd murmured something about storage racks in the basement and Peake had said more would have to be built because old Kimmelshue, the previous director, had filled most of them with earlier culls from the collection.

The mind boggled. If Kimmelshue had kept in William Carver Ewing and Everett Winstanley, what in God's name had he weeded out?

At the foot of the stairs, Buntrock paused to get his bearings. Abruptly remembering that this was also presumably where Roger Shambley had got his, he moved away from the landing.

To his left stretched caverns measureless to man in the form of a large Victorian kitchen; to his right, beyond a sort of minikitchen adjunct, was a closed door. Buntrock automatically tried the closed door first.

The lights were on inside and as soon as he stuck his bony head around the door frame, all the colors and patterns of Victorian excessiveness beat upon his optic nerves and clamored for simultaneous attention. The rooms upstairs were models of harmonic taste and order compared to the chaotic anarchy of texture and design down here, with its clash of different cultures. Clinging to the door for support, Buntrock's disbelieving eyes traveled from the syrupy farmyard scene over the fireplace, to the modern art posters thumbtacked to turkey red walls, down to the layered scraps of patterned carpet on the floor.

When he spotted the twentieth-century tape deck and portable television beside the nineteenth-century pasha's mattress heaped high with silken cushions, the bizarre incongruities were explained. The janitor's room, he realized.

Of course. Lo, the wonder of innocence!

With a shudder that lent his fuzzy sweater a fleeting resemblance to ruffled egret feathers, he pulled the door closed again and moved stilt-leggedly through the kitchen in search of old Kimmelshue's storage racks.

Upon entering the Breul House, Elaine Albee immediately headed for the attic to see if that art expert on loan from another police division had learned anything pertinent from Shambley's papers, while Sigrid and Jim Lowry invited Benjamin Peake into his own office for yet a further discussion of his relationship to Dr. Shambley.

"Relations were quite minimal," said Peake. The dark suit he wore was impeccably tailored and a turquoise tie made his blue eyes seem even bluer as he leaned back in his chair with careless grace. "Jacob Munson put him up for trustee back in the fall. I think it was his first trusteeship and, just between us, it went to his head. Got it in mind that he was actually supposed to *do* something."

He laughed deprecatingly. "Well, of course, he was supposed to be using some of Erich Breul's papers to document the price of original art works in the 1880's, here and abroad, for his new book."

"Yesterday, Miss Ruffton implied that Dr. Shambley's research had taken a different course," Sigrid said, "and, if you recall"—she paused to consult her notes—"you referred to him as a 'busybody and a snoop with delusions of mental superiority.' Would you explain that, please?"

Peake smiled. "I thought I just did. Roger Shambley seemed to think he ought to be a new broom, clean sweep, stir up the old cobwebs."

"And did he?" asked Sigrid. "Stir up old cobwebs?"

"He tried, but he was going about it all wrong. Now I don't know how much you've heard about the Breul House's financial difficulties but I assume Nauman's told you—"

"I prefer to hear your version," Sigrid interrupted coldly.

"Certainly." Peake glanced at Detective Lowry, but that young man had his eyes firmly fixed on the notebook on his knee and his face was a careful blank.

"Well, then, perhaps we should start with the terms of Erich Breul's will," Peake said and pedantically described shrinking endowments, capital outlays, and dwindling grants. "It's simply a matter of attracting more money, but Shambley had begun to act as if the fault lay with the staff. As if we weren't already doing everything humanly possible."

"Why did he ask for a set of your inventory sheets?" Sigrid asked.

Peake shrugged petulantly.

"We've heard that he made certain insinuations."

"Look," said Peake defensively. "I don't give a damn what you've heard. That was an honest mistake. There was nothing unethical or illegal about what happened when I was at the Friedinger. I was caught in the middle up there. And you can go through our inventory sheets with a fine-tooth comb. There hasn't been a straight pin deaccessioned from the Breul House since I took over. If anything's missing, it didn't happen on my watch."

Cautiously, because this was the first mention she'd heard of the skeleton in Peake's closet, Sigrid said, "It would help us clarify things if we had your side of what actually did happen at the Friedinger."

Giving his side took Benjamin Peake almost fifteen minutes, an intense quarter hour in which he used nearly every technical and aesthetic art term Sigrid had ever heard in order to rationalize his actions. When he ran out of breath, she mentally translated his account into layman's terms for her own benefit.

According to Peake, the Friedinger had been presented with an opportunity to acquire an important Ingres. In order to finance the purchase, it was decided to sell (in museum talk "deaccession") some of the lesser pictures, including two cataloged "School of Zurbarán." Consequently, the pictures were sent to auction and sold, and a month or so later, the new owner jubilantly announced that his hunch had paid off: exhaustive scientific and aesthetic analysis conclusively proved that the pictures were not merely "School of Zurbarán" but authentic works by Zurbarán himself.

In view of the soaring values for that artist's work after the Met's splashy Zurbarán show, the two pictures were now worth more than the Ingres they were sold to help purchase.

Peake's immediate superior was technically responsible for approving the deaccessioning of any of the Friedinger's holdings, so public ridicule fell heaviest on him; but since the action had been based on Dr. Benjamin Peake's supposedly expert recommendation, Peake's resignation was also accepted. Very unfair, Peake claimed, since he was pressured from above to find things to sell and had relied on the advice of subordinates who claimed to know more about the Spanish master than he had.

From the way Peake glossed over certain details, Sigrid gathered that there had also been allegations of impropriety concerning other, lesser pictures that had been deaccessioned and sold through private galleries, but nothing quite as spectacular as the Zurbaráns.

Once more Sigrid remembered Shambley's cock-of-the-walk attitude Wednesday night, the electricity in his big homely face, the pointed look he had given Peake when he learned that she was a police officer.

"Robbery, may one hope?" he'd asked. "How appropriate." He had also informed her that publicity came in many forms.

Publicity, Sigrid wondered, or notoriety?

Her flint gray eyes rested on Benjamin Peake as she considered what he'd just told them about the Friedinger in the light of Shambley's insinuations.

Peake stirred uneasily behind his gleaming desk, unable to meet her gaze, and Lowry, who'd endured that unblinking basilisk stare more than once himself, felt a small twinge of sympathy for the man.

At last Sigrid dropped her eyes and turned through her notebook for yesterday's interviews. "We've been told that you and Miss Kohn had a later confrontation with Dr. Shambley in the library, a confrontation overheard by Mr. Munson."

"Our conversation was hardly a confrontation," Peake protested with a nervous laugh. "It was only artsy hypothetical cocktail-party nonsense."

"What was his hypothesis?" asked Sigrid.

"I'm afraid I really don't remember."

Sigrid let it pass for the moment. "You stated that you left here Wednesday night around eight-forty?"

"That's correct," Peake said, relaxing a little. "Mrs. B—that is, Mrs. Beardsley—volunteered to stay and lock up after the caterers had gone. There was no need for both of us to stay."

"Where was Dr. Shambley when you left?"

The director shrugged. "So far as I knew, in the attic."

"Alive and unharmed?"

Peake looked at her sharply. "Certainly! That's right, isn't it? I mean, he died much later in the evening, didn't he?" He appealed to Jim Lowry for confirmation.

"The medical examiner's office says sometime between eight and eleven-fifteen," Lowry told him.

"Well, there you are," Peake told Sigrid. "You saw him go upstairs around eight, didn't you?"

"He could have come down again before you left," she said mildly.

"Ask Mrs. Beardsley. She'll tell you."

Sigrid nodded. "What did you do after you left here?"

"Went home," he said promptly. "It'd been a long day."

"Can anyone verify that?"

Peake hesitated. "No." He started to amplify and then stopped himself. "No," he repeated.

Before Sigrid or Jim Lowry could push him further on that point, there was a brisk knock on the office door and Mrs. Beardsley opened it without waiting for a reply.

"Dr. Peake!" she exclaimed, her long face full of self-important concern. "Lieutenant Harald! Someone's stolen Mr. Breul's gold-handled walking stick!"

Oblivious to the stares and speculations of curious docents, the tall mannequin stood as serenely as ever in the well of the curving marble balustrade, his face turned toward the female figure on the landing above his head. He still wore a gray pearl stickpin in his tie, but there was no longer a cane in his gloved hand.

"Who saw it last?" Sigrid asked.

Four other docents had gathered and they murmured together uncertainly, but Mrs. Beardsley said firmly, "I definitely remember that I brushed a piece of lint from the collar of his overcoat on Wednesday night and straightened his stick at the same time."

"When Wednesday night?"

"Shortly before the party began. You know how one will look around one's house to make certain everything's in proper order before one's guests arrive?"

Her unconscious choice of words revealed her deep involvement in the place, thought Sigrid. She recalled glancing at the two mannequins during the party and again yesterday, but she couldn't have sworn to the presence of a walking stick. She glanced at Jim Lowry, who shook his head.

"Call Guidry and see if the mannequin's in any of the pictures she took of the hall yesterday," Sigrid directed. Then, turning back to Mrs. Beardsley and Dr. Peake, she said, "Describe the cane, please."

Peake looked blank. "It was black, I believe, and had a solid gold knob."

"And was about so long," said Mrs. Beardsley, stretching out her plump hand a few feet from the floor.

"Would you like to read how it's listed on the inventory?" asked Miss Ruffton, efficient as ever.

She handed Sigrid a stapled sheaf of papers labeled *Second Floor*. A subdivision under *Bedroom & Dressing Room—Erich Breul, Sr.* was *Wardrobe—Accessories*, and Miss Ruffton pointed to a numbered entry: "2.3.126. Man's ebony stick. 95 cm., two threaded knobs: (a) gold plate over solid brass, acanthus design; (b) carved ivory ball."

As Sigrid read the description aloud, Mrs. Beardsley said, "So *that's* what that ivory thing is! I didn't realize one could change the knobs. How clever."

"Gold *plated?*" Peake sounded personally affronted.

Sigrid was silent, thinking of ebony's strength and hardness. And when weighted with a solid brass knob at one end? Until they learned otherwise, Erich Breul's missing walking stick sounded like a perfect candidate for the rod that had smashed Roger Shambley's thin skull.

Lowry hung up the telephone on Hope Ruffton's desk and reported, "Guidry says she'll have to make a blowup to be sure, but she doesn't think the cane's in any of the pictures and she's got a long shot of this hall and doorway."

After telling the staff members that they were free to continue with their normal routine for the moment, Sigrid walked with Lowry over to the Christmas tree where they could confer unheard. The gas logs wouldn't be lit until just before the students from Raleigh were due to arrive, so the hearth was dark and cheerless. Someone had already plugged in the tree, however, and a hundred or more tiny electric candles sparkled in the vaulted marble hall.

"I suppose it would be too much to hope that the search team found a blood-smeared walking stick yesterday?" Sigrid asked, bending for a closer look at one of Sophie Breul's glass angels.

" 'Fraid so," Lowry said glumly. "They noticed smears on that softball bat in Grant's room, but I didn't hear anything about a cane."

Sigrid turned to cast a speculative glance at the mannequin. It stood so near the concealed door beneath the stairs. Say Shambley had gone through the door on his way to the basement, she thought. And say further that he was accompanied by someone suddenly so moved to violence that he (or she?) had grabbed for the first implement that came to hand: the mannequin's walking stick.

The scene was so vivid in her mind that she could almost see it.

The only thing she couldn't see was who had actually wielded the stick.

"Albee helped search," Sigrid remembered. She glanced at her watch. "What's keeping her upstairs? Go check, Lowry. I'm going to take another look at that basement."

As Sigrid crossed the large basement kitchen, she heard noises floating down the passageway beyond. She had thought that Pascal Grant was still up in the attic, so who—? She paused to listen and the odd sound defined itself as a whistle that rose and soared above muffled thumps even as she listened, a bouncy and rather familiar tune. As she turned a corner and saw light spilling from a doorway, she recognized Gilbert and Sullivan's "I Am the Very Model of a Modern Major-General."

With catlike tread, she stole to the door and there was Elliott Buntrock, his lips pursed in music as he slid one picture after another from a large wooden storage rack, removed its brown paper covering for a quick examination, then carelessly recovered it.

Sigrid leaned against the doorjamb, one hand in the pocket of her loose gray slacks. "Found anything interesting?"

Buntrock jumped like a startled bird, but made a quick recovery. "Nothing worth keeping," he said cheerfully. "Biggest pile of junk you ever saw."

"I thought nineteenth-century art was outside your area of expertise."

"Good art is timeless. You don't have to be an expert to recognize it. All you have to do is trust your eye."

"As Peake trusted his at the Friedinger?" she asked sardonically.

"Ben Peake couldn't tell his armpit from his—" He broke off with a laugh and undid another picture.

"What about Roger Shambley? Could he tell undoubted Raphaels from Gerard Dows and Zoffanies?"

Buntrock leaned the picture against the others, put his hands on his hips, and straightened up to give her his full attention.

"Well, well, well!" he said, cocking his head to look down at her from his full six foot two. "And here I thought Oscar was merely becoming eccentric in his old age. A policewoman who actually knows her Gilbert and Sullivan."

Sigrid shrugged. "Tarantara, tarantara," she said modestly.

"Now don't show off," he admonished.

She laughed and came over to look at the last picture he'd uncovered. It was a bathetic sickroom scene: an expiring young matron, a doctor who held her limp wrist with a hopeless air, the grief-stricken young husband being comforted by his innocent curly-haired toddler and a couple of weeping older women. There was a bronze title plate at the bottom of the picture frame but it was written in old-fashioned German script and Sigrid didn't recognize any of the words. Nor the artist's name.

"Probably part of Mrs. Breul's dowry," Buntrock hazarded. "Godawful, isn't it? Picasso painted scenes like this when he was about fifteen."

"Are all the pictures like that?"

"This is one of the better ones. Most of them are ladies, either at their spinets or spinning, or landscapes oozing with moral uplift, like the one hanging over the hearth in the janitor's room. Have you been in there?" A mock shudder shook his bony frame.

"Not yet. I keep hearing that it's an interesting experience."

"Don't bother," he advised her. "You'd find it a visual nightmare."

Buntrock watched as Sigrid pulled another picture from the rack.

"So how long've you known Oscar?" he asked.

"Since April. Do you think Shambley examined these pictures?"

He ignored her question and pounced on her answer. "April? That's when Riley Quinn was poisoned, wasn't it?"

"Yes."

"And in the process of catching his killer, you also caught one of the greats of American art?"

"Is he?"

"He must be. After all, I once called him the master of effortless complexity in an article I wrote for *The Loaded Brush*."

Sigrid pulled a picture of a snow-covered mountain from the rack. It depicted a late afternoon when the snow was cream and rose. Long purplish shadows stretched across the slopes, and the needles on a scrub pine in the foreground looked almost real. "Why? What makes a Nauman abstract a better picture than, say, this snow scene? It looks effortless enough."

Buntrock started to laugh, but something in her steady gaze stopped him. Instead, he found himself answering seriously. "Effortlessness is one thing, a breezy want of substance is quite another. True art's always been made for an elite, Lieutenant. The elite of the eye. It places visual *demands* on the viewer and it rewards with visual delights. That snow scene demands nothing. It's only meant to soothe and please or, at worst, *edify*, for God's sake.

"Nauman goes to the core of experience and makes visible the invisible. His pictures are more than the merely fungible formulations of generic abstraction, and they're never *ever* tricked-up literary sentimentality like *that* thing!"

Caught up in the heat of his rhetoric, Buntrock flung out a hand and thumped the offending canvas scornfully. "Nauman's pictures deal with critical masses and elemental tensions. His best are like the moment before the big bang!"

Buntrock's arms fluttered erratically as be searched for the precise phrases, as if he expected to pluck them from the walls of this cramped storage room. "It's as simple as that, Lieutenant: Oscar Nauman makes the invisible visible. Either you see it or you don't."

He flexed his bony shoulders and assumed his contemplative pose. "Nauman was the quintessential risk-taker in his time," he said with a valedictory air. "He may no longer be on the cutting edge. The parade does move on. Modernism gives way to postmodernism as day yields to night. But his place within the matrix of aesthetic discourse is secure. And do you know what triggers his genius?"

A bit dazed, Sigrid shook her head.

"He knows what to leave out!" Buntrock said triumphantly. "He is the master of elision."

She had listened without comment and when he finished, she formally inclined her head—rather an interesting head now that he looked at it closely—and said, "Thank you."

Buntrock was intrigued. She was almost like a Nauman painting herself: a seemingly simple surface that concealed unexpected complexities. "Don't you like his work?" he asked.

"It's not that. There are things that I can like that I don't understand. That's not the point. It's the things I don't like that I *want* to like that give me trouble."

"Ah," he smiled. "I think we're not talking about art anymore."

There were hurried footsteps out in the kitchen and Lowry's voice called, "Lieutenant?"

"Down here," she answered.

"Could you come up? They've found something interesting in Shambley's briefcase."

Sigrid turned to go. "If *you* find something interesting among these pictures, you will share it, won't you?"

In a series of jerky movements, Buntrock threw up his hand and touched his thumb to his little finger. "Scout's honor."

A faint expression of surprise flitted across his bony face. "Oddly enough, I mean it," he said and rearranged his long fingers to form a Vulcan peace sign.

Oddly enough, thought Sigrid as she joined Lowry and started up to the attic, she believed him.

In the attic, Elaine Albee introduced Sigrid to Dr. Ridgway of Special Services, who immediately described how she'd found Roger Shambley's briefcase under the desk. "Inside were the usual papers, and this."

"This" was a heavily-embroidered pink satin envelope lined in white satin and tied with red cords. It measured approximately twelve inches long by seven inches wide and although it was now empty, they could clearly see that it had once held something that had left an imprint upon the lining, a rectangular object that measured ten by four and a half inches.

"Any guesses?" asked Sigrid.

"Could be anything," said Dr. Ridgway. "A diary, letters, maybe even a jeweler's box. I haven't come across anything here that fits though."

In fact, she reported, she'd been through everything on Shambley's makeshift desk and had found nothing untoward among the murdered man's papers. "It seems to be the usual scholarly hodgepodge of raw data right now," she said, running her fingers through her extravagantly curly hair. "He had cross-referenced Erich Breul's bills of sale for various pictures with what similar pictures were fetching in the U.S. at the time. He wanted to check what a middleman like Bernard Berenson got for some of the pictures he represented as compared with dealing directly with the owners as Breul did, for instance."

"You've matched those bills with the actual pictures?" asked Sigrid.

"Only on the inventory sheets," said Dr. Ridgway. "Shambley seems to have already checked them off himself, but I'll redo it, if you like."

"I would."

"Okey-doke," she said.

As Dr. Ridgway returned to her work, Sigrid drew Albee and Lowry aside and asked Albee about yesterday's search of the basement. Lowry had already told her about the missing cane and the policewoman shook her blond head. "We were specifically looking for anything that could have been used as a weapon so I'm sure it would have been noticed if it was there."

Sigrid looked around the large attic and saw that Mrs. Beardsley had rejoined the docents who, with Pascal Grant's help, were still laboriously checking the attic's inventory. She carried the embroidered satin envelope over to the senior docent.

"Have you ever seen this?" she asked.

"It's Sophie Breul's glove case," said Mrs. Beardsley. "How did it get up here?"

"Where's it normally kept?"

"Why, down in her dressing room, of course."

She led the three police detectives down to the second floor, to the dressing room that connected Sophie Breul's bedroom to her bath. With barely a moment's hesitation, Mrs. Beardsley went straight to a chest of drawers and opened the second one from the top.

A whiff of lavender drifted toward them as a puzzled Mrs. Beardsley said, "But *here's* her glove case!" and drew out an identical envelope of embroidered pink satin. "I didn't realize there were two."

Sigrid reached for the new one. Inside were several pairs of kid gloves, all imbued with the scent of lavender. She lifted the first satin case to her nose. It was musty and smelled like an old bookstore.

"This didn't come from that drawer," she told the others.

Matt Eberstadt and Bernie Peters finished up at the New York Center for the Fine Arts before noon, grabbed a sandwich in a nearby bar and grill on York Avenue, then headed over to the Guggenheim Museum on Fifth Avenue.

Afternoon sunlight shone through the barebranched trees of Central Park and slanted on the luxurious apartment buildings on the other side of Fifth Avenue. There, uniformed and gloved doormen opened their doors for residents who emerged from double-parked limos with piles of beautifully gift-wrapped boxes. Santa's little helpers.

"What're you getting Frances for Christmas?" asked Bernie as they passed a nursemaid wheeling an enormous English pram, its tiny occupant buried in a nest of pale pink wool.

"I don't know. Maybe a fancy new robe."

"Didn't you give her that last year?"

"Did I?" They paused for a light and the big detective sighed. "Yeah, I guess I did. I don't know. What're you giving Pam?"

"Diamond earrings," Bernie said happily. "Soon as she got pregnant this last time, I just knew it was going to be a boy, so I put them on layaway and I've been paying on 'em all along. Next week, they're mine."

"Diamond earrings! God, I hope Frances doesn't hear about them," groaned Eberstadt as they neared the Guggenheim.

Their visit to the Fine Arts Center had added little to their knowledge of the dead man. Tuesday had been the last day of classes until after New Year's, so the only colleagues to be found were some instructors who hadn't turned in all their grade cards.

Dr. Aaron Prawn, head of nineteenth-century American studies, summed up Shambley's career through tightly clenched, pipe-gripping teeth. "Ambitious. Perhaps a bit too. But definitely on his way. A bit of a barracuda? Yes. But one has to be to get anywhere in the nineteenth century these days. Junior colleagues loathed him, of course. Goes with the territory."

Unfortunately, Shambley had been on leave this semester so no one had seen enough of him lately to report on his last movements. The divisional secretary remembered that he'd been in Wednesday morning to pick up his mail, but she'd been busy with a student and had merely exchanged season's greetings with him.

They were luckier at the Guggenheim. Among the scraps of paper in Shambley's pocket had been a receipt from the museum's bookstore and one of the clerks there remembered Dr. Shambley.

"I was in one of his classes at the center last spring," said the girl, a part-time student who worked full-time during the holiday break. "I knew who he was, but he didn't remember me."

Eberstadt found that hard to believe. His own hairline had receded to the very top of his head where wiry gray curls ran from ear to ear across his bald dome like some sort of steel-wool tiara. He was half bald by necessity; the girl must have paid a hair stylist good money to clip that same area of her platinum white hair to a flat half-inch stubble while the rest of her hair fell to her shoulders.

How many of Shambley's students could have had hairstyles like that?

Bernie Peters was more interested in whether she was wearing a bra beneath that turquoise silk shirt. "Do you remember what he bought?"

She looked at the sales slip and nodded. "Two Léger posters at fourteen ninety-eight each, plus tax."

"Léger?" asked Eberstadt, stumbling over the pronunciation. He pulled out his notebook and pen. "How do you spell that?"

"Fernand Léger," she said, spelling it over her silky shoulder as she led them through aisles crowded with artsy souvenirs and art books—some of them heavy enough to give you a hernia, thought Peters—to the Guggenheim's collection of posters. "French painter. I thought it was kinda strange that Dr. Shambley would want cubist posters when his field's nineteenth-century American. Of course, he *did* want early Léger and not the mechanistic things from the twenties and thirties that he's really famous for."

She pulled a plastic-wrapped cylinder from one of the bins. "This is it. I'm not supposed to open it though unless you're going to buy it."

There was a small reproduction of the artwork on the outer wrap. To the detectives' untutored eyes, it looked like a picture of two faceless mannequins constructed of Dixie cups and paper chains. They were drawn in heavy black lines. One figure was red, the other bright blue.

"He bought *two* of 'em, just alike?" asked Peters.

"Uh-huh. He got kinda pissed when we didn't have two different examples from that period. It was like maybe he was doing his Christmas shopping or something. But then he kinda laughed and said it didn't matter; that he'd just hang one of them upside down. Weird, right?"

Her loose shirt fell forward as she bent to return the poster to its proper slot, but Bernie Peters noted with only half his attention that she wasn't wearing a bra. The other half recalled the search he'd helped conduct yesterday.

"I think I saw those posters in the Breul House basement," he told Matt Eberstadt.

Seated across the library table from the two female detectives, Mrs. Beardsley had grown weary of the way one had to say the same thing three different ways before the police moved on to a different question. Beyond the possibility of a trunk in the attic, she had no idea where Sophie Breul's extra glove case had spent the last seventy years, nor what that satin case had held, and she had told them so. At length.

This was rapidly becoming, she decided, a delicate question of etiquette.

On the one hand, police officers were, by their very calling, of a lower socioeconomic order. One must, of course, treat everyone—even one's inferiors—graciously although a certain distance was allowed.

On the other hand, Miss Harald—*Lieutenant* Harald, Mrs. Beardsley reminded herself sharply—had been met on a social level and she was, after all, a personal friend of the famous Oscar Nauman.

So one could hardly snub her with impunity. Not even when she made gross insinuations.

"Now *really*, Lieutenant Harald!" She stiffened in one of the leather library chairs. I don't know with whom you've been gossiping, nor do I wish to be told. Under the circumstances, I suppose everyone becomes suspect. Nevertheless, it's simply ridiculous to suppose that one—that *I*—would resort to violence."

"But Dr. Shambley did fill a vacancy on the board of trustees that you had hoped for, didn't he?" asked the lieutenant.

"I let it be known that my name could be considered," Mrs. Beardsley admitted. "One is seldom chosen immediately. It is quite usual to be passed over the first time or two."

"Will you ask to be considered now that the seat is vacant again?"

"Certainly," said Mrs. Beardsley firmly. "Why not? Everyone knows my devotion to the Erich Breul House is unchanged."

"Yes," agreed the police officer. "We've heard that you're often the first to arrive in the mornings and the last to leave at night."

Her tone sounded more conciliatory and Mrs. Beardsley unbent slightly. "One can't claim too much credit for that when it's merely a matter of walking across the square."

"And you do have a key," mused Lieutenant Harald.

Mrs. Beardsley looked at her sharply. Such a drab-looking person today in that dark gray suit and no makeup. On Wednesday night she'd been rather striking in an odd way. Or was that only because one linked her with Oscar Nauman?

"Tell us again, please, what you did after the others left?" she was saying.

Mrs. Beardsley sighed and went through it all again: how all the guests had gone by eight-thirty, how she'd sent Dr. Peake on his way, how she'd overseen the caterers' departure. She did not try to describe how she loved being alone in this house, how she could almost imagine herself a member of the Breul family, or how alive they often seemed to her. Never mind if Pascal were in the basement or Dr. Shambley in the attic. As long as one didn't see or hear either man, one's imagination was free to see and hear the Breuls.

"No," she said again. "I didn't go down to the basement because I thought Pascal was still out; and Dr. Shambley had made it quite clear more than once that he did not wish to be disturbed when he was working. I ascertained that all the candles were snuffed, then I unplugged the Christmas tree and went home without seeing either of them."

Mrs. Beardsley braced herself for more questions on that point. Instead, the Harald woman sat back in her chair with a trousered knee propped against the edge of the gleaming table top and asked, "Why did Pascal Grant dislike Dr. Shambley? Some of the other docents have told us that he avoided the man whenever he could."

"Dr. Shambley made him feel uncomfortable," she hedged.

"How?"

Protective maternalism surged in Mrs. Beardsley's breast. "Pascal Grant couldn't hurt a fly," she told them. "Surely you see what a sweet gentle boy he is."

"That's why we don't understand what he had against Dr. Shambley," said the younger detective, smiling at her across the table.

Mrs. Beardsley approved of the blonde's tailored femininity, her coral lipstick and modest eye shadow, her Cuban-heeled boots and brown tweed jacket worn over beige-and-peach plaid slacks. So much easier to talk to, she decided. And really, weren't policewomen rather like nurses? One could discuss anything with nurses.

"It was painful for Pascal to speak of it," she said, bravely ignoring her own embarrassment, "but it seems there was a man at the shelter workshop where Pascal trained when he was twelve or thirteen." Her voice lowered. "A *sexual deviant*, if you please! And he took advantage of his position to force himself on some of the boys."

"And Shambley—?" asked Detective Albee.

"Oh, no!" exclaimed Mrs. Beardsley. "When I realized how uneasy Pascal was, I cross-questioned him quite thoroughly, for I would have denounced Dr. Shambley had that been the case. No, no, I'm quite certain he did not approach the boy; but evidently, there was some physical resemblance between Dr. Shambley and the man who had once abused him. Something about their eyes, I believe. Poor Pascal. His reactions are emotional rather than reasoned. But you must surely see from this that his instinct is to retreat, not attack. He simply avoided the man whenever he could."

The other two women were silent for a moment, then, absently tapping her pen against her knee, Lieutenant Harald said, "Getting back to your own movements, Mrs. Beardsley: you saw no one after the caterers left?"

"Not even," added the other officer, "Mr. Thorvaldsen when you crossed the square?"

"I'm sorry, Detective Albee, but when it's that cold, one doesn't linger outside to pass the time of night with casual pedestrians whom one may or may not know. I simply didn't notice."

"So when you say that you went home shortly after nine and didn't return," said Lieutenant Harald, "there's no one who can confirm your statement?"

Mrs. Beardsley inclined her head. "No one."

Once more they asked her about seeing Thorvaldsen leave the house at midnight and then they thanked her for her cooperation.

One with a completely clear conscience did not register relief at having done one's civic duty, Mrs. Beardsley reminded herself, and walked with quiet dignity from the library.

Sigrid glanced at Albee. "Well?"

"Oh yes," said Elaine. "I could see her deciding that he was a bug that needed to be squashed and just doing it. But only if he was hurting her precious house. And he wasn't."

"That we're aware of," Sigrid told her. "We still don't know where he found that glove case or what he took from it."

"And we may never know," sighed Jim Lowry, returning from the attic at the end of her comments. "The docents say there're more than a dozen trunks and wardrobe boxes full of Mrs. Breul's stuff up there and the inventory sheets don't go into much detail. Just 'apparel' or 'accessories.' And the case might have held a jeweler's box, but they don't think there was anything valuable still in it because all her good stuff was sold when the house became a museum."

Out in the long marble hall, there was a sudden babble and chatter of excited female voices and through the open doorway, they saw a bearded professor with a harried air as he shepherded his charges past the ticket table.

The art students from that Raleigh women's college, no doubt.

"This might be a good time to break for lunch," Sigrid said judiciously.

At the gallery off Fifth Avenue, Rick Evans mechanically set another painting on the easel, readjusted the two floodlights on either side, took a reading with his light meter, then focused his camera and clicked the shutter.

When he first came up from Louisiana in September, it had surprised Rick how strongly the art world depended upon slides. The first cuts in competitions were made by judges who looked at slides; grants were awarded, exhibitions decided, magazine articles written—all very often on the basis of photographic slides alone.

His grandfather spoke of this trend with contempt, but Hester Kohn merely shrugged her shoulders and asked Jacob to consider the cost of shipping fees, not to mention wear and tear on the artwork itself.

Rick set another large oil painting upon the easel. It looked a little top-heavy in composition, all those purple slashes at the top and empty unprimed canvas at the bottom, and he checked the label on the back of the stretcher to make sure it was right side up. He no longer tried to understand each picture. All he cared about now was making a technically perfect slide.

In the beginning, his grandfather had brought a chair into the workroom and sat beside him during these photography sessions and talked to him of each work's artistic strengths and weaknesses. "See how the dynamic forces play against the static, Richard," he would say, his words lightly accented with German and the smell of peppermint. Or, "Why do you think the artist placed the yellow so low? Why to buoy up the work and to relieve the dark weights above. Contraction and relaxation, *ja?*"

And if the picture touched a chord, he would go off and rummage through books in his office and come back with illustrations that showed how Vermeer, though a Dutch realist of the seventeenth century, used the same approach; or how Picasso or Matisse had dealt with the same matter differently.

"Do you see?" he would ask. "Do you see?"

"Yes, sir," Rick would reply, wanting to please. And he *did* see when his grandfather pointed it out, but when asked to critique a fresh picture, he always muddled it.

"*Mein Gott!*" Jacob had exploded one day. "The simplest thing in art and you do not see it!"

That day, he had grabbed Rick by the shoulders and fiercely swung him around to glare into his face. As their eyes locked, the anger had drained from the old man's face.

"Paul's eyes you have," he'd said sadly, "and in you they are blind."

After that, his grandfather continued to sit in on some of the sessions and to instruct as before, but the intensity had gone out of his lectures and he had stopped asking Rick to describe what he saw.

He could stand that, Rick thought, as he snapped the last exposure on the roll of film. What he couldn't stand was the look that had appeared on his grandfather's face when he and Hester had returned from the police station yesterday.

"You were there last night?" Grandfather had asked in a dreadful voice. "In that *Schwachsinnigen's* bedroom?"

"In his *room*," Rick had said, reddening under the scornful implication. "And he's not an idiot, Grandfather, just a little slow. We're friends."

"*Ja*, sure," his grandfather muttered wearily, and suddenly he looked his full eighty-two years, old and frail and utterly defeated by what fate had given him. He had touched the picture of his dead son, then sighed and laid it face down among the papers on his desk, swivelled in his chair, and turned his back on Rick. "Tell Hester to come in," he'd said stonily.

He would stay until after Christmas, Rick thought, sliding a fresh roll of film into his camera. After that, he would go home and let his mother pull strings for a job with one of the state bureaus in Baton Rouge. He would walk backcountry lanes again and take pictures of pelicans and swamps for wildlife calendars or tourist brochures.

And he would stop trying to deny to himself that he was what he was.

*   *   *

Next to a rent-controlled apartment, Zeki's, just west of Third Avenue, was that most precious urban find: an as-yet-undiscovered, good, midtown restaurant. Even Gael Greene was unaware of its existence. Although celebrities often lunched there, knowing they would not be bothered by gawkers, New Yorkers came for the Turco-Croatian cuisine of delicately spiced lamb and indescribable breads, not to see and be seen.

It was nearly two and the outer room was still crowded as Oscar Nauman passed through. He spoke to a couple of friends, nodded when the barman said, "The usual?" and found Jacob Munson at his corner table in the back.

"Sorry I'm late," he said, sliding into the chair opposite his dealer. "The garage down the block was full. You order yet?"

"*Nein.*"

Oscar looked across the snowy white tablecloth and frowned. "You feeling all right, Jacob?"

The old man shrugged. He looked shrunken today. His face was nearly as gray as his thin beard and his brown eyes had lost their elfin luster.

"Not coming down with something, are you?"

"It's nothing. A little cough. What are you? Nurse Nightingale?" Jacob asked irritably.

"That's better," Oscar grinned.

But as his glass of ale arrived accompanied by a martini, the grin faded; and when the waiter had taken their orders, he said, "What's with the drink? I thought your doctors said—"

"They did. Lean closer, my friend, and I'll tell you a secret: Jacob Munson is not going to live forever. Tomorrow he could drop dead; so why not a martini today?"

He lifted the glass and sipped long.

"Then who'll take care of my show?" Oscar asked lightly, determined to shake Jacob out of this puzzling mood.

"Elliott Buntrock will." He caught the waiter's eye across the room and signaled for another martini. "There's a Buntrock under every rock," he said bitterly.

"Jacob?"

"You're a lucky man, Oscar Nauman. When *you* go, you will leave behind you good work that will honor your name."

"What the hell's going on?" Oscar demanded.

Munson sank back in his chair. "Roger Shambley was killed Wednesday night." He twirled the stem of his empty martini glass back and forth between his wrinkled fingers.

The silence stretched between them. "So?" Oscar finally asked.

"So your lady policeman thinks my grandson Richard did it."

"What?"

"She's wrong, though. You will tell her this?"

"Jacob—"

"It was Benjamin or Hester or maybe both together," he said heavily. "I don't know."

As the waiter brought their food and another martini, a paroxysm of coughing shook his small frame and Oscar told the waiter to take away the drink and bring his friend club soda with a twist of lemon.

When Jacob was breathing normally again, Oscar said, "Talk to me, Jacob. What's happening at the gallery?"

"You know what Horace Kohn and I tried to build." Jacob stared at the savory chicken stew before him. "We never said *caveat emptor.* Never! What we sold we backed with our reputation and for better than a half century, Kohn and Munson Gallery has been trusted. Never a stain on its name."

"Yes."

"You remember Paul?" he asked abruptly.

Oscar remembered Paul Munson as a handsome, sweet-natured kid. Bright enough, but not the flaming meteor he'd become to his father since his plane had crashed sixteen years ago. Odd to think Paul would be nearing forty if he'd lived. "Rick reminds me of Paul," he said as he buttered a piece of crusty bread. "Same eyes."

"They are nothing alike," said Jacob, anger in every syllable. "Paul had an eye for art."

"I meant in looks," Oscar said mildly. "Same shade of brown. Besides, aren't you being a little hard on the boy? He's only been here three months."

"Three months, three years, it wouldn't matter. It's his mother's fault. Suzanne turned her back on the gallery."

Oscar occasionally had trouble remembering that there were two older daughters, Suzanne and Marta. He vaguely recalled that both had earned doctorates in other fields, but Jacob almost never spoke of them. All his pride had been bound up in Paul and when Paul died, Paul's friend, Benjamin Peake, had become his surrogate.

"She made him a photographer. She made him a"—his voice dropped lower—"a *Schwulen.*"

"A what?" asked Oscar.

The old man's face twisted with shame. "A faggot."

Oscar ate silently. There were so many different sexual proclivities in the art world that he was surprised that Jacob could still be homophobic. Or did tolerance stop when it touched him personally?

"He was with the janitor that night. In his bedroom."

"So what's the big deal, Jacob? It's not the end of the world."

"Only the end of my line," Munson said bleakly, drawing his fork through the sauce on his plate. "The end of the gallery."

"Oh, come on, Jacob. If the boy doesn't work out, Hester will keep things going. And it's crazy to think she had anything to do with Shambley's death. When Sigrid and I left Wednesday night, you and Hester were planning to share a cab back uptown."

"She got out at East Forty-ninth. Said she was meeting someone at the Waldorf. Yesterday when she came back from the police station, I made her tell me who. It was Benjamin."

Oscar stopped cutting his lamb and started to wonder if Jacob were experiencing the beginnings of senility. His voice was gentle as he asked if Jacob had forgotten that Hester and Ben—?

The art dealer interrupted with an impatient wave of his hand. "It wasn't about sex, Oscar. Wednesday night, Roger Shambley accused Hester and Ben of passing a piece of forged art through the gallery. Yesterday I asked Hester of this. First she said no; then she said there was no way Shambley could have proved it."

He pushed his plate aside with most of the food still untasted. "She may be a woman, but she isn't that stupid, Oscar. Shambley wouldn't have had to prove anything. A gallery's word is its bond and if that word becomes a lie—"

He gave a palms-up gesture of hopelessness.

Sigrid arrived at the gallery with Jim Lowry shortly before three. The soft-voiced receptionist informed them that Mr. Munson had not returned from lunch and that Miss Kohn, as they could see, was busy at the moment but if they wished to wait?

"Yes," Sigrid said and Lowry took a guide sheet from a nearby stand.

"Notebook pages?" he asked sotto voce. "Twenty-three hundred a sheet? Who's Ardù Screnii? Never heard of him."

Stunned, he began to circle the airy showroom, peering first at each matted and framed drawing and then at the price Kohn and Munson was asking for it.

Sigrid pretended to study the drawings, but she chose those that would give her reflected views of Hester Kohn, presently occupied with two customers. The dealer wore hot pink today and a chunky pearl-and-gold necklace.

From the conversation which floated through the nearly deserted gallery, Sigrid soon gathered that the man and woman were a husband and wife from Chicago and that he was a commodities trader. She also gathered that they expected more from an Ardù Screnii drawing than pure aesthetics.

"Of course," she heard Hester Kohn say, "you have to realize that the bottom line is whether you *like* a work. I mean *I* can't tell you something's going to go up."

"Yes," the man nodded sagely. "Yes, I know that but—"

"I can tell you how some things *have* gone up, but if you're buying one of these purely as an investment—"

"Oh, no, we *love* art," said his wife, a dark, intense woman in her early thirties. "Of course, my decorator's going to *kill* me. My taste is changing. Growing. I was always so—um—traditional, you know? And here I came home with this huge modern canvas and my decorator wouldn't let me hang it in the bedroom. Said it defeminized the room— it's all traditional antiques, you know? So I put it in storage. But if I get one of these Screniis, then it's coming out of storage. I don't care *what* the decorator says."

She was struck by a sudden thought. "I forget. Screnii was Albanian, wasn't he?"

"Bulgarian," said Hester Kohn.

"Oh, good!" said the woman. "I've always believed in the Bulgarians."

By way of the reflective glass, Sigrid saw Hester Kohn smile politely.

The man chuckled, even though he wasn't quite ready to give up the practical. "Still, a Screnii *is* an investment, isn't it? And a lot more fun than soybean futures."

There was a contemplative pause.

"Not that I'd even know what a soybean looked like if I came face to face with one."

"Aren't they like guyva peas?" the woman asked brightly.

Hester Kohn shrugged.

"Ah well," said the man, "what does it matter as long as I can buy low and sell them high? Now, I think my wife and I are going to have to do a little commodities trading on which one of these Screniis we want."

Ardù Screnii had died in the midsixties, Sigrid knew. He had eked out a living by teaching an occasional course at Vanderlyn, and Nauman was a little bitter that Screnii had never been able to sell one of his major paintings for more than fifteen hundred dollars during his lifetime.

As the two clients left, promising to come back the next day with their minds made up, Sigrid and Lowry approached Jacob Munson's partner. "Miss Kohn? We have a few more questions."

Hester Kohn sighed. "Yes. I was afraid you might."

When Matt Eberstadt and Bernie Peters returned to the Breul House, the docent on duty at the door informed them that Detective Albee could be found in the attic.

"Where's Lowry and the lieutenant?" they asked after they'd climbed to the top of the house and heard about Dr. Ridgway's discovery of the satin glove case in Shambley's briefcase.

"Over at Kohn and Munson Gallery," Elaine told them. "What's up?"

The two women listened intently as the men described how Shambley had bought two posters at the Guggenheim on Wednesday morning, posters Bernie Peters thought he remembered seeing.

"I haven't found any references to Léger in his papers," said Dr. Ridgway, "but I'll keep it in mind."

The three detectives went down the back stairs, avoiding a group of twenty or so young women to whom Mrs. Beardsley was giving a tour of the house.

In the basement, it took Peters a few minutes to regain his bearings, but he soon went to a box in one of the storage rooms and plucked out the rolled posters, still in their plastic wrap. He slit the paper on one of them and backrolled it so that it would hang straight.

It was just as the small illustration promised: a cubist depiction of two figures that, except for their vivid red and blue colors, reminded Elaine of the Tin Woodman in *The Wizard of Oz*.

They carried it upstairs and asked Dr. Peake if he or Miss Ruffton could speculate why Shambley should buy two identical Léger posters and stash them in the basement.

"Beats me," Peake said, lounging indolently in a chair beside Hope Ruffton's desk. "Léger's too modern. Clean out of Shambley's period. Most of his work was done in the thirties, and forties. He died in the midfifties, if I'm not mistaken."

His secretary was equally puzzled. "This looks familiar though. Now where have I seen—?"

The young janitor passed nearby on his way down to the basement and he gave them a shy smile as he skirted the mannequin dressed like Erich Breul.

"Just a minute, Grant," Dr. Peake said. "These detectives found some posters Dr. Shambley left in the basement. Do you know anything about them?"

Pascal Grant looked at the cubist poster and his face lit up. "I have pictures like that in my room."

"What?" exclaimed Peake, coming erect in his chair.

"*That's* where I saw it," said Hope Ruffton. "Those posters Dr. Kimmelshue had. The ones you told Pascal he could put up."

"Oh," said Peake. "Those."

He sank back lazily into the chair again. "For a minute there—" He smiled to himself at the absurdity of what he'd almost thought for a minute.

"Want to see them?" Pascal Grant asked the detectives. Golden curls spilled over his fair brow and he brushed them back as he looked up at Eberstadt with a friendly air.

"Naw, that's okay," said Peters.

He and Eberstadt started toward the front door. "We've still got a couple of alibis to check. Drop you somewhere, Lainey?"

"No, thanks," she said, remembering Mrs. Beardsley's explanation of Grant's unease with Shambley. "One thing though—when you were checking out Shambley's background, did anybody happen to mention if he was gay?"

"No," Eberstadt said slowly, "but when we asked if he was living with anybody . . . remember, Bern?"

"Yeah. They said no. That Shambley couldn't decide if he was AC or DC, so he wound up being no-C."

"Interesting," Albee said. "I'll hang on to the poster and bring it back to the office later. The lieutenant'll probably want to see it."

By the time Matt Eberstadt and Bernie Peters reached the sidewalk, Elaine Albee was already halfway down the basement steps to talk with Pascal Grant again.

"I suppose I may as well tell you," said Hester Kohn. "If I don't, Jacob will."

She led them to the small sitting room she'd created around the window corner of the large office that had once belonged to her father, and Sigrid and Jim Lowry were invited to take the blue-and-turquoise chairs opposite her plum-colored love seat. The upholstery seemed impregnated with her gardenia perfume, which, coupled with a pair of highly chromatic red and orange abstract pictures on dark green walls, gave the office a sensual, subtropical atmosphere.

She loosened her pink jacket button by button and a languid smile touched her lips when she saw how Lowry's eyes followed her fingers.

As an interested spectator, Sigrid usually enjoyed watching other women operate, but it was almost three and she didn't feel like wasting more time. "What would Mr. Munson tell us?" she asked crisply.

"That he didn't drop me at my apartment near Lincoln Center Wednesday night," Hester replied. "I met Ben Peake after the party. We talked about an hour, then I went home. Alone. And before you ask, no, I can't prove it."

"You'd just seen Dr. Peake," said Sigrid. "Why did you meet again so quickly?"

"There were private things we needed to discuss."

"Things Shambley had brought up in the library?" Sigrid asked.

"Ben told you about that?"

"He gave us his version—" Sigrid said carefully.

Hester Kohn interrupted with a ladylike snort and ran her fingers through her short black hair. "I'll bet he did!"

"—and no doubt, Mr. Munson will have his own version of what he overheard Shambley say," Sigrid finished smoothly.

The seductive languor disappeared from Hester Kohn's body and she became wary and all business. "There's no need to question Jacob about this."

"No?"

"No." She cast a speculative woman-to-woman look at Sigrid. "Oscar and Jacob have been friends for as long as I can remember. Even since I was a little girl. Oscar could tell you how much this gallery means to Jacob."

Her words contained a not-too-subtle threat, which Sigrid coldly ignored. "And not to you, too?"

"Of course to me," she answered impatiently. "But it's different for Jacob. He's old-world with a capital O and that means things like honor and *mano*. It's going to kill him to admit there's ever been anything a little under-the-table with the gallery, but to admit it to a *woman*—!"

Her hazel eyes slid over Jim Lowry's muscular body. "He might talk to you," she told him.

"He's chauvinistic?" asked Sigrid.

"He's a gentleman," Hester Kohn corrected with a grimace. "That means women are ladies. You charm ladies, you marry them, you have sons with them, but you don't take them too seriously or admit them to power. Look around the gallery, Lieutenant Harald: We represent two female artists. And both of them are dead.

"Jacob used to think that Paul and I would marry and Paul would run the business. Then when Paul died, and it was too late to rope in

Suzanne or Marta, he half adopted Ben Peake and tried to make *him* marry me. Thank God, *my* father had a different attitude about daughters."

Bright spots of angry red flamed in her cheeks. "Every time I really think about it, I feel like screaming. Men made the tax laws, Ben Peake and his friend came up with the figures, and all I did was sign the appraisal, but who does Jacob blame the most? Three guesses."

"I'm sorry, Miss Kohn," said Jim Lowry, "but I don't understand. Tax laws? Appraisal?"

"It's absolutely routine," she said defensively. "Anyhow, half the galleries in the country are doing it, too."

Abruptly, it dawned on her that neither detective knew what she was talking about. "I thought you said Ben told you."

"I said he gave us his version," Sigrid reminded her. "And we still have to hear Mr. Munson's."

With an angry sigh, Hester Kohn sank back into the cushions of the plum love seat. "This happened a couple of years ago while Ben was still at the Friedinger. One of the patrons there was in serious need of a large tax write-off. Basically, the way it works is that a donor gives a nonprofit institution a work of art. An independent appraiser estimates how much the work is worth and the donor then lists that figure in his tax returns as a charitable donation."

"The appraiser—you, in fact—inflates the figure?" Sigrid asked.

Hester Kohn nodded.

"But why would the institution that's getting the artwork go along with that?" asked Lowry.

"What do they care?" Her voice was cynical. "They're getting a donation they otherwise wouldn't and next time, it might be a really important gift. Besides, if they decide to deaccess, it's usually worth at least half the appraised price."

Sigrid looked at her inquiringly. "Only in this particular case—"

"In this particular case, it was worth about a quarter of what Jacob Munson said it was worth."

"You signed his name to an appraisal statement?" asked Lowry.

"He's the judge of artistic merit in this firm," Hester Kohn said with bitterness. "I'm just the business and financial side. My signature wouldn't have sufficed. See, Jacob isn't asked to appraise things very often because everyone in the business knows he's so goddamned straight-arrow. He might come down on the high side, but his figures are usually within two or three thousand of the true value. The tax people know this, too, and they haven't bothered to question him in years."

"So how much kickback did you and Peake get?" Sigrid asked.

"I had a pool put in at my house in Riverhead," she said candidly. "I believe Ben bought a car."

"And Shambley threatened to blow the whistle on you?" asked Jim Lowry.

Hester Kohn shrugged and plucked a piece of lint from the dark purple upholstery. "Ben thought so, but I wasn't that sure. Roger Shambley was so effing devious. He never came straight out and said what he meant. It was all hypothetical and insinuating. Frankly, I thought he was sounding us out to see if we'd go along with some scheme he was hatching."

"Oh?"

She nodded. "Sort of as if he were saying he knew we'd bent the rules once before and got away with it and maybe we could do something for him. Or with him. It wasn't clear."

"So you and Dr. Peake didn't feel threatened by him?"

"Not really. *I* certainly didn't." She crossed her shapely legs and adjusted the hem of her short pink skirt. "Neither of us wanted Jacob to find out about that tax scam, of course, but it's not like we were going to go to jail or anything if it came out. Appraisals are subjective judgments, right?"

"You forged your partner's name," Lowry pointed out.

"Ye-s," she admitted, "but if it came right down to it, Jacob would claim it was his signature. He'd rather hush it up and say he'd made an honest mistake than let the gallery's name be dragged through the mud with one of its owners up for forgery."

She stood up and walked over to stare through the window at the buildings of midtown Manhattan. A wave of gardenia reached the two police officers as she turned back to face them. "Look, I know I've been rather flip about it and Jacob really does make me furious at times, but go easy on him about what Ben and I did, okay? He's an old man and the gallery's all he has now."

"What about his grandson?" asked Lowry.

She shook her dark head. "He's a sweet kid, but Richard Evans doesn't know art from artichokes. Wouldn't surprise me if he went home for Christmas and never came back."

"One moment, *acushla*," said Francesca Leeds from her suite high in the Hotel Maintenon. She removed a heavy gold-and-amber earring and then returned the receiver to her ear. When she spoke, her voice was like warm melted syrup, so pleased was she to hear Oscar's voice on her private line again.

"It's been almost two years. How many people did you have to call to find my number?"

"None," Nauman replied, making her pulse quicken before he added, "It was on the gallery's Rolodex."

"Beast! You're supposed to say it's engraved on your heart."

He laughed. "Elliott Buntrock just called. He wants to have a short meeting here at the gallery tomorrow afternoon. 'Talk turkey' was how he put it. Think you and Thorvaldsen can make it?"

Francesca looked at the calendar on her desk. "What time?"

"Three-thirty?"

"Four would probably be better for Søren."

"Four it is. See you."

"Ta."

She replaced the receiver and tilted her head so that the thick coppery hair fell away from her face as she slipped the stud of her earring through the lobe again.

The nice thing about parting amicably with someone, she thought, was the free and easy friendship that often continued afterwards. The rotten thing was when the parting was more amicable on *his* part than yours. And the rottenest thing of all was feeling jealous of your replacement when you knew that if you both walked into a room together, nine men out of ten wouldn't notice her.

Except that the tenth man would be Oscar.

The interview with Jacob Munson was as difficult as Hester Kohn had predicted.

It began awkwardly when Sigrid, trailed by Jim Lowry, walked down the hall to Munson's open door and found Nauman there, too, just hanging up the phone on Munson's desk. At least Nauman hadn't said anything flippant when she introduced Lowry, and Lowry gave no sign that the artist's name had special curiosity value for him. But when Nauman heaved his tall frame up from the chair, Munson had underlined the personal aspects of the case by insisting that Oscar should stay.

"You *und* Miss Harald, you have no secrets."

"Just the same, I'll wait outside," Nauman said and took himself off.

Munson sat behind his cluttered desk looking like an elderly elf who'd just learned that Santa's workshop was jobbing out its toy production to Korea. He went through the motions of hospitality halfheartedly, offering them drinks, which they refused, and peppermints, which Lowry accepted.

"Wow!" he breathed as the pungent minty oils peppered his tastebuds.

Normally, Jacob Munson would have beamed and offered to share the name of the candy company who imported these particular mints, but not today.

His answers to their questions were monosyllabic. Yes, he and Hester had left the party together. Yes, Hester had gotten out near the Waldorf and he'd gone on home alone. No, there was no one to say what time he'd arrived at his upper West Side apartment, nor could he say when his grandson had come home, as he'd already gone to sleep.

"Besides," he added, twisting the thin strands of his gray beard, "you know where my grandson was and what he was doing."

"Yes," Sigrid said wryly, thinking bow busy Rick Evans and Pascal Grant must have been hauling Shambley's body all over the Breul House.

Munson adamantly refused to discuss what he'd heard Shambley say to Benjamin Peake or Hester Kohn. "You must ask them," he said, drawing his small frame up with Prussian militancy.

"Miss Kohn has told us about the forgery," Sigrid said.

She had thought it was impossible for his stiff shoulders to become more rigid. She was wrong.

"Then you know all there is to know," he said. "I will not discuss this further without my lawyer."

And from that position, he would not budge.

Nauman was still waiting out in the main part of the gallery when they emerged from Munson's office, and he looked up expectantly.

Sigrid glanced at her watch, saw it was almost five-thirty, and sent Lowry to the phone to check in.

"Ready to call it a day?" Nauman asked.

"Unless something's come up," she said.

They watched while Lowry spoke to headquarters on the receptionist's telephone.

"Nothing that can't wait till tomorrow," he reported.

As she dismissed him, she caught the look of hesitation on his face. "Something, Lowry?"

"Just that—well, ma'am, Eberstadt and Peters have checked out all the stories we've been given."

"Yes."

Her gray eyes were like granite and Jim Lowry lost his nerve. Let someone else ask her, he decided.

"Nothing, ma'am. See you tomorrow?"

"What was that about?" asked Nauman, watching the younger man step out into the cold night air and pull his collar up to his ears.

"I think he wanted to ask if you had a proper alibi." She smiled as she put on her heavy coat and gloves.

"Me?"

"I suppose I'll have to go on record tomorrow and tell them that all your movements are accounted for."

"*All* my movements?" he laughed.

"Well," she emended. "Enough of them anyhow."

They browsed through a few stores along Fifth Avenue, not really intent on Christmas shopping, but open to felicitous suggestions. Sigrid bought a new camera case for her mother. Anne Harald was a photojournalist and her old case had banged around all over the world so much that it was ratty and frayed.

A cutlery store reminded her that Roman Tramegra had recently grumbled about his need for proper boning knives. She found a set with wicked-looking thin blades.

Nauman saw a delicate cloisonné pin enameled to look like a zebra swallowtail and immediately bought it for Jill Gill, an entomologist friend who raised butterflies.

By seven their arms were laden with packages, so they walked to the garage west of Fifth Avenue, dumped everything into Nauman's bright yellow sports car, and drove down to the Village for an early dinner.

Over their wine, Nauman brought up Shambley's death and Jacob Munson's reaction. "He told me everything," he said.

Sigrid held up a warning hand. "Nauman, wait. You do understand that anything you tell me—"

"—can and will be used against me?"

"Yes."

"I know. It's okay."

"I know he's your friend," Sigrid said. "And he seemed like a nice old man Wednesday night, but he wasn't very cooperative today."

"You might be uncooperative, too, if you were eighty-two years old and just found out that your only grandson's gay and your business partner's a partner in murder."

"What?"

In short terse sentences, Nauman repeated the things Munson had said at lunch.

"He doesn't have trouble hearing, does he?" Sigrid asked.

"No, why?"

"I just wonder if he misheard what Shambley actually said. Hester Kohn didn't pass forged paintings; she forged Munson's name on an inflated appraisal so someone could get a big tax write-off for a charitable donation."

Sigrid swirled the red wine in her glass thoughtfully. "Or at least that's what she told me this afternoon."

As the waiter brought their check, she glanced at him in sudden mischief. "By the way, Nauman, what are fungible formulations?"

"Oh, God!" he groaned. "Buntrock's been at you, hasn't he?"

She smiled.

"Elliott's all right as far as this new breed of *helden*-curators goes," Nauman warned, "but aesthetic sensibility is only a meager compensation for the loss of innocence."

In his office at the Erich Breul House, Benjamin Peake sat in the deepest concentration he'd attained since assuming the directorship. Shambley's Léger poster had touched off such an unlikely train of speculation. All the same . . .

He found one of the house's brochures and scanned it, but the information he sought wasn't there; so he swivelled in his chair and took down a copy of *Erich Breul—The Man and His Dream*, that fulsome confection whipped up by the first director sixty years ago. He'd skimmed through it when he took over the house, but it seemed like so much puffery that he'd never bothered to read it carefully. He thought he recalled, though, that the book held a chronology.

Yes, there it was. Erich Breul's life laid out from birth to death. And there was Erich Jr.'s birth in 1890, his graduation from Harvard in 1911, his departure for Europe in the fall, and his fatal accident in 1912.

Peake turned to the section on Erich Jr., but it was sketchy and, except when describing the youth's Christmas visit with his Fürst relatives in Zurich, lacked necessary details. He had arrived in Paris in September of 1912 and died in mid-November.

1912, thought Peake. Just before the Armory Show of 1913 blasted the American art world into modernism. Picasso was in Paris then. Picasso, Braque, Derain, Matisse, Juan Gris and, yes, Léger, too. All the iconographers of modern art poised on the brink of greatness. Nothing in the book suggested that the dutiful young Erich Jr. harbored bohemian leanings, but he was his father's son so surely it wasn't outside the realm of possibility that he'd seen an avant-garde exhibit in that brief two and a half months before he'd died.

Could that be why Shambley had ransacked the house? wondered Peake. Was that why he wanted the inventory sheets and why he accused me of being too lazy to see what was under my nose?

Peake replaced the book and turned back to the inventory file. Not the attic, he thought, the basement. He ran his finger down the itemized list and there it was: "*B.8.4. Steamer trunk. EB Jr.*"

It was really too absurd, he told himself as he got up and walked through the inner door to the butler's pantry. On the other hand, Shambley *had* been on his way down to the basement Wednesday night, right?

Twenty minutes later, he closed Erich Jr.'s trunk in disappointment and brushed the dust of the storage room from his trousers knees. *Well, you knew it was a million-to-one chance*, he thought wryly.

Nauman drove Sigrid home and when they carried in her packages, they found Roman Tramegra positively radiant.

"Come and have some champagne!" he boomed. "I ordered a case for the holidays, but we must celebrate *tonight*! I did it, I *did* it, *I DID IT*!"

"Did what?" asked Sigrid, disentangling herself from his effusive bear hug.

"Sold my very first *mystery* story!" He waved a long blue check at them. "*Mostly Male* magazine bought it—five hundred dollars for fifteen hundred words. What a glorious, *glorious* Christmas present!"

He shepherded them into the living room and filled two more crystal champagne flutes from a bottle that was by now nearly empty. On the table beside the ice bucket was an ornate and expensive-looking arrangement of blue spruce and white poinsettias.

"You *are* celebrating," said Sigrid, clinking glasses with Roman and Nauman.

"Oh, those aren't *my* flowers," Roman told her. He fumbled through the greenery and located a small white envelope. "They came for you."

Puzzled, Sigrid opened the envelope and found one of Søren Thorvaldsen's personal cards. On the reverse, he'd written, *Please accept my apology.*

"Thorvaldsen?" Nauman growled, shamelessly reading the card over her shoulder. "What'd he do? Why's he apologizing?"

In creating from his own home "A Museum for the edification and pleasure of the public so long as its stones shall endure," it was Mr. Breul's sincerest wish that he might refute those cynics who hold that life has become squalid and ignoble in this new century of ours. Instead of the weariness and boredom induced by more formal museums, visitors to the Erich Breul House are charmed and refreshed by the air of peace and dignity and beauty throughout. Every room invites, every room welcomes the visitor as if he were a cherished guest in the private home of a gentleman of taste and discrimination.

And so he is!

ERICH BREUL — THE MAN AND HIS DREAM,
PRIVATELY PUBLISHED 1924 BY THE FRIENDS AND
TRUSTEES OF THE ERICH BREUL HOUSE

NINE

THE DAY DAWNED gray and freezing and Sigrid's mood wasn't helped when she reached work and found that Mick Cluett had called in sick again and that Bernie Peters was taking a half day of personal leave.

"One of his daughters fell off her bike this morning and knocked out a tooth," said Matt Eberstadt.

"I thought kids watched cartoons on Saturday morning," Sigrid said, diverted by the thought that the Peters children might be part of a healthier national trend.

"Their TV's in the shop," said Eberstadt.

He described to her what they had learned of Shambley at the New York Center for the Fine Arts and how they'd found the posters he'd purchased at the Guggenheim.

"Matt thinks Shambley might have been bisexual," Elaine Albee chimed in. "And you remember what Mrs. Beardsley said about Pascal Grant feeling uneasy around him?"

Sigrid nodded.

"Well, I decided to have another talk with him. He's got all these reproductions of modern art up in his room—says they remind him of jazz. He's really a nice kid and so good-looking, I wondered if maybe Shambley was trying to lay him."

"And instead of flowers and candy," jeered Lowry, "he brought art posters?"

"It could fit," Eberstadt contended. "Shambley told the girl at the museum shop that he could hang one of the posters upside down and it wouldn't matter. Sounds like he was talking about somebody two cards shy of a full deck, doesn't it?"

"A love triangle?" Sigrid said. "Is that what this is all about?"

"Rick Evans said he and Grant were together when Shambley was killed." Lowry nodded judiciously. "And we know what *that* means, but what if Evans knew Shambley was going to try to cut him out and—"

"No way," said Elaine Albee. "Oh, there might be some latent adolescent stirrings, but Pascal Grant says he and Evans were listening to jazz and I don't think he was lying. I don't think he knows *how* to lie. He's such an innocent. Look how quickly he fell apart when we questioned him Thursday."

"You may be right about Grant," Sigrid said, "but Jacob Munson is convinced that his grandson's gay and he's not happy about it."

She repeated the pertinent things Nauman had told her about his lunch conversation with Munson.

"Oh," said Lowry. "So that's what he meant when he said we knew where his grandson was when Shambley was killed. And what he was doing there. I thought he was talking about them moving the body."

"I did, too," Sigrid admitted.

"I asked Grant about that again," said Elaine. "He said Rick didn't want anyone to know he'd been spending the night there because, and I quote, 'People would say it was sex.' "

"And you're sure that it wasn't?" asked Sigrid.

"Not on Pascal Grant's part," Elaine said sturdily.

They moved on to the possibility that Shambley might have tried to blackmail Hester Kohn and Benjamin Peake over Munson's forged signature on an inflated tax appraisal, and considered that relatively minor crime in the light of Munson's assertion that they had instead authenticated and sold forged paintings through the gallery.

It was hard to know which was true, they decided, when everyone who'd known Dr. Roger Shambley agreed that he insinuated, suggested, and implied but very seldom said precisely what was on his mind.

"Look at Thorvaldsen," said Lowry. "A self-made millionaire like him, he has to be sharp, right? Yet, according to him, he went sneaking back to the Breul House Wednesday night and cooled his heels for an hour, all because Shambley offered him a deal. At least he *thinks* Shambley offered him a deal. But he doesn't know what and he doesn't know why."

"Or so he says," Sigrid cautioned. "Don't forget he also hinted to me that Shambley might have caused him a problem if he stirred up trouble right now. He might have gone there expecting to pay blackmail for all we know."

"We checked out Lady Francesca Leeds' story," Matt Eberstadt reported. "And Hope Ruffton's. Both were where they said they were unless a lot of people are lying."

"That takes care of all the checkable stories," said Lowry in his capacity as recorder for this case. He read from his notes, "Of the people there that night, the ones in the clear are Leeds, Ruffton, the Hymans, the Herzogs, Buntrock, that pianist and the caterer's people. Munson, Hester Kohn, Thorvaldsen, Mrs. Beardsley, Peake, and Mr. Reinicke can't prove their movements."

Lowry paused and Sigrid said dryly, "You've omitted two people: Oscar Nauman and me."

There was an interested silence.

"For the record, Professor Nauman and I were together during the pertinent time period. If it becomes necessary, I can supply corroboration. Question?"

"No, ma'am," said Lowry.

"Moving on then." Sigrid laid out the blowups Paula Guidry had made of the great hall on Thursday morning. "As you see, the mannequin's cane is missing. Until we have reason to think otherwise, I think it's safe to say that's our weapon. So whose place is worth a search warrant?" she asked them.

They went down Lowry's list, from Jacob Munson—"That old guy?" said Elaine. "He may be old, but he's feisty," Jim told her—to Winston Reinicke. "Lainey has a theory about him," Jim grinned.

Lieutenant Harald was not amused by their byplay. This was where she missed Tillie the most. By this time, he would have provided a timetable with each suspect's movements and motives carefully logged.

"Has anyone heard when Tildon's expected back?" she asked abruptly.

"They keep saying sometime after New Year's," said Matt. "I talked to him two days ago. He was supposed to go to Chuckie's Christmas play last night, his first time out except to see the doctor."

Elaine Albee gave Sigrid a sympathetic glance. "You miss him, too, right?"

"I miss his thoroughness," she answered, with a pointed look at Eberstadt. "I don't suppose Peters remembered that he was supposed to interview the Zajdowicz woman this morning."

Eberstadt patted his pockets. "Yeah, he gave me the name of the place and the time. I wrote it down."

He found the scrap of paper. "Haven Rock on Staten Island. They told him to come after eleven o'clock. That's when the priest finishes confession. Want me to go?"

"No," Sigrid decided. "I'll do it."

The rest home was in West New Brighton on the north side of Staten Island, so she took the ferry instead of driving to Brooklyn and crossing the Verrazano Bridge.

The sun had burned through the earlier clouds and even on this cold December day, the open rear deck of the boat held many camera-snapping tourists. The ferry still offered one of the most spectacular views of lower Manhattan; and although city lights made it much more breathtaking after dark, daytime wasn't bad either, thought Sigrid. She stood close to a bulkhead out of the wind and watched the stretch of choppy gray water widen between boat and shore.

As the ferry moved out into upper New York Bay, away from the shelter of land, several passengers who had burbled about the smell of clean salty air abruptly fled inside to search for hot coffee.

Most cameras were pointed back toward the twin towers of the World Trade Center, but a few telephoto lenses were already focussing on the Statue of Liberty off to starboard. No one was paying attention to Brooklyn on the port side of the boat and Sigrid was stirred by a sudden memory of her Great-uncle Lars. He had often treated her and cousin Hilda to rides on the ferry that once ran between Brooklyn and Staten Island before the Verrazano Bridge was built.

If Albee or Lowry had been with her, she would have kept silent; but since she was alone, Sigrid turned to a nearby tourist and pointed toward what would still be the country's fourth largest city if it hadn't been annexed back in 1898.

"Brooklyn," she said.

The Japanese woman smiled and nodded and a couple of her friends looked up at the thin woman with inquiring faces.

"The tall building is the Williamsburgh Bank," she said, imitating Great-uncle Lars's clear didactic tone. "Five hundred and twelve feet high. The tallest four-sided clock in the world."

"Ah!" said the women. They spoke to their men. A ripple went through the group, then fourteen cameras swung toward Brooklyn.

When Sigrid was escorted to the correct building, a priest was still working his way down Barbara Zajdowicz's corridor, offering to hear those who wanted to confess and bestowing a quiet blessing on those who did not.

The guide with whom a receptionist at the main office had provided her was a white-haired resident, gossipy and plump and proud of his continued mobility into his ninth decade of life. As loquaciously proud of Haven Rock as if he were a majority stockholder and she a prospective customer, Mr. Hogarty described the various facilities: how residents usually began with an apartment, moved into a comfortable single room in this building when they needed medical monitoring and could no longer manage alone, and, if necessary, finished up in a medical ward for the totally bedridden.

"Me, I'm still in my own apartment," Mr. Hogarty bragged, "but a lot of my friends are over here."

"Here" was a clean-lined series of interlocking squares. The residential rooms reminded Sigrid of a solid block set down inside a square greenhouse. Each room opened onto the wide window-lined corridor, a common area hung with flowering baskets and green plants and made homey with clusters of sofas and easy chairs all along its length. It was a pleasant area and one that invited residents and their guests to sit and converse and look out at the small courtyard garden. The clear glass windows were curved to catch every ray of winter sun, and several of the people basking in the bright sunlight exchanged greetings with Sigrid's guide when they passed.

As they found two unoccupied easy chairs and sat down to wait for the priest to emerge from Mrs. Zajdowicz's room, Sigrid asked Mr. Hogarty if he knew the woman personally.

"Barb? Oh sure. See, she used to be in me and the wife's canasta club, but then she had that first little stroke a couple of years ago and got religion and—" He broke off and gave a humorous shrug. "I mean, we're all religious here. Me and the wife, that's why we picked Haven Rock. Because it's run by the Catholics, see? But when Barb had her stroke, even though it wasn't a big one—well, you probably know how that can turn things on in your head that weren't there before?"

Sigrid murmured noncommittally.

"Well, that's what happened with Barb, see? So she quit playing cards and started going to confession every week and to mass every time it was offered. The wife said to me it was like being on retreat with the nuns, the way she talked; but the wife and her'd been friends ever since the beginning—we moved into our place the same week Barb did, see, in the next apartment—and they stayed friends. The wife passed away last spring and Barb kept having more of these little strokes, see, so they moved her over here. I try to get over a couple of times a week even though she don't know me half the time."

He shook his head. "Bad when the mind goes. The wife, she was sharp as a tack right up to the day she passed away. Beat me in cribbage that very morning, but Barb— Well, you'll see. Although she's usually pretty good after Father Francis has been here. You a friend of the family or something?"

"I didn't think she had any family," Sigrid parried.

"Well, she didn't, far as I ever heard. Me and the wife, we both come from big families but we only had the two boys. Dick, he's the oldest, he lives right here on Staten Island. Got grandchildren of his own, even. But not Barb. She just had a sister and brother and none of 'em ever had kids. None that lived anyhow."

Sigrid's mental antennae quivered. "She had children that died?"

"Not her. She told the wife her and her husband couldn't have babies. But seems like the sister had a couple of miscarriages or the baby died getting born or some female trouble like that. She never talked about it till after her first stroke. Least that's when the wife first mentioned it to me, see, 'cause Barb'd get on these crying jags about those poor innocent babies and how the sister oughtn't to have done it." He lowered his voice. "See, the sister wasn't married."

The door of Barbara Zajdowicz's room opened and a middle-aged priest came out.

"How's she doing today, Father?" asked Mr. Hogarty as he and Sigrid walked toward him.

"Much as usual, Harry," said the priest. He smiled and nodded at others across the corridor, but did not break his progress to the next room.

As Sigrid started to follow Mr. Hogarty into his friend's room, she saw an unwanted sight. At the far end of the corridor, a tall redheaded man in sheepskin jacket and cowboy boots with a camera case slung over his shoulder paused to compare a room number on the nearest door with something scribbled on his notepad. He saw her at almost the same instant and his homely face took on the look of an excited terrier spotting its prey.

"Yo! Lieutenant Harald," he cried and loped around a passing wheelchair. William "Rusty" Guillory of the *Post*.

"Two minds with but a single thought." His free hand fumbled with the zipper on his camera case. "Didja talk to her, yet? Does she know anything about the babies? What've you got for me?"

"What're you doing here, Guillory?" she stalled.

"Same as you." He took two quick pictures of her before she could protest. "Got her name off the deed and ran it by a snitch in Social Security."

Mr. Hogarty's curious face appeared in the doorway behind her and the reporter craned for a view of the interior. "Who're you?" Guillory asked.

"Hold it, Guillory," Sigrid said firmly. "You'll have to wait out here. I was just going in to interview Mrs. Zajdowicz now."

"Talk fast huh, Lieutenant? If she's got anything good, I can still make the second edition."

Without promising, Sigrid stepped inside the room and closed the door on Rusty Guillory.

"Here she is now, Barb." Mr. Hogarty's gossipy nature was clearly piqued by the appearance of yet a second visitor for his old acquaintance.

Sigrid stretched out her hand to the woman in the wheelchair. "Mrs. Zajdowicz? I'm Lieutenant Harald of the New York City Police Department."

"Police?" breathed Mr. Hogarty.

Barbara Jurczyk Zajdowicz bore the ravages of her age and her illness. Her short straight hair was completely white, her blue eyes were faded, and the years had cut deep grooves in her gray face, but time could not efface the basic structure of her rangy frame and there was a residual impression of strength in her prominent jaw and broad brow. She wore a maroon skirt and cardigan, a white blouse that was pinned at the collar with a lovely cameo, and sturdy black lace-up oxfords. The footrests of her chair were folded up so that her feet touched the floor as she walked herself forward to give Sigrid her left hand.

Her hand was considerably larger than Sigrid's and bare of rings, except for a wide gold band that hung loosely on her fourth finger, trapped forever by the enlarged knuckle. Her right hand held a rosary and lay curled in her lap in what Sigrid recognized as stroke-induced weakness; and when she spoke, her words were so slurred that it was difficult to understand.

"She says did Angelika send you?" interpreted Mr. Hogarty, who'd had more practice. "That's her sister."

"I know," said Sigrid. "No, Mrs. Zajdowicz. I came because a trunk was found in the attic of your old house a few days ago. Can you remember? Do you know anything about it?"

The old woman looked at Sigrid for a long moment, then made a gesture with her left hand. "Go 'way, Harry," she said thickly.

"But, Barb—" he protested, his face dropping.

Again came that dismissive shooing wave of her hand. "Out."

Sigrid detained him for a moment as he neared the door. "There's a reporter out there, Mr. Hogarty. He'll probably ask you questions, try to make you speculate about certain things which he may later twist for his own purposes. I'd caution you to choose your words carefully."

Mr. Hogarty brightened immediately and bounded through the door with such eagerness that Sigrid realized she should have saved her breath.

She sat down beside Mrs. Zajdowicz.

"Angelika?" asked the woman.

"Your sister's dead, Mrs. Zajdowicz. Like the babies."

"Ah." She closed her eyes and her rawboned fingers began to tell the beads of the rosary. A moment later, Sigrid saw tears seep from beneath those wrinkled lids.

"Mrs. Zajdowicz. Barbara," she said gently. "Were they your sister's babies?"

The old woman nodded. Her eyes opened. "Sister. Sorry. So sorry, Sister. Father . . . bless me, Father, for she has sinned—" She crossed herself with her left hand and her words became unintelligible.

"Who sinned, Barbara?" Sigrid asked urgently. "Angelika? What happened to Angelika's babies?"

"Died," Barbara Zajdowicz said, enunciating as clearly as she could. "Wrong . . . but we . . . couldn't let . . . anyone know. Gregor. He kill her."

"Your brother Gregor killed the babies?"

Mrs. Zajdowicz twitched her rosary beads impatiently. "No. Gregor. Such shame . . . on family. We said . . . woman troubles. Gregor . . . stayed downstairs."

"You're saying Gregor would have killed Angelika if he'd known she was pregnant? So you kept it from him? How?"

"She . . . fat like me."

Too much newsprint had been devoted to stories of large women suddenly surprised to find themselves giving birth for Sigrid to doubt that a sister built like Mrs. Zajdowicz could have gotten away with illicit pregnancy.

"Who was the father?" Sigrid asked. "Was it your husband? Karol?"

"Karol . . . he cried . . . babies for you, he said. But every time . . . died."

Her words were still badly slurred, but Sigrid was becoming used to her speech patterns.

"How did the babies die, Barbara?"

"Sin . . . she sinned . . . Karol . . ."

"Did Angelika kill her own babies?" Sigrid asked.

"They should been . . . *mine!* Not . . . Angelika's." Her rheumy blue eyes glared out at Sigrid, then they filled with tears. "Poor . . . little babies. So little. The shame . . . Sister—"

She held out her rosary to Sigrid. "Pray me, Sister," she pleaded and Sigrid wasn't sure if Mrs. Zajdowicz had confused her with Angelika or a nun, since she was dressed today in navy slacks and a boxy black jacket.

"Who put those babies in the attic?" Sigrid asked. "You or Angelika?"

"Pray me, Sister," Mrs. Zajdowicz wept. "Pray me."

Sigrid looked around helplessly, then saw the call bell on the wall beside the woman's bed. She went over and pushed it. While she waited, she took a shiny white card from her purse and gently pressed it against Barbara's fingers; first the left hand, then her curled right hand. After the card was carefully tucked into her notebook, she sat holding the sobbing woman's hands until the nurse came.

"What's going on?" said Rusty Guillory, when Sigrid emerged. He had managed a couple of hasty pictures of the distrait Barbara Zajdowicz before the nurse closed the door again. "Didja give her a heart attack or something?"

A small crowd had gathered in that section of the corridor and as Sigrid's eyes fell upon Mr. Hogarty, the plump little man looked embarrassed and scuttled away.

"Hey, wait a minute!" called Guillory. "We didn't finish."

"Yes, you did," said Sigrid. "Come on, Guillory. Give it a rest."

"Then give me a statement," he countered. "What'd she tell you?"

"She's confused and unhappy," Sigrid told him. "She's had several strokes, her speech is badly slurred, and her mind's not very clear."

"But you got something out of her. I know you, Lieutenant."

Sigrid looked at the circle of avid faces that ringed them. Resigned, she said, "Put your coat on and let's go. You want to make your deadline, don't you?"

They walked through the now-buzzing corridor. "It's not much of a story and we'll probably never know what really happened," she warned.

"That's okay," Guillory said cynically. "Feel free to speculate. I'm going to."

"She and her husband lived there with her unmarried sister Angelika and their bachelor brother Gregor. She says the babies were Angelika's and that they all died at birth. That's all I could get out of her."

"Was it incest, adultery, or good old-fashioned fornication?" Guillory went right to the tabloid heart of things.

"She says her brother would have killed Angelika if he'd known she was bringing shame on the family name," Sigrid said. "I believe her."

"What about the husband?" he persisted.

"I can't go on record about that. She wasn't clear enough."

"So who killed the babies?"

"Fifty years ago, no prenatal care, unattended birth, they could have just died," said Sigrid. "Why does it always have to be murder?"

"Murder sells more papers. You know that, Lieutenant. Besides, didn't the M.E.'s office say the mummified one was born alive?"

"But there's still nothing to say it wasn't a natural death." She pushed open an outer door and walked toward the parking lot. Despite the noontime sun, the wind was biting.

"So who put them in the attic?" asked Guillory, looking at his watch. "Santa Claus?"

Sigrid shrugged. "Sorry, Guillory. I'm all out of speculations."

Rusty Guillory slung his camera case inside the car. "If I make the next ferry, I'll just squeeze in under the next deadline. Need a lift?"

"No, thanks, I have a car."

She waited until Guillory's car was out of the lot before walking back to the dark-clad man who lingered indecisively near an evergreen tree beside the gate. "Father Francis, isn't it?"

"Yes. They say you're a police officer."

"Lieutenant Harald," she said, reaching into her shoulder bag for her gold shield.

"They say you're here because of those poor baby skeletons found over in New York. That it was Barbara Zajdowicz's old house?"

"Yes."

The priest was perhaps half an inch shorter than she and his troubled eyes were nearly level with hers.

"Father Francis, did she ever discuss this with you? About her sister? Or the infants?"

He drew back. "I can't answer that."

"I'm not asking you to break the sanctity of confession," Sigrid assured him. "I meant outside confession."

He hesitated. "I really never talked with her until after her first stroke. You have to understand, Lieutenant. Strokes, Alzheimer's, hardening of the arteries—sometimes it's hard for them to keep in touch with reality. Or for me to know where fantasy begins. Everything's so different today. People have babies out of wedlock all the time—actresses, singers, career women—no one hides it anymore. Sometimes we forget what it was like fifty years ago."

"Some things haven't changed though, have they, Father Francis?" Sigrid said. "Things like jealousy and spite?"

"No," he sighed.

"She killed them, didn't she? They weren't born dead, no matter what she told Angelika."

"I'm sorry, Lieutenant." He moved away. "I can't talk to you about this."

*   *   *

Back at the office, Sigrid gave Bernie Peters the card she'd used to take Barbara Zajdowicz's fingerprints. Peters stopped talking about his daughter's newly reimplanted front tooth and developed the latents with special emphasis on the old woman's right fingers, which he then compared to the prints found on the old newspapers.

At a little after two, he brought them into Sigrid's office, where she was going over the case with Lowry's records.

"We wouldn't go to court without finding more characteristics," he said, "but see the double bifurcation at one o'clock on both of these latents and the delta at high noon?"

Sigrid looked through the magnifying glass and agreed they seemed identical. "So what do we have? Evidence that in 1938, Barbara Zajdowicz put one of the bodies in that attic trunk. A woman who's now eighty-seven, mentally confused, and confined to a wheelchair." She sighed. "Write it up as soon as you can, Peters, and we'll send it along to the DA's office. Let them decide what to do about it."

Elaine Albee and Matt Eberstadt breezed in at two-thirty from their interview with Søren Thorvaldsen, flushed and excited by a brief taste of life aboard a Caribbean cruise ship.

"It was getting ready to sail when we caught up with him—the *Sea Dancer*," Albee reported. "And he invited us to ride out into the bay and take his launch back with him. He wanted to hear how the engines ran or something."

"They'd just installed a new generator," said Eberstadt.

"So he gave us a pass and we got to stand on deck and throw confetti and streamers and listen to the band play 'Anchors Aweigh' with a reggae beat."

"They had a buffet already set out like you wouldn't believe," Eberstadt told Peters, who was listening enviously. "Frances would put me on lettuce and water till Christmas if she ever heard about the salmon and—"

"Oh, and those luscious chocolate-dipped strawberries and pineapple slices!" Albee interrupted him.

"Then we went up to the bridge—what a view!—and Thorvaldsen gave us a tour of the owner's suite, one flight down with its own private deck. Talk about luxury!"

"We saw one of Oscar Nauman's paintings," said Elaine Albee, with a wary glance at Sigrid. She wondered how the lieutenant would react if they told her that Thorvaldsen had tried to pump them about her. "It was very colorful."

"Did you happen to remember why you were there?" Sigrid asked coldly.

Eberstadt virtuously produced Thorvaldsen's typed and signed statement. "He had a stenographer come up to his suite and went through the whole evening again, but it doesn't add doodly to what he told you Thursday night."

He read from Thorvaldsen's statement, " 'Dr. Shambley implied that it could be to my benefit if I met with him again that night at the Erich Breul House. I assumed he meant to offer me the private opportunity to add something choice to my art collection. As I have occasionally bought works of art under similar circumstances, this did not strike me as an unusual request. I cannot say positively that this is what he meant. I saw no such piece of art that night, nor did I see Dr. Shambley. I went in through the unlocked front door, waited in the library for approximately one hour, and left at midnight without seeing or speaking to anyone.' "

Sigrid had listened silently with her elbows and forearms folded flatly on the desk.

"When we first got there," said Albee, "we talked with Thorvaldsen's secretary, a Miss Kristensen. She gave us the name of a security guard who was on outside duty Wednesday night, Leon Washington. She says Washington saw Thorvaldsen enter his office building around ten-thirty and then leave again about fifteen minutes later."

"Convenient," Sigrid said.

Elaine Albee shrugged. "Who knows? We stopped by his place on our way back here and woke him up. He wasn't happy about telling us, but he says he'd stashed a coffee thermos in an empty warehouse across the street and was taking an unauthorized coffee break—"

"Coffee, my ass," Eberstadt interjected.

"—so he saw Thorvaldsen but Thorvaldsen didn't see him. And yeah, he may be lying, but he seemed too worried about the possibility of losing his job to be acting."

Matt Eberstadt nodded. "He said Miss Kristensen promised she wouldn't let it get back to Thorvaldsen and that's all he really seemed to care about."

Bernie Peters sighed. "If the guard's telling the truth, that definitely puts Thorvaldsen out."

"Whether or not he's lying, it's still hard to put Thorvaldsen there." Sigrid leaned back in her chair with her left knee braced against the edge of the desk. "Francesca Leeds said she left him between ten and ten-fifteen; Evans and Grant said they found Shambley's body between ten-fifteen and ten-thirty. Even if he had the full half hour to get back there, from the restaurant four blocks away, get inside, kill Shambley and then leave by the basement door, it'd be awfully tight."

"And why would he hang around there for another hour and a half?" asked Elaine Albee.

"Looking for the picture Shambley promised him?" Lowry guessed.

"With Grant and Evans running all over the place?"

"Up and down the *back* stairs," Lowry reminded her. "They never said they were in the main rooms."

Despite Lowry's reservations, the others were willing to strike the Danish ship owner from their dwindling list.

"Reinicke, Munson, Kohn, Beardsley, and Peake," said Lowry. "I move to strike Reinicke, too. I can't see him tying the dog up somewhere while he goes in and bops Shambley over the head just because the guy sneered at his taste in art. He didn't seem to be that thin-skinned."

Sigrid listened with only half an ear as they bounced theories off each other. "That's probably all it really was," she told them.

"Ma'am?" said Eberstadt.

"What Lowry said about a bop over the head. A simple whack with a weighted cane that happened to be handy. One blow, not a shower of them. If Shambley's skull had been half as thick as his skin, he might not have suffered anything other than a simple concussion."

"Unpremeditated," mused Albee.

"He was at the party for less than an hour," Sigrid said, "but in those few minutes, he insulted Reinicke and Thorvaldsen and half threatened Kohn and Peake with public disgrace. He didn't seem to care what he said; but at a party, of course, he could get away with it. Although," she added, "Thorvaldsen almost threw a punch at him."

"So," Peters said, "if he mouthed off to the wrong person—"

"Bop!" Lowry grinned.

"If we eliminate Reinicke," said Sigrid, "I could see Benjamin Peake or Hester Kohn flying off the handle. And even Mrs. Beardsley or Jacob Munson might be pushed. But why then and there?"

They didn't see her point.

"Look," she said. "Assume that Shambley says something that so enrages or scares the killer that he or she grabs up the cane and starts after him. At that point, Shambley's already passed through the door under the main staircase and started down the basement stairs when the blow lands on his head. Why? His study was in the attic. Elliott Buntrock went through the paintings stored down there and he's certain that none of them are worth much more than the canvas they're painted on. So why was Shambley going to the basement?"

"Oh, crap!" said Albee. "You don't think it's simple B and E, do you? That he left the door open for Thorvaldsen and a burglar came in? In that case, he could have been trying to get help."

"Great," Peters groaned. "So instead of four suspects, you just widened the field to half a million."

"I don't know." Eberstadt shook his head. "I've got a gut feeling about those two kids down there—Rick Evans and Pascal Grant. You sure that janitor's not stringing you along with that innocent look, Lainey?"

"And what about that empty glove case in Shambley's briefcase?" asked Lowry. "That's got to mean something, doesn't it?"

In a half-empty coffee shop on Fourth Avenue, Pascal Grant savored a forkful of fruitcake and drank from his glass of milk as be listened to Rick Evans talk about Louisiana.

"You'd love it out there in the country, Pasc. No subways or drug pushers every ten feet, no crowds of people hassling you all the time. We could go camping and fishing back in the swamps."

"Yeah, but Rick—" He carefully speared two green cherries and a piece of citron with his fork and ate them one by one.

Christmas carols drifted down from a speaker high on the wall overhead.

"Is it money? You don't need much in Louisiana," Rick said earnestly.

"Yeah, but you'll be taking pictures. What'll I do?"

"You'll help me. Or you can do what you do here. In my town, people are always griping because they can't find anybody to do chores or odd jobs. You can be a gardener. Work outdoors all day long if that's what you want."

"I'd like that," Pascal said, smiling at Rick across the scarred Formica table.

"Great!" said Rick. "Then you'll come with me next Saturday? The day after Christmas?"

Pascal's smile faded and his fork explored a raisin. "Mrs. Beardsley won't like it."

"Mrs. Beardsley doesn't own you, Pasc. You own yourself just like I own myself."

"But you're not a dummy," Pascal blurted, his blue eyes miserable. "People may not like me in your town. Your mother won't like me."

"Sure she will. And you'll like her. I called her last night and told her all about you and she said I could bring anybody home I wanted to. And besides, as soon as we're earning enough money, we could move into a place of our own. Maybe even out in the middle of nowhere where nobody'll bother us and you can play your jazz tapes as loud as you want."

The thought of open country was bewildering to someone who'd only known the city, but Pascal had never had a friend like this, someone who did not merely put up with him but actually seemed to like him unconditionally and as he was. The lure of that friendship and the fear of losing it were irresistible and outweighed any nebulous fears about Louisiana's alien landscape.

Pascal put out his hand and shyly touched Rick's. "Okay," he said.

When Sigrid got home at five-thirty, she was surprised to find Nauman and Elliott Buntrock wrestling with an eight-foot Christmas tree in her living room.

"I thought you had a summit meeting at the gallery," she said.

"You didn't hear what happened with Thorvaldsen?" asked Nauman, holding the tree perpendicular while Buntrock crawled around under the lower branches, tightening the screws of the stand.

"No," said Sigrid.

"One of his ships sailed today."

She nodded. "I know. Two of my detectives rode out into the bay and then came back with him in his launch."

"They should have stayed on a little longer," said Nauman. With his foot he nudged aside a large, much-taped cardboard box so that Buntrock would have more space for his flying elbows. "The Coast Guard was waiting for it just beyond the Verrazano Bridge."

"What?"

"They took down some of the bulkheads in the engine room and found over six million dollars in fifty- and hundred-dollar bills. A lot of them marked so they could be traced, according to the news bulletins we heard at the gallery. Drug money. On its way to buy a fresh shipment in the Caribbean."

"They confiscate speedboats and fishing boats when they're involved in drug deals," said Buntrock from somewhere beneath the tree. "Do you suppose they'll confiscate the *Sea Dancer?*"

The telephone rang out in the kitchen and Roman Tramegra stuck his head around the corner a moment later. "Ah, Sigrid, my dear. I *thought* I heard you come in. Telephone."

"Lieutenant!" came Albee's breathless voice. "Did you hear about Thorvaldsen? The feds have arrested him."

"So I just heard," said Sigrid.

"This must be what he meant when he said he went back to the Breul House because he didn't want Shambley to cause any controversy right now. Wow!"

Sigrid waited until Albee ran out of steam, then observed, "It's certainly interesting, but I don't see that it affects Shambley's murder. Do you?"

There was a moment of silence, then Albee admitted that she was probably right and rang off.

As Sigrid hung up the kitchen phone, it finally registered on her that Roman was surrounded by take-out cartons, plastic containers, and green-and-white grocery bags from Balducci's. He seemed to be arranging a long snakelike creature on his largest platter.

"What in God's name is that?" she asked.

"Smoked eel. Neapolitans *always* have eel at Christmas, but I wasn't sure what to do with a fresh one, so I got smoked. Isn't it *sumptuous*? I know it should be skinned and cut, into perfect little ovals, but then we'd lose the *effect*." He straightened the tail. "I thought a bed of red lettuce with strands of alfalfa sprouts for seaweed? What do you think?"

"Roman, are we having a party tonight?" she asked.

"A tree-trimming party. Didn't I *tell* you?"

"No," she said mildly.

"Oh, my dear!" he rumbled. "I'm *so* sorry. I was *certain*—" He curved the eel around a mound of tortellini salad and paused to consider the result. "It's such a *little* party—hardly worth calling it a party at all—but we *do* want to celebrate our first Christmas tree, don't we? I'm such a *child* about Christmas! See what you think of my wassail."

He filled a glass from a nearby bowl and passed it to her across the cluttered counter. Sigrid sipped cautiously. Roman might be a child about Christmas but this was no child's drink. She tasted tart lemon juice tamed by sugar, rum, and some sort of fruity flavor. "Peach brandy?"

"Do you like it?"

Sigrid nodded, beginning to feel slightly more festive. "Who's coming?"

"Just family, so to speak. Oscar, of course. And, as you see, he brought along his friend. Amusing chap. A bit too fey though."

Sigrid almost choked on her drink at this pot calling the kettle black.

"And Jill Gill and—"

"What about ornaments?" Sigrid interrupted. "I don't have any. Do you?"

"I bought new lights and fresh tinsel." He smeared two crackers with pâté and handed one to her. "Goose liver."

"Umm."

"And your mother sent down that *enormous* box out by the tree. She said it hadn't been unpacked in her last eight moves, but she's sure it's tree ornaments."

Since Anne Harald averaged three moves per every two years, no amount of unopened boxes would surprise Sigrid. She refilled her glass and wandered back out to the living room, where Elliott Buntrock had emerged from the shrubbery. He wore black jeans and a black shirt topped by a white sweatshirt that bore the picture of a large yellow bulldozer with the words "Heavy Equipment Is My Life."

"My glass is empty," he complained and headed for the kitchen.

Roman had decked their halls with bayberry candles but he hadn't yet lit them, so the woodsy smell of the fresh pine tree filled the room as Nauman turned to her and, with a flat, deadpan Brooklyn accent, said, "Hey, lady, where's yer mistletoe?"

She smiled and went into his arms.

Even without mistletoe, it was a very satisfactory kiss.

"What happens to your show now that Thorvaldsen won't be underwriting it?" she asked.

"Elliott had already decided I'm not postmodern enough for the Breul House. He's talking about using Blinky Palermo or someone like that to put the place back on New York's cultural map."

"Blinky *who*?"

"Don't ask."

"But what about you?"

"I let Jacob and Elliott talk me into a three-gallery midtown extravaganza," he admitted, "and Francesca's going to line up a new set of sponsors. It's starting to sound like a cross between Busby Berkeley and *Pee-wee's Playhouse*. I may go to Australia for the year. Want to come?"

She laughed as the buzzer went off in the entry hall announcing the arrival of Anne Harald and Jill Gill at her outer gate.

The next hour was a happy jumble of untangling light cords, testing bulbs, and running extension cords from badly placed outlets, helped along with generous servings of Roman's wassail.

Jill Gill had brought with her a selection of Christmas records ranging from Alvin and the Chipmunks and the Norman Luboff Choir to Gregorian chants; and Sigrid took a bittersweet trip down memory lane when Anne opened the carton of ornaments and lifted out a crumpled tinsel star. All at once she was three years old again and her father was holding her up in his strong young arms to place that same star on the very top of their Christmas tree.

She had been so young when he was killed that her memories of him were fragmentary, and suddenly here was a new one that she hadn't even known she possessed.

Anne leaned over and a faint mist of familiar jasmine followed as her lips brushed Sigrid's cheek. "I know, honey," she whispered.

Candles glowed from a dozen different clusters around the warm room. Nauman struggled to relight his pipe, Buntrock and Roman were debating the aesthetics of icicles slung on in clumps (Buntrock's method) or carefully draped one by one (Roman's), and Jill brought a fresh platter of canapés hot from the oven.

Elliott Buntrock beamed as he savored the ambience. "How utterly postmodern this is!"

"Late postmodern," Nauman corrected.

Later, when everyone else had left and Roman had stumbled off to bed, Sigrid walked out to Oscar's disreputable yellow sports car with him. It was midnight and the temperature was frigid, but for once the air was so clear that the brighter constellations shone through the city's reflected glow.

At the car, Nauman unlocked the passenger door, but Sigrid touched his arm regretfully. "I can't go home with you. I promised Roman I'd help him clean up before work in the morning."

"I know," he said. "But I have something for you and it's too cold to stand out here on the sidewalk."

As soon as they were inside, Oscar switched on the engine and started the powerful heater; then he turned and gently traced the contours of her chilled face with gentle fingers. In this dim light, for a fleeting moment, the memory of other faces flickered between his hands—women he had known, women he had slept with, women he had even loved for a little space of time.

And now this woman.

For the first time, he had admitted to himself that she had it within her to be the last. And for the first time he was both awed and apprehensive by what be felt for her.

Half angered by the powerful emotions she aroused in him, he reached into the space behind her seat and drew out a flat package wrapped in brown paper. "Here," he rasped. "Merry Christmas."

"Nauman?" She looked at him, puzzled by his sudden belligerence.

He shrugged and stared through the windshield.

Bewildered, Sigrid undid the paper and found a cardboard folder approximately ten inches wide by eighteen inches tall. Inside was a drawing.

Silently, Oscar turned on the interior light so that she could see, and he heard the sharp intake of her breath as she realized what she held.

It was a sheet of light gray paper with a textured surface that was exquisite to touch; and on it was her own portrait, drawn in delicate silver point and highlighted with touches of white.

A taxi lumbered past, an ambulance wailed in the distance, and from the river a block away came the lonesome hoot of a tugboat's horn; but Nauman's small car was a pool of silence.

At last Sigrid turned to him. "It's like something Dürer would have done," she whispered brokenly. "Is that how you see me?"

"Just like Dürer," he said and leaned forward to touch the tear that glistened on her cheek.

Paris.

. . . add my condolences to the Ambassador's and hope it may somehow comfort you to know that it was not a cold, indifferent stranger that personally supervised the packing of your son's possessions, but a father like yourself; moreover, one who has also had to submit to the heaviest burden Providence may lay upon the shoulders of any father.

As a pen more gifted than mine has written, "What is the price of a thousand horses against a son where there is one son only?"

I pray God may strengthen you in this hour of darkness.

LETTER TO ERICH BREUL SR., DATED 12.15.1912,
FROM MR. LEONARD WHITE, PERSONAL ASSISTANT
TO THE HONORABLE MYRON T. HERRICK,
AMBASSADOR TO FRANCE
(FROM THE ERICH BREUL HOUSE COLLECTION)

TEN

Sunday, December 20

CONSCIENCE, DUTY, AND sheer willpower kept Sigrid from burying her groggy head back under the pillow when her alarm clock went off ninety minutes early the next morning. Getting up at any hour was always a chore, but she had promised Roman that if he'd leave the mess, she would help him clean up before she went to work; so she dragged herself out of bed and into the shower.

After so much wassail the night before, Roman had professed himself uninterested in doing anything other than putting away the leftovers and trundling off to his bed in what had once been the maid's quarters beyond the kitchen.

Ten minutes in the shower restored the outer woman and Sigrid headed toward the kitchen to see what hot black coffee could do for the inner. As she passed through the living room, she gathered up a handful of dirty glasses and plates and carried them out to the sink.

Roman had cleared himself space on the green-and-white tiled counter and was seated there with newspapers and coffee. His miniature countertop television was tuned to the morning news.

"There's your friend," he said, pouring her a cup of coffee by way of greeting.

She paused to watch Søren Thorvaldsen arrive in handcuffs at the federal courthouse. A moment later, cameras panned over the *Sea Dancer* tied up in custody as belligerent vacationers streamed down her gangways. While the camera lingered lovingly on the stacks of paper money uncovered in the engine rooms, Sigrid opened the refrigerator for juice, encountered the glassy eyes of the Saran-Wrapped eel, and closed the door again, all desire for juice abruptly gone.

When the program moved on to another story, Roman clicked it off and rose with a sigh. "How art the mighty fallen," he said portentously. "I'll begin on the dishes if you'll bring in the rest."

"Deal," she said and carried a large tray out to the living room for the demitasse cups and saucers that had accompanied Roman's *bûche de Noël*. Christmas trees with their lights extinguished always looked vaguely forlorn to Sigrid. There was something sad about shimmering tinsel when it reflected only cold winter daylight.

Two trips with the tray cleared out most of the disorder and five minutes with the vacuum took care of cracker crumbs, stray tinsel, and a crushed glass ball. Afterwards, she poured herself a second cup of coffee and began to dry the pots and pans while Roman continued to wash by hand the things he couldn't fit into the dishwasher.

An unquenchable optimist, he announced that his sale of that short mystery story had finally convinced him that he was ready to begin writing the full-length murder mystery he'd been planning since the first day they met back in April.

"In fact," he said, scouring vigorously with steel wool, "I finished the first chapter yesterday morning. Now if I were to average three pages a day, I could be finished by Easter."

"Three months?" Sigrid asked dubiously. "I thought a book took at least a year."

"That's for serious writers," he told her.

"And you're not?"

"My dear, I'm forty-three years old. I have a certain flair for the English language, a certain facility, but *depth*? I fear not."

He rinsed a copper saucepot and handed it to her. "Writers with something profound to say write poetry, writers with something serious to say write novels, but writers with nothing to say write genre fiction. *I* shall become a mystery writer."

He handed her another wet pot. "Don't look so sad. I shall try to be a very *good* mystery writer."

Sigrid smiled. "Tell me about your plot."

"Actually, I don't have one yet," he confessed. "That's the one drawback. I don't want to write suspense or thrillers or, God *forbid,* one of those dreary down-these-mean-streets-a-man-must-go sort of social tracts. No, I want to write classic whodunits, elegantly contrived puzzles, and for that you need a cast of several characters who all have equally good motives to kill the same person. But that's almost impossible anymore. I've been doing some research and there are no *good* motives left."

"No good motives for murder?" Sigrid snorted. "Roman, I'm a homicide detective. Believe me, people kill for a thousand different reasons."

"And most of your cases, dear child, are open-and-shut, no? Domestic violence. The husband enraged at his wife's nagging; the wife who simply *refuses* to be battered any more; addicts killing for drug money. I've been *so* disappointed to see how really ordinary most of your work has been. Oh, I won't say you haven't *occasionally* had interesting puzzles, but usually, it's for money or power, is it not?"

He finished with the pots and pans and began to wipe down the stove and surrounding countertops.

"Well, yes," Sigrid admitted. "But—"

"And most of the time, as soon as you find *one* person with a solid motive, that's the killer, isn't it?"

"So what's your definition of a good motive?" she asked, nettled.

"One that would work for more than two or three people," he said promptly. "Like your babies in the attic in last night's *Post.* Even though that was a dreadful picture of *you,* the story itself would make a *smashing* murder mystery. Just *think*: everyone connected with those babies had a reason to kill them—both sisters, the brother, even the husband. If I were using them in a book, I should probably add in a grandmother and a crazy nurse or priest."

Roman paused with the wet dishcloth in his hands. "Illegitimacy used to be such a *wonderful* reason for murder! Along with miscegenation and incest. Nowadays, if it's not drugs or mere lust, it's for something as pointless and bizarre as a parking place or a pair of designer sunglasses.

"People used to kill for *noble* reasons—for revenge or honor or to usurp a throne. Today, everyone lets it 'all hang out.' " His lip curled around the phrase disdainfully. "You can't build a believable mystery around simple *scandal* for its own sake anymore. Can you *imagine* trying to write *A Scandal in Bohemia* today? Instead of hiring Sherlock Holmes to retrieve that picture of himself with Irene Adler, the king would probably be trying to peddle the negatives to *The National Enquirer.*"

Sigrid laughed. "And would probably be turned down because both parties in the picture were fully clothed."

As she dressed for work, Sigrid thought about the remaining suspects in Roger Shambley's death in light of Roman's insistence that most contemporary homicides were committed for gain. She had to admit that Shambley's shadowy threats carried little weight in today's tolerant atmosphere. And yet . . .

She brushed her hair, put on lipstick and eyeshadow, and even rooted out a red-and-gold silk scarf to add color to her charcoal gray suit, but all the time, her mind kept switching back and forth between Matt Eberstadt's reservations about Rick Evans and Pascal Grant, and her own unanswered question of why Shambley had been killed on the basement steps.

She put on the shoulder holster she'd begun using when her wounded arm made a purse impractical back in October; and her subconscious threw up something that she'd overlooked till then: what had Rick Evans done in those few minutes between the time he left Pascal Grant's room and the time young Grant met him over Roger Shambley's body?

The more she thought of it, the surer she became. She glimpsed at her clock. Still a little early but Albee was usually an early bird, thought Sigrid, and began punching in numbers on her phone.

Elaine Albee answered on the second ring. She sounded a little dubious when Sigrid outlined her theory, but she procured the address Sigrid wanted.

"You're the boss," said Albee, and promised to meet her there as soon as she could get the search warrant.

When Sigrid arrived at the apartment building in the West Eighties, she discovered that Jim Lowry had come along, too.

"I'm the recorder on this case, aren't I?" he grinned.

The building was one of those solid old brick co-ops with a daytime doorman and a well-tended elevator that rose smoothly to the eighteenth floor.

It was only a few minutes before ten when they rang the bell, but soon there was a flicker of movement behind the peephole, then the door was opened by Jacob Munson, still in his robe and slippers and holding the art section of the *New York Times*.

"Lieutenant Harald?" he said, surprised to find them on his threshold.

"May we come in?" she asked. "This is Detective Lowry, whom you met on Friday, and Detective Albee. We'd like to talk to your grandson."

"Richard? *Ja*, sure." He led them down a dim hall lined with framed black-and-white drawings into a large sitting room bright with a half-dozen modern paintings on the walls and numerous small sculptures and art objects atop cabinets, tables, and windowsills. The bookcases were filled to overflowing with art books of all eras and a Mozart sonata cascaded in a ripple of crisp harmonics through the room.

It was a room of culture, a room that had filled up slowly and judiciously over the long years with objects and pictures that represented careful winnowing, a room that had probably been familiar to the adult Nauman while she was still a child in grade school. Imagining Nauman here made Sigrid sad for what she now must do.

"Please sit," said Munson, gesturing to comfortably shabby couches and chairs. "My grandson is asleep, but—"

"No, I'm awake, Grandfather," said Rick Evans from the doorway. "What's up?"

He wore jeans and an LSU sweatshirt and he looked very young and vulnerable with his bare feet and sleep-tousled hair.

"We'd like to talk to you again, Mr. Evans," Sigrid said. "About the statement you signed Thursday."

Rick glanced at Munson. "The lawyer said I wasn't supposed to talk to you without her."

"You may call her if you wish, but this is only to clarify things you already told us."

"Should I, Grandfather?" he asked.

Jacob Munson fingered his thin gray beard. "No tricks?" he asked.

"No tricks," Sigrid promised. "If at any time he wants to stop, then he can say so. We'll take him downtown and you can invite your lawyer to be present."

Rick's eyes were apprehensive as he sat down upon a nearby leather hassock.

Munson folded his paper, placed it neatly on the morning pile beside his chair, and prepared to listen.

Sigrid turned to the young man. "You've told us that on Wednesday night at approximately ten-fifteen, you were visiting Pascal Grant in his room in the basement of the Erich Breul House when you heard a strange noise. Is this correct?"

"Yes, ma'am," he said in his soft Southern voice.

"You said that you went outside to investigate, carrying a softball bat; that you heard a noise which you identified as footsteps in the passage to the service door; that someone unknown to you left by that door; and that when you returned to the main kitchen, you saw Pascal Grant bending over Shambley's body. Correct?"

"Yes, ma'am," he repeated.

"Who did you think had gone down that passageway, Mr. Evans?"

"I told you. I don't know," he said. His brown eyes met her steady gaze and then darted away.

"How long would you say that you were out of Pascal Grant's sight?"

"I-I'm not sure. Two minutes, maybe three."

She sat silently, then held out her hand to Albee, who gave her the legal document.

"This is a search warrant, Mr. Munson. It gives us the authority to search your apartment. If you've no objection, we'll begin with your grandson's room."

"No!" cried Rick, springing to his feet.

Munson looked up at his daughter's son and his face was terrible in its aged, pitiless intensity. "Why not, Richard?"

The youth made a hopeless gesture and sank back down on the hassock.

Sigrid nodded to Albee and Lowry.

"That your room through there?" asked Lowry.

"Yes, sir." His shoulders slumped in defeat.

As the other two detectives disappeared down the hall, Munson asked Sigrid if she would like coffee or tea.

"Nothing, thank you."

"I assume you've heard about Thorvaldsen?"

She nodded.

"Shocking," he said and sat back in his leather chair with a weary air.

The Mozart sonata came to an end and was replaced by Handel. Otherwise the room was silent.

She did not expect Lowry and Albee to be gone for more than a few minutes and she was right. After all, how many places were there to hide something as long as a gold-headed walking stick?

"Mein Gott!" Munson exclaimed, when Lowry returned, carrying the cane carefully by the handkerchief-wrapped tip. "Richard, *was ist das?"*

Rick Evans swallowed hard, then stood up manfully and said, "I guess I'd better put my shoes on. And maybe you could call Miss Difranco, sir, and tell her I've been arrested for killing Dr. Shambley?"

"Oh, don't be an ass," Sigrid told him. She turned to Munson. "You'd let him do it, wouldn't you? Your own grandson."

Munson glared back at her, his small frame rigid with anger. "I disown him!" he said. "He is a disgrace to my blood."

Rick was bewildered. "Grandfather—"

"No! I have no grandson who is *ein Schwuler."*

Rick flushed and drew back as if he'd been struck. "I'm *not!"*

"What did you see when you stepped out of Pascal Grant's room Wednesday night?" Sigrid asked softly.

"Not *see,"* Rick quavered, trying to hold back the tears. "I smelled something. Peppermint. All the way down the passageway, the smell of peppermint. And then when I got home, I saw the cane in the umbrella stand and there was blood on the knob."

Grief-stricken, he looked at her and shook his head. "I couldn't believe my eyes. It was just there in the umbrella stand for anyone to walk in and see, and he was in bed sleeping like a baby."

"Schwul," growled Munson.

"That's what set you off, wasn't it?" Sigrid asked him. "What did he do? Taunt you that your grandson was a homosexual and that he would prove it to you?"

Jacob Munson gave a short laugh and glared at her defiantly. "Now I'll call Miss Difranco and tell her you've arrested me, *ja*?"

"Yes," Sigrid said, and wondered how she was going to tell Nauman.

No. 14 Sussex Square

Dearest Friend,

We are so sorry you do not feel you can join us for Götterdämmerung *tomorrow night, but Henry and I do understand. To think of hearing Wagner without Sophie beside me in our box to translate certain of the passages is almost insupportable. How much more unbearable for you!*

You are very kind to give me her Ring *scores. I cannot think of any keepsake of hers I should rather have had, and I shall always treasure the memory of the happy hours we spent poring over them in her music room, our two voices blending together in the songs of the Rhine maidens as the gold goes back to the river bottom.*

With affectionate gratitude,
Jean

LETTER TO ERICH BREUL SR., UNDATED, FROM
MRS. HENRY BIGELOW
(FROM THE ERICH BREUL HOUSE COLLECTION)

EPILOGUE

Tuesday, December 22

". . . ANYBODY ASK YOU *who I am, who I am, who I am . . .*"

The jazz version of an old Southern folk carol floated through the basement room and Pascal Grant sang along as he folded his few clothes into neat bundles and fit them in the canvas bag Mrs. Beardsley had given him for Christmas.

She seemed sorry that he was leaving the Breul House, but had surprised him by saying, "I think you'll make an excellent gardener, Pascal."

"If anybody ask you who I am," he warbled, "Tell 'em I'm a child of God."

He put his tapes in the side pocket because he planned to carry the player in his free hand; his little television was wrapped in a shirt and tucked into the middle compartment.

On the radio, a tenor sax picked up the melody line. *"The little cradle rocks tonight in glo-or-ry, the Christ Child born in glory."*

He and Rick weren't leaving till tomorrow, but he wanted to be ready. So much had happened that sometimes his head got dizzy thinking about it—Rick's grandfather in jail for hitting Dr. Shambley and killing him even though he didn't mean to, then Rick's mom and aunt flying in to look after Rick and Mr. Munson, and Rick's mom saying maybe he and Rick ought to go on down to Louisiana because Mr. Munson was going to pay to get out of jail and since he was mad at Rick somebody had to feed her two dogs and the cat.

Two dogs and a cat! thought Pascal, dazed with happiness. He'd never even thought about having a pet before.

"Mary rock the cradle, peace on earth . . ."

When everything that was his was crammed inside his new suitcase and old knapsack, Pascal looked all around him and suddenly remembered that Mrs. Beardsley had said, "Now, Pascal, you must leave your room *exactly* as you found it."

Well, he knew what that meant.

Very carefully, he took down the posters that Dr. Peake had said he could have and rolled each one tightly, secured them with rubber bands and carried them out to the storage bin in one of the storerooms. He hated to give them back, but there was no room in his cases.

Finally, he took everything out of the trunk with men's clothes and laid on the bottom the paper picture with the funny monkey head. On top of that, he laid the two brightly colored cloth pictures, then put everything back in the trunk and closed the latch.

Mrs. Beardsley was standing on the stairs as Pascal Grant returned from the storage rooms and her heart melted at the sight of his beautiful face. She was rather sad that he was leaving the Breul House, but the city was becoming so crazy and he was so vulnerable. Surely Louisiana would be better for him.

As joyous music surged through the open door in final chorus, she smiled fondly. "All packed?"

"Yes, Mrs. Beardsley. And I did everything you said, too—put my room back just like I found it."

"That's nice, dear."

"If anybody ask you who I am, tell him I'm a child of God."

A HIGHLAND CHRISTMAS

ONE

MORE AND MORE people each year are going abroad for Christmas. To celebrate the season of goodwill towards men, British Airways slams an extra one hundred and four pounds on each air ticket. But the airports are still jammed.

For so many people are fleeing Christmas.

Fed up with the fact that commercial Christmas starts in October. Fed with carols. Dreading the arrival of Christmas cards from people they have forgotten to send a card to. Unable to bear yet another family get-together with Auntie Mary puking up in the corner after sampling too much of the punch. You see at the airports the triumphant glitter in the eyes of people who are leaving it all behind, including the hundredth rerun of *Miracle on 34th Street*.

But in Lochdubh, in Sutherland, in the very far north of Scotland, there is nothing to flee from. Christmas, thought Hamish Macbeth gloomily, as he walked along the waterfront, his shoulders hunched against a tearing wind, was not coming to Lochdubh this year any more than it had come the previous years.

There was a strong Calvinist element in Lochdubh which frowned on Christmas. Christmas had nothing to do with the birth of Christ, they said, but was really the old Roman Saturnalia which the early Christians had taken over. And as for Santa Claus—forget it.

So there were no Christmas lights, no tree, nothing to sparkle in the dark winter.

P. C. Hamish Macbeth was feeling particularly sour, for his family had taken off for Florida for a winter vacation. His mother had won a family holiday for thinking up a slogan for a new soap powder—"Whiter Than The Mountain Snow"—and Hamish could not go with them. Sergeant Macgregor over at Cnothan was ill in hospital with a grumbling appendix and Hamish had been instructed to take over the sergeant's beat as well as do his own.

Hamish's family were unusual in that they had always celebrated Christmas—tree, turkey, presents and all. In parts of the Highlands, like Lochdubh, the old spirit of John Knox still wandered, blasting anyone with hellfire should they dare to celebrate this heathen festival.

Hamish had often pointed out that none other than Luther was credited with the idea of the Christmas tree, having been struck by the sight of stars shining through the branches of an evergreen. But to no avail. Lochdubh lay silent and dark beside the black waters of the loch.

He turned back towards the police station. The wind was becoming even more ferocious. The wind of Sutherland can sound frightening as it moves up from ordinary tumult to a high-pitched screech and then a deep booming roar.

Hamish decided to settle down with a glass of whisky in front of the television. He was just reaching up for the whisky bottle in one of the kitchen cupboards when he realized he had not checked the answering machine. He went through to the police office. There was one message, and it was Mrs. Gallagher saying she wanted him to call on her immediately as she wished to report a burglary.

Hamish groaned. "This is all I need," he said to the dingy, uncaring walls of the police office. He loathed Mrs. Gallagher. She was a tough, wiry old lady who ran her small croft single-handed. She lived out on the Cnothan road and was generally detested. She was described as crabbit, meaning "sourpuss." Mrs. Gallagher never had a good word to say for anybody. She had a genius for sniffing out the vulnerable points in anyone's character and going in for the kill.

In the far north of Scotland in winter, there are only a few hours of daylight. Hamish glanced at his watch. "Three o'clock and black as hell already," he muttered.

The wind cut like a knife as he climbed into the police Land Rover. As he held the wheel tightly against the buffeting of the wind and drove along the curving road out of the village, he realized that he had never questioned Mrs. Gallagher's bitterness. It had simply been one of those unpleasant facts of his existence since he had started policing in Lochdubh.

At last he bumped up the rutted track leading to the low croft house where Mrs. Gallagher lived. Bending his head against the ferocity of the wind, he rapped at the door. He waited as he heard her fumbling with locks and bolts. What was she afraid of? Most crofters didn't bother locking their doors.

Then he saw the gleam of an eye through the door, which she opened on a chain. She had always had all those locks. How on earth could anyone manage to get in and burgle her?

"Police," he said.

The chain dropped and the door opened wide. "Come ben," she said curtly.

He ducked his head and followed her in.

As in most croft houses, the kitchen was used as a living room with the parlour being kept for "best." That meant the parlour was usually only used for weddings and funerals. Mrs. Gallagher's kitchen was cosy and cheerful, belying the permanently sour expression on her face. She had a mass of thick crinkly pepper-and-salt hair. The skin of her face was like old leather, beaten into a permanent tan by working outdoors. Her eyes were that peculiar light grey, almost silver, you still see in the Highlands. Emotions flitted over the surface of such eyes like cloud shadows on the sea and yet rarely gave anything away.

"What's been taken?" asked Hamish.

"Sit down and stop looming over me," she snapped. Hamish obediently sat down. "My cat, Smoky's been stolen." Hamish had started to tug out his notebook, then left it alone.

"How long's the cat been gone?"

"Twenty-four hours."

"Look here, Mrs. Gallagher, it's probably strayed, gone wild or been killed by the fox." Like "the devil," it was always "the fox" in the Highlands of Scotland, where crofters had no sentimentality about an animal they damned as the worst piece of vermin in the countryside.

"Havers!" said Mrs. Gallagher. "If I say it is stolen, then it is stolen and it is your duty to get it back."

"I'll have a look around for it," said Hamish, struggling to rise out of the low chair on which he was sitting. "Is there any sign of a break-in? Any doors, locks or windows been tampered with?"

"Not a sign. But they could be too cunning for the likes of you. I want you to get a SOCO team out here," said Mrs. Gallagher. Hamish, who watched police soaps as well, knew she meant a Scene of Crime Operatives team. "Smoky was here with me. He didn't go out."

"Did you go out yourself?"

"Yes, I went to feed the sheep."

"And wouldn't Smoky nip out after you?"

"No, Smoky never goes out until dinnertime." Hamish interpreted "dinnertime" to mean midday. In most houses in and around Lochdubh, dinner was still in the middle of the day and high tea, that is, one course followed by bread and scones and cakes and washed down with tea, in the early evening.

"I cannot order a forensic team frae Strathbane for a missing cat," said Hamish. "Anyway, they chust wouldn't come."

"Your trouble," said Mrs. Gallagher, "is that you are lazy. That is why you are still unmarried. You are too damn lazy to get off your scrawny backside to even court a lassie."

Hamish stood up and looked down at her. "I will look around outside for your cat and post a notice at the police station," he said evenly. "That iss all I can do." His Highland accent became more sibilant when he was angry or distressed.

"You have not even checked the doors or windows to see where they might have got in!" shouted Mrs. Gallagher. "I'll report you."

"Do that." Hamish put on his cap and let himself out.

The wind had died as suddenly as it had sprung up. It was still blowing hard far up in the sky, for ragged black clouds were tearing across a small cold moon. He set off over the surrounding fields calling "Smoky!" but there was no sign of any cat.

He wearily returned to the croft house and knocked on the door. Again he waited and called out "Police" in answer to her sharp demand to know who was there. "Have you got a photo of the cat?" he called. After some time, the door opened on the chain. She handed a photograph to him. "I want a receipt," she said. He wrote out a receipt and went on his way.

The next day, Hamish forgot about the cat. He had a more important burglary to investigate in a neighboring village.

Cnothan, less rigid on the subject of Christmas than Lochdubh, had planned to decorate its main street with fairy lights. Now they were gone. He set out, enjoying the faint glow from a red sun which shone low on the hills. All was still after the gales of the day before. Smoke rose up from cottage chimneys in straight lines. The waters of the sea loch were flat and still, one great mirror reflecting the clouds and mountains above.

Hamish did not like Cnothan, the least friendly place in the Highlands. He marvelled that Cnothan of all places should want to brighten the place up with lights. He went to the home of the chairman of the parish council, a Mr. Sinclair, who had reported the burglary. The door was opened by Mrs. Sinclair who told him he would find her husband at his shop in the main street. The shop, it turned out, sold electrical goods. Hamish grinned. Nothing like Highland enterprise when it came to making money.

Mr. Sinclair was a smooth, pompous man. There is not much of a pecking order in the north of Scotland and so often the shopkeeper is head of the social world. He had an unlined olive face, despite his age which Hamish judged to be around fifty. His unnaturally black hair was combed straight back and oiled.

"Was the shop burgled?" asked Hamish, looking around.

"No, we didnae have the lights here," said Mr. Sinclair. "They were kept in a shed up by the community hall."

"Maybe you'd better take me there."

"You'll need to wait until I'm closed for lunch. This is my busiest season."

Hamish looked around the empty shop. "Doesn't look busy now."

"Temporary lull. Temporary lull."

Hamish looked at his watch. Ten to one. Oh, well, only ten minutes to wait. Sod's law, he thought bitterly as a woman came in at exactly two minutes to one and started asking about washing machines.

It was quarter past one before she finished asking questions and left without buying anything. "I hate that sort of woman," grumbled Mr. Sinclair after he had locked up and led the way up the main street at a brisk trot. "I think they come in just to pass the time. Here we are."

The door of the shed was open. A smashed padlock lay on the ground. "Did they take anything other than the lights?" asked Hamish.

"Yes," said Mr. Sinclair. "They took the big Christmas tree as well."

"Och, man, someone must hae seen someone carrying a great big tree!"

"You can ask. I've asked. Has anyone seen a thing? No."

Hamish squatted down and studied the ground. "There's no dragging marks," he said. "Must have been more than one o' them. How big was the tree?"

"About eight feet."

"Aye, well, one man would ha' dragged it. So it was several of them. And no one saw them. So it stands to reason they must have gone up the back way." He stood up and looked down at Mr. Sinclair from his greater height. "I never heard afore that the folks of Cnothan wanted anything to do with Christmas."

"I was elected chairman of the council this year and I managed to persuade them. I was backed by the minister. We took up a collection."

"And your shop supplied the lights?"

"Yes. Do you mind if I get home for something to eat?"

"You run along. I'll let you know if I find out anything."

Behind the community hall, Hamish noticed common grazing land.

There was a gate leading into it. Hamish bent down again. There were little bits of fir needles on the ground. So they had gone this way. Where to? Who would want to take a Christmas tree and lights?

After searching around some more, he went into a cafe and ordered a sausage roll and a cup of coffee. The roll was greasy and the coffee, weak. He approached the slattern who ran the cafe and asked, "Are there folks in Cnothan who were against having Christmas lights in the main street?"

She blinked at him through the steam from a pot on the cooker behind her. With her wild unkempt hair, her thin face and red eyes, she looked like one of the witches who had appeared to the other Macbeth.

"Aye, there's some o' those," she said.

"Like who?"

"Like Hugh McPhee. He went on and on about them."

"And where can I find him?"

"Down at the fishing shop by the loch."

At the bottom of the main street lay the loch, one of those products of the hydroelectricity board. Hamish could remember his mother telling him about how people had been moved out of their villages to make way for these artificial lochs. But they had all been promised that water power would mean cheap electricity and only found out too late that the resultant electricity was not cheap at all. There was a drowned village under Loch Cnothan at the far end. There was something dismal about these man-made stretches of water, he reflected. There weren't any of the trees and bushes around them that you found in the natural ones. At one end of the loch was a great ugly dam. The sun was already going down when Hamish reached Mr. McPhee's shop.

Mr. McPhee sat like a gnome behind the counter of his dark shop among fishing tackle.

Hamish explained the purpose of his visit. "So what's it got to do with me?" asked Mr. McPhee. He was a small gnarled man with arthritic hands.

"I heard you were against the whole business o' the lights," said Hamish.

" 'Course I was. It was that man, Sinclair. Get's hisself elected tae the council and afore you know it, he's got an order for the lights."

"So you weren't objecting on religious grounds?"

"No, you'll need tae go tae Bessie Ward for that. She says the lights are the devil's beacons."

"And where will I find her?"

"Her cottage is at the top o' the main street. It's called Crianlarich."

"Right, I'll try her."

Back up the main street. It was bitter cold and the light was fading fast. He found a small bungalow with the legend CRIANLARICH done in pokerwork on a small wooden board hung over the door on two chains.

He rang the doorbell, which played a parody of Big Ben.

"What is it? Is it my sister, Annie?" asked a solid-looking matron on seeing a uniformed policeman.

"No, nothing like that," said Hamish soothingly. "I am asking questions about the missing Christmas lights."

"Whoever did it was doing the work of the Lord," she said. "You'd best come in."

Hamish followed her into a highly disciplined living room. Church magazines on a low table were arranged in neat squares. Brass objects on the mantel glittered and shone. Cushions were plumped up. Against the outside streetlights, the windows sparkled. The room was cold.

Hamish took off his cap and balanced it on his knees. "I am asking various prominent residents of Cnothan if they might have any idea who did it," began Hamish.

"I neither know nor care." Mrs. Ward sat down opposite him. Her tight tweed skirt rucked up over her thick legs, showing the embarrassed Hamish support hose ending in long pink knickers, those old-fashioned kind with elastic at the bottoms. "The Lord moves in mysterious ways," she added sententiously.

Hamish was about to point out that the Lord did not break padlocks but did not want to offend her. "You look like a verra intelligent woman tae me," he said. Mrs. Ward preened and a coquettish look appeared in her eyes as she surveyed the tall policeman with the hazel eyes and flaming red hair. "Have there be any strangers around here?"

"There's some come and go for the forestry. It's all the fault of that awful man, Sinclair. You know the reason he forced through the collection for the lights? Because he sold them."

"But if there was enough in the collection for the lights," said Hamish, "it follows that some of the people here want them."

"I blame the incomers," she snapped. "Godless lot."

Hamish did not bother asking who the incomers were. She probably meant people who had settled in Cnothan during the last twenty years. Once a newcomer, always a newcomer. That's the way things were in Cnothan. And you never really got to know anyone in Cnothan. In other villages, he called in at houses on his beat for a chat. He had never dared make an unofficial call on anyone in Cnothan. He surmised that such a respectable house-proud matron would not have anything to do with a theft. He was suddenly anxious to take his leave. But Mrs. Ward pressed him to stay for tea and he weakly agreed.

After he left, he took in great gulps of fresh air outside. He felt he had been trapped in that glittering living room forever. He decided to go back to Lochdubh.

In friendly Lochdubh where everyone gossiped freely, he would have more chance of picking up news of any strangers in the area. He was sure it was the work of strangers. Surely even the most rabid Calvinist would not stoop to crime.

Back in Lochdubh, he parked the Land Rover and walked along to the doctor's cottage. Angela Brodie, the doctor's wife, answered the door to him. "Come in, Hamish," she said, putting a wisp of hair back from her thin face. "I'm just decorating the Christmas tree."

"I'm glad someone in Lochdubh has a Christmas tree," remarked Hamish.

"Come on, Hamish, you know a lot of us have them behind closed doors." She led the way into the cluttered sitting room. The tree was half decorated and Angela's cats were having a great game swiping at the brightly colored glass balls with their paws. Angela gave a cluck of annoyance and scooped up the cats and carried them out to the kitchen.

"So what have you been up to?" she asked when she returned.

Hamish told her about the theft of the Cnothan lights.

"There was a lot of feeling against having the lights by some of the older residents," said Angela. "Might not one of them have taken them?"

"No, I don't think so. You see a large Christmas tree was taken as well. If someone wanted to stop the lights and tree being put up for religious reasons, then they'd probably have smashed the lights and chopped up the tree. Someone's probably down in the streets of Inverness or somewhere like that trying to sell them. In fact, when I get back to the police station, I'll phone the police in Inverness and Strathbane and ask them to keep a lookout for the missing lights."

Hamish passed a pleasant hour helping Angela with the decorations and then went back to the police station. He went into the office and played back the messages on the answering machine. There was a curt one from the bane of his life, Detective Chief Inspector Blair, asking him to phone immediately on his return.

Hamish rang police headquarters and was put through to Blair.

"Listen, pillock," said Blair with all his usual truculence, "there's some auld biddie in your neck o' the woods, a Mrs. Gallagher."

"What about her? She's only missing a cat."

"Well, find the damn animal. She's complained about you, right to Superintendent Daviot. Says you're lazy and neglecting your duties. Says you're a disgrace to community policing."

Hamish sighed. Community policing were the current buzzwords at Strathbane.

"So you get out there and find that cat, dead or alive."

"Yes."

"Yes, *what*?"

"Yes, sir."

Hamish rang off. He decided to eat first and then tackle the horrible Mrs. Gallagher again.

An hour and a half later, he knocked once more at Mrs. Gallagher's cottage. Frost was glittering on the grass round about and his breath came out in white puffs.

He waited patiently while the locks were unlocked and the bolts were drawn back.

She let him in. He was about to give her a row for having made trouble for him at headquarters, but he noticed she had been crying and his face softened.

"Look, Mrs. Gallagher," he said gently, "I was not neglecting my duties. But you must know what it's like. The cat could be anywhere. And why would anyone break in and steal a cat? And how could anyone break in with all the locks and bolts you have? You even have bolts on the windows."

"Someone did," she said stubbornly.

"Have you ever been burgled afore?"

"No, never."

"So why all the locks and bolts?"

"There's a lot of evil people around. And unintelligent ones, too. If you had any intelligence, you wouldn't still be a policeman."

"I choose to stay a policeman," said Hamish, "and if you expected that remark to hurt, it didn't." It was amazing how little anyone knew of Mrs. Gallagher, he reflected, even though she had been in Lochdubh longer than himself. But then she was damned as a nasty old woman and that was that. It must be a lonely life and she had been crying over the loss of her cat.

"Let's start again, Mrs. Gallagher," he said firmly, "and stop the insults or we won't get anywhere. The mystery here, and it iss where I would like to start, is why you bar and bolt yourself in and why you should immediately think that someone had broken in."

She sat very still, her red work-worn hands folded on her aproned lap. "Can't you just find Smoky?" she pleaded at last.

"I'm giving a talk at the school tomorrow and I'll ask the children if they'll help me to look for Smoky. School's nearly finished. But you have not yet answered my question." He looked at her shrewdly. "Who iss it you are afraid of, Mrs. Gallagher?"

She studied him for a long moment with those odd silver eyes of hers. Then she said abruptly, "Will you be taking a dram with me?"

"Aye, that would be grand."

A flash of humor lit her eyes. "I thought you didn't drink on duty."

"Only on a cold winter's night," said Hamish.

She went to a handsome dresser against the wall and took out two glasses and a bottle of malt whisky. She poured two generous measures, gave him one and then sat back down in her chair, cradling her glass.

"Slainte!" said Hamish, raising his glass with the Gallic toast.

"Slainte," she echoed.

The peat fire sent out a puff of aromatic smoke and an old clock on the mantel gave an asthmatic wheeze before chiming out the hour.

"So," said Hamish curiously, "what brought you up here?"

"My father was a farmer. I was brought up on a farm."

"Where?"

"Over near Oban. I knew I could make a go of it myself."

"You must know country people and country ways. Why all the security?"

A little sigh escaped her. "I always thought one day he would come back."

"He?"

"My husband."

"I thought you were a widow."

"I hope I am. It's been a long time."

"Was he violent?"

Again that sigh. "There you have it. Yes."

"Tell me about it."

"No, it's my business. Finish your drink and go."

Hamish studied her. "Was he in prison?"

"Get out of here, you tiresome man. I'm weary."

Hamish finished his drink and stood up.

"Think about it," he said. "There's no use asking the police for help and then withholding information."

But she did not reply or rise from her chair. He stood looking down at her for a few moments and then he put on his cap and let himself out.

His Highland curiosity was rampant. Why had he never stopped before to wonder about Mrs. Gallagher? She would appear in the village from time to time to stock up on groceries. If someone tried to speak to her she would be so cutting and rude that gradually she had come to be left alone. In the morning he would visit one of the older residents and see if he could find out some facts about her mysterious husband.

TWO

THE FOLLOWING DAY, before he was due to talk to the local schoolchildren, he set out to call on Angus Macdonald. Angus was the local seer, credited with having the gift of second sight. Hamish was cynical about the seer's alleged powers, guessing that Angus relied on a fund of local gossip to fuel his predictions.

He went out to the freezer in the shed at the back of the house and took out two trout he had poached in the summer. The seer always expected a present.

The day was cold and crisp and so he decided to walk up the hill at the back of the village to where Angus lived. Hamish thought cynically that Angus kept the interior of his cottage deliberately old-fashioned, from the oil lamps to the blackened kettle on its chain over the peat fire. His fame had spread far and wide. The dark, old-fashioned living room, Hamish was sure, added to the legends about Angus's gifts.

"It's yourself, Hamish," said Angus, looking more than ever like one of the minor prophets with his shaggy grey hair and long beard.

"Brought you some trout for your tea, Angus."

"Fine, fine. Chust put them down on the counter there. A dram?"

"Better not, Angus. I'm going to give a talk to the schoolchildren and I don't want the smell o' whisky on my breath."

"Sit yourself down and tell me what brings ye."

"Now, now," mocked Hamish, "I thought the grand seer like yourself wouldnae even have to ask."

Angus leaned back and half closed his eyes. "She isnae coming back this Christmas."

Hamish scowled horribly. He knew Angus was referring to the once love of his life, Priscilla Halburton-Smythe.

"I didn't come about that," said Hamish crossly. "Mrs. Gallagher's cat is missing." He opened his notebook, took out the black-and-white photograph of Smoky and handed it to the seer.

"It iss grey and white, that cat," said the seer.

"You've seen it?"

"No, I chust know."

"So tell me about Mrs. Gallagher. I wasn't around when she came to Lochdubh. There's something about her husband. Know anything about that?"

"I thought she was a widow."

"So you don't know everything, Angus."

"No one can know everything," said Angus huffily. "You will need to give me a bittie o' time to consult the spirits."

"Aye, you do that," said Hamish, heading for the door.

The seer's voice followed him. "I find a bit o' steak does wonders for the memory."

Hamish swung round. "I gave you two trout!"

"Aye, but there's nothing like a bit of steak for helping an auld man's memory."

"Aren't you frightened of the mad cow's disease?"

"Not me," said Angus with a grin.

"Aye, you've probably got it already," muttered Hamish as he walked down the frosty hill.

The village school only catered for young children. The older ones were bused to the high school in Strathbane. There was a new school-teacher, a Miss Maisie Pease, and it was she who had suggested that Hamish talk to the children. She was a small, neat woman with shiny black hair, a rather large prominent nose and fine brown eyes like peaty water. Hamish judged her to be in her thirties.

"Now, Officer," she began.

"Hamish."

"Well, Hamish it is, and I'm Maisie. I feel that children are never too young to learn about the perils of drugs, as well as all the usual cautions about not talking to strangers."

"Right. Are the children ready for me?"

"They're all in the main classroom."

Hamish walked with her along a corridor to the classroom. As he neared it, he could hear the row of unsupervised children. When he pushed open the door, there came a frantic scrabbling of small pupils rushing back to their desks. Maisie followed him in.

"This is P. C. Macbeth, children," she said. "I want you to sit quietly and pay attention."

Hamish looked round the faces of twenty-four children, ranging in ages from five to eleven years old, rosy-cheeked Highland faces with bright eyes.

He started off by talking about the evils of bullying and of stealing. He warned them against talking to strangers or accepting lifts from strangers and then moved on to the subject of drugs. Not so very long ago, he reflected, such a talk would have been unnecessary. But drugs had found their way even up into the Highlands of Scotland. He then asked for questions.

After a polite silence, one little boy put up his hand. "Is wacky baccie bad?"

Hamish, identifying "wacky baccie" as pot, said, "Yes, it is. It's against the law. But a lot of people will tell you there's nothing to it. It's better than booze. But it's not. You can get sicker quicker and it destroys short-term memory. Just say no."

Another boy put up his hand. "My brither wants to know where he can get Viagra."

"Ask Dr. Brodie," said Hamish. The boy relapsed, sniggering with his friends. So much for the innocence of youth, thought Hamish.

He then asked them what Santa Claus was bringing them. He was answered by a chorus of voices calling out that they wanted dolls or mountain bikes or dogs or cats. Hamish was glad that the children were not going to be denied Christmas, however Calvinistic the parents, although in the Lochdubh way, it would probably be celebrated behind closed doors.

"I'm going to talk to you now about pets," said Hamish. He thought briefly of his own dog, Towser, long dead, and felt a pang of sadness. "Don't ask your parents for a dog or a cat unless you're very sure what looking after an animal entails. A dog, for instance, has to be house-trained, walked and fed, possibly for the next fifteen years of your life. A cat even longer. It's cruel to want an animal as a sort of toy. If I were you, I'd wait until you're a bit older. Dogs have to be properly trained up here or you'll have some animal worrying the sheep.

"While I remember," he said, "someone or some people have stolen the Christmas lights that were meant to decorate the street in Cnothan. I want you to let me know if you hear anything about strangers in the Cnothan area. There's a bit o' detective work for you. Ask your older brothers or sisters or your parents and if there's anything at all, let me know. Also, Mrs. Gallagher has lost a cat. I'm going to pass round a photograph of the cat and I want you all to study it carefully and then search for this cat. There'll be a reward."

Schoolteacher Maisie then showed him out. "I see you don't have the classroom decorated," said Hamish.

"We were going to make some paper decorations but you know how it is. Some of the parents objected. They said they didn't mind giving their children a present, but that they were against what they call pagan celebrations. It's hard on the children because they all watch television and they are all in love with the idea of a Christmas tree and lights and all those things. Oh, well, it's only at Christmas that they get stroppy. Other times, this must be the nicest place in the Highlands."

"It is that," said Hamish. "Maybe you'd like to have a bite of dinner with me one night?"

She looked startled and then smiled. "Are you asking me out on a date?"

Hamish thought gloomily about his unlucky love life and said quickly, "Chust a friendly meal."

"Then that would be nice."

"What about tomorrow evening? At the Italian restaurant? About eight?"

"I'll be there."

"Grand," said Hamish, giving her a dazzling smile.

Mrs. Wellington, the minister's wife, was just arriving and heard the exchange. She waited until Hamish had left and then said in her booming voice, "I feel I should warn you against that man, Miss Pease."

"Oh, why?" asked the schoolteacher. "He's not married, is he?"

"No, more's the pity. He is a philanderer."

"Dear me."

"He was engaged to Priscilla Halburton-Smythe, daughter of Colonel Halburton-Smythe who owns the Tommel Castle Hotel. He broke off the engagement and broke her heart."

Miss Pease had already heard quite a lot of Lochdubh gossip, and the gossips had it the other way round, that Priscilla had broken Hamish's heart.

"Oh, well," said Miss Pease, "he can't do much to me over dinner."

"That's what you think," said Mrs. Wellington awfully. "Now about the Sunday school . . ."

Hamish walked along the waterfront and met one of the fishermen, Archie Maclean. The locals said that Archie's wife boiled all his clothes, and certainly they always looked too tight for his small figure, as if every one had been shrunk and then starched and ironed. The creases in his trousers were like knife blades and his tweed jacket was stretched tightly across his stooped shoulders.

"Getting ready for Christmas, Archie?" Hamish hailed him.

"When wass there effer the Christmas in our house?" grumbled Archie.

"I didn't think the wife was religious."

"No, but herself says she's having none of those nasty Christmas trees shedding needles in her house, nor any of that nasty tinsel. You ken we've the only washhouse left in Lochdubh?"

Hamish nodded. The washhouse at the back of Archie's cottage had been used in the old days before washing machines. It contained a huge copper basin set in limestone brick where the clothes were once boiled on wash-day.

"Well, the neighbors have been dropping by tae use it tae boil up their cloutie dumplings. But dae ye think I'll get a piece. Naw!"

Cloutie dumpling, that Scottish Christmas special, is a large pudding made of raisins, sultanas, dates, flour and suet, all boiled in a large cloth or pillowcase. Some families still kept silver sixpences from the old days before decimal coinage to drop into the pudding. Large and brown and steaming and rich, it was placed on the table at Christmas and decorated with a sprig of holly. It was so large it lasted for weeks, slices of it even being served fried with bacon for breakfast.

"In fact," said Archie, "the only one what's offered me a piece is Mrs. Brodie."

"Angela? The doctor's wife?"

"Herself."

"But Angela can't cook!"

"I know that fine. But herself says she's going to try this year. Herself says it's surely chust like a scientific experiment. You measure out the exact amounts."

"It never works with Angela," said Hamish. "Her cakes are like rocks. Come for a dram, Archie. I've been talking to the schoolchildren and it's thirsty work."

They walked into the Lochdubh bar together.

When they were settled at a corner table with glasses of whisky, Hamish asked, "Do you know any gossip about Mrs. Gallagher?"

"Her, out the Cnothan road? Why?"

"I've been thinking. We all know her as a sour-faced bitch. But why?"

"Cos she's a sour-faced bitch. Postman says she's got the place like Fort Knox wi' locks and bolts."

"I mean, what soured her? Was she always like that?"

"I think so. Good sheep. Doesn't have dogs. She just whistles to the sheep, different whistles and they do what she wants. She had one friend."

"Who?"

"I don't know if the woman iss still alive. She bought the croft from her. Mrs. Dunwiddy. She went to live with a daughter in Inverness. Wait a bit. Maybe two years back now, someone says to me that Mrs. Dunwiddy had a stroke and she's in an old folks home in Inverness. What's she done?"

"She done nothing. She thinks someone's pinched her cat."

"Gone wild probably or the fox got it."

"That's what I told her."

"So what d'ye want to know about her for?"

"Curious. That's all. I think she's a verra frightened woman."

"Listen, Hamish, if I lived up there and never spoke to a body except to do a deal for sheep at the sales at Lairg, I'd get frightened as well."

"I think there's more to it than that. Oh, and if you hear of someone selling Christmas lights, let me know. Cnothan's had theirs stolen."

"There's a lot o' Free Presbyterians o'er there."

The great essayist Bernard Levin once described the Free Presbyterian as the sort of people who thought that if they did not keep the blankets tight over their feet at night, the pope would nip down the chimney and bite their toes.

"Maybe," said Hamish. "But I doubt it. The lights were taken along with a tree out of that shed at the community hall. The padlock was smashed. Any loose elements roaming the countryside?"

"Haven't heard. Don't get them in the winter."

"If you hear anything, let me know."

Hamish returned to the police station to collect the Land Rover and drive to Cnothan.

He was once more examining the shed when Mr. Sinclair came up to him. "You're not wearing gloves," he accused.

"Why should I?"

"You'll be destroying fingerprints."

Hamish sighed. He knew Strathbane would not send out a team of forensic experts to help solve the mere theft of a Christmas tree and lights.

Ignoring Mr. Sinclair, he set out, stooped over the ground, following the trail of pine needles. He went through the gate into the common grazing ground. No more needles. There must have been more than one. He could imagine them getting it over the gate and then lifting it onto their shoulders. He set off up the hill, doubled over, studying the ground. He guessed they would go fast and in a straight line.

Mr. Sinclair stood watching him until the tall figure had disappeared over the crest of the hill. "That man's a useless fool," he said to the frosty air. "It's a pity Sergeant Macgregor is off ill." He quite forgot that Sergeant Macgregor would have considered such a trivial theft not worth bothering about. Mr. Sinclair was feeling particularly righteous. He had supplied a new set of lights, which were being put up on the main street at that moment, and he had not charged for them.

Hamish spent the rest of the day searching over the common grazing ground until he came upon the peat stacks on the other side of the hill. There, in muddy, watery ground, he came across tire tracks. They could have been made by one of the locals, but as he studied them, he saw a little cluster of pine needles and some marks made by, he thought, running shoes. He counted the different footprints. Four sets of them. They'd probably come to thieve peats and then thought they might stroll over towards the village to see if there was anything they could lift. He stood studying the prints, trying to build up a mental picture of the robbers. There had been a lot of petty theft over towards Lairg, tools lifted from garden sheds, things like that. He decided to put a full report into headquarters and ask for a printout of areas of recent petty theft in Sutherland. That way he might find the area they were operating from. Because of the pettiness of the other thefts, not much police work had gone into finding the culprits. They would possibly be unemployed, hard drinkers, the sort who preyed on farmhouses and cottages during agricultural shows when they knew people would be away from home.

As Hamish prepared a meal for himself that evening, he thought about the schoolteacher. It would be pleasant to talk to someone new. He stopped, about to drain the potatoes into the colander. There had been something wrong in that classroom. He had picked up at one point a little atmosphere of fear. Then he shrugged. He would ask Maisie Pease about it.

The following morning, he decided to run down to Inverness and do some last-minute Christmas shopping. The presents he had already bought for his family were waiting at the police station, but he needed to buy a few little presents for his friends in the village. He would phone in regularly to his answering machine just in case anything cropped up.

It was ten o'clock when he set off and the sun was just struggling up over the horizon. It was one of those unexpectedly mild winter days when a west wind blows in over the Gulf Stream.

As all the main stores in Inverness are crammed into the centre of the town, he found the main street as full of shoppers as ever. Inverness was always busy. Finally, when he had accumulated a supply of various presents, he returned to the police Land Rover. He phoned his answering machine but there were no messages. It was then he remembered Mrs. Gallagher's friend, Mrs. Dunwiddy.

He went to the central police station and asked if he could use the phone. Hamish had his mobile phone with him, but he wanted to phone around to old folks homes in the area and so he wanted a warm desk, a phone book and a police phone where the cost would not appear on his own phone bill.

On the sixth try, he landed lucky. Yes, they had a Mrs. Dunwiddy, but she was very frail and rambled most of the time. Nonetheless, he said he would call and see her.

He found the old folks home out on old Beauly Road. What was it like, he wondered as he parked in the gravelled drive, to end up in one of these places when you were old? He walked inside. There was a lounge to the right where several elderly people sat staring at a television set. The lounge was decorated with glittering colored chains of tinsel. An overdecorated Christmas tree stood beside the television set, dripping with glass balls and tinsel. Somehow, the festive decorations made the television watchers seem older, more frail and forgotten.

He went to the reception desk, produced his identification and asked for Mrs. Dunwiddy. "She has a few good days still," said a brisk woman, "but I don't think this is one of them. She's in her room. I'll take you along."

"Do any of her family visit her?" asked Hamish as he followed her along a thickly carpeted corridor.

"She's got a son and a daughter. They don't come often. You know how it is. This place is expensive and these days, people feel they've done their duty by paying out. Sad. Here we are. Visitor for you, dear."

Mrs. Dunwiddy sat in a wheelchair by the window. She was staring out with blank eyes at a bleak winter lawn at the back of the building.

"I won't be long," said Hamish. He pulled up a chair and sat down next to Mrs. Dunwiddy. The woman who had ushered him in said, "There's a bell on the wall if you need anything, Officer." Then she left.

"Mrs. Dunwiddy," began Hamish. Her old eyes did not flicker.

"I don't know if you remember," said Hamish, "but you sold your croft and house to a Mrs. Gallagher."

Silence.

"I'm worried about Mrs. Gallagher," said Hamish. "She lives up there by herself, been on her own since she moved in. She's got the place bolted and barred. What is she frightened of?"

Silence.

"I thought you might know something, that she might have said something."

She could have been carved out of rock.

Hamish gave a little sigh. He must ask if there was any pattern to her good days and try again. On the other hand, it was a lot of trouble to go to for a nasty woman. He decided there was nothing he could get out of her that day. He rose to leave.

"Cat," she said suddenly.

Hamish turned. One frail trembling hand had risen and was pointing at the window. He looked out. A black cat was sliding slowly on its belly towards a starling which was tugging at a worm. Hamish banged on the window and the cat fled.

Hamish sat down again. "Mrs. Gallagher?" he said gently. "Remember her?"

"Alice," she said, her voice like dry autumn leaves blowing across a tarmac road.

"Alice Gallagher?"

"Bastard."

"Who?"

"Said he beat her. Said she ran away."

"Her husband?"

"Have you washed your face, Johnny? You're going to be late for school."

Hamish tried to get more out of her but her brain had retreated to the past. He quietly left.

As he crossed the hall, he once more looked in the lounge. There they sat with the television set blaring. What a Christmas!

He had a sudden idea. He went back to the desk. "Miss—?"

"Mrs. Kirk," she said.

"Well, Mrs. Kirk, is anything ever done to brighten up those folks in the lounge?"

"They have the television."

"I just thought of something. Could I arrange a wee concert for them, for Christmas day?"

"I don't see why not. Could you wait and I'll get our director."

After a few moments, Hamish was ushered into an office where a small, bespectacled man was sitting behind a desk.

He rose and held out his hand. "I am John Wilson. You were saying something to Mrs. Kirk here about a concert?"

"Aye, just an idea. For Christmas."

"What sort of concert?"

"I know a retired couple, used to be on the halls. They can still play and sing all the old songs. Old people like that."

"I'll need to look into our budget," he began fussily.

"No charge."

"Well, in that case, it does seem a good idea. In fact, we have other homes like this. If they're any good, we might employ them to do the rounds."

"Oh, they're good," said Hamish. "I'll arrange it for the afternoon of Christmas day."

"That's very kind of you, Officer. May I ask why you are doing this?"

Hamish smiled. "Because it's Christmas."

He then drove to a housing estate at the north of the town, home of Charlie and Bella Underwood.

Bella answered the door. She was in her seventies, but her hair was dyed a flaming red and she was heavily made up. "Hamish!" she cried. "God, it's been ages. Come in, darling! Charlie, it's Hamish!"

A dapper little man came out to meet them. "What brings you, Hamish?"

"It should be a friendly call," said Hamish when they were all seated over a fat teapot in the Underwoods' kitchen. "But I'm afraid it's because I've got a business proposition for you."

"Business?" asked Bella. "We've been out of the business for a while."

Hamish explained about the old folks home. "You see," he said, "you know all the old sing-along songs. Can you still perform?"

"Course we can," said Bella. "You're a gem, Hamish."

"I'll be paying you for this myself, but if that Mr. Wilson likes you, you could get more work."

"Keep your money, Hamish," said Charlie. "We'll do it for nothing."

Pleased with his outing, Hamish returned to Lochdubh. He would tackle Mrs. Gallagher in the morning. In the meantime, there was his dinner with Maisie to look forward to. He washed and dressed carefully in his one good suit, brushed his flaming red hair until it shone, and then strolled along the waterfront towards the Italian restaurant. Great stars burned in the Sutherland sky overhead and their reflections twinkled in the black sea loch like the missing Christmas decorations.

He pushed open the door of the restaurant and went in. He was greeted by the waiter, Willie Lamont. Willie, in the heady days when Hamish had been elevated to police sergeant before being demoted again, had been Hamish's sidekick, but he had married the beautiful daughter of the restaurant owner and left the police force.

Willie conducted him to a table at the window. "I'm waiting for a lady," said Hamish. "I'll order when she arrives."

Willie whipped out a bottle of cleaner and began scrubbing at the table. "The table was clean already," protested Hamish, remembering how Willie, a fanatical cleaner, had scrubbed out the police station instead of paying attention to his duties.

"It's a real grand cleaner," said Willie. "It's called 'SCCRUBB.' I sent away for it."

"Willie, Willie, it's taking the polish off the table."

"Oh, michty-me, so it iss. I'll just get some polish."

"No," said Hamish firmly. "Leave it until we've eaten."

Willie's face twisted in anguish. "Just a wee scoosh o' wax," he pleaded.

"Not even one." Hamish rose to his feet. "Here's my lady."

Maisie Pease joined him. "This is very nice," she said, looking around.

She sat down in a chair and then shrank back as Willie darted up to the table and shot a spray of liquid wax from a canister and then began polishing fiercely.

"Go away, Willie!" shouted Hamish. "And bring the menus." Muttering, Willie went off.

"What a strange waiter," said Maisie.

"Oh, he's all right. Just a bit keen on cleaning."

They were the only customers in the restaurant. They ordered food and wine, but the hovering presence of Willie unnerved Maisie. She knocked over a glass of wine, she dropped spaghetti on the table and dropped her bread roll on the floor, and there was Willie each time, mopping and polishing and complaining. Hamish at last stood up and marched Willie into the kitchen and threatened to punch his head if he came near the table again unless they called for him.

"I'm sorry about that," said Hamish. "He'll leave us alone now."

"Tell me all about Lochdubh," said Maisie. "I'm just getting to know it and the people."

So Hamish told her about the people in the village, and she watched his thin attractive face and wondered if he was the philanderer that Mrs. Wellington had said he was.

Then Hamish said, "I had a feeling when I was giving that talk that someone was frightened. Just a feeling. Any bullying going on?"

"Not that I know of. But it's early days for me. It could just be that maybe some of the children were lying."

"What about?"

"I don't know if it's true, but some of them come from very strict religious homes. So when you asked them what Santa Claus was bringing them, they all replied, but in some of the homes, there won't be any Christmas presents."

"That's sad. I know some of them are against Christmas but I didnae think they would take it out on their children."

"I'll ask about."

They talked of other things and then Hamish walked her back to her cottage, which was attached to the schoolhouse. She smiled and thanked him for dinner. He smiled back and then turned and walked away.

Maisie went slowly indoors. He hadn't even tried to kiss her. He hadn't suggested a second date. Philanderer indeed!

THREE

HAMISH DID NOT want to visit Mrs. Gallagher. But the idea that someone had been living in solitude and fear on his beat nagged at him. The wind had come back and as he drove off, a ragged cloud of crows rose up from the field behind the police station and scattered out over the loch. Low clouds scurried over the mountaintops. Hamish wondered if the Romans had held their Saturnalia at just this time as a sort of drunken wake to the death of the year. On such a day it seemed as if the grass would never grow again or the sun shine.

Mrs. Gallagher was out in the fields. As he approached, he could see her striding back towards the house. She had seen his arrival and waited at the door for him.

"Well?" she demanded.

"No news."

"Then I have no time for you."

"I would like to speak to you for a little bit."

"Why?"

"I want to talk to you about your husband."

She ducked her head suddenly to hide her face. She stood like that for a long moment and then took a ring of keys out of the pocket of her old tweed coat and began to unlock the door.

"Come in," she said curtly.

Hamish removed his cap and followed her in.

She turned to face him. "What about my husband?"

"Can we sit down?"

She nodded. She took off her coat and hung it on a peg by the door.

"It's like this," said Hamish when he was seated. "I have reason to believe that you are still afraid of your husband."

"What's that got to do with my missing cat?"

Hamish studied her and then with a sudden flash of Highland intuition, he said, "For some reason, you live in fear of him, and when Smoky disappeared, you were frightened he had come back to take your cat away. That's the sort of thing he would do—destroy something you loved."

Her face was now a muddy color. "You know him," she whispered. "You've met him."

"No. But did you never think of appealing to me for help? You could have taken out an injunction against him. Was he ever in prison?"

There was a long silence. The wind howled around the low croft house like a banshee.

Then she said, "He was arrested for armed robbery. We were living in Glasgow at the time. I saw my chance to get free and took it. My mother had died and left me money. I managed to keep that fact from him. I drew out all the money and came up here."

"Look, what's his full name?"

"Why?"

"Because," said Hamish patiently, "I can check up on him. I can find out where he is and what he's doing. He could be dead. Think of that. The man could be dead and here are you, talking to no one and living scared."

"Hugh," she said. "Hugh Gallagher."

"Last address?"

"Springburn Road, number five-A."

Hamish scribbled rapidly in his notebook. "And when was he arrested?"

"In nineteen seventy-eight. In March. It was the eighteenth when they came for him."

"Right, I'll get onto that right away."

He stood up. She rose as well and clutched at his dark blue regulation sweater. "You won't let him know where I am."

"No, no," he said soothingly. "I've told the schoolchildren to help look for your cat, so if you see any of them about, don't be chasing them off."

She sank back in her chair and covered her face with her hands.

"You should have friends," said Hamish.

"You can't trust anyone," she said from behind her hands.

Hamish left and drove back to the police station. He phoned Strathclyde Police Headquarters in Glasgow and put in a request to find out what had become of an armed robber called Hugh Gallagher, arrested in March of 1978 for armed robbery.

They said they would phone him back. He fed his sheep and hens and decided to drive up to the Tommel Castle Hotel to see if there was any news of Priscilla Halburton-Smythe.

He was welcomed by the manager, Mr. Johnston. "Come to mooch a cup of coffee, Hamish?"

"Aye, that would be grand."

"Come into the office. Herself won't be home for Christmas."

Hamish blushed. "I didn't come here to ask that. But I thought she would come home to see her parents."

"She's working for some big computer firm and they've sent her to New York."

So far away, thought Hamish. So very far away.

"So how's business?" he asked with well-manufactured cheeriness.

"Business is booming. We're fully booked for the Christmas period."

"No news about the old Lochdubh Hotel down by the harbour?"

"Some Japanese put in a bid but then the Japanese recession hit. Then other folks seem to think there isn't room up here for more than one hotel."

"It's a grand building. Could do for a school."

"So how's policing?"

"Nice and quiet."

"No juicy murders for Christmas?"

"God forbid. I've got the case of the missing cat and the case of the missing Christmas lights at Cnothan."

"Ach, Cnothan! That's such a sour wee place they probably took away the lights themselves, them that thinks Christmas is sinful."

"I think it was youths. Petty theft. Anyway, Cnothan may be a sour place but at least they wanted to put up some decorations. Look at Lochdubh, as black as the loch."

"Well, Mr. Wellington the minister was all for putting up a tree this year on the waterfront but he came up against Josiah Anderson."

"What! Him that lives in that big Victorian house?"

"The same. A real Bible basher. I'm sorry for that wee daughter o' his."

"He's got a wee daughter?"

"So you don't know everything. Josiah and his wife were trying for years to have children."

"Probably didn't know how to go about it," said Hamish maliciously. "They should have asked me and I'd have given them a map."

"Anyway, the wife went down to Inverness for the fertility treatment and she had a girl. Josiah was fifty when the bairn was born and the wife,

Mary, forty-five. The wee girl, Morag, she must be about nine now. What a life for her, they're that strict. No presents for her."

"She goes to the village school?"

"Aye."

"I gave a talk to the kids there and asked them what Santa was bringing them and they were all expecting something."

"What child wants to be different from the others?" asked Mr. Johnston.

"What does Morag Anderson look like?"

"Like a waif. All eyes. And clean. Oh, so clean. I think they scrub her every morning."

Hamish's hazel eyes narrowed. "Sounds like cruelty to me. I'll have to talk to the schoolteacher."

"I've heard you've been romancing her—dinner at the Italian place."

"Have I no private life?" mourned Hamish.

"Aye, well, if you'd wanted a private life you wouldn't have chosen to live in Lochdubh. But I'm in a generous mood. If you want to take her for lunch, I'll let you have it on the house."

Hamish drank his coffee, then headed for the schoolhouse. He looked at his watch. School would be breaking up any minute for the Christmas holidays. The children were singing carols, their voices carried towards him on the wind. He waited in the Land Rover until he saw them streaming out. Then he got out and went into the schoolhouse.

Maisie Pease was clearing up papers on her desk. She looked up and blushed when she saw him. "Why, Hamish! What brings you?"

Ask me out again, a voice inside her was urging. But Hamish perched on the side of her desk and said, "You've got a pupil here, Morag Anderson."

"Yes, and I won't believe for a moment she's in trouble. She's my star pupil."

"No, she's not in any police trouble. I heard an unsettling piece of gossip about her parents, that's all. Seems they're a bit too strict. No Christmas for Morag."

"I can't really do anything about that, Hamish. I would be interfering with their religious beliefs."

"Nonetheless, I would like to talk to them."

So you're not going to ask me out, thought Maisie huffily. "I can't stop you," she said curtly. "Go ahead. Have a word with them if you want."

"I thought maybe since it's just noon you would like to come with me and then we could have a bite of lunch."

"At the Italian place?"

"No, I'll take you to the Tommel Castle Hotel."

"Oh, Hamish. That's so expensive."

"Think nothing of it. My treat."

Maisie's face was now flushed with pleasure. "I'll get my coat."

Most of the houses in Lochdubh were eighteenth century when the then Duke of Sutherland had hoped to expand the fishing industry. But there were a few large Victorian villas built in the last century when the lesser orders copied their queen by having holiday homes in Scotland. But now that people who could afford it usually preferred their holiday homes to be in Spain or some other sunny country, the villas were no longer holiday homes but residences of the middle class. Josiah Anderson owned a clothing factory in Strathbane. Hamish opened the double iron garden gate and ushered Maisie inside.

"What are the parents like?" he asked in a low voice.

"A wee bit severe. I've met them on parents day. Morag always has top marks so I've never had any reason to talk much to them."

Hamish rang the brass bell set into the wall beside the door. When he found himself looking down at Mrs. Anderson when she opened the door, he was surprised. He realized he had seen her about the village, had exchanged a few words with her in the general store, knew she was Mrs. Anderson. But he had forgotten, and had conjured up a picture of a grim matron.

Mrs. Anderson was small and neat with permed hair and a rosy face. She looked startled at the sight of Hamish. "Nothing wrong?" she cried.

"Just a friendly call," said Hamish.

"Come in. My husband's in the sitting room."

They followed her into the sitting room which was large and dark, high-ceilinged, full of heavy furniture and impeccably clean.

"Josiah," said Mrs. Anderson, "here's our policeman and Miss Pease, Morag's schoolteacher."

He rose to greet them. He was wearing a charcoal grey three-piece suit with a white shirt and striped tie. His black shoes were highly polished. He had thinning grey hair, thick lips, small watchful eyes and tufts of hair sprouting from the nostrils of a large nose.

"What's up?" he asked.

"Just a friendly call," said Hamish again.

"Sit down, sit down, Officer. Mary, get tea."

"It's all right," said Hamish. "We won't be long. We're on our way for lunch."

They all sat down. Hamish looked at Maisie as a signal for her to begin.

"Christmas is very important for little children," said Maisie.

"That is because each year they are brainwashed into a state of greed," said Mr. Anderson.

"I don't think that's true," said Hamish. "There's an innocent magic about it. I hope Morag isn't going to be left out."

Mrs. Anderson opened her mouth to say something, but Mr. Anderson held up his hand. "Our Morag is a sensible girl. She knows such things as Santa Claus and presents are pagan flummery."

"It's a bit of a burden to put on a wee girl," protested Hamish. "All her friends at school will be excited about it."

"I see you will need to talk to Morag herself. Get her, Mary."

Mrs. Anderson went out to the foot of the stairs and called, "Morag, come down here a minute."

They waited until Morag came into the room. She looked at Hamish and her face turned white and her eyes dilated.

"Now, then, Morag," said her mother quickly, "there's nothing to be afraid of. Constable Macbeth and Miss Pease have called because they are worried you might be feeling left out of the Christmas celebrations."

"I beg your pardon?" said Morag faintly.

In the rest of the modern world, when people didn't understand what you were saying, they said "What?" or "Excuse me?" But in the Highlands, they still used the old-fashioned "I beg your pardon?"

"They're worried that you might feel different from the other children because we don't have anything to do with Christmas."

Morag stood there and slowly color returned to her face. "Oh, no," she said softly. "I don't bother about it."

"Are you sure?" asked Maisie.

"Oh, yes."

"There you are," said Mr. Anderson. "You're a good girl, Morag. You can go to your room." He turned to Maisie. "You may think we're a bit hard about Christmas but we have our religion and we live by it. Morag gets plenty of presents on her birthday."

Maisie looked helplessly at Hamish. He indicated to her that they should leave. But as Mrs. Anderson was showing them out, he turned and looked down at her. "Did you never think it might not be a good idea to let Morag make up her own mind about what she wants to believe in when she's older?"

"No, children need to be guided young. As you can see, she is not troubled at all. She has everything a little girl could desire. She has her own room and bathroom and a little sitting room at the top of the house where she can entertain her friends."

"Does she bring friends home?"

A shadow crossed Mrs. Anderson's face. "Not yet, but she will when she is older. She is a very happy, self-sufficient girl. She does all the housekeeping for her part of the house herself. She volunteered. And she even asked if she could cook some meals for herself."

They thanked her and left. As they drove towards the Tommel Castle Hotel, Hamish said, "That was one very frightened little girl."

"People are always frightened by the sight of a policeman."

"Not of me. She saw me in the classroom and I was with you. I thought for a minute she was going to faint."

"I tell you what it could be. Mr. Patel? He sometimes catches little kids stealing sweets from his store. He doesn't call you, he calls me. I see the parents and the matter's settled. Maybe Morag took something and thought the forces of law and order had descended on her. I mean, imagine her parents' reaction if they found their precious child was a thief."

"Could be. There's such a thing as a child being *too* good. But her strict upbringing doesn't seem to have affected her studies."

"No, she's bright and she likes learning. She has a terrific imagination. She writes very colorful essays."

"I'd like to see some of them."

"You're worrying too much, Hamish. How did you ever get time to catch all those murderers I've heard you arrested if you fret so much over a wee schoolgirl?"

"I'm curious," was all Hamish would say.

When they entered the dining room of the hotel, the maître d', Mr. Jenkins, who had once been butler to the Halburton-Smythes, ushered them to a table. "You're to have the cock a leekie soup, followed by the venison," he said. He flicked a napkin open and spread it on Maisie's lap and departed.

"How odd," said Maisie. "Don't they give you a menu here?"

"It must be a set meal for lunch."

Maisie glanced around. Some diners were holding large leather-bound menus. She decided not to comment on it. Perhaps the maître d' knew that Hamish liked the set menu.

"Would you like some wine?" asked Hamish.

"That would be nice. Can you drink and drive?"

"Not really and I shouldn't be driving you around in the police vehicle, either. But I'll get us a couple of glasses. Excuse me a minute."

Hamish went through to the hotel office and said to Mr. Johnston, "It's kind of you to give me lunch. I want to order wine but that snobby scunner Jenkins'll make a fuss."

Mr. Johnson laughed. "You don't want your date to know you aren't paying for it. Okay, I'll bring you something."

Hamish returned and sat down. Soon Mr. Johnston arrived, bearing a bottle of claret which he deftly opened. Hamish introduced him to Maisie. "We keep a special claret just for Hamish," said Mr. Johnston.

"I hope you're not going to live on baked beans for a month after paying for this," said Maisie.

"Och, no. I've got a bit saved up." Hamish thought about his bank account, which was sinking rapidly into the red after his Christmas shopping. Maisie was just gathering courage after they had finished their soup to invite Hamish out for a meal, when he said suddenly, "Are you doing anything on Christmas day? I mean, are you going to be with your family?"

"No, my parents are dead and my sister's in Australia. I was going to cook a small turkey and toast myself. Would you like to join me?"

"If you'll join me in something first." He told her about the old folks home in Inverness and ended by saying, "I thought of dropping down there on Christmas day to hear the concert."

"Of course I'll come," said Maisie delightedly, "and then when we get back you can join me for Christmas dinner."

Hamish beamed at her. It looked as if it was going to be a good Christmas after all.

In the hotel office, the phone rang. Mr. Johnston picked it up. "It's me, Priscilla," came Priscilla Halburton-Smythe's voice. "How are things?"

"We're fully booked. Do you want me to get your father or mother for you?"

"No, I spoke to them yesterday." There was a pause and then Priscilla said, "I've just phoned the police station. Hamish isn't there. I didn't bother leaving a message, but you haven't seen him, have you?"

"Yes, he's right here in the dining room."

"Well, if I could . . ."

"He's having lunch with his lady friend."

"Oh, who's she?"

"Maisie Pease, a right pretty lass, the new schoolteacher. I think there'll be wedding bells soon. Do you want me to get Hamish to the phone?"

"No," said Priscilla quickly. "Don't bother." She asked some more questions about the hotel and then rang off.

The manager looked at the now silent phone. He felt guilty but, on the other hand, he told himself, how was Hamish ever going to get over Priscilla if she kept jerking his chain?

Hamish drove Maisie back to her cottage and then made his way back to the police station. He switched on the answering machine. The first was only a silence and then a click as someone rang off. The second was from Strathclyde Police from the policewoman who had been searching the records for Mrs. Gallagher's husband. "I've got something," she said. "Ring me."

Hamish phoned up Glasgow and was put through to her. "I don't know if this is good news or bad, Hamish," she said, "but he's dead."

"That's good news. When and how?"

"He got knifed in a drunken brawl in the Govan area two years ago."

"Thanks," said Hamish. "That wraps that up."

He set off once more, heading towards Mrs. Gallagher's croft. No more lame ducks, Hamish Macbeth, he told himself severely. Give her the good news and then leave her alone, apart from still trying to find out if her cat's about.

"Macbeth!" he called loudly as he knocked on the door.

She opened the door on the chain. "Have you found Smoky?"

"No, but I've got some news for you about your husband. Can I come in?"

She dropped the chain and held open the door.

In the kitchen she turned to face him. "He's dead," said Hamish.

She sat down abruptly as if her legs had given way. Hamish took off his cap and placed it on the table and sat down opposite her.

"How? When did he die?"

"Two years ago. A drunken fight in Govan. He got knifed."

"Thank you," she said faintly. Then she said, "I'm a silly old woman. If only I'd asked for help before."

"He probably terrorized you. What were you about to get involved with a man like that?"

"I didn't know he was a man like that," she snapped, all her old crustiness returning.

"Like I said, I lived on a farm near Oban with my parents, well, just outside Oban that is. He stopped by one day on his motorcycle. He wanted to know if we did bed-and-breakfast. My mother said, yes, even though we didn't have a sign on the road. She usually only catered for a few regulars who came year after year. He said he would book in for two nights." Her silver eyes grew dreamy as she seemed to look down some long tunnel into a bright past where life had still been innocent.

"He was very good-looking, tall with fair hair. He said he was up from Glasgow. I'd led a very sheltered life but I'd been to the cinema and like the other girls, we were all mad about James Dean. Hugh had this big shiny motorbike and he wore a leather jacket. He took me to the cinema and dancing. He stayed two weeks instead of two days and by the end of the two weeks, he'd asked me to marry him. I was over the moon. He said he had a good job and worked as a salesman. I wanted a church wedding but Hugh said he was in a rush because he had to get back to his job. My parents were upset, but I was twenty-one so there was nothing they could do to stop me. We got married in the registry office and then he went off to Glasgow and I packed up and followed him down on the train. He'd said his parents were dead. Would you like some tea?"

Hamish shook his head. "His flat was a bit of a shock. It was in a tenement in Springburn, dark and sordid. He said, don't worry, he had something in mind. We'd soon be out of there. Then things began to fall apart. My father phoned and said money from the farm office was missing and only Hugh could have taken it. Of course, I stood up for Hugh and we had a row and he told me never to come back to the farm again until I had come to my senses. Then one day when Hugh was out, his parents came by. Yes, parents! The father was drunk and the mother was a slattern. Hugh came home and threw them out. I asked him why he had lied to me. He said he was ashamed of his parents and that his father used to beat him.

"Oh, I believed him because I wanted to. Then the police came for him. He had stolen the motorbike. He got a short prison sentence and when he came out, he stopped keeping up any front for me. He would get drunk and beat me. And yet I still loved him and pride stopped me from going back to my parents. But things got worse. All sorts of villains started calling round. Then one day Mother phoned and said my father had died. I went back for the funeral. Hugh asked me if he had left me anything and I said no, truthfully. He had left everything to my mother. Mother sold the farm and moved into a little house in Oban. She was never the same after my father's death. She got cancer and a year later, she was dead, too. She left everything to me. Hugh hadn't come up with me. I saw the lawyers and got the money she'd left and said that any other money from the sale of the house was to go into an account in Oban in my name. But I meant to tell Hugh about the money. I was always hoping he would reform."

A dry sob escaped her. "I went back to Glasgow. He was entertaining his friends. There were bottles everywhere. Hugh had a raddled woman sitting on his knee. I cracked. I said I was leaving him. He turned ugly.

He got everyone out and then he beat me with his belt. I'd brought back some family photos and he threw them on the fire. He said I couldn't leave him. He'd always find me. Then the police broke in during the night and arrested him for armed robbery. I stayed only as long as the trial, only as long as it took to learn he was going to prison, and then I left for Oban. I stayed until my mother's house was sold and then came up here. I decided that people were no good. I'd stick to my croft and my sheep. That Mrs. Dunwiddy was friendly while I was negotiating the sale with her, but she asked too many questions so I never saw her again."

"Mrs. Dunwiddy's down in an old folks home in Inverness. She had a stroke. I believe her mind's gone," said Hamish, not elaborating further because he didn't want the touchy Mrs. Gallagher to know he had been trying to find out about her.

"Oh, dear," she said vaguely.

"So now your worries are over, you should get about and meet people."

"I'm too set in my ways to start socializing, young man. And my worries aren't over. What about my cat?"

"Still searching," said Hamish getting to his feet. He looked down at her helplessly. There was nothing that could be done to combat years of isolation and sourness.

FOUR

HAMISH PUT IN a request to Strathbane for a list of all petty crimes in the Highland area in the past month. Then he decided to go over to Cnothan and make some more inquiries. The day was cold and still. It never snowed on Christmas day but he found himself hoping that just this year there might be a light fall to delight the children. As he passed Mrs. Gallagher's croft, he saw her out in the fields. She seemed to be shouting something. He stopped and switched off the engine and rolled down the window.

"Smoky!" she was calling. "Smoky!"

Her voice echoed round the winter landscape, and the twin mountains above Lochdubh sent back the wailing echo of her voice. He drove on slowly, looking right and left, suddenly hoping that he would see a grey-and-white cat. But only a startled deer ran across his path and then with one great leap vanished among some stunted trees at the side of the road.

He drove on until he reached Cnothan. He noticed lights had been strung along the main street and two men were erecting a tree in a large tub at the bottom of the street. He called in at Mr. Sinclair's shop. "Oh, it's you," said Mr. Sinclair.

"I see you've got the lights up. Did that mean another collection?"

"No, it did not! I paid for those lights out of my own pocket, so that should shut up those who said I only wanted the lights to make a bit of money."

"No more thefts in Cnothan?"

"Not that I know of. Isn't one theft enough for you?"

"Just wondered. Any news of strangers about the place?"

"Look, I've been too busy with the customers to notice anything."

Hamish looked thoughtfully at him. He wondered if by any mad chance Mr. Sinclair had taken the lights himself and then because of the fuss had handed them back, claiming to have supplied new ones.

He went out of the shop and strolled down towards the loch. He stood for a moment watching the men working on the tree and then he went into the bait shop. Mr. McPhee looked up. "You again."

"Yes, me. I'm still checking around to see if any strangers have been spotted, probably four young men in a four-wheel drive."

"See nothing like that."

Hamish looked around. "You can't do much trade this time of year."

"It's better than sitting at home looking at the telly. I hate Christmas, and that's a fact."

"What will you be doing for Christmas?"

"Sitting getting drunk and trying not to put my foot through the telly. Do you know they're going to show *The Sound of Music* again? It's enough to drive a man mad."

"I tell you what, me and the schoolteacher from Lochbudh are going down on Christmas day to a concert at an old folks home to try and brighten the folks up. Why don't you come with us?"

"I'm not that old. I'm only sixty-eight."

"I'm not old either. But it would be a bit o' fun."

Mr. McPhee peered at him and then said, "Aye, it might be fun. What time would ye be leaving?"

"I'll let you know. Wait a bit. I'll let you know now." Hamish took out his mobile phone. He phoned the Underwoods' number. Bella answered. "What time's the concert to be held, Bella?"

"Three in the afternoon, Hamish. We went to see that Mr. Wilson and he seemed awfully pleased at the idea."

"I'll be there myself with some friends."

"Good. See you then."

Hamish rang off. "I'll pick you up at two o'clock."

Mr. McPhee looked quite animated. "Dearie me," he said, shaking his head. "I don't know when I last had an outing since the wife died."

"When did she die?"

"Two years ago." Bleak loneliness stared out of his eyes. For some reason, Hamish found himself thinking again about Mrs. Gallagher. What a miserable lonely life she led!

"That's fine," he said to Mr. McPhee. "I'll see you Christmas day."

He asked various locals about the village if they had seen any youths about and then drove home to the police station. There was a fax waiting for him from Strathbane. He studied the list of petty thefts. They seemed to be spread all over the place. He studied the list again closely. Any youths who would take lights and a Christmas tree were not experienced thieves. They probably roamed around picking up stuff that was easy to lift. His eyes settled on the thefts in the Lairg area. A crofter had had a toolbox taken from a shed, another, a generator, a third, a supply of cut planks with which he had intended to build a henhouse.

He would take a drive over to Lairg in the morning.

Maisie Pease was on the phone with a friend in Inverness. "I'm telling you, Lucy," she said with a giggle, "I never thought I would end up with the village policeman. Yes, he's quite good-looking. We're going down to some old folks home on Christmas day for a concert, just the two of us, and then I'll make him Christmas dinner, and then who knows what will happen!"

Hamish went along to the general store to buy some groceries early next morning. As he was paying for them, he asked Mr. Patel, "Do you get many of the schoolchildren pinching stuff?"

"Not so many," said the Indian shopkeeper, his white teeth gleaming in his brown face. "I've got these mirrors up, so I usually catch them. Och, it's nothing for you to go worrying about, Hamish. I deal with it myself."

"Know a wee lassie called Morag Anderson?"

"Aye, I ken them all."

"She ever take anything?"

"Come on, Hamish, that lassie's a saint. Always polite. Beautiful manners."

Hamish took his bag of groceries.

"Does the shopping for her parents, does she?"

"No, her mother does that."

"Just buys sweets?"

"Never. She says she isn't allowed sweets."

"No Christmas, no sweets. What a life! What does she buy?"

"Just some cat food."

Hamish froze. It couldn't be, could it?

"Hamish," chided Mr. Patel, "there's a queue behind ye."

"Sorry." Hamish left and stood outside the shop.

"What's up with you, Constable?" demanded a voice. "Standing there like a great loon. Shouldn't you be about your duties?"

Hamish found himself confronted by the Currie sisters, Nessie and Jessie, twins and spinsters of the parish. They both wore tightly buttoned tweed coats and woolly hats over rigidly permed hair. "What are you standing there gawking at, gawking at?" said Jessie who had an irritating way of repeating everything.

Hamish suddenly smiled blindingly down at them. "At your beauty, ladies."

"Get along with you," said Nessie. "It's not our beauty you're after but that new schoolteacher."

"She should be warned, she should be warned," said Jessie.

"Have the Andersons a cat?" asked Hamish.

"What? Them at the big villa at the end?" asked Nessie.

"Yes, them."

"I've never seen one, never seen one," said Jessie. "I shouldn't think so. Herself is verra houseproud, verra houseproud."

"Just wondered," said Hamish, ambling off. He went to the police station and stacked away his groceries.

Now let's go for a mad leap of the imagination, he thought. The saintly Morag steals Mrs. Gallagher's cat. How can she hide it from her parents? Well, her mother had bragged about her having her own separate apartment at the top of the house.

So I could just go along and ask Mrs. Anderson if she has a cat. If she says no, ask her why Morag is buying cat food. I suddenly wish I didn't have to do this. I suddenly wish it was someone else.

He hoped he was wrong. The thought of telling Mrs. Gallagher made him quail. He had no doubt she would press charges. His heart was heavy as he left the police station and walked along the waterfront. He had a weak hope they might not be at home. But the factory at Strathbane would be closed for Christmas and no doubt Mr. Anderson would be at home, just as he had been when Hamish first called.

He rang the bell. Mr. Anderson answered the door. He drew down his brows in a scowl. "If you've come here again to lecture us about Christmas, I'll report you to headquarters."

"I would like to speak to you and your wife. It's a case of theft."

Mr. Anderson looked taken aback. "You'd better come in."

Hamish walked into the dark sitting room where Mrs. Anderson was knitting. She looked up, startled, and a steel knitting needle fell to the floor.

"This officer is here to talk about a theft," said Mr. Anderson, "although what it's got to do with us is beyond me."

"May I sit down?" Hamish took off his cap and sat down before they could say anything. "It's like this," he said. "Mrs. Gallagher who lives out on the Cnothan road, her cat's disappeared."

Mrs. Anderson goggled at him. "What on earth has that got to do with us?"

"Have you got a cat?"

"No, we haven't got a cat!" raged Mr. Anderson. "How dare you come here and imply—"

"Then why is Morag buying cat food?" said Hamish in a flat voice. They both stared at him.

Then Mr. Anderson went to the foot of the stairs and shouted up, "Morag! Come down here!"

They waited in silence until Morag came in, small and neat in a crisp white blouse and block-pleated skirt.

"This officer says you have been buying cat food," said her father.

Morag turned pale. "I was buying it for someone."

"Who?" asked Hamish gently. "I shall check with the person you say you are buying the cat food for."

Huge tears filled Morag's eyes and she began to sob. The atmosphere in the room was electric.

Mrs. Anderson left the room and went upstairs. Morag stood sobbing.

"Will ye no sit down, lassie?" suggested Hamish.

But she continued to cry. Hamish glared at her father. Couldn't he do something or say something?

Mrs. Anderson came back, a smile on her face. "Och, there's no cat up there," she said triumphantly. "All you've done is give Morag a fright."

"It still doesn't explain the cat food," said Hamish. "Mind if I have a look?"

"Oh, go on!" shouted Mrs. Anderson. "But a complaint about you goes straight to Strathbane today. Terrorizing children! You're a monster."

Hamish went up the thickly carpeted stairs. He went into Morag's bedroom. It was white and clean; white bedspread, white flounced curtains. He searched around and under the bed. Then he tried the sitting room and the bathroom without success. There was a door on the landing. He pushed it open. It was a box room full of discarded old furniture and old suitcases. Over by the window, he saw a bowl of water and a bowl of catfood.

"Smoky!" he called.

A faint meow came from one of the suitcases. He noticed it had airholes bored in the sides. He lifted the lid and a small grey-and-white cat blinked up at him. "Come here," he said in a soft voice. He picked up the cat, which snuggled under his chin, and went slowly downstairs.

Mrs. Anderson screamed when she saw him with the cat and Mr. Anderson began to shout and rave at his daughter. She was a limb of Satan. How could she do this after all they had done for her?

"I wanted something to love that would love me back," said Morag, now past crying.

"Did you go into Mrs. Gallagher's house and take the cat?" asked Hamish.

"No," she said, her voice little above a whisper. "I was walking up by her croft after school and I saw the cat. It came up to me. It likes me. Smoky *loves* me. I thought I would take Smoky home and play with him for a bit. That's all. Then I was frightened to take him back."

Hamish turned to the parents. "Look here. No harm done. I've got the cat. Why don't I just tell Mrs. Gallagher I found it wandering by the road? You don't want charges against Morag."

"There will be no lying!" thundered Mr. Anderson. "You will take Morag and that animal to Mrs. Gallagher. It is up to her to punish the girl."

Hamish looked at him in disgust. "Aye, I'll do that and then I'll be back to have a word with you. Get your coat, Morag, and put a scarf on. It's cold out."

He walked with the now silent Morag along the waterfront to where the police Land Rover was parked outside the station. "I want you to take Smoky and hold him on your lap, tight," he ordered. "Cats are sometimes scared if they're not used to motors."

Morag gently took the cat from him and climbed into the passenger seat. In a bleak little voice, she asked, "Will I go to hell?"

"Och, no," said Hamish, letting in the clutch. "Don't you have the telly?"

She shook her head miserably.

"Well, it was on the news. Hell's been abolished. Fact. Trust me. You read your Bible, don't you?"

A nod.

"I mean the New Testament?"

Nod, again.

"Don't ye know the bit about there being more rejoicing in heaven over the entrance of one sinner than that of an honest man, or something like that?"

Her wide eyes looked up at him, startled.

"I am the law," said Hamish grandly, "and I wouldnae lie tae ye."

When they got to Mrs. Gallagher's croft, he said, "Give me the cat and wait there. No running away."

Cradling Smoky against his chest, he knocked at the door. Only one lock clicked and the door was opened.

"Oh, God, it's Smoky," said Mrs. Gallagher. Tears of relief coursed down her face. Hamish was beginning to feel like Alice in the pool of tears.

"I want to talk to you about it," said Hamish, following her in.

She looked at him sharply. "Smoky hasn't been wandering the fields. He's well fed and clean."

"Aye. Let me tell you the story."

He sat down and told her all about Morag, about her strict parents, about how she seemed to have every material comfort but nothing in the way of love. "She said she only wanted something to love that would love her back. Wait!" He held up his hand, seeing the anger on Mrs. Gallagher's face. "I was going to lie to you. It's bad enough you bitching to grownups, but I didn't want you taking your spite out on a wee girl. I wanted to tell you I had just found Smoky wandering about, but those parents from hell made me bring the girl up here, and you can press charges if you want and give the poor bairn a criminal record."

"She's outside?"

"Yes."

"Bring her in."

"All right," said Hamish wearily. "What a Christmas!"

He went out to the Land Rover and said to Morag, "You'd best come in and apologize."

Morag climbed down and then stood looking up at him, her eyes wide with fright. "She's a witch. Everyone says so."

"She's only something that rhymes with it. Witches were abolished in the eighteenth century. I am the law and that is the fact, so stop having these stupid ideas."

They went into the croft house, Hamish gently nudging Morag in front of him.

Morag stood before Mrs. Gallagher. "I am so very sorry," she whispered.

Mrs. Gallagher looked at Hamish. "Get out of here, Officer, and let me have a word with the girl." Hamish hesitated. "Go on. I'm not going to eat her."

Hamish reluctantly went outside and got into the Land Rover. He had given up smoking some years ago and now he was glad there were no shops nearby. He had a sudden sharp craving for a cigarette. He waited and waited. At last he could bear it no longer. He went back to the croft house and walked in.

Mrs. Gallagher and Morag were sitting in front of the television set.

Morag had Smoky on her lap. Mrs. Gallagher stood up and said to Hamish, "A word with you outside."

Hamish walked out with her, and Mrs. Gallagher turned to him. "You can go back to her parents and tell her that Morag's punishment is that she's to come up here every afternoon during the school holidays. Tell them it's a community service."

Hamish grinned and bent down and kissed her on the cheek. "I'll pick her up at five o'clock," he said. He marched off to the Land Rover.

Hamish drove off whistling. Now for those parents.

When he followed Mr. Anderson into the sitting room, the angry words he had rehearsed died on his lips. Mrs. Anderson had been crying. Her eyes were red and swollen. More tears, thought Hamish. What a day for tears!

"It has turned out all right," he said evenly, "but no thanks to you. Mrs. Gallagher wants Morag to go to her every afternoon during the holidays as a sort of community service. Morag is with her at the moment and will be home at five. Now, she was wrong to take the cat, but it seems to be that a lassie with no friends and grim parents needed something to love."

"But we do love her. We give her everything!" cried Mrs. Anderson.

"Aye, she's got her own wee flat where nobody ever comes. She sees the other children getting excited about Santa Claus and knows there is no Christmas for her, no fun. Now I know your minister and he's a good man, and I don't think he would like you to be torturing a wee girl by forbidding Christmas. She does well at school and I bet you take it for granted. I bet you think that because she's got her own flat, she owes you. There's more to life than material things. To try to get your child sentenced in a criminal court over a damn cat is beyond my comprehension. You could have ruined her life. You had her when you were both on in years, so she doesn't have young parents to take her on picnics or to the movies."

"The movies are the work of the devil," said Mr. Anderson heavily. "Naked lewd women—"

"Aw, shut your face, you dirty auld man!" Hamish shouted, losing his temper completely. "Haff you neffer heard o' Walt Disney? You go on banning everything in her life that's fun and she'll run away from ye as soon as she's old enough. I've seen it happen time and again. And parents like you sit there and wonder why and neffer look at their own behavior. If you're thinking of reporting me to Strathbane, forget it. I'll deny everything about that cat and so, if I'm not mistaken, will Mrs. Gallagher. Oh, for God's sake, lighten up. This place is like a morgue.

I'm going now, but I'll be checking on ye. And if you persecute Morag over this, I'll have the Royal Society for the Protection of Children on your doorstep. Good day to you."

He marched off. As he drove to the police station, he said, "Movies the work o' the devil! Havers!"

"Have you ever seen *Star Wars*?" Mrs. Gallagher asked Morag.

"No, Mrs. Gallagher."

"Call me Alice. It so happens I have a video here."

Mrs. Gallagher put the tape in the video machine and sat back with a sigh of pleasure. It was nice to have someone to watch things with. She didn't need to worry about Morag gossiping or being cruel. She was just a little girl. Not like a grownup. But grand company for all that.

Hamish went back at five o'clock to pick up Morag. She waved goodbye to Mrs. Gallagher and shouted, "See you tomorrow, Alice!"

"So it's Alice, is it?" asked Hamish.

"I had a grand time," said Morag.

"Well, she needs the company."

The happy look left her face. "My parents are going to be mad at me."

"It sometimes doesn't do to let people know the whole truth," said Hamish cautiously. "What did you do this afternoon?"

"We watched *Star Wars*."

"Aye, well, I would keep quiet about that. Just say you're keeping the old lady company, helping about the croft."

"Dad doesn't approve of the movies."

"No, he doesn't. So go easy. You've got off lightly."

He went into the house with her. "Afore I go," he said sternly to Morag's parents. "We could get round this Christmas business and ye could be helping with a bit o' Christian work. There's a concert for the old folks down in Inverness on Christmas day. I'm taking Miss Pease, the schoolteacher, and Mrs. Gallagher and Morag, I am sure, would like to come. It would cheer the old folks up to see a girl like Morag. She seems to have a way with old people. And she would be doing her Christian duty."

He waited for a rant of protest, but Mr. Anderson said wearily, "I can see nothing against that."

"Right, I'll drive you all down. And I think Morag's been punished enough. Mrs. Gallagher will be down to pick her up at noon tomorrow."

Hamish made his escape. He'd better rent that bus from the garage. They'd never all fit into the police Land Rover.

*   *   *

Maisie was studying a cherry red dress. It looked nice and festive and would do for Christmas day. She dreamily pictured the long drive down to Inverness with Hamish. In her mind, he put his hand on her knee and said, "I've been thinking of settling down." Ah, well, when you got a man on his own, there was no saying what could happen.

The next day Hamish, realizing all the business about Morag had delayed his visit to Lairg, drove over there to see if he could find out anything. The day was even colder than the one before, with a steel-blue sky above and unmelted frost sparkling on the trees and grass.

He dropped into various shops on the main street until in the butcher's, a woman heard him questioning the butcher and turned round and said, "There were a couple of lads trying to flog boxes of Christmas lights."

Hamish took out his notebook. "Can you give me a description?"

"One o' them had dyed blonde hair and one o' thae rings through his nose. T'other was squat and dark. The fair one was wearing a red anorak and jeans and the dark one, an old tweed coat and jeans as well."

"What were they wearing on their feet?"

"We used to call them 'sandshoes,' then they were called 'sneakers,' now they're called 'running shoes.' Them white things."

"Thanks. Any other distinguishing marks? Tattoos? Funny haircuts?"

"They were wrapped up so I don't know about tattoos. What d'you mean, funny haircuts?"

"Spikes or shaved all over or something like that?"

"The dark one was going a bit bald. That's all."

Hamish went out of the shop and worked his way down the street, stopping to talk to the locals, asking questions, until one man volunteered that he had seen two men answering the description Hamish had given, getting into a small truck. No, he hadn't noticed the registration, but it was old and muddy and painted blue.

Hamish decided to search outside Lairg. He dropped in at the croft houses at Rhianbrech outside Lairg but no one there had seen anything, then past the station, always looking right and left. Then he went back through Lairg and out on the Lochinver road, cursing the rapidly failing light.

His eyes were getting weary with straining into the surrounding wilderness and he was tired of driving along at ten miles an hour. He decided to put his foot down and go on into Lochinver for a cup of tea. Then he saw a glimmer of white across the moorland. He stopped abruptly and climbed out of the Land Rover. In the gloaming, he could just make out a white trailer. He set out across the moorland. The sun had gone down and great stars were beginning to twinkle against a greenish sky.

As he approached, he saw the blue-painted tailgate of a truck parked beside the trailer. There was a dim light shining through the curtained windows. Hamish did not feel like tackling two, possibly four, young men on his own. If I were in a film, he thought, I would render them all helpless with a few well-placed karate chops. But this wasn't a film, yet he was reluctant to phone for backup unless he had some proof.

He silently crept up. The back of the truck was covered with a tarpaulin. He looked underneath it and in the fading light saw boxes and boxes of Christmas lights. On the other side of the truck, he found a Christmas tree lying on its side.

He quickly and quietly sprinted back to the Land Rover and phoned headquarters at Strathbane. "I'll go on into Lochinver," he said after he had given his report. "I don't want one of them looking out of the window and seeing a police vehicle."

He set off for Lochinver and parked by the waterfront and waited, cursing the long distances in the Highlands. He hoped the police contingent wouldn't come racing along the Lochinver road with lights flashing and sirens blaring.

At last four police cars arrived and Hamish's heart sank when Detective Chief Inspector Blair heaved his bulk out of the leading car.

"I would have thought this would have been too small a case for you, sir," said Hamish.

"I think these are the lads responsible for a chain o' thefts across Sutherland," said Blair. "Just tell us where they are, laddie, and get back to yer sheep."

Hamish stood his ground. "It's dark and you won't find them without me."

"Oh, all right. Lead the way."

Hamish drove off and the police cars fell in behind him. Curtains twitched in cottage windows. He found himself hoping that none of them had a girlfriend in Lochinver. In these days of mobile phones, villains could be communicated with just when you didn't want them to be.

He pulled up down the road and peered across the moorland. The trailer was still there. He hoped they were all inside. He got out and set off without waiting for Blair and the others. But he knew they would be quickly behind him. Blair was not going to let Hamish Macbeth take any credit for this.

When he reached the trailer, Blair's truculent voice whispered in the darkness. "All right, Macbeth, knock on the door and then leave the rest tae us."

Hamish knocked on the door. "Who is it?" called a voice from inside. "Police!"

Then loud and clear he heard a dog give a warning bark. He knew that bark. It was his dead dog, Towser. He threw himself on the ground to the side of the door just as a shotgun blast shattered the door and would have shattered one Highland policeman had he been standing in front of it.

"You're surrounded!" he yelled, getting to his feet. "And we're armed. Throw out that gun and come out with your hands in the air."

There was silence from the trailer. Hamish cursed. He had never thought for a moment that they would be armed.

The door was kicked open and the men emerged, one by one, their hands on their heads. Blair took over and ordered them to lie on the ground, where they were handcuffed. The charges were announced: theft and attempted murder of a police officer. The men were led off to a police car.

"You're a fool," Blair snapped at Hamish. "Putting our lives at risk by failing to tell us they were armed."

"I didn't know and you didn't know," protested Hamish. "And it was me that was nearly killed."

"But you knew that shot was coming. How?"

Hamish grinned. "Highland intuition."

"Crap," muttered Blair.

After they had gone, Hamish found his hands were trembling. He drove back into Lochinver and went into a hotel bar and ordered a double whisky. Then he ordered a pot of coffee. The germ of an idea was forming in his brain. He waited for a couple of hours and then set out for the trailer again. A forensic team was just packing up.

"That truck with all the lights in it shouldn't be left there," said Hamish. "Someone might pinch them. Are the keys to the truck around?"

"They were in the ignition."

"Right, maybe it would be a good idea if one of you could drive the truck to the police station where I can take care of them."

"I suppose we could do that." One of them said, "You two, go with this officer and take that truck and leave it at Lochdubh police station. It is Macbeth, isn't it?"

"Aye."

"I've heard of you."

"Wait a bit. Could you take the tree as well?"

"Come on. Who's going to take a big tree like that?"

"You never know."

"Okay. Boys, put that tree on the back of the truck."

*   *   *

After the lights had been stacked in the police office and the tree stacked at the back of the police station, Hamish said goodbye to the two forensic men. He then made himself a meal and went to bed. Tomorrow was Christmas Eve and he had just had an outrageous idea. But he would need help.

In the morning Hamish went along to the local garage to see the owner, Ian Chisholm. "I want to hire that Volkswagen minibus of yours," he said. "I'm taking some folks down to Inverness on Christmas day. Is it still working?"

"Good as new. Come and see."

He led the way through to the yard at the back. The old minibus stood in all its horrible red-and-yellow glory, Ian having run out of red paint and gone on to yellow. His wife had made chintz covers for the passenger seats and it looked, as Hamish thought, as daft a conveyance as ever.

"I'll take it," he said.

He made his way back to the police station and saw the small figure of Morag running towards him. "Glad to see you," said Hamish. "Tell your parents and Mrs. Gallagher that we'll be leaving at one-thirty from the war memorial on the waterfront. What's up? You look a wee bit strained. Parents been giving you a hard time?"

"No, they say Mrs. Gallagher's punishment enough. It's not that."

"So what is it?"

"Mrs. Gallagher's a Roman Catholic."

Hamish privately cursed all religious bigotry everywhere. If the Andersons knew that Mrs. Gallagher was a Catholic, their precious child would not be allowed anywhere near her.

He forced his voice to sound casual and not reflect the rage and frustration he felt.

"I would not be bothering them with such a thing at Christmas. Sometimes it is better not to trouble people with facts that would distress them."

"So it's all right not to tell?"

"Oh, yes."

And God forgive me for encouraging a wee lassie to lie to her parents, thought Hamish as Morag scampered off. Then he quietened his conscience by reflecting that he hadn't exactly told her to lie, he had just advised her not to say anything.

He walked on. As he passed Patel's, none other than Mrs. Gallagher emerged. She had two carrier bags and Hamish could see they were full of Christmas decorations. "That's nice," he said, indicating the bags. "Getting ready for Christmas?"

"Why don't you mind your own business?" demanded Mrs. Gallagher. "Haven't you got any work to do?"

"I've told Morag I'm picking you up at the waterfront at one-thirty tomorrow. Chust make sure you don't die o' spleen afore then," snapped Hamish.

She glared at him and then the anger died out of her face and she let out a surprisingly girlish giggle. She was still giggling as she walked to her car.

"Whit's up wi' that old crone?" asked a voice at his elbow. Hamish looked down and saw Archie Maclean. "I havenae seen that woman laugh afore," remarked Archie. "Whit happened? Did she see someone slip on a banana skin and break a leg?"

"Never mind her. I need some help, Archie. Come into the police station and have a dram."

Archie's face brightened. "Grand. But don't be telling the wife."

In the police station, Hamish poured two glasses of whisky. "Listen to me, Archie, I need you and some of the more liberal-minded fishermen to help me."

FIVE

THAT AFTERNOON, A group of children met outside Patel's to share sweets and talk about what they hoped to get from Santa Claus. A red-haired little boy called Sean Morrison said, "Folks say Morag has been visiting Mrs. Gallagher."

There was an amazed chorus, "That old witch! Maybe she'll put a spell on her."

Then Kirsty Taylor, a blonde who already had a flirtatious eye heralding trouble to come, said, "I bet you, Sean, you wouldn't have the guts to go out there and ask for Morag."

"Bet you I could."

"Bet you can't."

"I'll go if you all come wi' me," said Sean.

Kirsty danced around him, singing, "Cowardy, cowardy custard."

"If you don't come," shouted Sean, "you won't know I've been there!"

So it was decided they would all go. Sean would knock at the door and they would hide.

"Who can that be?" asked Mrs. Gallagher as she heard the knock at the door.

"I'll go if you like," said Morag.

"No, it's all right." Mrs. Gallagher opened the door and looked down at the trembling figure of Sean. "Is Morag here?" he asked.

"Come in," said Mrs. Gallagher.

*　　*　　*

"He hasnae come out," whispered Kirsty. "Maybe she's putting them both in the pot to boil them for her supper. I'll creep up and peek in the window."

The others clutched one another as Kirsty crept up to the window. At last she came running back, blonde hair flying, cheeks red in the frosty air. "They're sitting at the fire eating fruitcake," she gasped. "Fruitcake with icing on top."

Mrs. Gallagher opened the door and saw the group of schoolchildren, all professing to be friends of Morag. Mrs. Gallagher knew from Morag that the girl craved friends and was shrewd enough to know why this lot had come round. She knew her local reputation.

"Come in," she said. "There's plenty of cake and lemonade. But first, you've got to give me your phone numbers and I'll phone your parents and let them know where you are." She wrote down the phone numbers and names and went to the phone in her parlour. When she returned to the kitchen, Morag was surrounded by chattering children.

"I'll give you all some cake," said Mrs. Gallagher, "and then you can all help me to put up the Christmas decorations. I'm a bit late this year."

When had she last put up decorations? she wondered, looking back down the years. She cut generous slices of fruitcake while Smoky purred on Morag's lap.

Hamish phoned Maisie Pease. "I'll be setting off from the war memorial tomorrow," he said. "Pick you up at one-thirty."

"Grand, Hamish, I'll see you there."

She rang off and then stared at the phone. How odd? Why wasn't he picking her up at the schoolhouse? She looked through to her neat kitchen where a large turkey lay waiting to be roasted. She had bought a large one to make it look really Christmassy in a Dickensian way. It was too large, she thought. She would be eating turkey for a month.

Jessie and Nessie Currie set out arm in arm for their usual tour of the village. They liked to keep an eye on everything that was going on. As they passed Chisholm's garage, Ian was hosing down the minibus.

"It'll freeze in this weather," said Nessie.

"Freeze in this weather," echoed the Greek chorus that was her twin sister.

"Just getting it ready for Macbeth," said Ian.

"And why would he want a bus?" asked Nessie.

"Don't know. But he's booked it for Christmas day."

The sisters headed for the police station, eyes gleaming with curiosity. Then Nessie grabbed her sister's arm. "Look at that!"

Angela Brodie was pushing a pram along the waterfront. "Herself is past having the babies," exclaimed Nessie.

"Herself has never been able to have the babies, the babies," said Jessie.

They crossed the road and stood in front of Angela. "Who does the little one belong to?" asked Nessie.

"Me!" said Angela with a smile, and pushing the pram around them, headed for home.

"It is the fertility treatment," said Nessie.

They went to the kitchen door of the police station. Jessie peered round Hamish's tall figure. The kitchen seemed to be full of fishermen.

"What's going on, what's going on?" asked Jessie.

"Crime prevention meeting," said Hamish curtly. "What can I do for you?"

"You hired a bus for the morrow," said Nessie. "Why?"

"I'm taking some people down to an old folks home in Inverness for a Christmas Day concert."

The sisters looked at each other. Then they said in unison. "We'll come."

Hamish wanted to be rid of them. "All right," he said. "The bus leaves the war memorial at one-thirty."

"We'll be there."

I don't want them, thought Hamish, but if that pair is determined to come, there'll be no stopping them.

At two in the morning on Christmas day, there was a wickedly hard frost, which turned the whole landscape white. Silently and quickly Hamish and the fishermen set to work. Archie paused in his labours to whisper to Hamish, "What will you say if Strathbane finds you out?"

"I'll say I'm testing them," Hamish whispered back. "To see if they work. It's the one day only."

Christmas day. Morag struggled awake and switched on her bedside light. She knew she should not hope that Santa had brought her anything, but she wistfully thought it would be wonderful if just this year he had decided to stop at her home.

She climbed out of bed and drew back the curtains. Then she let out a gasp. It was snowing, large feathery flakes falling down from a black sky.

But not only that. She rubbed her eyes and looked again. The Anderson house was at an angle so that the windows faced down the waterfront. Fairy lights were winking and sparkling through the snow, and by the memorial was a large Christmas tree, also bedecked in lights.

She hurriedly washed and dressed and was about to rush from her room when she saw a bulging stocking hanging on the end of her bed. Wondering, she tipped out the contents. There was a giant bar of chocolate, a small racing car, nuts and oranges. Santa must have come. Her parents would never have allowed her chocolate.

She went into the sitting room. Four packages wrapped in Christmas paper stood on the coffee table. Eagerly, she opened them up. Three labels said TO MORAG FROM HER MOTHER AND FATHER. In one package was a smoky blue Shetland scarf, in another, a bright red sweater, and in the third, a doll with blonde hair and blue eyes. The fourth package was from Mrs. Gallagher and contained a handsome wooden box of tubes of watercolors and brushes, and along with it came a large drawing book.

She was about to run and find her parents, when she distinctly heard sleigh bells outside and a great voice crying, "Ho, ho, ho!"

"Santa!" Morag ran to the front door and jerked it open. The snow fell gently and the lights of a transformed Lochdubh glittered and sent their reflections across the black loch. She looked up at the sky but there was no fleeing sleigh. Then she saw the parcel lying on the doorstep. The label said TO MORAG FROM SANTA WITH LOVE.

She carried it into the sitting room and squatted down on the floor with the parcel on her lap and opened it up. It was a large stuffed grey-and-white cat, like Smoky, with green glass eyes.

Morag ran up to her parents' bedroom and threw open the door. Her parents struggled awake as the small figure of their daughter hurled herself on the bed, hugging them and kissing them and saying, "It's wonderful! I've never been so happy in all my life!"

And Mr. Anderson, who had been prepared to break the news to his daughter that there was no such person as Santa Claus, followed by his usual lecture on the pagan flummery of Christmas, found his eyes filling with tears as he hugged his daughter back and merely said gruffly, "Glad you're happy."

In the police station, Hamish Macbeth put the tape recorder with the sound of sleigh bells and "Santa's" voice along with the chain of small gilt bells he had borrowed from Angela on the kitchen table. Time to get a few hours' sleep before the journey to Inverness.

In the cottage next to the schoolhouse, Maisie Pease had a leisurely bath, and then began to dress with care, first in satin underwear and then in the cherry-red wool dress. She looked thoughtfully at the large sprig of mistletoe hanging over the living room door. She would point at it shyly and he would gather her in his arms. "You're looking bonnie," he would say before his lips descended on hers. She gave a happy little sigh and went to look out of the window. Where had all the lights come from? They sparkled the length of the waterfront. The snow was falling gently and she hoped it would not thicken and stop them from going.

She tried to eat breakfast, but excitement had taken her appetite away. How slow the hands of the clock moved. She waited and waited as the sky reluctantly lightened outside. She looked out of the window again. The snow had stopped and a little red winter sun was struggling over the horizon. Ten o'clock in the morning. Three hours to wait. Maisie switched on the television set and prayed for time to speed up.

Angela Brodie opened the door to the Currie sisters. "Happy Christmas!" cried Angela. "Come in and have a glass of sherry."

The sisters came in and sat down in Angela's messy kitchen. Nessie handed Angela two small parcels. "For the baby," she said.

Angela looked at them in amazement. "What baby?"

"Yours. The one you were pushing in the pram."

Angela blushed with embarrassment. "I'm sorry. I never thought for a moment you would believe me. It was a cloutie dumpling. I'd been using Mrs. Maclean's washhouse. I'm sorry I've put you to expense. Let me pay you."

"That will not be necessary, not necessary," said Jessie. "We'll just put them away. Someone's always having a baby, a baby."

"Sherry?"

"No," said Nessie, "we're going down to Inverness with Macbeth. He's taking us in Chisholm's bus. It's a concert he's organised at an old folks home."

"What a surprising man he is. Can anyone come? We're not having dinner until this evening."

"The bus leaves the war memorial at one-thirty."

"I'll see if my husband wants to come and maybe join you."

Maisie Pease stared at the carnival-painted bus and then walked round it, looking for the police Land Rover. On the other side, she found Hamish with a group of people.

"Maisie!" he cried. "Are we all set?"

"Yes," she said eagerly.

"Right, I think that's everyone," said Hamish. "All on the bus."

Maisie watched in dismay as the Currie sisters, Dr. Brodie and his wife, Angela, Mr. and Mrs. Anderson, Morag and Mrs. Gallagher all climbed aboard. Hamish was at the wheel. There would be no chance for any intimate talk.

Then she brightened up. They would be alone for dinner that evening.

Despite the odd assortment of villagers, there was a festive air on the bus. Angela laughed at the chintz-covered seats. The bus sped out of Lochdubh under a now sunny sky. Snow lay in a gentle blanket everywhere. It was a magic landscape, thought Morag, clutching the stuffed cat on her lap as she sat next to Mrs. Gallagher.

They stopped in Cnothan and picked up Mr. McPhee. Maisie groaned inwardly. How many more?

The Currie sisters were flirting awfully with Mr. McPhee, whose old face was beginning to assume a hunted look.

He moved his seat to the back of the bus. Thwarted, the Currie sisters began to sing carols in high, reedy, churchy voices. Hamish was amused this time to hear Jessie repeating the last line of every lyric and falling behind her sister.

When they were finally silent, Hamish, his eyes twinkling with mischief, called to Mr. Anderson to give them a song. To his surprise he began to sing "The Road to the Isles" in a clear tenor. Morag sparkled when her father finished and was given a round of applause.

At last Hamish drew up outside the old folks home and they all climbed down.

A piano had been set up in the lounge. Residents of the home sat around. Bella and Charlie were already at the piano dressed in striped blazers and straw boaters.

Mrs. Dunwiddy exclaimed, "Is it really you, Alice?"

"One of her good days," Mrs. Kirk whispered to Hamish.

They all sat down and were served with sweet sherry and slices of Christmas cake. The lights were switched off except for a light over the piano and the glittering lights on the tree.

Bella and Charlie were really good, thought Hamish as they belted out all the old songs, Charlie playing and both singing, their voices still full and strong. Elderly faces beamed, arthritic fingers tapping out the rhythm on the arms of chairs.

Morag sat clutching her father's hand and thought her heart would burst with happiness. In that moment, she decided that she would be a policewoman when she grew up and be as much like Hamish Macbeth as possible.

Only Maisie felt let down. It was not that Hamish was ignoring her. It was just that he treated her with the same friendliness as the rest of the party. She thought of the large turkey that she had cooked the night before so that it only needed to be heated. Would Hamish think it excessive? There had been a television program on world famine, and then thinking of those stick-like people and the sheer waste of that overlarge bird, Maisie felt guilty.

The concert finished at five and then after more sherry and cake, they all climbed back on the bus.

As Hamish drove out of Inverness on the A-9, it began to snow again, great gusts of white whipping across his vision.

He wondered what on earth he would do with this busload if he got stuck. He called back to Mr. McPhee, "Would you mind if I went straight to Lochdubh? I can put you up for the night." He remembered Maisie's dinner and said over his shoulder, "Is that all right with you, Maisie?"

"Oh, sure," said Maisie, sarcastic with bitter disappointment. "Why not bring everyone?"

Hamish missed the sarcasm in her voice and said warmly, "That's really good of you."

"Yes, it is," said Angela. "I'll drop off at our place and pick up the turkey and dumpling. Everything's ready. We'll have a feast."

"If we ever get there," said Hamish.

Morag crept down the bus and clutched her father's arm. "Daddy, can we go, too?"

He looked down into her wide pleading eyes and bit back the angry refusal. "Well, just this once."

And it will be just this once, thought Maisie angrily. She thought of the boyfriend down in Inverness that she had jilted. She had been cruel. She would phone him up and make amends.

Hamish was often to wonder afterwards how he had ever managed to drive that bus to Lochdubh or how the old vehicle had managed to plough up and down the hills as the storm increased in force. He let out a slow sigh of relief as they lurched over the humpbacked bridge that led into the village and saw the Christmas lights dancing crazily in the wind.

It was only after Angela and Dr. Brodie had collected their contributions to the meal that Maisie began to brighten up. As the women helped her in the kitchen and the men laid the table and then went out into the storm to make forays to collect more chairs, she was surrounded by so many people thanking her that she began to get a warm glow. Her spirits sank a little as Mr. McPhee grabbed her under the mistletoe and gave her a smacking kiss, but lightened again as soon as everyone was seated round the table in front of large plates of turkey and stuffing, chipolatta sausages, steaming gravy and roast potatoes. Bowls of vegetables were passed from hand to hand. Wine was poured, although the Andersons and Morag stuck to cranberry juice.

Hamish rose to his feet. "A toast to Maisie for the best Christmas ever!"

Everyone raised their glasses. "To Maisie!"

When the turkey was finished and the plates cleared, Angela said brightly, "The dumpling's heating in the oven. I'll get it if some of you ladies will help me with the plates."

Hamish watched nervously as the large brown dumpling was carried in and placed reverently in the middle of the table. Angela's lousy cooking was legendary.

"Would you do the honours, Hamish?" said Angela brightly.

Hamish reluctantly picked up a knife and sank it into the pudding. He cut the first slice and spooned it onto a plate and then filled the other plates. It looked good, but with Angela's cooking, you never could tell until you'd tasted it.

Custard was poured over the slices. Here goes, thought Hamish. He cautiously took a mouthful. It was delicious! What an odd Christmas, he thought. For once in her life, Angela's got it right.

Mrs. Gallagher and Mr. McPhee had discovered a mutual interest in birdwatching and were chatting busily. The Currie sisters who had strict Christian beliefs were talking happily about the iniquities of the world to the Andersons. Morag was telling Angela about her Christmas and Maisie was flushed and happy at the success of her dinner party.

"Who can that be?" demanded Mrs. Wellington, the minister's wife.

"Why don't you answer the phone and find out?" suggested her husband patiently.

Mrs. Wellington picked up the receiver.

"Hullo, Mrs. Wellington, this is Priscilla."

"Merry Christmas. Where are you?"

"In New York."

"Would you believe it? The line's so clear you could be next door. Everything all right?"

"Yes, fine. Look, I've been phoning the police station. I've been trying to get hold of Hamish to wish him a happy Christmas. Do you know where he is?"

"You could try the schoolteacher's place. He might be there."

There was a long silence.

Then Priscilla said, "Have you her number?"

"Wait a minute. I'll look in my book."

"Who's that?" asked the minister.

"It's Priscilla. She wants to talk to Hamish. I'm getting her the schoolteacher's number."

"Maybe you shouldn't have suggested he might be there."

"Oh, why?"

The minister sighed. "You wouldn't understand."

His wife gave him a baffled look and then located the number in her book and picked up the receiver again. "Are you still there? It's Lochdubh six-o-seven-one."

At the schoolhouse the table had been cleared away and a ceilidh had started in the living room, that is, everyone performing something or other. The Currie sisters had taken up positions in front of the fire and were singing in high, shrill voices.

"I'll get some coffee," said Maisie.

"I'll come and help you."

One last try, thought Maisie. She stopped right under the sprig of mistletoe and smiled up at Hamish invitingly. He put his arms about her and smiled back. Maisie tilted back her head and closed her eyes. At that moment, the phone rang loudly and shrilly.

Hamish released her. "You'd better answer that. I'll get the coffee."

Cursing, Maisie picked up the phone.

"Priscilla Halburton-Smythe here," said a voice as cold as the snow outside. "I wish to speak to Hamish Macbeth."

"I'll see if he's here," said Maisie haughtily.

"Who is it?" asked Hamish.

"It's for you." Maisie went back to join the others.

The phone was in the little cottage hall. Hamish picked it up. "Lochdubh Police," he said automatically.

"It's me, Priscilla."

Hamish sank down on the floor, holding the phone.

"It's yourself. How's New York?"

"Oh, you know, very bustling, very energetic as usual. I'm just about to go out to have dinner with friends."

"Bit late, isn't it?"

"I'm five hours behind you, remember?"

"So you are. Merry Christmas. How did you know where to find me?"

"Merry Christmas, Hamish. Mr. Johnston told me you were romancing the schoolteacher and so I assumed you'd be there."

"Why on earth would he say a thing like that? We're just friends."

"Just a cosy evening for the two of you?"

"No, there's a lot of people here. I'm just one of the guests. I'll tell you what happened." Hamish told her about the cat and the lights and the visit to the old folks home.

"Sounds like fun," said Priscilla.

"Will you be back for the New Year?"

"No, I'll be here for another six months."

"Now what'll I do if I get the murder case and havenae my Watson?" teased Hamish.

"I'll give you my number. You can always phone me. Write it down, and the address."

"Wait a bit." Hamish found a notepad on a table in the hall with a pen. "Fire away," he said.

She gave him the number and address and then said, "There are a lot of cheap fares to the States nowadays, Hamish. You could always hop on a plane."

"I could always do that," said Hamish happily, forgetting in that moment all about the state of his bank balance.

"Why aren't you over at Rogart with the family?"

Hamish told her about the soap powder competition and Priscilla laughed. "It is good to hear you, Hamish, and it would be good to see you again."

"Aye, well, you never know."

They wished each other a merry Christmas again and said goodbye.

Maisie looked up as Hamish came into the room. His face looked as if it were lit up from within. "We were just discussing sleeping arrangements," she said. "It's too bad a night for Mrs. Gallagher to get back home so Mr. and Mrs. Anderson have kindly offered to put her and Mr. McPhee up for the night."

"What about Smoky?" asked Morag anxiously.

"Smoky will be fine," said Mrs. Gallagher. "I've left him plenty of food and water."

So the party broke up. Hamish stood with the others outside the schoolhouse. The snow had stopped and lay white and glistening under the sparkling fairy lights.

Maisie watched them all go and then went indoors to phone the boyfriend she had so cruelly jilted.

Hamish walked along to the police station. He felt very tired. He took out his key but as he bent to unlock the kitchen door, he heard a faint noise from inside. He went to the police Land Rover and took out a hefty spanner to use as a weapon. Then he softly unlocked the door, threw it open and clicked on the kitchen light. A small dog trotted up to him and started sniffing at his trousers. It had a label attached to its collar. He squatted down by the animal and read the label. "To Hamish from Archie. Merry Christmas."

Hamish groaned. The fisherman knew there was a spare key to the police station kept in the gutter above the kitchen door. He must have let himself in with the dog while Hamish had been in Inverness. Hamish didn't want another dog. Once you've broken your heart over one dog, you don't want another. And it was such an odd dog. It was a mongrel, small and rough haired with floppy ears and blue eyes. Hamish could not remember ever having seen a dog with blue eyes. It licked his hand and jumped up to lick his face.

"Have you eaten?" asked Hamish. The dog wagged the stump of its tail energetically.

"I'd better give ye something." Hamish poured a bowl of water and then searched in the cupboards. Then he remembered he had a steak out in the freezer. By the time he had defrosted it, cooked it and chopped it up for the dog, he felt exhausted. He got ready for bed and then fell facedown and drifted off into a dream where he was walking along Fifth Avenue in New York with Priscilla on his arm.

And then the phone rang from the police office. He came awake and sat up. The dog was sitting on the end of the bed looking at him with those odd eyes. He was tempted to let the phone ring and let the answering machine pick up the call, but he remembered the weather and was frightened it might be a report of someone stranded up on the moors.

He went into the police office and picked up the phone. It was Detective Jimmy Anderson from Strathbane. "Is that you, Hamish?" he said. "Well, you'd better move your arse and get thae lights down."

"Why?" asked Hamish, too sleepy to deny anything about the lights.

"There's a man called Sinclair over in Cnothan. Someone told him that Lochdubh was all lit up and he's fuming that they're his lights that the forensic boys said you took to the station. Blair heard about it and he's planning to get over there first thing in the morning."

"He won't manage it," said Hamish. "The roads'll be blocked."

"Hamish, he thinks he's got you this time. He was talking about taking the helicopter. He was drinking all day and I tried to tell him the super would be furious at him for getting a helicopter out, all that expense for some Christmas lights, but he's determined."

"I'll see to it." Hamish dressed hurriedly and then began to phone round the village.

Hamish and his army of fishermen worked all night, taking down the lights, carefully packing them back into the boxes, taking down the

Christmas tree and propping it back up against the wall of the police station. Other villagers came out to help. Word flew from house to house that Hamish Macbeth was in trouble and that his superior officer was about to descend from the skies like the wrath of God.

Even Mr. Patel set to work, making sure the lights were all correctly packed so there would be no sign they had ever been taken out of their boxes.

At last the work was finished and everyone crowded into the police station for a celebration party. Mr. Patel presented Hamish with tins of dog food, for Hamish had told him about the dog.

"What are ye going to call him?" asked Archie.

Hamish longed to say that he didn't want another dog, but the dog looked at him and he looked back at the dog and said instead, "I don't know. Where did you find him?"

"I found the poor wee soul wandering up on the moors," said Archie, "and I thought, that's the very dog for Hamish."

"But Archie, someone may be looking for it."

"Don't think so. It was running up and down the road as if it had been dumped out of a car. Why not call it Frank?"

"Why Frank?"

"You know. Ol' Blue Eyes."

"Frank," said Hamish to the dog.

He turned to Archie. "He doesn't like it."

Another of the fishermen laughed and said, "Look at the lugs on it," referring to the dog's floppy ears.

"What about it?" said Hamish to the dog. "Like the name Lugs?"

The dog wagged its tail and put a paw on Hamish's trouser leg.

They all raised their glasses. "To Lugs!"

"Shh!" said Hamish, holding up a hand for silence. He opened the kitchen door and stepped outside. The sky was turning pale grey. He could hear the sound of an approaching helicopter.

"He's coming, boys!" shouted Hamish.

They scattered out of the police station while Hamish changed into his uniform.

Blair crouched forward in the helicopter. "Can ye see any lights?" he roared at the pilot.

"Nothing but a few house lights!" the pilot shouted back.

Blair was sobering up rapidly and a little worm of fear began to gnaw his stomach.

"Set down on the front!" he yelled.

The pilot landed next to the Chisholms' bus. Blair climbed down and ducked under the still rotating blades. He glared up and down the waterfront. Not one single Christmas light winked back at him.

He marched to the police station and walked right in. Hamish, neat in his uniform, was sitting at the desk in the police station typing something on the computer.

"Where are those lights?" demanded Blair.

"The Cnothan lights?" said Hamish innocently. "Look about ye, sir. Boxes and boxes of them."

Blair ripped open one of the boxes and glared down at the neatly packed lights. "I'll need to put in a report about that box," said Hamish. "You're destroying the evidence."

"Look, here, Macbeth, I had a report you had thae lights strung up all over the village."

Hamish looked suitably amazed. "Now who would go saying a thing like that?"

Blair stamped out. He went from house to house, demanding to know if anyone had seen any lights, but all shook their heads.

Beside himself with worry and rage, he went back to the police station. Hamish held out the phone. "You're just in time. Superintendent Daviot on the line."

"What the hell are you about taking out the helicopter?" roared Daviot. Blair opened his mouth to lie, to say he had heard of a crack house in Lochdubh, anything, but Daviot was going on. "It's all round Strathbane that you heard Macbeth had put up Christmas lights from that robbery all over his village. Well, did he?"

"There's nothing here, sir. But you see—"

"Listen to this. The pilot will be charging double because it's Christmas and I think the cost should come out of your wages. Return here immediately!"

Blair put down the phone. He walked to the door of the police office. "I'll have you yet, Macbeth," he threatened. Then he looked down with a comical look of pure outrage. Lugs was peeing into his shoe.

He raised his foot to kick the dog but it scampered under Hamish's desk and lay on his boots.

Blair squelched out.

"Come out of there," said Hamish to the dog. "Do you know something, Lugs? I'm going to keep you after all.

"Merry Christmas, you lovely wee dog. It's turned out the best Christmas yet!"